Somewhere Beneath Those Waves

Sarah Monette

PRIME BOOKS

SOMEWHERE BENEATH THOSE WAVES

Prime Books
www.prime-books.com

For more information, contact Prime Books.
prime@prime-books.com

ISBN: 978-1-60701-305-1

For Elise, who carries the Moon.

Contents

CONTENTS

INTRODUCTION

ELIZABETH BEAR

I am hardly without bias where Sarah Monette is concerned.

She is my co-author on (so far) three novels, a number of short stories, and the occasional bit of tomfoolery. She is my confidante in matters personal and my co-traveler in matters professional. She is my writing partner: a person I turn to for critiques, perspectives, and that all-important voice that tells me I'm being impenetrable again.

But most importantly, she is my friend, and one of the best friends I've had in my life.

Honesty compels me to acknowledge that friendship, even when I am not here to celebrate it. What I am here to celebrate, rather, is her work—or, as I find myself thinking of it, her *early* work. Because as I write this Sarah is brilliant, and imaginative, and not yet forty—and surely she has many more stories to tell.

I could tell you that her prose is lapidary—but you hold this book in your hands. In a moment, you will see that yourself. I could tell you that her ideas are fantastical and chilling, but . . . the same applies. I could tell you that she has studied the craft of horror and fantastic fiction from the pens of masters and mistresses of the genre. But you can see the results for yourself.

9

So instead, I will talk briefly about a few of the stories, and what they mean to me.

This collection opens with my favorite of Sarah's stories to date, "*Draco campestris*," which is named for a necklace created by Elise Mattheson and which inspired me to write a dragon story in response, to which Sarah penned another, and so on. (I believe it's currently my turn.)

I may be too in love with this story to speak sensibly about it—its non-traditional structure, the way its themes emerge from the narrative like the patterns of a fugue. I find myself speaking in musical metaphors a lot when discussing Sarah's work, possibly because the words so clearly evoke melodies to me. If "*Draco campestris*" is a melody, then, it is a grating and discordant one, full of the cries of strange birds and the rasp of scale on stone.

This is a story of details, told in details, and it must be reconstructed as the taxonomist reconstructs legendary creatures from their bones.

And what we learn from those dry bones of narrative is that this is also a love story. A great and tragic love story about two awkward, inarticulate people, the sort that inspires operas and ballads and tear-jerking stage productions for generations to come.

Only Sarah would build a love story that way, like a paleontologist assembling a fossil skeleton—half by guesswork and half by a profound understanding of how the living animal might have worked, *had* to have worked. If you're reading it for the first time, I envy you.

"Under the Bean Sidhe's Pillow" is a love story too, an even more unlikely one. It is a story of how immigrants bring their stories with them, and how stories need to be told. It's brief, a page or two, and it echoes with perfect loneliness and perfect devotion—from the point of view of a banshee who has started to be a bit affected by the stresses of her job.

Not all love is the romantic sort. There's the love that washes the dead, as well.

"The Watcher in the Corners" is a ghost story, and it's sort of a running joke between Sarah and me that I do not like ghost stories, do not understand them, have very little sympathy for their aims. But "The Watcher in the Corners" isn't just any ghost story. It's a story about brave young woman in a bad, real world where men, bad and good, had the power to treat their families as possessions—a world that is still very real, for some of us.

What I'm getting at is that Sarah's stories are often—usually—the stories of awkward outsiders, people who in some way do not fit the expectations of their societies. They are people who are too strong, too introverted, too queer, too transgendered, too haunted, too political, too feral. Her heroes and heroines are aliens in their own worlds, bemused and lonely, and still trying to find connection to other people—some way, some how.

So, what you hold in your hands is the first non-themed collection of the short fiction of one Sarah Monette, poet of the awkward and the uncertain, exalter of the outcast, the outré, and the downright weird. There is nothing else quite like it. And no matter how strange and alienated you may feel, there is room in her world for you.

DRACO CAMPESTRIS

i.

THE MUSEUM OWNS eighty-nine specimens of the genus *Draco*. It is unlikely that there will be any additions to the collection, for the adit to that array of Arcs has become increasingly unstable in the last two centuries. For that same reason, very little work has been done with the specimens since the last of the great dragon hunters willed his collection to the Museum one hundred thirty-two years ago. They were once a prized exhibit, but since the great taxonomic scandal under the previous Director, they have been an embarrassment rather than a glory. There is a cavernous hall in the sublevels of the Museum where the dragons stand shrouded in layers of yellowing plastic, unvisited, unwept, unremembered.

Their great eye-sockets are full of darkness deeper than shadows.

ii.

THE LADY ARCHANGEL was no longer in favor with the Empress.

That much was certain, and the Museum buzzed and rustled with the rumors that strove to create the story around that fact. The visitors chattered of it while the tour guides looked remote and superior and squirreled away every tidbit to be shared later over tea. The curators speculated, in slow, disjointed conversations; the visiting scholars asked nervously if there was any danger of an uprising, for the Lady Archangel was popular, and the papers reported unrest in those parts of the Centre where her charity had been most needed and most freely given.

No, said the curators, the tour guides, even the custodians. There had been no uprising in the Centre since the short and bloody reign of the long-ago Emperor Carolus, and there would not be one now. But when the scholars inquired as to the probable fate of the lady herself, they were met with grim headshakes and the sad, gentle advice to concentrate on their research. Whether it was sin or treason the Lady Archangel stood accused of, if she could not prove her innocence, she would be beheaded at the culmination of Aquarius. Such was the penalty for falling when one climbed as high as the Lady Archangel had climbed, and though the Empress was just, she was not merciful. She could not be, and hope to maintain her rule.

It was not for mere poetry that her throne was called the Seat of Dragons.

iii.

The Director has a dream. So she says, and no one in the Museum would dare to say otherwise, no matter how much they may doubt her ability to dream. Everyone knows she does not sleep.

Perhaps it is only a metaphorical dream, but even so, her shining coils are restless with it, her great yellow eyes (which only blink when she remembers that they ought to) hypnotizing. There are rumors that they were the eyes of a basilisk, and somehow that seems more likely than the idea that the Director can dream. Her metal claws score gouges in the vat-grown teak of her desk, and when she leaves her office, the tithe-children come creeping to sand and polish, as they have been doing for years, so that no unwary visitor may catch a splinter in the soft pads of his or her fingers.

When the Director speaks, there is only the faintest harshness in her voice to tell you that she is not a flesh-and-blood woman, nor—if the stories whispered in the Museum halls are true—ever was. When she speaks of her dream, that metallic rasp is louder, more strident; the matter is not merely important to her, but in some queer way, vital.

iv.

VISITORS COME to the Museum from all Arcs of the Circumference. It is the second-most popular tourist attraction of the Centre, after the Empress's palace (and that only in the summer months, for in the winter the Gardens of the Moon is closed to the public), and far ahead of such delights as the Tunguska Robotics Works and the People's Memorial of War. Visitors come on two legs, on four, on the sweeping sinuosity of scaled, legless bodies. There are perches in front of every exhibit for those who come by wing, whether feathered or membranous, and the Museum does its best to accommodate those whose habitual method of locomotion is aquatic. Parties of schoolchildren are allowed, although they are expected to be clean and quiet and capable of obeying the Museum's rules.

The most popular exhibit in the Museum is the mechanical orchestra of the Emperor Horatio XVI, bequeathed by him to the Museum on his death-bed. His death-bed is also an exhibit, though few visitors penetrate far enough into the Domestic Arts wing to find it.

Horatio XVI's mechanical orchestra is kept in perfect working condition by the curators, although it has not been played in over a hundred years. The sixteen rolls of its repertoire—imported, like the orchestra itself, from Arc ρ29—stand in a glass cabinet along one side of the orchestra's specially built hall. Each is five feet long and, mounted on its steel spindle, heavy enough to kill a man.

Nearly as popular as the mechanical orchestra is the Salle des Joyaux, where the Museum keeps—along with a number of stunning examples of the jeweller's art—the Skystone, sacred to the aborigines of Arc v12; the black Blood of Tortuga from Arc κ23; the cursed Hope Diamond from Arc σ16; and the great Fireball Opal, donated to the Museum by the Mikado of Hekaiji in Arc φ05.

Many visitors spend hours enthralled by the illuminated manuscripts of the Pradine Cenobites, brought out of Arc τ19 mere days before the eruption of Mount Ephramis closed that arc permanently. Others marvel over the treasures of the Arms and Armor Wing: the armor of the spacefarers from Arc θ07; the porpentine gloves characteristic of the corsairs of Wraith (ξ22) the claymore of Glamis (σ03); the set of beautifully inlaid courtesan's stilettos from the Palace of Flowers (α08).

It is considered advisable to purchase a map at the ticket window. Assuredly, the stories of visitors becoming lost in the Museum, their dessicated corpses found years—or decades—later, are merely that: stories. But all the same . . . it is considered advisable to purchase a map at the ticket window.

v.

HE WAS THE GREATEST taxonomist of twenty Arcs. His enemies said bitterly that formaldehyde ran in his veins instead of blood. Unlike the stories whispered about the Director, this was a mere calumny, not the truth.

He was pleased and proud to be part of the Director's dream (he said at the Welcome Dinner organized by the Curators' Union), and if there was any irony in him, the curators did not hear it.

All that season, the taxonomist, impeccable in suit and crisply knotted tie, assisted by a series of tithe-children, none of whom he could distinguish from any of the others, clambered among the bones of the eighty-nine dragons, scrutinizing skulls and teeth and vertebrae, recovering from the mists of misidentified obscurity *Draco vulcanis, D. campestris, D. sylvius, D. nubis*; separating a creative tangle of bones into two distinct specimens, one *D. maris*, the other *D. pelagus*; cleaning and rewiring and clarifying; entirely discrediting the identification of one specimen as the extinct *D. minimis*. It was merely a species of large liazard, said the taxonomist—any fool could see that from its teeth—and should be removed from the collection forthwith.

Meanwhile, the Director ordered the Salle des Dragons opened and cleaned. The tithe-children worked industriously, washing and polishing, commenting excitedly among themselves in the sign-language that no outsider has ever learned. They found the armatures where they had been carefully stored away, found the informational placards, beautifully written but entirely wrong. They found the tapestries, artists' reconstructions worked in jewel-colored yarns by the ladies-in-waiting of the current Empress's great-grandmother. These, they cleaned and re-hung, and the Director gave them words of praise that made their pale eyes shine with happiness.

Swept and garnished, the Salle was ready for its brides, and as the summer waxed and ripened, the taxonomist and the tithe-children brought them in, one by one, bearing them as tenderly across the threshold as if they came virgin to this marriage.

vi.

THE DRAGON LIES piled like treasure on the stairs, cold and pale and transparent as moonlight, its milky eyes watchful, unblinking. It is visible only on rainy days, but even in full sunlight, the staff prefer the East Staircase.

The tithe-children, though, sit around the ghost dragon during thunderstorms, reaching out as if they could touch it, if only they dared.

vii.

ONCE, AS THE TAXONOMIST was making comparative measurements of two *D. anthropophagi* skulls, a tithe-child asked, "Are there any dragons still alive, mynheer?"

He was surprised, for it was not customary for the tithe-children to speak; he had not even been certain that they could. "Perhaps, although I have never seen one."

"I would like to see a living dragon."

The taxonomist looked at the tithe-child, its twisted body, its pale, blinking eyes. He said nothing, and the tithe-child turned away from his cold pity. It would never see a living dragon, would never see anything that was not catalogued, labeled, given a taxonomy and a number and a place in the Museum's long halls. But it had dreamed, as every living creature must.

The taxonomist returned to his measurements; the tithe-children, watching, wondered what *he* dreamed.

viii.

ONE DOES NOT WANDER in the Museum after dark. Even the tithe-children stay in their rookeries; the security guards keep to their strait and narrow paths, traveling in pairs, never any further from each other than the length of a flashlight's beam. And of all the Museum's staff, it is the security guards who are hardest to keep. For they, who see the Museum's night-veiled face, know more clearly than any of the daytime staff the Museum's truth, its cold, entrapping, sterile darkness. They know what its tall, warped, and shining doors shut in, as well as what they shut out.

In the reign of the Empress Heliodora, a security guard committed suicide by slitting his wrists in the main floor men's bathroom. No one ever knew why; the only suicide note he left, written in his own blood across the mirrors, was: *All things are dead here.*

Later, the mirrors had to be replaced, for although the tithe-children cleaned and polished them conscientiously, the reflection of those smeared letters never entirely came out.

ix.

IT WAS a sultry afternoon in mid-August when the taxonomist descended the ladder propped against *D. campestris*'s horned skull, turned, and found the lady watching him.

She was a tall lady, fair and haggard, dressed with elegant simplicity in gray. The taxonomist stared at her; for a moment, recognition and memory and pain were clear on his face, and it seemed as if he would speak, but the lady tilted her head infinitesimally, and he looked over her shoulder, seeing the two broad-shouldered men in nondescript suits who stood at the door of the Salle, as if waiting for someone or something.

His gaze met hers again, and in that glance was exchanged much that could not be spoken, then or ever, and he bowed, a formal, fussy gesture, and said stiffly, stiltedly, the pedantic mantle of his profession settling over him, "May I help you, mevrouw?"

The lady smiled at him. Even though she was haggard and no longer young, her smile was enchanting, as much rueful as charming, and heart-breakingly tired. "We loved this room as children," she said, lifting her eyes to gaze at the long, narrow wedge of *D. campestris*'s skull. "I remember coming here with my brother. We believed they were alive, you know." She waved a hand at the surrounding skeletons.

"Indeed."

"We thought they watched us—remembered us. We imagined them, after the Museum had closed, gathering in a circle to whisper about the people they'd seen that day and make up stories about us, the same way we made up stories about them." Her face had lost some of its haggardness in remembering, and he watched her, almost unbreathing.

"Indeed."

"Tell me about them. Tell me about this one." She pointed at *D. campestris*.

"What do you wish to know?" he said, his gaze not following the graceful sweep of her arm, but remaining, anxiously, on her face.

"I don't know. We never read the placards, you see. It was so much more interesting to make up stories in our heads."

Their eyes met again, as brief as a blow, and then the taxonomist nodded and spoke: "This is *Draco campestris*, the common field dragon. This specimen is an adult male—you can tell because his wings are fully fledged. He is thirty feet long from snout to tail-tip and would probably have weighed well in excess of three tons. The wings are merely decorative, you understand, primarily used for display in mating rituals. The only dragon which can fly is *Draco nubis*, the cloud dragon, which is hollow boned—and much smaller than *campestris* in any event. Contrary to popular belief, *campestris* does not breathe fire. That would be *vulcanis*," he pointed at the magnificent specimen which dominated the Salle, "which must breathe fire because it would otherwise be unable to move fast enough to catch its prey."

"Yes," the lady murmured. "It is very large."

"*Campestris*, like the other dragons, is warm-blooded. They are egg-layers, but when the kits hatch, the mother nurses them. It is very rare for there to be more than two kits in a *campestris* clutch, and the sows are only fertile once every seven years. Even before that Arc was lost, sightings of them were very rare."

"Yes," the lady said sadly. "Thank you."

He took a step, almost as if he were being dragged forward

by some greater force. "Was there something else you wanted to know?"

"No. No, thank you. You have been very kind." She glanced over her shoulder at the doors of the Salle, where the men in suits still waited. She sighed, with a tiny grimace, then straightened her shoulders and defiantly extended her hand.

The taxonomist's startle was overt, but the lady neither flinched nor wavered. Slowly, gingerly, he took her hand. He would have bent to kiss it, if she would have allowed him, but her grip was uncompromising, and they shook hands like colleagues, or strangers meeting for the first time.

Then she released him, gave him a smile that did not reach the fear and desolation in her eyes, and turned away, walking down the Salle toward the men who waited for her.

The taxonomist stood and watched her go, as unmoving as the long-dead creatures around him.

At the door she paused, looking back, not at him, but at the great skeleton towering over him. Then one of the men in suits touched her arm and said something in a low voice. She nodded and was gone.

x.

EVEN THE MUSEUM cannot preserve everything, though it is not for want of trying. The Director is vexed by this, perceiving it as a failing; tithe-children and curators are allied in an unspoken conspiracy, tidying the riddles and fragments out of her way on her stately progresses through the departments and salles of the Museum.

But always, when she has gone, the riddles come out again, for scholars love nothing more than a puzzle, and the tithe-children have the gentle persistent curiosity of *Felis silvestris catus*, as that species is classified in those arcs to which it is native, or to which it has been imported. It is as close as they come, curators and tithe-children, to having conversations, these attempts to solve the mysteries left by the receding tides of history and cataclysm:

A fragment of a ballad from Arc ψ19: *The Dragon Tintantophel, the engine of Malice chosen*... But Arc ψ19 has been lost for centuries, and no one from that array has ever heard of Tintantophel.

A pair of embroidery scissors, sent to the Museum by one of its accredited buyers in Arc ρ29 with a note saying *provenance to follow*. But the buyer was killed in the crash of the great airship *Helen d'Annunzio*, and the provenance was never discovered.

Two phalanges from the hand of a child, bound into a reliquary of gold wire. This object was found in one of the Museum's sublevels, with no tag, no number, no reference to be found anywhere in the vast catalogues.

And others and others. For entropy is insidious, and even the Museum's doors cannot bar it.

xi.

THE TITHE-CHILD SAID in its soft, respectful voice, "I saw in the papers today that the Lady Archangel was beheaded last week."

The taxonomist's face did not change, but his hands flinched; he nearly dropped the tiny *D. nubis* wing-bone that he was wiring into place.

"They say she came to the Museum last week. Did you see her, mynheer?" There might have been malice in the great pale eyes of the watching tithe-children; the taxonomist did not look.

"Yes," he said, the words grating and harsh, like the cry of wounded animal. "I saw her."

Then the taxonomist did dream, the tithe-children saw, and they did not speak to him of the Lady Archangel again.

xii.

YOU WHO VISIT the Museum, you will not see them. They are not the tour guides or the experts who give informative talks or the pretty girls in the gift shops who wrap your packages and wish you safe journey. They are the tithe-children. Their eyes are large, pale and blinking, the color of dust. Their skin is dark, dark as the shadows in which they live. The scholars who study at the Museum quickly learn not to meet their eyes.

They might have been human once, but they are no longer.

They belong to the Museum, just as the dragons do.

QUEEN OF SWORDS

HER PREDECESSORS' PORTRAITS hang in the antechamber of her bedroom. "A reminder," the king says. There is space for her portrait to hang beside them.

The ghosts come to her for the first time on her wedding night, after the sated king has departed for his own chamber.

They call her sister.

They stand just inside the doorway, Queen Katharine and Queen Isobel, each wearing a wedding gown as sumptuous as that which hangs now in the new queen's wardrobe, each cradling her own severed head in her bloodstained hands, and they call her sister.

They whisper to her in voices like the tapping of branches at the window. They tell her she is beautiful, as they were; they tell her that she will recognize her own successor merely by the light in the king's eyes. They tell her not to be jealous, not to be afraid. They tell her they will welcome her gladly to their company. The queen imagines standing next to Queen Isobel, the weight of her own head in her hands. She imagines calling her successor sister and shivers.

The dead queens appear after each of the king's conjugal visits. They drift closer and closer as the weeks go by, trading bits of their unceasing threnody back and forth. Once, she tries to speak to them, but they will not break their chain of words to answer.

In the fourth month of her marriage, the new queen and her physicians determine that she is pregnant. The king is delighted.

"I thought I was cursed to marry only barren women," he tells her that night, his weight pinning her to the bed. He expects no response, and she offers none.

Later, alone, she waits, heavy with guilt. She has succeeded where Queen Katharine and Queen Isobel failed. They called her sister, and she has betrayed them.

But the dead queens do not come, and eventually she sleeps.

She wakes in the middle of the night. Queen Katharine and Queen Isobel are standing at the foot of her bed.

"He will have an heir."

"The murderer—"

"—*our* murderer—"

"—will have an heir."

"Our sister will grow heavy with his child."

They start toward the new queen, one on each side of the bed.

"She will bear *his* child."

"She will not be our sister."

"She will be his."

"His forever."

The ghostly queens stand beside the bed, close enough to touch. The new queen grips her hands together, her knuckles turning white.

"She is not his."

"She is ours."

"*Ours.*"

"She is *our* sister."

"He will not have her—"

"—will not keep her—"

"—we will not let him."

"Please," the new queen whispers. "Please let me be."

When the servants find her in the morning, she is lying in a great, clotted darkness of blood. Her body is already cold.

One month later, the king begins to look for his fourth wife.

———✕———

Letter from a Teddy Bear
on Veterans' Day

1.

It is early morning, barely dawn. It rained all night, and it will be raining again soon. The air tastes green and fresh and heavy. The park is deserted. I walk along the path, carrying the teddy bear in my left hand, as if it were something as normal as a newspaper. Somewhere ahead of me, the Wall is waiting.

2.

It was July and raining; there was a thunderstorm working up. You'd been dead for three months. I was in my room; I was reading. One of the guys who had served with you came to your funeral. I can't even remember his name, but he'd had both his legs amputated at the knee, and he was in a wheelchair. He was the only person who talked to me like I was old enough to understand what was going on. He gave me *All Quiet on the Western Front* and said, "This is about what happened to your brother and what happened to me." I read it that night, and then I read it again, and then I went to the library, and I started reading like it was life. I read everything I could get my hands on, including a lot of stuff the librarians didn't think a thirteen year old kid should be reading. But everybody in town knew about Dad, and Mom just said, "It's educational, ain't it?" and hung up the phone.

That day I was reading *A Separate Peace*, lying on my bed with a headache throbbing in my eyes. It'd be another two years before anybody figured out I needed glasses. But the headache was all right; it was like the book and like what was happening in my mind. I heard a crash through the wall, from your room, a crash that felt like the Last Trump. I lay there for a moment, my tongue thick in my mouth and my heart banging in my chest, and then I got up and went out into the hall.

Your door was open; it hadn't been open since you'd gotten on the plane in Knoxville. I looked in. Mom was on her knees, leaning into your closet, throwing things into a big cardboard box. The crash had been your track trophy missing the box and breaking against the floor. The little running figure that had been on top of it was halfway across the room, lying hard and cold and helpless between the bed and the hall door, as if he'd been struck down trying to escape.

"Mom?" I said.

She sat back on her heels and pushed her hair out of her eyes and said, "Yes."

"What?"

"Yes, I'm throwing out all his things. I refuse to have a goddamn shrine in my house for the rest of my life." The glare she gave me was like a dog getting ready to bite. She wasn't crying; she wasn't anywhere close to crying. I knew she'd broken your trophy on purpose.

"Mom, shouldn't you—"

"Get out," she said.

I stood there, the book still in my hand, one finger still marking my place. I stared at her.

"Didn't you hear me? *Get out!*"

I went back to my room and closed the door. The thunder started about ten minutes later, and for a while it was like there was another war on, between Mom and the thunder. Everything of yours that was breakable, she broke.

She dragged the cardboard box out to the curb in the rain, and then another one, and then another. And then she went into the kitchen and started dinner. We both knew Dad wouldn't be home until midnight or maybe later, and he'd be drunk. So it was just Mom and me, and she'd make dinner, and we'd eat it, and then we'd each go into our own room and die by inches. I don't know what Mom did in her room; I never did know. She had let you go in there sometimes, but you had never told me what you all talked about. I'd thought I could ask you later, when I was older.

3.

VETERANS' DAY is November eleventh. That's a bad day at work. Even my patients are restless, and the other wards are hell, where there are people who can follow a calendar and who understand that this should be their day. It isn't their day, and they know it. Nothing we do can make it their day. Nothing anyone can do can make it their day ever again.

You died on April twenty-second. I can take a day of vacation then, and I always do. I tell everyone that I'm going home to see Mom and Dad, and that always works. They know about you a little bit; I keep having to explain to people why I work where I do, as if intelligence ought to exempt me from trying to help those still trapped in the wreckage.

I lie, of course, when I say I'm going home. I haven't been back there since I went to college, except for funerals. Dad's luck finally ran out the year after I graduated. He went off the road in his Ford late one night, dead drunk as usual. The car hit a telephone pole, and by the time the ambulance got there, he was just dead. I think I'd been expecting it to happen since he showed up drunk for your memorial service. Mom and I didn't speak to each other at Dad's funeral; she looked straight through me and defied me to remind her that I, too, was her son. I returned the favor.

4.

I DREAMED of you again two nights ago.

5.

THE WALL IS BLACK. It's not the color of a scar, but that's what it is: psychic scar tissue made visible, tangible, cold and hard and real. There is no way to describe the action of the Wall against the ground. Its black, silent presence is verbless; it is the place for people who do not have verbs. The blackness of the Wall eats action as the blackness of a black hole eats light.

6.

YOU VOLUNTEERED FOR VIETNAM. You were eighteen; you didn't know any better. I was twelve; I knew even less. I thought anything you did was right by definition. In my experience you had never done anything wrong. You knew Communists were evil, and there was a great hunger in you to do battle with darkness and sin. You never got to read *The Lord of the Rings*; you were not warned about the price of victory, even for the good and pure of heart.

7.

IN THE VA HOSPITAL, there is a lounge with a long bank of windows. On sunny days when we wheel our patients in, we try to put them where they'll be able to feel the sunlight as long as possible. Even plants respond to sunlight.

8.

Mom didn't care if I read at the table; it saved her from having to talk to me. I sat there with my book and turned pages, because it was good camouflage, but I wasn't reading. All I could think of was your things out there in the rain in those boxes, and how the scavengers would start coming by tomorrow, and they'd take away anything that looked worthwhile, and then the garbage men would take the rest, and that'd be it. Nobody who knew you would have anything of yours, and the people who had your things wouldn't care at all about who they'd belonged to. I thought about the rain hitting the pages of your books. She'd ripped all your paperbacks in half before she threw them in the boxes; I'd seen the pages sliding out of the box and falling around her in the rain. I thought about the paper puckering and the words blurring and dissolving, and when I remembered to, I turned a page in *A Separate Peace*. Mom ate like some kind of machine, her hands and jaws moving, her eyes blank and fixed, like they were made of glass and filled with mercury. If you broke them, her tears would poison you.

9.

The names on the Wall do not accuse, or even stare. It would be better if they did. Statues would be easier against the conscience. Statues can look back at an observer, or even simply look at each other. They can give, however fleetingly, the impression that death is not lonely. The names are simply signifiers that have nothing left to signify. They are unforgiving because there is nothing left in them that can forgive.

10.

I dream of you in Vietnam, although I have never been there. I dream of you in the jungles and the heat, dream of you cutting your way through greenness turned hostile, dangerous, alien. I dream of you with the other soldiers in your unit; sometimes the man who came to your funeral is there, but I always dream of him in his wheelchair, the stumps of his legs covered by a quilt in the pattern called the Delectable Mountains. In my dreams, you talk to them and laugh, but I can never hear your voice.

11.

USUALLY WHAT I DO on my Veteran's Day—your Veteran's Day—is go to the local cemetery. It's an old place, full of silence. I look at the gravestones of the soldiers who are buried there; I read their dates and think about yours. I remember the fantasies I used to have, that you were still alive, a POW or a monk in Tibet or wilder, even more impossible things. In my dreams, you were always dead, beyond the reach of fairytales, but lying awake, staring at the night outside my window, I told myself stories, and I still don't know if they made things better or worse.

12.

AFTER DINNER, we washed the dishes. We didn't say anything; we didn't need to. Then Mom went into her room and slammed the door. She probably locked it, too. She usually did, and I never knew if it was just to keep Dad out, or if she was keeping me out, too. She sure as hell wasn't letting me in.

13.

I CATCH MY first glimpse of the Wall, black against the green, and suddenly become aware that there is somebody standing beside the path. I turn my head, my heartbeat accelerating. But the man beside the path isn't going to hurt me. He's wearing camouflage pants; his dogtags gleam against his naked chest. Half of his head is gone in a red and gray ooze that stains his neck and shoulder.

His remaining eye looks at me. It is brown, so I know that he is not you; your eyes were blue.

14.

I THINK OF YOU when I look at my patients. I wonder if it would be better if you were one of them, if you were alive and I could touch you. I look at their wives when they come to visit, at the hope in their eyes that turns to pain every single time, and I think, no, it's better that you're dead, that I can't even pretend that I will ever see you smile again. But when I wake up at five in the morning and know, because my eyes and pillow are wet, that I've been dreaming of you, I know that anything would be better than this emptiness, and I would give anything to be able to touch your hand again, even if you didn't know I was touching it.

15.

A FEW PACES further on, there is another soldier, and then a pair, and then I am walking through a crowd of men, all of them wearing uniforms, all of their dogtags so visible it hurts. I know that if I stopped, I could read the names on those gleaming tags, and the names would burn themselves into my memory. I turn my face away and refuse to read their names, refuse to know them. I think that I see my patients in the crowd, their faces younger than the faces I know, their eyes bright and quick. But I do not stop even for them. I would stop for you, if I saw you, but no matter how hard I look, you are not there. I am struck by a horrible fear: would I recognize you if I saw you? I last saw you in the flesh when I was twelve. I have no pictures of you. When you are in my dreams, you have a face, and I know that face to be yours, but no matter how true they are, dreams are not real, and I don't know whether my dreaming mind has ever succeeded in catching your real face.

16.

I WENT to my room, and put my book on the bed. I sat there for a while, watching it get dark out the window and listening to the rain and thinking about your stuff in those boxes and about what Mom would do to me if she caught me sneaking out there. I thought it was pretty likely she'd throw me out of the house, tell me that if I didn't want to do things her way, I could go live with Aunt Cindy in Lenoir City. You'd remember the way she used to say that. That summer I could feel the threat in the air all the time, although she'd quit saying it out loud. I think that's because it had quit being a joke.

Your door was still open; I'd seen that before I went into my room. And I remembered the way you'd gone out the window to meet your friends. After three-quarters of an hour, I eased my door open again and went into your room.

I hadn't been in there since you enlisted, and you'd never really wanted me in there anyway. But I remembered the way it had been, with your posters on the walls and your books in the one bookcase by the bed. Mom had ripped all the posters in half and thrown them out, like the books, and she'd stripped your coverlet off the bed, along with your sheets. There was no personality left in the room, nothing of who you'd been and what you'd thought about. Mom had said she didn't want a shrine, but she'd turned the room into something worse. When I read about the aftermath of battles, that's what I see: your room in the darkness, and how empty it was and how horrible.

I didn't dare shut the door behind me, in case Mom heard it, or came out of her room and noticed. I walked across from the door to the window as if there were someone sleeping in the room, someone I might wake if I wasn't careful. I eased the window up, one inch at a time, and only realized when I'd pushed it all the way open that I was holding my breath.

I knew how you'd gotten out; I'd watched you do it once or twice on nights when you'd co-opted me to be your alibi. But I'd never done it myself, and I sat there for some time in the window, wondering whether I could or not. But the rain was still coming down, still obliterating your memory out there in those cardboard boxes. Finally, I swung one leg over the sill and leaned out toward the tree.

It was a big dogwood; I couldn't remember a time when it hadn't been exactly as it was, wrapping the side of the house in its embrace, green and white and laughing or bare and brown and hungry. The nearest branch was just far enough from the window that I don't think either Mom or Dad ever imagined you could use it to get out of the house. Every time I'd watched you do it, my heart had been up in my mouth, and it was even worse when it was me, when it was my hands reaching, my left leg gripping the inside of the window sill, my body swaying out against gravity. There was a moment when I was sure that I was going to fall, that I was going to free Mom from having to look at the way my face was almost but not quite yours. And then my fingers reached the branch, and my hands locked against it as if the tree itself could negate the whole world and teach me how to fly.

I swung myself gracelessly from the house to the tree, scraping my hands and arms, bruising my legs, getting spider webs in my hair and dogwood leaves down the back of my shirt. When you had done it, it had looked so easy, so effortless.

I nearly fell twice climbing down, and when I was finally standing on the ground, my heart was racing and I was trembling all over. But Mom's window was on the other side of the house; she wouldn't see me.

I crossed the yard in the rain. The boxes were clumped sadly by the curb. I had to force myself to push the flaps back on the nearest one, and then I found that I couldn't look inside. I couldn't bear to look at your remains. The Army hadn't found enough of your body to send it back home, or at least that's what we were told. These cardboard boxes were all that was left. Blindly, I stuck my hand inside. My face was wet, and my hair was dripping down my neck. My fingers came in contact with something damp and soft, and I pulled it out.

Between the rain and the dusk, I could scarcely make it out. It was your teddy bear, the one you'd given up when I was six and you were twelve. Teddy bears were for babies, you said, but when Mom suggested you give it to me, you said, "It's *mine*," and it went in your closet. Standing out there in the rain, I remembered how that had made me feel, how small and stupid and worthless, as if I had to be something even more contemptible than a baby. And then the next day, you'd taken me to a movie, some stupid science fiction thing that Mom wouldn't have let either one of us see if she'd known, and I'd felt ten feet tall.

My fingers tightened around the teddy bear, and I walked back to the house. It was only at the foot of the tree that I realized I couldn't climb back to your window holding the bear in one hand. I tucked the front of my T-shirt into my shorts and put the teddy bear in my shirt. It lumped against my stomach, squashy and damp and neglected, and I climbed up.

Getting back in your window was even worse than climbing out had been, but I did it. I'd come too far to give up now, and I knew that if Mom caught me, she'd make me take the teddy bear back out to the boxes, or she'd do something else to destroy it. I could imagine her burning it: the stench of scorching plush, her face, remorseless and inexorable, lit from beneath by the flames. I crept back across your room, back along the four feet of hall that separated your door from mine, back into my own room. I eased the door shut behind me, and started breathing again.

And started looking for a place to hide the teddy bear from Mom.

17.

Sometimes when I dream of you, you are in my apartment, wearing your fatigues and dogtags, prowling through my living room as if it were a Vietnamese village. You look at the books on my shelves, pick up the knickknacks on my end table and turn them over as if they puzzle you. You go into the kitchen and inspect my refrigerator; you go into the bathroom and look in my medicine cabinet. The night before last, for the first time you came into my bedroom. You never used to remind me of a cat, but you prowled around my bedroom like a cat looking for another door. You seemed both restless and unhappy. You came and stood by the bed for a long time, staring down at me. I couldn't read the expression on your face. Then you went prowling away again, opening my closet, looking through my dresser drawers. You found the teddy bear. You picked it up, turned it over the way you turned over my bookends, and put it back down with a little, tired sigh. You didn't recognize it. It meant nothing to you.

18.

The dead men crowd around me as I walk. They do not touch me, do not even reach for me. Only their eyes yearn toward me, yearn toward warmth and memory. They do not remember who they are. They cannot read their own dogtags. I feel a cramping, agonizing need to read their tags, to tell them their names. But at the same time, I know they won't remember what I tell them. The dead cannot remember themselves; that's why the living have to. And I cannot be memory for all these men, although I could destroy myself finally in the process of trying. I cannot even be memory for you. I have lost you somewhere. The teddy bear is nothing but a teddy bear, a conglomeration of fabric and stuffing and glass as dead as you are. Nothing green and vital can grow from this teddy bear; it is not a magic talisman that can keep you near me or even let me pretend any more that you belong to me.

19.

I COME to the Wall. The dead men press their hands against the panels and turn to me, terrible pain in their eyes.

"I can't help you," I say and flinch at the sound of my own voice. They can't hear me; the only sounds they listen for are their own, the names they can no longer remember.

20.

MOM DIED a year ago. Cancer: it took her fast, devoured her body as if she were her own funeral pyre of dry wood and kerosene. I visited her in the hospital in Knoxville. We stared at each other, and I realized that while I look like Dad, and like you, I have her eyes.

I was the only mourner at her funeral; everyone else who had loved her was dead.

21.

I HID your teddy bear for years, moving it from secret place to secret place around my room. When I went to college, it went with me, packed in the bottom of a box full of sheets and pillowcases. I hid it from my roommate, knowing that I could never face explaining why I had brought a ragged, mildewy teddy bear with me. I liked my roommate fine, but when I was eligible to move into a single, I did. It was my secret—*our* secret—and I would rather have died myself than desecrate it by sharing it.

22.

I DON'T KNOW WHERE your name is on the Wall and no longer believe that it matters. I choose a panel near the middle and leave the teddy bear in the border between the Wall and the path. I leave the dead men clustering at the Wall and walk away.

I look back. Like Orpheus, like Lot's poor stupid wife. But this isn't a story. There's nothing there.

⸺⊗⊗⊗⸺

UNDER THE
BEANSIDHE'S PILLOW

THE BEANSIDHE does a lot of wailing during the crossing.

Not just for her own family, and insofar as a creature of her nature can feel guilt, she feels guilty. She is the O'Meara Beansidhe; in all the years of her existence she has cried O'Meara deaths and O'Meara deaths alone. But the grief is too much, death crammed upon death, and she wails for Mary Sullivan's baby just as loudly as she wails for James O'Meara, whose mother's death in childbirth she wailed for sixty-seven years ago. But it is James O'Meara's coat she takes, after his daughter has laid him out; in its inside pocket is the acorn he picked up as he was leaving the dooryard of his house for the last time. He didn't tell his daughter about it, didn't tell his pinch-faced grandchildren. He didn't tell the Beansidhe, either, but she knew.

She wraps his coat around her and wails for all the death she feels coming. For all the dead who soon will be.

The immigrants huddle together in the lower decks and even those with the Sight pretend they cannot hear her.

If a Beansidhe can hate, she hates them. Hates them for leaving Ireland, hates them for dragging her with them. Hates their pain, her addiction and poison, that lured her onto this terrible floating hulk so like the emptied-out carapace of a dead beetle. Hates them for holding her here with their grief, with the dying of their dreams. And she hates them most because a Beansidhe should not hate; they are changing her, making her less than she was. It is a Beansidhe's nature to cry death, not to grieve. Not to *care*. And yet she cannot seem to stop caring, now that she has started, as if James O'Meara's acorn has been planted in her own heart and has started to sprout.

Beansidhes do not sleep, neither do they dream. She curls up in a corner, in the reek of the bilge and the rats, tasting salt, tasting death, and pillows her head on James O'Meara's ragged coat. In the pocket of the coat, where she can sneak her hand under and touch it, is the acorn. James O'Meara's acorn. James O'Meara's dream.

And when she reaches America, although it is against her nature, she will plant it for him.

The Watcher
in the Corners

Lilah Collier was washing the windows the first time the sheriff showed up.

It was April 9, 1930, a beautiful sunny Saturday in Hyperion, Mississippi, and Lilah was taking advantage of the weather. She had been the Starks' housekeeper for four months, ever since she and her husband Butch came into town, and since Butch drank more of his paycheck than he brought home, she was hanging onto this job like grim death, even if she didn't much like Cranmer Stark *or* his pale, nervous wife Sidonia. So she cooked for their fancy dinner parties and kept their house spotless, and if Mrs. Stark didn't want the help talking to her little boy, then all right the help would keep her goddamned mouth shut. She felt sorry for Jonathan, a pale, silent child who always did as he was told, but not sorry enough to risk her job.

She was in the guest bedroom when the doorbell rang, and came panting down the stairs, only to pull up short when she recognized a lawman's silhouette against the frosted glass. She wiped the sweat off her face, made a futile attempt at smoothing down her hair, braced herself for whatever disaster Butch had caused this time. Opened the door.

And the sheriff, a stocky, tired man with watchful blue eyes, said, "Mrs. Collier, I hate to trouble you, but is Jonathan in the house?"

"Jonathan? No, sir, he's out with his mama."

"You seen him today?"

"No, sir. Mrs. Stark, she left me a note. They was gone when I got here. What's the matter?"

"Mrs. Collier, may I come in?"

She stood aside, her heart banging against her ribs, and when he hesitated in the front hall, led him back to the kitchen.

He sat down when she did, sighed, and said, "Mrs. Collier, it seems like Jonathan Stark has gone missing."

"Missing?"

"Straight out of the middle of Humphreys Park, from what his mama says. Now, we got men searching, but we're also trying to figure out what might make him run off. If he *did* run off. So, when did you see him last?"

Lilah told the sheriff what she knew. She'd given Jonathan his dinner early the night before, since his parents were having company: tomato soup and a cheese sandwich in his room. An hour and a half later, when there was enough of a lull in the dinner preparations, she'd gone up to get the tray. He'd been sitting upright in bed with the lamp on. She'd said good night to him, and he'd said good night back, being a polite child, and she'd gone out, and that had been that. No, she hadn't seen him at all on Saturday. Saturdays were her half days, and she hadn't come in until noon, when Mrs. Stark and Jonathan had already left.

"You sure of that, Mrs. Collier?"

"Sure of which?"

"That you didn't see him today."

"I done told you twice, they were already gone when I got here."

"And what were you doing this morning?"

"My own cleaning. Do I need an alibi, sheriff?"

"Not 'cause I suspect you, Mrs. Collier, just so as I don't have to start."

"My husband was home. We left the house together—matter of fact, he drove me here."

"Anybody else see you?"

"I was washing windows, so you might ask the neighbors. And Maddie Hopper can probably tell you I arrived when I said I did."

"She already has."

"Said you didn't suspect me, sheriff."

He put his pencil down and rubbed his eyes. He looked like a man who didn't get enough sleep. "So far, Mrs. Collier, there ain't nothing to suspect nobody of. But little boys don't just vanish into thin air, and they don't have that generous variety of enemies that adults might do. We're asking these questions of any adult that knows Jonathan Stark, for the pure and simple reason that we ain't got nowhere else to start."

"His daddy's a powerful man," Lilah observed.

"Don't I know it. And, yes, I think it's a kidnapping, and, yes, I think we're gonna be hearing from somebody here in another hour or so saying what it is they want. But it bugs the shit out of me, begging your pardon, that they could grab him in broad daylight in the middle of Humphreys Park and not have nobody the wiser. So I'm covering all my bases." He looked her squarely in the eyes then. "Do you know anything that might help us?"

"Like what?"

"Damned if I know. Like anything that might explain where he went or why somebody took him or *anything.*"

"I don't know nothing to explain that, sheriff. I'd tell you if I did."

"I hope you would, Mrs. Collier. I sincerely do. Thank you for your time."

He left her sitting there in her clean kitchen, gooseflesh crawling up and down her back.

No communications from kidnappers were received, not in the next hour, not in the next two weeks. No one was found who seemed to have any motive for harming Jonathan Stark; even his father's enemies were equipped one and all with unassailable alibis. No one was found who had seen him after his mother's last sighting of him at 12:30 p.m. in Humphreys Park. The park, which was not large, was searched with a fine-toothed comb, and the pond was dragged. No evidence of Jonathan Stark was discovered, although a remarkable assortment of other things came to light. As far as anybody could tell, Jonathan Stark *had* vanished into thin air.

Sidonia Stark took to her bed; Cranmer Stark took to drink. Lilah Collier took to cleaning the Stark house with a passion that surprised her. She had instructions to do nothing to Jonathan Stark's room—not even to dust—and she obeyed, but the rest of the house became antiseptically spotless.

She began to have the feeling, alone on the first floor of the Stark house, that she was being watched. She told herself she was being stupid and high-strung (her father's phrase for such airs was "being missish," and it was a good way to get a casual clout across the back of the head), but every day she talked herself out of it, and the next day by noon the feeling would be back again. Something watching, something small and white. She'd find herself glancing around, as if she could catch it in a corner, but she never saw anything, never anything that wasn't the curtains or a lace doily or her own dust rag left on a side-table. She sometimes got a feeling, towards dark, that there was something cloudy in her peripheral vision—sometimes on the left, sometimes on the right—but it was never something she was sure of. "Missish," she grumbled to herself, and was glad to leave the house for the dubious security of Butch's car.

And then, in the middle of June, the sheriff showed up again. Cranmer Stark had driven Sidonia to Memphis to consult a nerve-specialist; taking advantage of their absence—and desperate for something to keep herself occupied against the watchfulness filling the house—Lilah was washing the curtains, and she had to rinse soap suds off her hands before she could answer the door.

"Mrs. Collier," the sheriff said.

Lilah only realized after she'd done it that she'd glanced at the height of the sun in the sky, only realized it as she was thinking, We got another two hours before it really gets bad. "Sheriff Patterson," she said, controlling the impulse to weep with gratitude at the sight of another human face, the sound of another human voice. "They ai—Mr. and Mrs. Stark aren't home."

"I know that. I don't want to talk to them. May I come in?"

Oh, thank God, Lilah thought. Even being arrested for murder would be better than being alone in the Stark house any longer. "Come on back to the kitchen. You want some coffee?"

"You're a good woman, Mrs. Collier. I'd love some."

So Lilah made coffee, and the sheriff sat at the kitchen table, looking at the clean counters and the sultanas on the windowsill.

"What can I do for you, sheriff?" Lilah said when she'd given him the coffee and sat down herself.

"I ain't suspecting you, Mrs. Collier," he said, "but I want to ask you again about April eighth."

"You can ask, sheriff, but I can't give you no new answers."

"I just want to hear it again." He sipped the coffee. His eyebrows went up appreciatively, and he said, "I do wish you'd give lessons to my wife. Now. April eighth."

"There was a dinner party."

"Who?"

"High society folks," Lilah said and shrugged. "Three married couples, and a couple men on their own, and Mrs. Stark's cousin Renee from Oxford, and the lady who owns the gravel pit."

"Miss Baldwin, then. So what happened?"

"I did dinner. Or-derves and soup and salad and beef burgundy and a chocolate mousse. The party seemed pretty happy. Nobody fighting or nothing."

"When'd you leave?"

Lilah thought back. "Everybody was gone by ten, and I was doing the washing up—I can't abide to leave it overnight—when Mr. Stark comes in and says, 'You had a long day, Lilah. Why don't I run you home?'"

"Did he? Had he ever done that before?"

"No, sir."

"Done it since?"

"No, sir."

"Could you tell me about what time that was?"

"'Levenish, I'd guess. I'd got all the big stuff done, and I was just as happy not to have to walk. So I said, 'Them plates'll keep,' and he drove me home. Sheriff, what is it you're after?"

"Now, just bear with me. Tell me again when the last time you saw Jonathan Stark was?"

"I took up his dinner at five, I guess. His mama was in with him, showing him her pretty dress and letting him smell her perfume. So I put the tray on that big deal table they got in his room and went back down. Then, I guess it was six-thirty or so, I'd got the soup simmering and the beef in the oven, and the mousse to chill in the ice-box, and there wasn't nothing more I could do for another fifteen minutes at least, so I went back up for the tray."

"And he was there."

"Yes, sir. And alive. He was sitting up in bed and hanging on to that ratty toy bunny that drove Mr. Stark so wild."

"Did he say anything?"

"His mama was on him pretty sharp about not talking to me or Mr. Wilmot who comes about the lawns and such. He did say good night, but I think that was it."

"Are you sure?"

"Why? I mean . . . "

"Excepting his mama, you seem to be the last person who saw or spoke to Jonathan Stark. And, forgive me for saying it—and please don't repeat it—we ain't getting no manner of help out of his mama at all."

"She's a pretty nervous lady."

"She says she can't remember nothing about that Saturday morning. Not what he was wearing, not what they said to each other—and I *can't* believe that a boy and his mama could walk to Humphreys Park without a single word being passed between them."

"D'you think she's lying?"

"I don't know. Like you say, she's a nervous lady. But she ain't helping. And, Mrs. Collier, I got to say, I don't think this *is* a kidnapping."

"You think he's dead." Lilah's hands were ice-cold, and she was thinking of that feeling in the house, that feeling of being watched that got worse as the day darkened.

"I'm *afraid* he's dead. Did he say anything to you? Anything at all, even if it don't seem important." He held a hand up. "I know if it'd seemed important, you would've told me at the time. But *anything.*"

"God, sheriff, let me think." Lilah forced her mind off the emptiness of the house and back to that Friday night. "I was in a hurry, and I wasn't paying much heed to Mr. Jonathan. Sometimes kids say things, you know, and you answer 'em, but you ain't rightly listening?"

"Yeah," the sheriff said heavily. "I know."

"I could smack myself for it now. But we both knew he wasn't supposed to talk to me, and he was a quiet little boy anyways. Never said much at all."

"Mrs. Collier—"

"I'm trying. Lemme think. I came in and said, 'You done, Mr. Jonathan?' And he said, 'Yes, Mrs. Collier.' The tray was on the table where I'd left it. He was in bed, with his rabbit."

"What was he wearing?"

"His pajamas, I think. Blue striped." She shut her eyes, to remember better. "I went over to pick up the tray . . . and he *did* say something. Christ Jesus, I can hear his voice in my mind, but I can't remember the words."

"Was it about the party? About his parents?"

"It was about his mama looking so pretty," Lilah said and opened her eyes. "That's what he said. He said, 'My mama's the prettiest lady in town.'"

She took a deep breath. "I said, 'Yes, Mr. Jonathan,' because, well, I wasn't giving her no competition. And he said, 'Do you think Daddy thinks so?' And I said, 'I'm sure he does, Mr. Jonathan.' And then I said good night and he said good night, and I went out the door. I'm sorry, sheriff. That don't help you much."

The sheriff said, "And you never saw him again?"

"No, sir, like I said. Saturdays I don't come in 'til noon, and they were already gone."

"Would Mrs. Stark have gotten the boy his lunch?"

"Lunch?" Lilah said blankly.

"You do the cooking, don't you, Mrs. Collier?"

"Well, yes, sir. 'Cept Saturday morning, but I think Mr. Stark mostly takes 'em out to the Magnolia Tree."

"Magnolia Tree," the sheriff said, making a note. "And for Saturday lunch?"

"Well, I do that. Baked eggs at one o'clock, regular as clockwork. That's how Mr. Stark is."

"Did they go out to the Magnolia Tree on the ninth?"

"I don't know, sheriff."

"Where was Mr. Stark that Saturday? Do you know?"

Lilah could feel her eyes widening, and her mouth was dry as cotton. "I don't know, sheriff. Cross my heart and hope to die, I don't got no idea."

"Thank you, Mrs. Collier. I got one other question, and you can say no, and that's just fine."

"What is it?"

"I'd like to see Jonathan's room. I don't got a warrant, and you're within your rights to refuse."

"This ain't my house. I can't tell you what you can and can't do. But ain't it illegal for you to go wandering around without Mr. Stark says it's okay?"

"Mr. Stark says he don't want his wife bothered, and he says since Jonathan was kidnapped out of Humphreys Park, there ain't no point in me mucking up his boy's room. Mr. Stark ain't gonna say it's okay until sometime after Hell freezes over. But I'd dearly like to look."

Although raised to distrust and dislike the police, Lilah Collier had been alone or almost alone in that house for over two months, and she was quick enough to see where the trend of the sheriff's questions was leading. She said, "Okay, but if he finds out, I was at the grocery store and you just walked in."

"That's fine, Mrs. Collier. You don't have to come with me."

"I think we might both be happier if I did. This way, sheriff."

They climbed the stairs together. The sheriff said, "Mrs. Collier, are you the only help the Starks have?"

"Me and Mr. Wilmot, who comes on Tuesdays to do the lawns and the flowerbeds. Why?"

"No reason." But he was looking around uneasily. "There ain't nobody else home?"

"No, sir." And she couldn't help asking, "Do you feel it, too? Like you're being watched?"

The look he gave her was answer enough.

"It gets worse toward evening," she said, almost babbling with relief. "And it's been *terrible* today, I think 'cause there's nobody else home. I ain't dared ask Mrs. Stark if she feels it, and . . . and I ain't dared ask Mr. Stark neither." They were at Jonathan's door, and she stopped with her hand on the knob.

"Has the house always been like this?" the sheriff asked. " 'Cause you're right. I can feel it."

"Just since . . . since after he disappeared."

Lilah opened the door.

It was the first time she'd been in the room since the eighth of April. Dust was everywhere, and the room smelled musty and unpleasant. There was a tang to the air, so faint that Lilah almost thought it was her imagination, the smell of something rotting. The sensation of being watched was heavy and cold, like water deep enough to drown in. Lilah and the sheriff both glanced over their shoulders, and neither advanced so much as a step into the room.

"Did the boy always leave his room this neat?" the sheriff asked.

Lilah looked around carefully, looked twice at the bed. "He was tidy-minded, for a child so young. But he couldn't manage the sheets like that. He'd do his best, but the bed was always rumpled a little, even if it was just that you could see where his knees had been when he was getting the top straight."

The sheriff grunted. His eyes traveled around the room again. He said, "Mrs. Collier, you mentioned a toy rabbit. I don't see it."

"Ain't it on the bed? That's where he kept it." But she looked for herself, and the dingy, ragged bunny was nowhere to be seen.

"He wouldn't have taken it with him?"

She shook her head. "That bunny drove Mr. Stark wild. He couldn't stand it that a son of his would be carrying it around. Jonathan wasn't allowed to take it out of his bedroom, and he did what his daddy said. Always."

"Could it've fallen off the bed?"

They looked at each other. Lilah saw her own feelings mirrored in his face; he didn't want to go into that room either. She supposed it should have made her feel better—less missish—to know that a middle-aged sheriff had the creeping, crawling horrors the same way she did, but it didn't. It made her feel ten times worse.

Finally, she said, her tongue dry and dusty in her mouth, "I'll look."

She walked into the room slowly, her heart thudding wretchedly in her chest. The sheriff stood in the doorway. Step by step, she walked around the bed, to the side not visible from the door. "Nothing," she croaked.

"Jesus," the sheriff said and armed sweat off his forehead. "Mrs. Collier, I hate to say it, but will you check under the bed?"

"I think you oughta swear me in as a deputy first," she said, and they both yelped with laughter. Then Lilah, knowing she would have had to, even if the sheriff had said nothing, slowly bent and lifted the counterpane. She straightened up again in a hurry, all but gasping for breath. "Nothing," she said. "Just dust. It ain't here."

"Christ on a crutch," the sheriff said. "You come on out of there, Mrs. Collier. I ain't doing no more without I got a warrant."

"Yes, sir," Lilah said and left the room, gratefully and fast.

They went back down to the kitchen. The sheriff said abruptly, "How old are you?"

"Sixteen," Lilah said. She was past the point where she could lie to Sheriff Patterson. He'd felt the wrongness in Jonathan's room.

"Christ. I ain't leaving you here by yourself. This house ain't no place to be alone in. You write a note—tell 'em you took sick or something. I'll drive you home."

"And it ain't so far off the truth, neither," Lilah said, finding the pad of paper she used for shopping lists. "Sheriff, what do you reckon happened? What's the *matter* with this house?"

"That's a question for a preacher," the sheriff said. "But you want the honest truth, I reckon Jonathan Stark never left this house, and I further reckon he was dead a long time before Saturday noon."

"Me, too," she said, shivering.

Lilah left her note ("SORRY MRS. STARK. FEELIN BAD. GONE HOME. COME IN ALL DAY SATERDAY. L COLLIER"), and climbed into the front seat of the sheriff's car. "Never thought I'd be glad to be riding in one of these," she said, and he laughed.

"Where'm I taking you?"

Suddenly, Lilah could bear the thought of her own empty house no better than she could bear the Starks'. "Take me up to the pit office, if you'd be so kind. I'll just meet my husband."

"You're sure?" he said, giving her a sideways look.

"I can talk to Emmajean 'til he's done."

"Okay," the sheriff said, and she knew he understood.

He didn't leave her at the gate, as she'd expected, but drove up to let her out directly opposite the office door. She stopped halfway out of the car and said, "Sheriff, you got somebody you can go talk to or something? Or you can come in and Emmajean'll give you coffee. Ain't as good as mine."

He smiled. "Thanks, Mrs. Collier, but I got to go down to the station and figure out how I'm going to persuade any judge in this county to give me a warrant to take a look at Cranmer Stark's house. There's plenty of people around, though, don't you worry."

"All right. Thanks, Sheriff."

"Thank *you*, Mrs. Collier. You been a world of help." She got out, closed the door. He drove away. Lilah went in to talk to Emmajean, although later she could not remember one word Emmajean had said. She kept hearing Jonathan Stark, the words she hadn't heeded at the time, but that now wouldn't leave her alone. *My mama's the prettiest lady in town. Do you think my daddy thinks so?*

Butch's shift ended at six; Emmajean had passed the word that Butch Collier's wife was waiting for him, but it was six-thirty when Butch came sauntering into the office like he owned the world. "What's happening, Lil?"

Lilah hated it when Butch called her "Lil," just as she hated the way he would make her wait for him, purely because he could. Today, she didn't care, almost nauseated with gratitude only from knowing that she wouldn't have to be alone all night.

"Nothing much, Butch," she said. "Let's go home."

"Sure thing. Stay pretty, Emmajean."

"You, too, Butch," Emmajean said sweetly. Lilah bit the inside of her lower lip hard, and did not laugh. Butch almost never noticed jokes at his expense unless someone laughed at them.

In the car, heading out the gravel drive, Lilah made her mistake. When Butch asked, "What's the matter, Lil? Why'd you leave work?" she didn't answer, I came over funny, or even, There was nobody home and I got spooked. She told him the truth.

She told him because it was killing her to keep it all pent inside, not thinking about its effect on him. She had forgotten Butch's desire to see himself as a hero, a character out of the pulp magazines he read in the same habitual, thoughtless way he cracked his knuckles. He said, "Lilah! Are you serious?"

"What d'you mean?" she said, belatedly wary.

"Do you really think Mr. Stark killed his little boy and buried him in the cellar?"

"'Course not," Lilah said. "Don't be silly." But, of course, it was what she thought, she and Sheriff Patterson both, and she couldn't entirely keep that out of her voice.

"They ain't back yet, are they? You said they was going to Memphis today."

"Butch, what are you thinking?"

He swung the Model T in a wide, looping turn. "You got a key, don't you? We can go look!"

"You're crazy!"

"Sheriff Patterson'll be grateful. Maybe he'll make me a deputy or something."

"Butch, we can't break into their house!"

"We ain't. You forgot your purse. And if the basement door ain't latched right, that ain't *our* fault."

"Butch, please!"

But Butch was more pig-headed than a pig, and Lilah knew from experience that no argument of hers would make him change his mind. She could only hope, noticing uneasily that the last of the sun was disappearing below the horizon, that the atmosphere of the house would do the job. And she hoped it would do it quickly.

Butch, however, noticed nothing spooky about the house at all. Lilah felt it the instant she opened the back door, moving out at them like a wall of ice; Butch walked in like it was his own house. "Nice things," he said, then looked back. But he was looking for Lilah, not for the watcher in the corners. "You coming?"

She wanted to say no. No, Butch, thanks, think I'll wait in the car. But she knew if he figured out she was too scared to come in, she would never hear the end of it, and Butch would never again pay the slightest attention to anything she said. And that would last a lot longer than the ten minutes it would take for Butch to look at the cellar and get bored. "Coming," she said, amazed at how clear and normal her voice sounded. She walked into the house.

The cellar door was in the back hall, under the stairs, a place (Lilah now realized) that she had been avoiding, completely unconsciously, for weeks. The house was full of twilight around them, and the thing in Lilah's peripheral vision was more than a cloud. When she turned her head, it wasn't entirely gone, although that might just have been the shadows.

"Butch," she said, and now her voice was trembling. "I really don't think this is a good idea."

"Don't be such a scaredy-cat. This the door?"

Before she could say yes, no, or maybe, he'd opened it. That smell of rotting that she had noticed in Jonathan's room was here as well, and, though still faint, it was distinctly stronger.

"*Something's* down there," Butch said with satisfaction. "They got lights?"

"Yeah, there's a bulb," Lilah said, "but, Butch, don't—"

Butch found the cord, yanked it. For Lilah, the light made everything worse. It was harder than the dark, uglier, and anything it showed her would be true beyond any possible hope of redemption. Butch, oblivious, started down the stairs. It was the last thing in the world she wanted to do, but Lilah moved into the doorway to watch his progress.

"It sure does stink," Butch called up. "I think he's really down here, Lilah. I ain't kidding."

Oh, I believe you, Butch, she thought. That cloudy thing that she couldn't quite see was down at the foot of the stairs now. She said, "Butch, come on up and we'll call Sheriff Patterson. I don't think he needs a warrant if we call him in."

"Just wait a minute, Lilah. It'll be better if I can find him first."

"Come on, Butch." Without wanting to, she started down the stairs, as slowly as she had walked across the floor in Jonathan's room. She did not love Butch Collier—didn't even like him much—but she knew her duty toward him, and her duty right now said she had to get him out of the cellar before something horrible happened. "Let's just go call the sheriff, huh?"

"My Christ, Lilah, what're you scared of? The boogeyman?"

"'Course not," Lilah said. Butch and that cloudy shape, small and white, were converging on the same patch of floor. "But I don't think it's safe. The Starks come back and find us in their cellar . . . *we* might disappear next, Butch. I ain't kidding."

Butch knelt, putting his face on a level with that small, white, cloudy presence; Lilah reached the bottom of the stairs and froze there. She told herself she was being silly, that Jonathan Stark had been a meek, mild, sweet-tempered little boy, and that even if his spirit was vengeful, those who had not killed him should have nothing to fear. But she'd lived with that watcher for over two months, felt it in every room, felt its strength increase from hour to hour as the day waned. Whatever her rational mind said, she was afraid. She clutched the bannister, licked her lips, said, "Butch—?"

Butch said, "Holy Christ, he's right here!" She saw the dirt swept aside by his broad, grimy hand, saw, unmistakably, the shapes of small fingers being uncovered.

Then, several things happened at once; Lilah was never able, no matter how carefully she thought them through, to put the pieces together in order. She knew that the front door slammed open; she knew that Butch, looking up, seemed finally to see the small, white watcher. She did not know what he saw—she never, first to last, saw the watcher's face—but she saw Butch's face change, saw his death before he could have fully known it was on him.

Butch Collier screamed.

Lilah, watching helplessly, sagged sideways off the stairs, ending up on her knees, still clutching the bannister as if it could save her. She heard footsteps along the hall, heard Cranmer Stark say, "Go *upstairs*, Sidonia! I'll deal with it." Then he appeared in the doorway.

"*What the hell is going on here?*" he demanded, in a roar like that of a beast, set his foot on the first step, and started down.

At the same moment that Lilah realized the white, watching presence was no longer beside Butch, she saw it, as clearly as she ever did, on the cellar stairs just below Cranmer Stark. Its back was to her, but she saw its child shape, saw the tilt of its head. It was looking at Cranmer Stark.

She didn't think he saw it fully. He saw *something*; he shouted wordlessly, tried (she thought) to dodge it, and pitched headfirst down the stairs. She was close enough to hear the crack when his neck broke.

Lilah, who only realized later that she was screaming, flung herself up the basement stairs, slammed and bolted the door behind her, and half-scrambled, half-fell into the kitchen to call Sheriff Patterson.

WHEN THEY UNEARTHED Jonathan Stark's body, they found his toy bunny clutched under one arm.

LILAH WAS in Sheriff Patterson's car again. He'd taken her statement, tried to talk to the hysterically weeping Sidonia Stark, got his deputies started on the basement. Then he'd come back to the kitchen and said, "Mrs. Collier, would you care to come with me?"

"Am I under arrest?" she asked when he opened the door for her.

"Nope." He got in the car, started it, said, "I believe you. I busted up enough fights with Butch Collier somewhere near the middle to know what he was like. And I was in that house today. I believe it happened just like you said." He turned left at the end of the Starks' street, away from the middle of town. "But, and I hate to say this, there's a bunch of folks in Hyperion who ain't gonna see it like I do. They're gonna see one woman and two men in a cellar, and only the woman comes out, and they're gonna say, we don't know nothing about who put that little boy down there, but we know what two men end up dead over when there's a woman in the room. They're gonna like it better than the truth. Now, those folks can't make me arrest you, but I can't keep them from lynching you, neither. You understand?"

"Oh, yeah," said Lilah. "I hear you, sheriff."

"So I was thinking—I got your testimony, and I think when Sidonia calms down some, she maybe is gonna tell us the truth. And the man who needed prosecuting is dead, besides. So if you was to just . . . vanish, people could think what they liked and nobody'd get hurt. And I can't believe you'll be sorry to see the last of this town."

"I'll be grateful," Lilah said. "I mean, it's a nice town and all, but . . . "

"I know," he said as they passed the city limits sign. "You'd always be thinking about whether you had to go past the Stark house on your way home."

"Yeah."

They drove in silence for a long time. He said at last, "Near as I can make Sidonia out, Cranmer was carrying on with Miss Baldwin. She says she knew it and didn't care, and whether that's true or not, I don't know. But the way I figure it, the little boy got out of bed and saw something he shouldn't've—or said something he shouldn't've, maybe—and his daddy . . . "

"Made him be quiet," Lilah said. "That's about all I ever heard the man say to the little boy. 'Be quiet.'"

"He might not've meant to," the sheriff offered after a cold moment.

"Maybe. But he still must've meant to hurt him."

"So," said the sheriff. "I hear you, Mrs. Collier. And the rest of it, he planned out like a snake. Buried the little boy in the basement, worked up that lie for his wife to tell, bullied her into telling it—I can tell you one thing, Sidonia was scared clean out of her mind by her husband. And it was a good lie. There wasn't nothing we could check, nothing to say it wasn't true. They didn't go to the Magnolia Tree—I got that nailed down this afternoon—but that ain't a crime, just like it ain't a crime for a woman to use her own kitchen or a man to go in and work on a Saturday morning. That's where he was. In his office, and the secretary he dragged in with him to testify to his whereabouts. He had it all worked out."

"Yeah." Lilah thought of Cranmer Stark on the cellar stairs, thought of the thing he maybe hadn't seen—but maybe had. She said, "If I was you, I'd tell Mrs. Stark to sell that house. Or burn it, maybe. If it was mine, I'd burn it."

"Me, too. Sidonia claimed she hadn't noticed anything funny . . . but she was looking over her shoulder the whole time. I was, too."

"I don't think it can hurt people 'cept in the cellar, and maybe only after dark. I mean, it had two months to get me or Mrs. Stark—or Mr. Stark—and it didn't." She shivered. "But it wanted to."

"I never saw the boy but twice. Was he . . . was he a mean little boy?"

"No. That's the worst thing. He wasn't mean at all." She gulped, feeling her eyes start to prickle with tears. "He just wanted his daddy to love him. And his daddy didn't love him, and his mama didn't love him, and I didn't love him, neither. Didn't nobody love him, and maybe that's enough to make anybody mad." She got a handkerchief out of her purse and cried. Sheriff Patterson drove and didn't say anything.

Finally, calm again, Lilah said, "Where're you taking me, sheriff? You planning to drive all night?"

"It's another fifteen minutes to the state line. That should give you as much head start as you need on any trouble I can't box up."

"Well," Lilah said with a sigh, "Arkansas can't be any worse'n Mississippi."

The state line was marked by a sign so weather-beaten that only the letters "ARKA" were legible. Sheriff Patterson pulled over. He said abruptly, "What do you think killed Butch? Do you think it was just fright?"

"I dunno," Lilah said. "I told you, he hadn't seen it, and he didn't feel it. I mean, you felt it—not right away maybe, but you felt it."

"Yeah," said the sheriff. "I felt it all right."

"Butch didn't. He didn't feel it at all until he looked up from . . . from the body. And if I got to guess, I think it was like it was too sudden. Like, my brothers knew a boy who died of jumping in a lake, because it was so cold and he went in all at once, and his heart just stopped. I think it was like that."

"You don't think . . . you don't think the little boy could have done it?"

"No," Lilah said.

"That's good," said the sheriff. "That's good to hear."

Lilah got out of the car, slung her purse on her shoulder. She started toward Arkansas, then suddenly turned and ran back to the car. The sheriff looked up at her.

"Burn the house," Lilah said. "Do it yourself. Do it tonight."

Sheriff Patterson looked at her a moment, silently; they both knew what had killed Butch Collier, and it hadn't been fright. Butch had seen the watcher's face.

The sheriff touched the brim of his hat, said, "Ma'am, you're a smart woman." He shifted into first, pulled the car in a long, slow loop just shy of the Arkansas state line, and started back for Hyperion.

Lilah watched until his tail-lights were no more than dim red sparks in the distance. Then she turned, squared her shoulders, and—sixteen years old and six hours a widow—walked out of Mississippi forever.

THE HALF-SISTER

I WAS CLEANING the lamps when the stranger knocked.

I knew it was a stranger, right off, because whoever it was didn't know about the postern door that's the only thing in the front wall that opens. They'd knocked at the ceremonial gate that hasn't been used since Father reached his majority and won't be again until Gunther comes of age in another twenty years—if Father hasn't quarreled irrevocably with Gertrude before then and disinherited the whole pack of them.

I stayed where I was, up to my elbows in lamp-oil and dirt, while Nanna creaked her way slowly across the hall. Nanna's terrible arthritis does not change the fact that she is the ranking woman in the household. Gertrude hates that, but she loses the argument every time she starts it. Lane outranked Nanna, but it didn't matter, with Lane lying there like a dead thing in her bedroom, without even the strength to turn her face to the wall.

Nanna wrestled the door open, and stuck her head out to shout at whoever it was. I could hear a mutter of explanations and apologies, but all of the greeting formulas got carried away by the wind, so I was completely unprepared for the man who stepped into the hall at Nanna's gesture of invitation.

He screamed *Southerner* from head to foot, from his braided hair and long mustaches to the expensive but completely inadequate boots on his feet. They were soaked right through. I suppose he was handsome, if you go in for that sort of thing, though there was too much cheekbone for my taste—too much crag. Craggy-faced men always think far better of themselves than they need to.

He said to Nanna, slowly and distinctly, as if she were some kind of idiot, "May I see Madalane, please?"

I knew who he was. My hands—big, lumpy-knuckled hands, short-nailed and filthy—clenched so hard that the rag twisted between them tore. Nanna and the stranger both turned to stare at me; from the way his head jerked around, he hadn't even realized I was there.

I stood up, conscious of my shabby dress, the strands of hair escaping from my hairpins. "You should not be here."

"You must be Karlin," he said, as if I'd said something normal and polite. "Madalane told me a great deal about you."

If he thought that would make me like him, he could have spared his breath. "And you're Gerard. Lane hasn't said a word about you."

His face darkened in hurt and anger. But I continued before he could find words: "Leave. Please. Leave Lane alone."

"Lane can make her own choices, Karlin," Nanna said, her pale eyes sharp for once. "You will not make them for her." She turned and hobbled slowly out of the hall.

I stepped out from behind the table where I had been seated and approached Gerard. Prince Gerard of Hylfeneth, he was, and by Southern reckoning, Lane was his wife, although I wasn't sure whether their marriage was binding under Northern laws. It was one of the many things Lane wouldn't tell me.

"Please," I said, though the word was dry and bitter in my mouth. "Just *go*."

"I can't," he said, spreading his hands as if he expected me to understand.

"Haven't you hurt her enough?"

"*Hurt* her?"

"If she dies," I said, "it will be because you have killed her."

For a minute, I thought he was going to hit me, and so did he. But he changed his mind, and ran his hand over his face instead.

"Karlin," he said at last, and if I could have liked him, I might have pitied the weariness in his voice, "I don't know why you hate me, but I don't think you have any idea of why Madalane left Hylfeneth."

"Don't I?"

"You don't know what we went through."

"You haven't sat with her every night for a month of nightmares. You weren't here when she came riding up the pass like something that had been dead for a week and was just too brute obstinate to admit it. You haven't argued with her over ever single bite of food she eats—and had to give the half of her meals to the pigs anyway. I have. So don't tell me what I don't know."

He looked as if each word was a separate nail being pounded into his flesh, and maybe he would have left then, maybe he would have gone and left Lane alone, except that a voice said, thin and shaky, "Gerard?"

We both turned. It was her.

I don't know how she did it. She hadn't been able to leave her room for weeks, even to escape from Father, but there she was, leaning in the doorway—white as a ghost but fully dressed.

"Lane," I said. "Lane, you oughtn't—"

"Gerard?" she said again, and then they were clinging together in the doorway, talking and laughing and crying all together in a horrible tangle, and I knew that she was going back. Going back to Hylfeneth, going back to him, going back to the life I'd thought and hoped and even prayed she'd renounced. I'd thought she'd begun to see me again, the way she'd seen me before some fool traveling peddler had infected her with dreams of Hylfeneth and she'd stopped seeing anything but the blood-red minarets and lace-spun bridges of the stories. I'd thought, when she came back, that the reality had cured her of the mindless dreams, that if we could just wait out the last throes of the fever, Lane would be back, my Lane who'd never laughed at me for being raw-boned and ugly and dark, who'd never called me goblin, who had shared with me things that this handsome hero would never understand. He didn't know the Lane I did. I'd thought Lane had realized that, too, but the radiance on her face told me I was wrong.

They were deciding to leave as I watched them. I could see it on their faces. They would go riding off into the clouds together, and Lane wouldn't have to face Father or explain herself to Gertrude or confront any of the remnants of a life she didn't want. She didn't even see me when she said goodbye, only her faithful half-sister—every heroine has one.

I don't know if there was something I could have said, some way I could have reached her. I lie awake nights, wondering. But there was nothing I could have told her that she didn't already know, and if what she knew was not enough to keep her here, then what use would any words of mine be?

She strode out ahead of Gerard, eager for the next adventure I suppose, and I caught his cloak and said, "When she dies, don't bring her body here."

I don't think he understood me, not really, but he understood something, because he nodded and said, a little awkwardly, as if he wasn't used to it, "Karlin, I'm sorry."

I shook my head. "She's made her choice."

He left then, following her as he would follow her anywhere, and I stayed behind, as I had stayed behind the first time she left. Stayed behind to keep the lamps clean and lit, to keep the household running, to keep carrying the responsibilities Lane had let fall.

I'm no heroine. I don't have a story. And Lane's story is not mine to tell, except for this: *she made her choice.*

ASHES, ASHES

SNOW FELL from the gray sky like ashes.

I stood at the window, defying the weather to affect my mood. After months of restoration and renovation, we were finally moving into the house where my husband had spent his childhood summers, the house of the grandmother he loved, who had died when he was fifteen. The house had been standing vacant ever since, and for a time we had despaired of rendering it liveable at all.

I wanted our success to be greeted with dazzling sunlight, but instead we had gray louring clouds and snow.

Martin came up behind me, his arms sliding around my waist, and kissed the back of my neck. "Penny for your thoughts, beloved."

"I was just watching the snow," I said. I turned in the circle of his arms and stood up on tip-toe to kiss him. "And thinking how glad I am to be here."

He smiled, his dark eyes crinkling at the corners. "Grandmother Louise would be happy. Do you want to take a walk?"

"Yes, I'd like that," I said. "Show me where you used to play." I let him help me with my coat.

The snow was falling slowly, big wet flakes that melted like kisses as they touched the ground. We chose a path that led down into the woods behind the house; I held closely to Martin's arm. The doctor had said I did not need to treat myself as if I were made of glass, but I could remember my grandmother and her sisters trading their cautionary tales whenever one of their daughters or daughters-in-law or granddaughters announced she was pregnant.

I was determined to be careful, more than willing to let Martin coddle me as if I were his child rather than his wife.

We followed the narrow path through the trees, our shoes rustling damply among the dead leaves.

"This must be lovely in the spring," I said.

"You don't find it lovely now?"

"Oh, it's pretty enough, I guess, but . . . I don't know. It's awfully bleak." *Barren*, I thought, but it was not a word I was prepared to say. Not now. Instead, I smiled up at him and said, "I like my landscapes brightly colored."

"I'll plant you roses," he promised, smiling back.

I heard the voices first as no more than the wind among the crumbling dead leaves. But they were voices, children's voices, and after a moment I could understand their words.

Ashes, ashes, we all fall down . . . ashes, ashes, we all fall down . . .

"Do you hear that?"

"Hear what?" said Martin.

"Those children."

"Children? What are you talking about?"

Ashes, ashes, we all fall down . . . ashes, ashes, we all fall down . . .

"Don't you hear them?"

We had both stopped in the middle of the path. I was holding onto Martin's arm with both hands. He was frowning, head cocked, listening but—I realized, my stomach tightening into a cold knot—not hearing.

"Just the wind, beloved." He started walking again; numbly, I followed suit. But I could still hear those small, thin voices, that dreary singsong chant: *Ashes, ashes, we all fall down . . .* And I heard it all the way back to the house.

I tried to put it out of my mind, tried to concentrate on our house, our child, the life Martin and I were building together. I found myself avoiding the windows that looked out on the woods, found myself stopped, listening, at odd times of day, for voices that I did not hear. One afternoon, while Martin was teaching, I walked down to the woods by myself, and the voices came rushing to meet me, as if I were a playmate they had been waiting for. *Ashes, ashes, we all fall down . . . ashes, ashes, we all fall down . . .* I fled back to the house, but even a long, hot shower could not entirely dispel my shivering.

That Saturday, I suggested to Martin that we go walking in the woods again. He was agreeable, and we started down the path together. It was snowing, and I was glad to have his arm to hold to.

The voices sobbed in my head from the moment we passed the first line of trees. When we'd safely reached the bottom of the hill, I stopped Martin and said, my voice unnaturally casual, "There they are again."

"What?"

"Martin, please. You really don't hear them?"

"Hear *what*?"

"The children. Singing." And I joined in: "Ashes, ashes, we all fall down . . . ashes, ashes—"

"I don't hear anything of the sort," Martin said, but his face had gone pale and his mouth was tight. "Come on. We'd better go home." He turned and all but dragged me back the way we had come; we were halfway up the hill before I could brace my feet and pull free of him.

"Martin."

For a moment, I thought he would simply keep walking, head down like an angry bull. Then he stopped, sighed heavily, and turned. "What?"

Nothing, I almost said. *You're right. I was imagining things.* But for once I stood my ground. "You know something."

"About your imaginary voices? No. But I'm starting to think I should call Dr. Baines when we get back to the house."

The cruelty in his voice took my breath away. He had never spoken to me like that before. "You think I'm hysterical," I said. "Pregnant women have their fancies, right?" It was another topic on which my grandmother and great-aunts could hold forth for hours.

"I didn't mean—"

"Go on back to the house then," I said, my voice high and shaking with anger. "Go call Dr. Baines. I'm going to take a walk." I turned and started away, half-blind with tears, but whether of fury or hurt I did not know.

I followed the voices, ignoring the path and Martin's voice behind me. Branches caught in my hair, snagged my stockings. I skidded down into a dry creek bed and only kept upright by scraping my hands raw on a half-dead tree. The voices did not get louder or clearer, but they were closer. I could feel them, like cold, cold fingers on the back of my neck. And all the while the snow fell, soft and silent, disappearing against the black branches, the gray and brown of the dead leaves and stones. *Barren,* I thought again and shivered.

Ashes, ashes, we all fall down . . . Children's voices, but not *young* children, not young enough still to enjoy that particular game. They sounded breathless, almost scared, and I thought for no reason of the wicked stepmother in the fairytale, who was forced to dance in red-hot shoes until she fell down dead.

And then I fell myself, landing awkwardly on one knee and my already abraded palms. I thought—a panic-stricken lightning bolt—of the baby, and became as still as if I had been turned to stone, all my attention focused inward. But there was no pain, no sense of slippage or loss, none of the wrongness I was sure I would feel, and after a moment I began to breathe again.

Cautiously, not yet ready to try to stand up, I looked around, seeing the tangle of dead tree branches and grape-vines leaning over one side of the creek bed (which was now becoming more like a ravine), the jumbled stones underfoot—it was no wonder I had fallen, and I was lucky not to have broken anything. The other bank had a decided overhang; I could see the interlaced tree roots holding it up. And near where I was crouched, there was a place where the roots had not held, and the bank had caved in, a long, ugly spill of rocks and red clay.

And something that was neither red clay nor rock.

I did not want to see, and yet I found myself moving closer, in a painful sideways hobble. It was the shape that caught my attention first, the smooth rounded curve that could never be the shape of a rock. And then I was crouched in front of that treacherous grade, snowflakes wet against my face and neck and the cold whisper of the voices making me shiver: *ashes, ashes, we all fall down . . .* I reached out, my hand shaking, and brushed dirt away from that smooth, strangely vulnerable curve.

I saw the truth before I saw the hollowed eye-sockets.

I lost myself for a moment; when my mind cleared, I was digging in the bank as frenziedly as any small animal who hears the cry of a hawk. The bones were jumbled together. I found two more skulls in close proximity to the first, along with a scattering of vertebrae and small bones that I thought were probably phalanges, and then sat back on my heels, realizing I was panting, dripping with sweat, that I'd torn all my nails back to the quick, and that the appropriate thing to do was return to the house and call the police. When you find human remains on your property, you aren't expected to exhume them yourself.

Human remains, I thought. *Ashes, ashes,* cried the voices.

And Martin knew something, something he did not want to know.

I knew in that moment that I did not want to know, either. This secret, buried like bones, was a terrible threat, like the rot that had weakened the tree roots here until the bank collapsed. I wanted to pretend ignorance, to cover these poor bones again and return to the house, to let Martin take me to Dr. Baines and be prescribed bed-rest and pampering. But as I reached out for that first handful of loose dirt, I thought, *What about our child?* What would I be condemning our child to? Growing up among lies and shadows, taught to fear and never told why, lest she, too, begin to hear the cold, pale voices that whispered 'round my head. *Ashes, ashes, we all fall down . . .*

I straightened my fingers, let the dirt sift back. I touched the skulls again, gently, in apology for my cowardice. Then I pushed myself to my feet, wincing at the pain of my cramped knees and ankles, and began slowly and cautiously to make my way back to the house.

I saw it even before I was clear of the trees, all the lights blazing. As I started up the steps, the door was flung open; Martin stood outlined against the spill of light, a looming shape like a troll in a fairytale, and for a moment I was afraid he would deny me entrance.

Then he was rushing to help me, trying almost to carry me into the house. I could not at first pick words out of what he said, only the overwhelming wash of his concern and fear. I pulled away from him as soon as we were inside. "I need to call the police."

"The *police?* Are you—"

I interrupted him ruthlessly, before my cowardice could keep me from saying the words at all: "There are three skeletons in our woods. Three dead children."

His hand, reaching out for me, froze an inch away from my arm. "Dead children?" he said in a dry whisper.

"Who are they, Martin? Who *were* they?"

"It can't be," he said, his face ashen, and slumped sideways against the wall.

I followed him, catching his shoulder, shaking him. "What do you know?"

"She said it wasn't true," Martin said, his voice thin and dreamy, his eyes very wide. A child's eyes, like the child's rhyme that had been echoing in my head for days.

"Who?" I said, more gently. "Who said?"

He looked at me as if he did not recognize me and said, "Grandmother Louise," and then slowly folded up, sinking down the wall to sit with his head against his knees and his arms wrapped around his shins. "Call the police."

I dialed with shaking fingers. And all the time I was on the phone—and it took a remarkably long time to convince them that I meant it when I said I had discovered human remains in the woods behind the old Shoemaker place—Martin did not move.

The silence in our house was as thick and choking as a London fog for the next week. The police exhumed the bones and took them away; the officer in charge promised that she would let us know what they learned. She could tell we were upset, but I suppose that anyone would be; she did not press us for explanations, accepting at face value my story of falling over the bones while out walking. My battered state lent credence to a tale that I myself found woefully implausible. But if any of the police officers heard voices in the woods, they did not mention it.

We waited for the officer's return like defendants waiting for a verdict, both of us shying away from each other when our paths crossed. Martin did not sleep in our bed; I stayed out of the living room and study. I seemed to spend half my time crying; he spent hours on campus, and I did not know what he did there.

It was Friday afternoon when the officer called and said she had something to tell us, if we would let her stop by after work. I said, *Of course,* assured her that six o'clock was a perfectly acceptable time, hung up the phone, my heart hammering in my chest.

Calling Martin was the second hardest thing I'd ever done.

The officer was prompt; I'd made coffee—though anything else seemed too social, too much like it belonged in an Addams cartoon. We sat in the living room, the officer in the armchair, Martin and I at opposite ends of the couch like semi-cordial strangers, all of us cradling our mugs in our hands as if for warmth, although the house was well-heated and well-insulated. The officer stirred cream carefully into her coffee, then looked at us and said, "You've helped us solve the three oldest missing persons cases on our books. Thank you."

"Then you know . . . " Martin stopped, cleared his throat. "Then you know who they are."

"There was never much doubt about it. Especially once we got the bones dated. Those are the Three Lost Children of 1922." Martin put his mug down, but not quite quickly enough to hide the fact that his hands were shaking; the officer continued, sympathetic but implacable: "Charles Weatherby, Marianne Bolton, and Alma Shoemaker."

"My grandmother's sister," Martin said. "Thank God she never had to know her sister was . . . "

"Yes, sir." She looked at me and saw I was still in the dark. "Alma Shoemaker disappeared in March of 1922, Marianne Bolton in June, and Charles Weatherby in October. The two girls were twelve years old, and the boy was eleven. In December, a thirteen-year-old girl named Juliet Laroux was assaulted, but she managed to escape. She identified her attacker, without hesitation, as Roderick Shoemaker."

"My grandmother's favorite uncle," Martin said thinly. "She swore he was innocent, you know."

"He never confessed to the murders of the other three, and he never came to trial."

"Lynched," Martin said, still in that same faint, faraway voice.

"And so no one ever found out what he had done with the bodies. Did he ever live in this house? Do you know?"

"No, he never lived here. But he visited. He was quite noted for . . . for his way with the children. Excuse me." He left the room in a rush. The police officer and I sat, holding our mugs, not speaking.

After a time she said, "Even if Roderick Shoemaker *was* innocent, ma'am, whoever did this is long dead. And there've never been any other disappearances like those. You don't need to worry . . . "

"Thank you," I said. "I know."

I managed to smile at her, but it felt as fragile as blown glass. And although I did not want to, I said, "How did they die?"

"We don't know, ma'am. We don't have enough to go on."

"No, I suppose not."

But I knew, although I did not think I would tell the police officer so. I remembered those cold, breathless voices, and like any child, I had sung that selfsame doggerel. He had strangled them: garotted them probably, making his own meaning out of a nonsense rhyme.

"Ashes, ashes," I murmured, and the police officer nearly spilled her coffee.

"Ma'am? *What* did you say?"

"I was thinking of the children's rhyme. You know. Ring around the rosies—"

"Why?" Her eyes were wide, and she looked less like a police officer and more like a frightened little girl.

"I beg your pardon?"

"The man who attacked Juliet Laroux. That was how she knew who it was. Because he was singing 'Ring around the rosies,' and she recognized his voice."

"Oh God," I said. "Oh dear God." And I am sure my eyes were as wide as hers.

"How did you know?" she whispered.

"You did hear them," Martin said from the doorway. He was white-faced but composed. "You heard them singing their murderer's favorite song."

"*Heard* them?"

"It was how I found the bones," I said. "I . . . followed the voices. Charles and Marianne and Alma. 'Ashes, ashes, we all fall down.'"

The officer drained her coffee in a gulp, as if she wished it were something much stronger. "I don't think I'll put that in the report, if you don't mind, ma'am."

"Not at all," I said faintly.

"And I think I'd best be going." She stood up, nodded to both of us. "Thank you for the coffee. Sir, ma'am."

Martin let her out and then came back, hesitating a moment in the doorway. I was afraid he would turn and leave, that this house would again become the separate territories of two frightened and hostile creatures. I stretched out a hand toward him. He crossed the room, slowly, and sat down beside me, this time close enough that our thighs were touching. A hesitation, and he put his arm around me. I leaned into his embrace, and some of the tension ebbed out of our bodies.

He said, "I'm sorry."

"For what?"

"For not believing . . . for trying to make you not believe."

"Martin—"

"She told me so many stories about him. She told me about playing Ring Around the Rosies with him, about the way he'd sing it coming up the drive. She was fifteen when he . . . when Alma . . . She had a crush on him, I think, and of course no one told her anything. I think she told herself so many times that he was innocent that she simply *believed* it, even when she knew the evidence. The truth." He managed a small, infinitely painful laugh. "I guess now I know why she hated Juliet Laroux so much."

"Martin, you don't—"

"I don't think she ever talked about him to anyone but me. I was her favorite grandchild, her only male descendant. She told me once I looked like her Uncle Roderick." He pressed his free hand against his mouth, as if to steady it. "You don't think . . . "

"No. And even if you do, it doesn't matter."

We were silent for a while, but peacefully. He said, "Do you want to move?"

"Move?"

"This house . . . you can't want to live here knowing—"

"It isn't the house's fault. And whatever happened here happened a very long time ago. I'd rather stay and push the darkness back."

"Beloved," he said, and his arm tightened around me. And after a time he began to speak of other things, the day-to-day realities of the life we were building, and I was able to relax, to believe what I had said. This was our house now. It did not belong to the past.

And yet. The woods behind our house are beautiful, but I do not want our child to play there. I do not want to think about what might be watching.

SIDHE TIGERS

AT NIGHT the tigers pace. In the hall outside the little boy's bedroom, they pace like patient, vengeful angels. They are pale green, like luna moths; their eyes are lambent milky jade. They are cold and silent; when he has to go to the bathroom at night, the tigers stare at him with their pale pale eyes, and sometimes they open their mouths, as if they were roaring, but they make no sound. Their breath is like the aftertaste of brandy and the cold sting of snow. They never come near enough to touch. He wants the tigers to like him, but he is afraid they don't. They brush against the walls with a distant shushing noise, and even in his room he can feel the soft, relentless percussion of their padding feet. The moonlight shining through the hall windows streams straight through them.

No one else can see the tigers.

The house is always cold. His desire for warmth causes his father to brand him a sissy-boy, a weakling. At night he hugs himself, because no one else will, and dreams of escaping this loveless house, these cold tigers.

Years later, his father dies. He goes back because he must, leaving behind lover, friends, work, passion—his adult life like a treasure, locked in a chest for safekeeping. The house is unchanged, his mother petrified in her harsh condemnation of the world and its inchoate yearning for love. She puts him in his old room at the top of the house, as if he had never left at all.

That night, he hears the tigers, the patient rhythm of their feet marking off the seconds until Doomsday. "You aren't real,"

78

he whispers to them, lying stiff and cold, afraid to close his eyes because then he might be able to hear them more clearly. But the tigers, unheeding, continue pacing until dawn.

A LIGHT IN TROY

SHE WENT DOWN to the beach in the early mornings, to walk among the cruel black rocks and stare out at the waves. Every morning she teased herself with wondering if this would be the day she left her grief behind her on the rocky beach and walked out into the sea to rejoin her husband, her sisters, her child. And every morning she turned away and climbed the steep and narrow stairs back to the fortress. She did not know if she was hero or coward, but she did not walk out into the cold gray waves to die.

She turned away, the tenth morning or the hundredth, and saw the child: a naked, filthy, spider-like creature, more animal than child. It recoiled from her, snarling like a dog. She took a step back in instinctive terror; it saw its chance and fled, a desperate headlong scrabble more on four legs than on two. As it lunged past her, she had a clear, fleeting glimpse of its genitals: a boy. He might have been the same age as her dead son would have been; it was hard to tell.

Shaken, she climbed the stairs slowly, pausing often to look back. But there was no sign of the child.

Since she was literate, she had been put to work in the fortress's library. It was undemanding work, and she did not hate it; it gave her something to do to fill the weary hours of daylight. When she had been brought to the fortress, she had expected to be ill-treated—a prisoner, a slave—but in truth she was mostly ignored. The fortress's masters had younger, prettier girls to take to bed; the women, cool and distant and beautiful as she had once been herself, were not interested in a ragged woman with haunted half-crazed eyes. The librarian, a middle-aged man already gone blind over his codices and scrolls, valued her for her voice. But he was the only person she had to talk to, and she blurted as she came into the library, "I saw a child."

"Beg pardon?"

"On the beach this morning. I saw a child."

"Oh," said the librarian. "I thought we'd killed them all."

"Them?" she said, rather faintly.

"You didn't imagine your people were the first to be conquered, did you? Or that we could have built this fortress, which has been here for thousands of years?"

She hadn't ever thought about it. "You really *are* like locusts," she said and then winced. Merely because he did not treat her like a slave, did not mean she wasn't one.

But the librarian just smiled, a slight, bitter quirk of the lips. "Your people named us well. We conquered this country, oh, six or seven years ago. I could still see. The defenders of this fortress resisted us long after the rest of the country had surrendered. They killed a great many soldiers, and angered the generals. You are lucky your people did not do the same."

"Yes," she said with bitterness of her own. "Lucky." Lucky to have her husband butchered like a hog. Lucky to have her only child killed before her eyes. Lucky to be mocked, degraded, raped.

"Lucky to be alive," the librarian said, as if he could hear her thoughts. "Except for this child you say you saw, not one inhabitant of this fortress survived. And they did not die quickly." He turned away from her, as if he did not want her to be able to see his face.

She said with quick horror, "You won't tell anyone? It's only a child. A . . . more like a wild animal. Not a threat. Please."

He said, still turned toward the window as if he could look out at the sea, "I am not the man I was then. And no one else will care.

81

We are not a people who have much interest in the past, even our own."

"And yet you are a librarian."

"The world is different in darkness," he said and then, harshly, briskly, asked her to get out the catalogue and start work.

SOME DAYS LATER, whether three or thirty, she asked shyly, "Does the library have any information on wild children?"

"We can look," said the librarian. "There should at least be an entry or two in the encyclopedias."

There were, and she read avidly—aloud, because the librarian asked her to—about children raised by wolves, children raised by bears. And when she was done, he said, "Did you find what you were looking for?"

"No. Not really. I think he lives with the dog pack in the caves under the fortress, so it makes sense that he growls like a dog and runs like a dog. But it doesn't tell me anything about . . . "

"How to save him?"

"How to love him."

She hadn't meant to say it. The librarian listened too well.

"Do you think he wishes for your love?"

"No. But he keeps coming back. And . . . and I must love someone."

"Must you?"

"What else do I have?"

"I don't know," he said, and they did not speak again that day.

SHE DID NOT ATTEMPT to touch the child. He never came within ten feet of her anyway, the distance between them as impassible as the cold gray sea.

But he was always there, when she came down the stairs in the morning, and when she started coming down in the evenings as well, he came pattering out from wherever he spent his time to crouch on a rock and watch her, head cocked to one side, pale eyes bright, interested. Sometimes, one or two of the dogs he lived with would come as well: long-legged, heavy-chested dogs that she imagined had been hunting dogs before the fortress fell to the locusts. Her husband had had dogs like that.

The encyclopedias had told her that he would not know how to speak, and in any event she did not know what language the people of this country had spoken before their world ended, as hers had, in fire and death. The child was an apt mimic, though, and much quicker-minded than she had expected. They worked out a crude sign-language before many weeks had passed, simple things like *food*, for she brought him what she could, and *no*, which he used when he thought she might venture too close, and *I have to go now*—and it was ridiculous of her to imagine that he seemed saddened when she made that sign, and even more ridiculous of her to be pleased.

She worried that her visits might draw the fortress's attention to him—for whatever the librarian said, she was not convinced the locusts would not kill the child simply because they could—but she asked him regularly if other people came down to the beach, and he always answered, *no*. She wasn't sure if he understood what she was asking, and the question was really more of an apotropaic ritual; it gave her comfort, even though she suspected it was meaningless.

Until the day when he answered, *yes*.

The shock made her head swim, and she sat down, hard and not gracefully, on a lump of protruding rock. She had no way of asking him who had come, or what they had done, and in a hard, clear flash of bitterness, she thought how stupid of her it was to pretend this child could in any way replace her dead son.

But he was all she had, and he was watching her closely. His face never showed any emotion, except when he snarled with fear or anger, so she did not know what he felt—if anything at all. She asked, *All right?*

Yes, the child signed, but he was still watching her as if he wanted her to show him what he ought to do.

She signed, *All right,* more emphatically than she felt it, but he seemed to be satisfied, for he turned away and began playing a game of catch-me with the two dogs who had accompanied him that morning.

She sat and watched, trying to convince herself that this was not an auspice of doom, that other people in the fortress could come down to the beach without any purpose more sinister than taking a walk.

Except that they didn't. The locusts were not a sea-faring people except in the necessity of finding new countries to conquer. They were not interested in the water and the wind and the harsh smell of salt. In all the time she had been in the fortress, she had never found any evidence that anyone except herself used the stairs to the beach. She was trying hard not to remember the day her husband had said, casually, *A messenger came from the lighthouse today. Says there's strangers landing on the long beach.* Little things. Little things led up to disaster. She was afraid, and she climbed the stairs back to the fortress like a woman moving through a nightmare.

Her louring anxiety distracted her so much that she asked the librarian, forgetting that he was the last person in the fortress likely to know, "Who else goes down to the beach?"

The silence was just long enough for her to curse herself as an idiot before he said, "That was . . . I."

"You?"

"Yes."

"Why? What on earth possessed you?"

His head was turned toward the window again. He said, "You spend so much time there."

At first she did not even understand what he was saying, could make no sense of it. She said, hastily, to fill the gap, "You're lucky you didn't break your neck."

"I won't do it again, if you don't want."

She couldn't help laughing. "You forget which of us is the slave and which the master."

"What makes you think I can forget that? Any more than I can forget that I will never see your face?"

"I . . . I don't . . . "

"I am sorry," he said, his voice weary although his posture was as poker-straight as ever. "I won't bother you about it again. I didn't mean to tell you."

She said, astonished, "I don't mind," and then they both, in unspoken, embarrassed agreement, plunged hastily into the minutiae of their work.

But that evening, as she sat on her rock beside the sea, she heard slow, careful footsteps descending the stairs behind her.

Come! said the child from his rock eight feet away.

Friend, she said, a word they'd had some trouble with, but she thought he understood, even if she suspected that what he meant by it was *pack-member.* And called out, "There's room on my rock for two."

Friend, the child repeated, his hands moving slowly.

No hurt, she said, and wondered if she meant that the librarian would not hurt the child, or that the child should not hurt the librarian.

Yes, he said, and then eagerly, *Rock!*

"What are you doing, this evening?" the librarian's voice said behind her.

"Teaching him to skip stones." She flung another one, strong snap of the wrist. Five skips and it sank. The child bounced in a way she thought meant happiness; he threw a stone, but he hadn't gotten the wrist movement right, and it simply dropped into the water. *Again!* he said, imperious as the child of kings.

She threw another stone. Four skips. The librarian sat down beside her, carefully, slowly.

She said, "What is the sea like, in darkness?"

"Much more vast than I remember it being, when I had my sight. It would do the generals good to be blind."

"Blindness won't teach them anything—they have never wanted to see in the first place."

"You think that's what makes the difference?"

"We learn by wanting," she said. "We learn by grieving."

Shyly, the librarian's hand found hers.

The child threw a stone.

It skipped seven times before it sank.

AMANTE DORÉE

"You are importunate, m'sieur."

In Nouvelle Orléans, the jewel of the Territoire Louisiane, the greatest American city of the Empire Français, to speak French with the hard drawl of an American could be a liability—or, if one carried it off well, a great asset. Annabel St. Clair worked hard to make her voice as much an asset as her hair or her skin or her brilliantly blue eyes.

"Mademoiselle St. Clair, please, I meant no insult."

M. Charpentier lied, and they both knew it. But Annabel was not here tonight for her pleasure, or even for her personal business. She was here on the business of the Emperor of France and the Americas, Napoléon IV—little though that august gentleman himself might know it. "Then shall we call it mere gaucheness and an apology accepted?"

"As you please, mademoiselle."

She liked seeing the flash of resentment in his eyes, the unspoken, unwilling acknowledgment that, although he was one of the wealthiest landowners in Louisiane and she a mere courtesan—what the Louisien nobility called an amante dorée—it was she who held the power this evening. To the child of threadbare, disapproving Boston respectability, that look was headier than wine. "You were inquiring, I believe, whether the gentleman who escorted me here intends also to escort me home?"

"Yes, mademoiselle."

"Considering the fact that he *is* a gentleman, surely that question was unnecessary."

"Mademoiselle St. Clair." The growl of rising temper, and she abandoned her game.

"But, m'sieur, tomorrow evening I am entirely free. And I would be most enchanted to have dinner, perhaps, with your friend." She did not look at the young man talking to Mme. Charpentier by the punch-bowl—the young man for whom M. Charpentier was but the grudging proxy—but she was keenly aware of him and had positioned herself carefully to give him her profile.

"You are most gracious," said M. Charpentier with a slight, sardonic bow. "And I am sure my friend would be very pleased with such an arrangement. But I know also that it would delight him to make your acquaintance now, even if only for a moment."

Is he so hungry, then? Good. That will make this business easier. She turned, smiled sultry promise into the young man's coffee-dark eyes, saw them kindle and flare in return. "That would be most acceptable, M'sieur Charpentier."

It was long past midnight the next night when Louis Vasquez left Annabel St. Clair's house, only slightly the worse for drink and wearing a sated smile that did not improve his looks.

Salomé came into Annabel's boudoir carrying a cup of hot milk sweetened with vanilla and honey. "Shall I brush your hair, chérie?" Her French was perfect Parisian, crisp and fluid; it was her employer who spoke the muddy Français Louisien.

"Please," Annabel said, accepting the milk.

"Was he very ennuyant?" Salomé asked as she began to separate Annabel's hair into thick swatches, her voice light but her eyes, when Annabel met them in the mirror, concerned.

Annabel shrugged a little. "No more than they ever are."

"Are you sore, chérie?"

"Nothing to signify. He was . . . eager."

"Will it be worth it?" Salomé picked up the brush and began to draw it through Annabel's long, heavy curls.

Annabel grinned. "It's always worth it, darlin'," she said, deliberately employing the American endearment to make Salomé wince. "But, yes, my talk with M'sieur Vasquez was most enlightening."

"And will your Oncle Jules feel the same way?"

"I think so," Annabel said, her smile now as sated and self-pleased as that of Louis Vasquez. "I think so indeed."

It was not so much that the government of Napoléon IV cared for the Bourbon pretenders who came and went like mayflies, as that they wanted to be able to keep a weather eye on them. It was unlikely, seventy years after the death of the last Bourbon king of France, that any of the pretenders were either legitimate or capable of a serious bid for the throne, but they could be, and often were, nuisances, lodestones drawing trouble from Spain and England, especially when they announced themselves in one of the American principalities.

Louis Vasquez could have been trouble, despite his Spanish blood, for he was young, handsome—the Hapsburg chin not in evidence—well-spoken, and plausible, but although he had puffed up his consequence with hints of royal blood and dreadful persecution, he had seemed to have no imperial ambitions. His imagination had been fired by tracts he had read about the western reaches of the empire; he spoke animatedly of prospecting for gold, of exploring the wilderness, of meeting Sioux and Iroquois. She had asked if he did not wish to return to Europe, and he had laughed and said, "Maybe in five years, ten years, if I do not find a beautiful American wife, hein?" And had pinched her, maybe a little more viciously than necessary. She had not been sorry to see him go, and was not sorry to think that he would not require further cultivation.

The next morning, as Annabel was writing a polite, opaquely worded note to convey these opinions to Jules Sevier, who was no more her uncle than he was the Prince de Louisiane, Salomé came into her boudoir to say, "There is a man who wishes to speak to you, mademoiselle."

"A man?" Annabel said, turning. "What sort of man?"

Salomé's mouth thinned. "I have his card."

Annabel accepted it, turned it over. The inscription on the front was stingy, merely *H. Quentin* and an address in a rather seedy part of town. On the back, equally stingily, someone with a perfect copperplate had written, *Louis Vasquez est mort.*

"Mordieu," Annabel muttered. A Bourbon pretender who was alive, self-important, and harmless was one thing; that same Bourbon pretender unexpectedly dead was potentially a much knottier problem.

"I will tell him you must not be bothered, mademoiselle," Salomé offered. "He is a shabby Anglais and should know better than to trouble you."

"Anglais? Truly?" It was not often one met with an Englishman in Nouvelle Orléans—or anywhere in Louisiane, for that matter.

"Yes, of course. He is not American. His manners are too good."

"I will see him," Annabel said—not that she wished to, but Sevier would want to know about any Anglais involved with Louis Vasquez, and if the young man was indeed dead . . . "Show him into the front parlor, please."

"Yes, mademoiselle," Salomé said, curtseying in protest. Annabel watched five minutes go by on her Limoges porcelain clock before following Salomé downstairs.

Monsieur H. Quentin was middle-aged, tall and slightly stooped. He was clean-shaven, which Annabel found more pleasing than the muttonchop whiskers currently en vogue, but his graying brown curls were untidy and overlong. Deep-set eyes of a light hazel were the only remarkable feature in a longish, indeterminate, but strong-jawed face. He was shabby, as Salomé had said, but clean and well-mended. He turned from his perusal of Annabel's delicately scandalous Japanese prints as she came in, and she said, "M'sieur Quentin?"

"Mademoiselle St. Clair, I appreciate your agreeing to see me this morning." His French was excellent, Parisian rather than Louisien. His hand, when he took hers, was as narrow and long-fingered as her own; he had a copyist's calluses, which made sense of his beautiful, impersonal handwriting.

"You bring word that Louis Vasquez is dead," Annabel said, dispensing with the civilities necessary in conversation with a Frenchman or a Louisien. "How?"

"That is indeed the great question. He dined here last night."

"Are you with the police, M'sieur Quentin?" Annabel said, very politely.

"No, mademoiselle," he said, equally politely; there were no Englishmen employed in any capacity by the governments of either Nouvelle Orléans or the Territoire Louisiane, and any resident of the city knew that as well as they knew to fear cholera in summer.

"Then I do not understand . . . "

"The police do not yet know that Monsieur Vasquez ate his last meal here. I thought you might perhaps prefer that they not learn that. Or, at least, not yet."

"Why do you imagine that I do not desire to help the police in their investigations in any way possible?"

The brightness in his eyes showed that he was enjoying the sparring as much as she was. "Because I, too, Mademoiselle St. Clair, know who Louis Vasquez was."

"So, m'sieur. And who was Louis Vasquez?"

His lips quirked up. "A young gentleman of interest to Jules Sevier, who is well-known, in certain circles, to have taken you under his wing."

"And are those the circles in which you move, m'sieur?"

"Yes."

She tilted her head, considering him. It was possible that he was lying, that he had come by the information in some other way, but that did not change the fact that he knew who—and what— Jules Sevier was. And it explained what an Anglais was doing in Nouvelle Orléans.

"My uncle Jules," she said, "has been most kind to me." It was a lesson Sevier himself had taught her: admit nothing, even when cornered.

"Your uncle?" Polite skepticism.

She smiled at him brilliantly. "My mother was a Sevier, m'sieur."

"Of course," he murmured. "And did your uncle Jules also wish to be kind to Louis Vasquez?"

She widened her eyes at him, conscious of exhilaration dancing along her nerves, conscious also that they were both very close to laughter. "Why, how could he wish such a thing, m'sieur, when he never so much as met the unfortunate young man?"

"Ah. I thought perhaps he might have. It would explain . . . certain things."

"Such as?"

"The young man was murdered, mademoiselle, but not robbed, and in Nouvelle Orléans that is very much a surprise."

"Sloppy," she said, remembering Louis Vasquez's exceptionally fine pocket-watch.

"Yes. And I find that rather disturbing."

"Sometimes, m'sieur, when one goes walking in this quarter at unwise hours of the night, one does simply get murdered, for no better reason than that one is there."

"Yes, but after one has gone to the trouble of ridding oneself of one's . . . interested followers?"

Which is how he knows that Vasquez dined here last night. Of course. "I do not know why anyone would put themselves to the bother of murdering Louis Vasquez."

"No?"

"He spoke of Saint François, not Paris. He wished, he said, to see Indians."

"And yet he was killed last night. And not, let me be perfectly clear, by any subject of our most gracious Queen. We were intrigued by the young man, but not homicidal."

"You would hardly be homicidal," Annabel said tartly. "And please, M'sieur Quentin. *Your* most gracious Queen. I am not English."

"But you are not French, either."

"I am Louisienne. And I cannot help you."

"Cannot or will not?"

"Cannot, although I do not expect that you believe me."

"It is the hazard of our profession."

"Truly. Courtesans are such notorious liars."

He colored slightly and murmured, "Touché, mademoiselle." They smiled at each other, very much like fencers after a touch. "Shall I inform the police?"

"As you wish," she said. "He was not murdered here, and not even the police of Nouvelle Orléans are stupid enough to believe that a woman would follow him through the streets to murder him—or that she would succeed if she tried."

"Your most obedient, mademoiselle," he said, bowing, and left. Something in his manner told her that the police would go unenlightened.

She went back upstairs to continue her letter to Jules Sevier—including now the news of Louis Vasquez's murder and the information that the English had been sufficiently interested in him to have him followed. She did not expect to see M. Quentin again, and if the thought caused her a certain amount of melancholy, she did not confess it to anyone.

LOUIS VASQUEZ'S DEATH was not of great moment to most of Nouvelle Orléans. He was not the first young Frenchman—nor would he be the last—to meet his death through foolhardy exploration of the city after nightfall, and most people were perfectly satisfied with that explanation. And those who knew of Louis Vasquez's potential second identity as Louis XVIII of France had no eagerness to advertise their doubts about the popularly accepted story. Their investigations proceeded, but quietly and very much under the table. They were not distressed by the young man's death (Jules Sevier said to his "niece"), but they were definitely disquieted; he had been murdered, neither by accident nor by chance, but without official sanction from the emperor or his ministers.

Annabel, on her knees before him—for Sevier had ever believed in combining business with pleasure—made no response. None was expected, and a few moments later, Sevier lost the train of his remarks, his clutching fingers dislodging the pink silk rosebuds twined in her hair.

SHE HAD ASSUMED she would not see M. Quentin again, but in the following week it came to seem as if she could not stir from her house without falling over him. At the symphony, at the opera, at balls: when she made discreetly careless inquiries, she discovered that he was generally known to be connected in some fashion with the English embassy. She wondered if he had been there all along and she had simply not noticed him, dismissed him as too shabby to be worth her while. It was a lowering thought, and she countered it by starting a fiercely vivacious flirtation with him. He surprised her by responding very much in kind, and with the air of a man who was long-accustomed to such things. She wondered even more what he had been before he came to Nouvelle Orléans.

Quentin was very glad to be summoned into Annabel's box at the opera from his seat in the pit; they argued about music in preference to discussing matters which would force one or both of them to lie. They danced together at the public balls, matched in lightness of foot as much as in height. And the moment inevitably came, having sought respite from the crowd and hellacious heat in a private parlor, when Quentin said to Annabel, out of a flurry of gentle, semi-nonsensical repartee, "Does an amante dorée ever stoop to kiss a man who cannot pay her?"

Annabel became very still. "Are you propositioning me, M'sieur Quentin?"

"Do you wish me to, Mademoiselle St. Clair?"

"I cannot imagine what might have given you that idea," she said, turning toward the closed jalousies.

"The way you look at me, mademoiselle. The way I know I look at you."

"M'sieur, you know what I am."

"I do," he said, and she heard the rustle of cloth as he approached. "And you know what I am."

"A spy and an Englishman."

"Just so. And you are a courtesan, an American, and a spy for the interests of the French emperor."

"It is true."

"We need tell each other nothing. Annabel—"

"Oh, this is foolish. I do not even know your Christian name."

"Horatio, but I dislike it. I like the way you say 'Quentin' very much."

"Quentin, I—" She turned and found he was much closer to her than she had expected, closer than she was prepared for.

"Annabel," he said gently, "you cannot be afraid of me."

"Of course I am not." But she felt herself take a step backwards regardless. Her pulse was pounding in her throat, and she could not quite keep her hands from coming up as if to fend him off.

"You know I will not hurt you. If you do not wish a liaison, you have only to say so."

But he was so close, and it was not the liaison that she did not wish. His hands caught hers gently; she had to tilt her head back only slightly to meet his lips.

For a moment, the kiss was perfect, their bodies pressing close together through the layers of their clothing. Then Quentin pulled back, his grip hard on her wrists, his eyes wide, dark, both shocked and intent. And then he moved, fast as a cat, pinned her against the wall, his hands clenching in the lace draperies of her bodice, tightening. He said, almost conversationally, "You are not a woman."

"I *am!*" Desperately, she kneed him in the groin and bolted past him, leaving a good foot of dyed lace twisted in his fingers. She clutched her bodice together with both hands, aware of the cacophony of the ballroom, knowing she did not dare to scream.

He had staggered against the wall, but not fallen. His face was ashen, his expression . . . she turned away. "I am sorry to have hurt you, m'sieur. You frightened me."

"What are you?"

"Exactly what you called me. A courtesan, an American, and a spy."

"But you . . . you . . . " He drew himself upright. "I beg your pardon. It would be best if I did not further impose upon you. I shall fetch your cloak."

She had taken her lower lip between her teeth to keep from saying anything; she stayed as she was, her shoulders straight but her head bowed, as he silently left the room and silently returned, putting her cloak on a chair by the door. Only when the door latched shut behind him for the second and final time did she sink to her knees, folding around the throbbing, aching hardness in her groin, her fingers catching the lace that Quentin had dropped on the floor. Soundlessly, Annabel St. Clair began to cry.

THE NEXT DAY, Annabel did not leave the house. Her servants went about their duties in silence; she knew how bad she must look by the fact that Salomé did not seek her out, did not ask. But on the Monday, she could not stay hidden. The scandal had not broken; Quentin had held his tongue. She did not want to receive a letter— or worse, a visit—from Jules Sevier, chastising her for neglecting her responsibilities. She went out in the evening, danced, laughed, flirted madly. When she came home, she did not drink herself into a stupor, despite the temptation.

And she was glad of it the next morning, when the first post brought her a message from Sevier.

He had a task for her.

He had reason to suspect that Spain was involved in the death of Louis Vasquez. Annabel frowned, rereading Sevier's note. It made no sense. The Spanish had maintained their independence from France by the skin of their teeth—and the surrender of their holdings in the New World. They pretended complaisance, but no citizen of France doubted the ardor with which they desired the return of Floride, Mexique, and Californie. There had even been, in recent years, some amelioration of the centuries-old hostility between Spain and England, as the two battered European powers began to jockey against the might of France. The last thing in the world Ferdinand VII would want to do was rid France of a young man who was at the least an embarrassment and at the most a potential disaster. And, moreover, a kinsman of his—assuming that Louis Vasquez's claims were true, which had never been established.

And whether his claims were true or not, Louis Vasquez was hardly the first Bourbon pretender to show up in Nouvelle Orléans. Many of the others had also met their ends in its sweltering streets—but not at the instigation of the Spanish. But the Spanish ambassador's secretary, Don Carlos Morado y Soto, was asking questions, poking around in the affairs of both the embassy treasurer and the spymaster. Clearly, he believed there was collusion somewhere. The question was, wrote Sevier, what did he *know*, and what did he suspect?

And, given her past history with Don Carlos, Sevier wanted Annabel to find out.

She pushed aside her accounts book and began to consider ways and means of accidentally encountering Don Carlos Morado y Soto.

DON CARLOS WAS the personal secretary to his Excellency the Ambassador: middle-aged, close-mouthed, and very good at his job. He also had a terrible weakness, of which neither his wife nor his employer was aware, and it was that weakness that had brought him into Annabel's orbit.

Like many of her other patrons, he considered her a godsend. She was beautiful, notorious; to be seen with her conferred upon a man that certain distinction which only other men appreciated. And yet, in bed . . . She guarded their secrets, and they guarded hers. It was—and Annabel admitted it—a particularly genteel form of mutual blackmail, but it provided her security. There were a shocking number of highly-placed men in Nouvelle Orléans who had a vested interest in keeping as silent as the tomb the fact that Annabel St. Clair was not what she seemed.

Once, Salomé had said severely, "Someday, chérie, you will drop one of these eggs that you are juggling."

"Yes, and all Nouvelle Orléans will go up in flames," Annabel had said, laughing. "It will be worth it."

It was not, however, an eventuality she sought, and thus the myriad careful games she played with her admirers, both those who did not know and those who did. And thus the very little effort it took her to manipulate circumstances in her favor. She would not ordinarily have chosen to attend a performance of the latest German opera, preferring the lighter and more mannered Italian style, but she knew Don Carlos's tastes, and her surprise when he presented himself at her box during the first intermission of *Tristan und Isolde* was entirely manufactured.

It was a simple matter to cut him out of the pack of her admirers, simpler still to ascertain what she already knew, that Doña Mercedes, Don Carlos's Haitian-born wife, had returned to the island for reasons Don Carlos did not mention but which Annabel knew had to do with a particularly ugly imbroglio in the Spanish embassy involving Doña Mercedes and the son of the Ambassador's stablemaster. It was a good time for Don Carlos to be proving himself virile, a very good time for him to be seen in the corridors of the embassy with an amante dorée. She wondered, tucking away a smile before it could become a smirk, if she should write a letter of thanks to his wife.

She promenaded with him through the inevitable soirée in the embassy's main hall, kept her smile pleasant and her eyes soft. She drank wine with him in his suite, an Amontillado as dry as

Don Carlos's voice when he spoke of his wife. She allowed him to take her into his wife's bedroom, to remove her clothing one careful button at a time, to remove the pins from her hair and run his hands through its sunlight length. At his asking, she spread herself for him across his wife's bed; whether he held his wife in any regard or not—a question Annabel was disinclined to ask—Doña Mercedes had grievously wounded his pride.

Don Carlos was a courteous lover, unlike some of her patrons who seemed to wish to punish her for the desires they found unacceptable in themselves. He was never rough, never sought to humiliate her; she thought, if she had asked it of him, he would even have been willing to take her face to face.

She did not ask; she preferred her face to be hidden, just as she preferred the question of her arousal and how she achieved it to be largely academic to the men who shared her bed. Many of them did not care if she reached climax. Others, gentlemen like Don Carlos, wished her to receive pleasure as well as give, and if they were incidental to that pleasure—well, they did not ask, and she did not tell them. Her own hand at her groin and a headful of reliable fantasies did the trick quite nicely. If that night in the Spanish embassy, the man she dreamed of had Quentin's face and sharp, English-cadenced voice, it was of no concern to anyone but herself.

If it had been Quentin, she would have wanted to see his face when he spent himself. If it had been Quentin, she would not have had to bite her lip to keep from crying out his name. If it had been Quentin, perhaps she would not have wished so painfully to escape his post-coital embrace, would not have had to let her nails dig into her palms to keep from betraying distaste or impatience.

Afterwards, when Don Carlos slept, Annabel slipped out of bed, donned her shift, and made a cautious pilgrimage to investigate his desk.

Don Carlos was a methodical man, and since he was doing nothing wrong, he had not hidden his notes. Between the single candle she dared light and the cold high moon riding full outside the window, Annabel was able to make out the gist of them.

There wasn't a great deal. Some odd errors in bookkeeping that might not have been errors, a stableman who thought he might have seen Louis Vasquez leaving the embassy very late one night: suspicious circumstances, but hardly what one might call proof of anything. Except that Louis Vasquez had had oddly close dealings with the Spanish for someone claiming to be the rightful king of France. She returned to Doña Mercedes's bed and the snoring weight of Don Carlos, and lay unsleeping, thoughtful, waiting until the approach of dawn would make it possible for her to whisper gently in Don Carlos's ear that she had to leave.

But not quite an hour later, she heard footsteps in the hall. The footsteps of an excessively large number of people for that time of night.

The conclusion to which she leapt might have been wrong, but she did not dare to test it. She elbowed Don Carlos viciously, already scrambling up, diving for Doña Mercedes's massive wardrobe.

"What?" said Don Carlos as Annabel closed the wardrobe behind her and someone pounded on the door of the outer room. She heard him curse, a startlingly pungent oath for a Spanish don, but he was quick-witted, and he must have feared this eventuality as much as she had. She heard him get up, drag his robe on, stumble, cursing, to the door.

Her Spanish was not very good, but good enough for her to follow the outline of the ensuing exchange. Someone demanded to know the whereabouts of the amante dorée. Don Carlos demanded to know what business it was of theirs. *Never you mind that. Where is she?* Annabel pressed her fists against her mouth, praying. *I sent her home,* Don Carlos said and added a particularly unflattering epithet. Coarse laughter; Annabel hated them, silently, fiercely. A further spate of Spanish which she did not understand at all. She heard men moving around Don Carlos's apartments; she gripped the lip of the wardrobe door as hard as she could, having no other way to hold it closed. Mere moments later, someone tried the door, and she heard him call to Don Carlos, *This wardrobe door is stuck.* Don Carlos's reply was something about the embassy carpenter that made them all laugh again. And then, blessedly, they were leaving, grumbling about the high fidgets Don Esteban worked himself into.

Annabel was very, very cold.

The door closed, and she heard Don Carlos returning to the bedroom. She stayed where she was, naked among Doña Mercedes's gowns. When Don Carlos opened the wardrobe, she did not look up at him.

"I am sorry, Annabella," he said; she realized distantly that he was apologizing for the vulgar name he had called her, and shook her head. It didn't signify. He offered his hand.

She took it, only then feeling the throb of her fingertips from holding the wardrobe door so desperately. She forced herself not to scuttle for her shift, but to walk calmly. Inside her head, she was screaming, raging, cursing in French and English. Because she could not doubt that she had been deliberately trapped, and if she had been trapped, there was only one person who could have done it, the person who had sent her to Don Carlos's bed in the first place: Jules Sevier.

She picked up her shift and said, "Why should anyone wish to disgrace you, Don Carlos?"

"I beg your pardon?"

"You cannot imagine this was an accident," she said with asperity, and felt better for being clothed.

"Don Esteban is—"

"Don Esteban is your spymaster. I know that, even if you do not. Why would he wish you to be caught in bed with . . . " *A man.* But she wasn't one, and wouldn't say it. "With me?"

Don Carlos's face had gone gray, ill. She was sorry, but she did not have time for his sensibilities. "Don Carlos, I must be out of the embassy as soon as possible. Please. Tell me who would wish to see you . . . "

"No one, Annabella. I swear it on my honor. I have no enemies here, nor wish to. I serve His Excellency, and—"

She saw it hit him; his eyes widened and his mouth went slack behind his neat half-imperial. "But it was only a favor for Don Maurice."

"Don Maurice . . . Monseigneur le *Duc*?" Her voice squeaked on the last word, but there was only one nobleman she knew of in Nouvelle Orléans whose Christian name was Maurice, and that was the Duc de Plaquemine who held sovereignty over Nouvelle Orléans and the surrounding territory.

Don Carlos shook himself back into his secretarial persona. "Monseigneur de Plaquemine came to me a week ago, after the death of a young traveler, a gentleman of mixed French and Spanish blood named Louis Vasquez."

"Ah, *merde*," Annabel said before she could stop herself, but Don Carlos didn't seem to notice.

"He said that he had heard rumors that we—Spain—had been involved in the death of Señor Vasquez. He was very much distressed, even when I assured him we had not. So I promised I would . . . " He swallowed hard. "Investigate."

And although he had found nothing as of yet, it was painfully obvious that that did not mean there was nothing to find. And that whatever it was, it was more valuable to Jules Sevier than she was.

"Thank you," she said, struggling into her gown as quickly as she could. "I think, if you abandon your investigations, this sort of thing will not happen again."

"Abandon my investigations? Then it is true? We connived at the murder of—"

"Of a Bourbon pretender." And because he had always been gentle with her, she lied, "He must have been a threat to the Spanish throne as well. You did say he was half-Spanish."

"Yes," Don Carlos said. He sounded dazed and not entirely convinced, but she had done the best she could.

"I must go." She did not say good-bye, neither *au revoir* nor *adieu*, because she did not want to force either of them to say what they both knew: she would not see Don Carlos again.

Getting out of the Spanish embassy unseen was a challenge, but not beyond her capabilities. A greater obstacle was the question of where she could go once she stood outside its gates. Habit, after a night such as this, dictated that she go to the Sevier townhouse and make her report. But Sevier had sacrificed her like a pawn on a chessboard, and she was not confident that he would be happy to see her. It was possible—for anything was possible in the service of Jules Sevier—that she had not been merely an incidental target in the scheme against Don Carlos.

She could not go home, either, because if Sevier did wish to be rid of her, her house would be watched, and she did not want to bring trouble to Salomé and the servants. She could not go to any of her admirers; even those who could be blackmailed into sheltering her did not deserve the trouble she would bring in her wake.

She *needed* to gain an audience with the Duc de Plaquemine, but showing up on his doorstep at dawn, with her dress crumpled and her hair hanging down her back like a madwoman's, was not the way to achieve that.

She thought of taking sanctuary in a church, like the heroine of a romance, but while it was true that she could walk into any church in the city and Sevier would be helpless to drag her out, it was also true that that would solve nothing, gain her nothing. It was not time she needed; it was access.

And she could get that access, she realized, if she had the gall to ask for it.

And if Quentin didn't have her arrested on sight.

She remembered the address that had been on Quentin's card and found it without great difficulty. The door of the boarding house was opened by a young woman with skin the same café au lait shade as Salomé's. She seemed more than a little surprised when Annabel asked for M. Quentin, but said, "Yes, mademoiselle," and invited her into the front parlor.

The parlor was as shabby as Quentin himself, but with that same air of dignity kept under trying circumstances. She did not have long to wait before Quentin came in; his coat had every appearance of having been hastily dragged on, and his fingers were covered with ink. She pretended that she did not feel the acceleration of her heartbeat, that her mouth had not suddenly gone dry. She could not have him; these schoolgirl airs were ridiculous and futile.

"Mademoiselle St. Clair. I did not expect to see you . . . "

Here? Annabel wondered. *Again?* He sounded wary, but not hostile. Not, as she had feared, disgusted. "M'sieur Quentin, I beg pardon for disturbing you at this hour of the day, but—"

He waved it off. "I am an early riser, mademoiselle. How may I be of service?"

She took a deep breath and plunged without preamble into her story, telling him what the events and discoveries of the night had led her to: "Louis Vasquez was not a Bourbon pretender. He was an adventurer, in the pay of Spain. I don't know what they hoped to accomplish, but I think he must have double-crossed them. That was why he wanted to go west, and that was why he was killed."

"Yes," Quentin said cautiously.

"But Monseigneur le Duc has asked the secretary of the Spanish ambassador to investigate the matter. Don Carlos has found nothing, but tonight—"

"Wait. Why would the Duc de Plaquemine—"

"I don't know. That's why I need to speak to him."

"Which brings you to me because . . . ?"

"Because, m'sieur." She stopped, swallowed hard. Told him, her voice growing smaller and smaller, about being very nearly discovered in Don Carlos's bed, about the involvement of Don Esteban Castillo y Blas, about Jules Sevier's inarguable culpability.

A pause, agonizing in the shabby parlor. And then Quentin began to laugh. "Only you, Mademoiselle St. Clair, could make the entire English embassy your go-between."

She felt her face heat; she knew she should carry it off with a high hand, smile and murmur something rich with innuendo. But she could not do it. She was tired and afraid, and she wanted Quentin's arms around her so much she could barely breathe through the pain in her chest. She said, "You are doing me a favor, m'sieur. I assure you I can return it."

"Enlightened self-interest," Quentin said and sighed. "It runs in the veins of spies, you know, instead of blood. I will see what I can do."

THE DUC DE PLAQUEMINE received the amante dorée in a long echoing colonnade behind the ducal palace. Annabel had managed to pin her hair up, thanks to the generosity of Quentin's landlady, but she felt small and grubby and very American before the sad-eyed elegance of the Duc.

He listened carefully, asked questions—and answered them, which was a courtesy she had not expected of him. Her understanding had been correct, however sketchy. Louis Vasquez had been hired by Don Esteban—who might or might not have been acting on behalf of Ferdinand VII—to claim the principate of Louisiane. If he had succeeded, which the Duc seemed to feel was unlikely but not impossible, he would have returned Floride, Mexique, and Californie to Spanish hands—"or, at least," the Duc said sardonically, "to Don Esteban's hands"—and with the French empire suddenly splintered and its former colonies now allied against it, it was possible that Napoléon IV would not have been able to muster a decisive response. He was not the military man his great predecessor had been.

But Louis Vasquez had had second thoughts. He had come to see the Duc, very privately, told him the truth and begged for his help in leaving Nouvelle Orléans. His plan had been to go to Saint François (which Annabel, in some last ineradicable American corner of her soul, still thought of as San Francisco), but his funds were not sufficient.

"I gave him a letter to the manager of the Banque Impériale in Saint François. In return, he was going to write an open letter, detailing the truth of his presence in Nouvelle Orléans, and give it to the bank manager to send to the newspapers of Nouvelle Orléans and Paris. And then the next night, he was killed."

"But your letter wasn't . . . oh."

"Yes, mademoiselle," the Duc said sadly. "The Spanish took the letter I had written off the body, which I did not know until this morning, when Monsieur Sevier came to return it to me."

"Oh," Annabel said again, uselessly.

"It seems that Don Esteban came to see him on Monday, and they reached an agreement. Don Esteban got rid of Sevier's embarrassment—Louis Vasquez and my most unfortunate letter—and in return, Sevier got rid of his. I am afraid, mademoiselle, that you were merely a means to an end."

"But Don Carlos wasn't going to find anything."

"Don Esteban did not care to risk it. Don Carlos is well connected, and fiercely loyal to King Ferdinand. He would not have kept silent if he had discovered that Don Esteban was harboring imperial ambitions of his own."

"Do you think . . . ?"

"I think very little is beyond the reach of Don Esteban Castillo y Blas, though much remains beyond his grasp. But you do not need to worry about Monsieur Sevier any longer. I will speak to him."

"Thank you, monseigneur."

"And perhaps, Mademoiselle St. Clair, I may have the honor of dining with you one day soon?"

His protection would not be adequate, not in the long run, but it would give her space to maneuver, to renegotiate a perilous treaty with Sevier. She wished to serve France, and she did not know of another way in which she could do so.

"I would be enchanted, Monseigneur," she murmured, dropping a curtsey and trying not to shiver. She knew what he was truly asking, just as he did. He knew what she was. Although she did not desire him, his patronage would be even more valuable to her than his protection. She was an amante dorée; although she had never had the arrogance to aim as high as the Duc de Plaquemine, she was not such a fool as to reject a treasure when it fell into her lap.

Desire, after all, was irrelevant.

Amante Dorée

On a rainy Thursday, a month after the death of Louis Vasquez, Salomé came upstairs and said, "Mademoiselle, that mad Anglais is on the doorstep again."

"M'sieur Quentin?" Annabel had written him a letter, detailing the truth of the machinations surrounding the unfortunate Louis Vasquez, and had expected never to hear from him again. "What does he want?"

"To speak to you, he says."

Annabel pinched the bridge of her nose. "I will see him."

This time before descending to the parlor, she wrapped herself in a thick shawl.

Quentin was standing, shabby and correct, beside the window, and the desire she did not feel for her patrons kindled inside the cage of her ribs. *Irrelevant*, she told herself, but the word was hollow and false. "Mademoiselle," he said and bowed. "You look unwell. I trust I am not disturbing you."

"Not at all, m'sieur." She had spent the previous night with a patron who was not as courteous as Don Carlos, or Monseigneur le Duc. But the aching brittleness she felt was not illness, nor even anything worth the mention. "Will you be seated?"

"Thank you."

They sat down, each of them poker-spined and expressionless. Quentin said in English, "With your permission, Miss St. Clair, I would like to tell you a story."

"A story, sir?" It was hard to speak English, got harder and harder every year.

"Yes. The story of an American. A young man of good if impoverished family, from Boston."

"There are many such young men." But her tongue was thick in her mouth, and she gripped her hands together so that they would not betray her.

109

"This one was named Martin Loftis. He seems to have been a wayward, unhappy boy, the cause of much grief and strife for his parents. But never more so than when he ran away."

"Did he?"

"At the age of sixteen. His parents succeeded, by the outlay of a great deal of time, expense, and energy, in tracing him as far as St. Louis, but there he apparently disappeared entirely. He has been given up for dead in the city of his birth."

"Good." She bit her tongue, appalled at the savagery in her own voice, appalled at how much wounds ten years gone could still hurt.

"He was a tall young man, even at sixteen. Slender. Blond. Remarkably good-looking, from all accounts."

"There are many such in Boston." But her voice wavered, and neither of them was deceived.

Silence, and then Quentin said, "Why do you do it?"

"Because I must," she said: a useless answer, but the only one she had ever found. "Why have you not betrayed me?"

"Because I could not." He hesitated, then said, "You are a very beautiful woman, Annabel St. Clair."

"Thank you, sir." But it was a compliment, nothing more, untainted by any hint of desire. Or love. Her heart ached, as brittle as her body. The slightest touch would shatter it in a thousand shards around her feet.

But that touch would not come from Quentin. He rose, bowed, reverted to French: "I shall not overstay my welcome when you are so clearly troubled by other matters. But I wished you to know . . . " Looking at his face, she thought there were many things he would have liked to have said, if there had been words for them. "I shall not tell anyone."

"Promise?" she said wryly, knowing as well as he did that he could make no such promise and expect to keep it.

And he smiled wryly back. "Spy's honor. Good day to you, mademoiselle."

"Good day, m'sieur."

She stood at the window, watching him go, and did not attempt to call him back. And though he glanced up to meet her eyes, he did not return.

Somewhere Beneath Those Waves Was Her Home

184. Figurehead. Wood. 35" x 18". American, ca. 1850. Figure of a woman holding a telescope and compass. Ship unknown.

THE SELKIE STANDS at the window, staring out at the sea. Behind her, in the rumpled bed, the artist snores. She's had better sex with her own fingers, but it doesn't matter. He wanted it, and it amuses her to cheat on Byron. In their stalemate—she cannot make him give back her skin, he cannot make her love him—she takes her pleasures where she finds them.

She sighs, running one palm over her velvet-short hair. It would've been nice if the artist fucked as pretty as he talks.

197. Figurehead. Wood. 34" x 17". American, ca. 1830-35. Figure of a woman in a hat. Ship unknown.

I FOUND a museum today. Not a surprise, really, but I'd given up on there being anything interesting to do in this town. The only bookstore for twenty miles was a rare and used dealer along the "picturesque" main street specializing in the most abstruse and technical aspects of naval history. I'd spent hours on the beach, staring at the water and the gulls. The water was dark; the gulls were blindingly white. And malicious, I thought. They would have appreciated me more if I'd been dead, and I saw that truth in their little, bright eyes.

But this afternoon I turned up a side street, and there was the sign: MARITIME MUSEUM. I'd taken it for a warehouse. It was open, and I needed something to do for at least one of the three hours remaining before I could legitimately go back to the apartment Dale had rented and begin to wait for him. I pushed open the door, and pushed hard, for like all the doors in this town it was balky and swollen with the breath of the sea.

I'd been in more than my share of maritime museums, as Dale had a passion for them. This one seemed indistinguishable from the multitude: bleak and dusty and full of ship models and scrimshaw and all the sad mortal paraphernalia of a long-gone way of life. I stood for a long time before a case of glass pyramids, once set in the decks of ships to allow light into the cramped spaces below. I wondered how long you would have to stay down there before you forgot that you could not reach up your hand and touch the sun.

The museum's collection was large, but not terribly interesting. "Thorough" would be the polite word. There was nothing there I hadn't seen better examples of elsewhere, and I was unhappily conscious that the museum was not occupying enough of the long brazen afternoon. I walked more and more slowly, carefully reading each word of each printed placard, and still I was calculating: how long to finish at the museum, how long to walk back to the apartment, how long to take a shower. How long I'd waited for Dale the previous night and all the nights before.

And then I turned a corner, stepped through a narrow doorway, and found myself in a long hall, its stretch of narrow windows admitting dusty sunlight and a view of the sea; a hall bare except for the double row of figureheads, mounted like the caryatids of some great invisible temple.

I started down the hall, reading the placard beside each figurehead and studying awkward proportions, stiff shoulders, clumsily carved faces. The collection was composed entire of women: naked, half-dressed, clothed in Sunday best; blonde and brunette and redheaded; empty-handed and holding books and holding navigational instruments. And all of them staring, their eyes seeming to seek for something lost and irreplaceable, something that they would never find in this half-neglected room.

There was a feeling of incompleteness about them. They had never been meant to be seen on their own, nor from this unnatural angle. Their makers had intended them to be part of a greater whole, had intended them to lean forward fiercely, joyfully, into the crash and billow of the sea. By rights they were the eyes, the spirits, of ships far vaster than themselves. This room was not where they belonged; this room was not their home.

The dust motes floating in the shafts of sunlight, the long shallow gouges in the floor boards, the cracking, yellowing plaster of the walls—I had never been in a room so sad. The figureheads seemed like mourners, standing at the edges of a grave which was the aisle I walked down. For a moment, I felt truly buried alive, in my marriage, in this town, in this dreary, dusty hall.

But even as my heart pounded against my ribs, my breath coming short from imagined suffocation, I looked into the face of a figurehead whose long wooden hair was entwined with strands of wooden pearls, and saw that I was not the one buried in this room. Nor was I the one for whom they grieved, the one for whom they watched. They were waiting for something that could not enter the museum to find them.

After I worked my way up one side and down the other, I returned to stand in front of one woman, the pale green of sea-foam, her prim Victorian maiden's face framing the wide-open eyes of an ecstatic visionary. I was staring into her eyes, trying to put a name to what I saw there, when I was startled nearly out of my wits by a man's voice asking, "Do you like the figureheads, miss?"

After the silence of the figureheads, the man's harsh voice seemed as brutal as the roar of a noreaster. I turned around. The door at the far end of the hall, marked Employees Only, was open, and a tall, gaunt old man stood with his hand on the knob. His hair was iron-gray, clipped short, and he wore jeans and a cable-knit sweater.

"Yes," I said, groping after my composure. "They . . . they are very beautiful."

"Aye," he said, coming toward me, and I had to repress the stupid impulse to back away, "they are. There's nothing like them made any more." When he reached me, he extended his hand. "Ezekiel Pitt."

I shook hands with him, although I didn't want to. It was like shaking hands with a tangle of hawsers, even down to the faint sensation of grime left on my palm and fingers when he let go. I refrained with an effort from wiping my hand on my jeans. "Magda Fenton."

"Nice to meet you, Miss Fenton," Ezekiel Pitt said politely, and I did not correct him. "I do most of the collecting for the museum, and I must admit the ladies have always been my favorite." His smile was unpleasant, the teeth prominent and yellow and wolf-like. His smell was musty and sweaty at once, and I gave in and backed up a step.

"Why do none of them have names?" I had noticed that on the placards; figurehead after figurehead was *ship unknown*.

"They're all from shipwrecks, these ladies," Ezekiel Pitt said. "Their names are beneath the sea, like their ships. I suppose you might call them widows."

"Yes, you might," I said, although it seemed to me, looking at their wide, blind eyes, that it would be fairer to call them lost spirits, sundered from their proud bodies, their unbounded blue world, their joyous wooden lives.

Ezekiel Pitt was crowding me again, and I did not like him. I moved toward the door, to finish my tour of this dismal museum and return to my dismal life. He stayed where he was; out of the corner of my eye, I saw him touch the green woman's face, caressing it like a lover. At the door, I stopped. I had one question more. "Why are they all women?"

He glanced up from the green woman and gave me a horrible, unbelievable, leering wink. "I only like the ladies, miss," he said.

I could stand him and his sad prisoners no longer; I fled.

179. Figurehead. Wood. 32" x 17". American, ca. 1840. Figure of a woman crowned with flowers. Ship unknown.

Byron Pitt stole the selkie's skin on an August afternoon when the sky was dull with heat, the sun as fake as an arcade token and not a cloud near to cover its shame.

Byron knows the old stories either far too well or not nearly well enough. He ran with her skin that first day, ran like an ungainly jackrabbit, and nothing—nothing within the limited compass of what she is allowed—will make him tell her what he did with it. She cannot hurt him, much as she would like to; she cannot leave him. She *could* refuse to have sex with him, but it would do her no good. Byron is willfully stupid about a lot of things, but not even he is foolish enough to believe she would stay with him one split-second past the moment she got her hands on her skin again. And although selkies can lie, it is not natural to them: she admits the truth of her own appetites. Even Byron is better than no one at all.

But he isn't enough. He could never be enough, even if she loved him as the stories say some selkies came to love their captors. And she doesn't even like him, although much to her own irritation, she finds him too pathetic to hate. She's all he's ever had, he tells her over and over again, and it's all too easy to believe.

She doesn't care about charity. She wants her damn skin back. Her life. Her home.

In the six months she's been trapped on land, she's trashed Byron's apartment twice, searching. Her skin isn't there. She's explored this dreary town as thoroughly as she ever explored the sunken ships that were her childhood playground. She knows everywhere Byron goes, and she's searched all those places, too. All of them except for one.

She knows her skin is in the Maritime Museum, the same way she knows, not quite in her head and not quite in her gut, where her sisters are, out in the cold Atlantic. It may not be true, this knowing, but it's real. These days, it's the most real thing about her.

But she can't go into the museum. The museum is Ezekiel Pitt's territory, and her fear of him is too deep for reason.

Ezekiel is Byron's uncle or cousin or something like that. He knows what she is, knew the moment he laid eyes on her, without Byron saying a word, and he doesn't care. He's not impressed, not appalled; he looks at her as if she's just another curio in the museum, and not even an interesting one. But the way he looks at Byron . . . Ezekiel Pitt may not care about selkies, but he understands Byron perfectly. He knows what it is to keep something that doesn't belong to you. Knows and gloats, and she knows it was Ezekiel who put the idea of catching a selkie into Byron's stupid head.

She fears him because she does not understand him and because whenever she sees him, she smells death in captivity, smells the truth, that Byron is never going to let her go. Ezekiel Pitt makes her want to submit, to let Byron take her self the way he took her skin, and that scares her most of all.

191. Figurehead. Wood. 45" x 15". American, ca. 1840. Figure of a woman using a telescope. Ship unknown.

THAT NIGHT, lying beside Dale's indifference, I dreamed of the figureheads. They were free from their mountings, standing at the windows of their prison, staring out at the clamoring surf. The moonlight showed the tears on their faces, showed their small pleading wooden hands pressed against the indifferent glass. And then, in my dream, like a gull I flew out from the museum, out over the dark and terrible sea. I flew for miles and miles without becoming tired or afraid, marveling in the beauty of the water and the night.

Then I dove beneath the waves. I seemed still to be flying, effortlessly, down through the water, and I knew I was a seal, as much at home in this element as gulls were in the air. I reached the sea floor and there danced in and out of the gaping, barnacle-encrusted hulls of sunken ships. These were the ships of the figureheads, their lives and their deaths, all here interred in the sand beneath the black weight of the water.

188. Figurehead. Wood. 37" x 22". American, 1865? Figure of a woman holding a broken chain. Ship unknown.

THE SELKIE SPENDS a lot of time on the beach. It drives Byron up the wall; he seems to be afraid that someone will figure out what she is and take her away from him. "Well, I can hope," the selkie said, and Byron winced and shut up.

She met the artist on the beach, let him think he was seducing her. She's learned a lot, these last few months, about the lies men tell themselves.

She pushes the cuffs of her sweat pants up and walks as far into the tide as she can in this stupid body that will drown if she lets it, or die of cold. She doesn't swim; without her skin, it's just a mockery.

She stands for a long time, until her feet start to go numb, and it's not until she turns back toward the land that she realizes she's not alone. There's a woman standing at the high tide line.

The selkie startles, splashing. The woman doesn't even seem to notice, and as the selkie wades back to dry land, she realizes that the woman is crying. The selkie skirts wide around her, light-headed with relief when she makes it to the public parking lot without attracting the woman's attention. She glances back, and the woman is still standing there. Staring out to sea, crying slow silent tears, as if the oceans of her body are trying to find their way home.

176. Figurehead. Wood. 39" x 19". American, ca. 1820. Figure of a Native American woman. Ship unknown.

I woke up hard, my breath caught in my throat, rolled over and looked at the clock. It was almost six a.m. I couldn't stand the stifling closeness of the bedroom any longer; I got up, dragged on yesterday's clothes, and escaped into the open. Dale always slept like the dead, and he wouldn't care even if he woke. I took the same path I'd taken for days, threading my way through the stiff, sullen town to the beach. I stood there, just above the undulation of seaweed that marked the high tide line, staring at the jeweled golden mystery of the sunrise, my mind, still half-dreaming, full of the memory of the figureheads, imprisoned in a hall as stifling as that bedroom, held away from the place where they belonged. The green woman's childlike face returned to me, her rapturous eyes.

Somewhere beneath those waves was her home. The rich strangeness, the terrible sadness of the dream returned to me, and I realized that I was crying, hot silent tears sliding down my cheeks; I licked one off my upper lip, but could not distinguish its taste from the salt miasma of the sea. I stared at the water until my eyes felt as sea-blasted and blind as the figureheads', and then I began to walk, aimlessly, blindly, my mind in the air with the gulls, in the deep water with the seals, in the dusty prison with the waiting women.

190. Figurehead. Wood. 30" x 18". American, ca. 1870-1890. Figure of a mermaid. Ship unknown.

THE SELKIE ANSWERS the phone: "Moonwoman Coffeehouse."

"Hi, Russet, it's me. Byron." Byron always has to name both of them when he calls her, as if he has to guard against the possibility that their identities might slip. She feels sorry for him, for the crippled understanding that thinks identity has anything to do with something as arbitrary as a name. *Russet* isn't her name anyway, but it'll do.

"Hello, Byron," she says warily.

"Look," Byron said, his voice a little too high, a little too fast, "I've been thinking. I think we should get married."

She wants to laugh at him, but she can't find the breath. Because marriage means Byron isn't getting tired of this horrible fake relationship, isn't coming to his senses. No, quite the opposite: Byron wants to make it *official*.

She hears herself say, "Well, we can't talk about it now, Jesus, Byron!" And watches her hand, small and broad and brown, hang up the phone. And then she starts to shake.

She looks up, and Shelly is staring at her. "You okay?"

"Yeah. Just Byron, y'know?"

Shelly says, "I wish you'd just go ahead and dump his ass," and the selkie gives her half a smile and a shrug and gets back to work.

She clears tables and scrubs counters all morning, remembering to smile at the regulars, remembering receipts and correct change and to keep out of Shelly's way as she works. She has the afternoon off. She doesn't have another meeting with the artist until next week. Byron won't be home 'til six. She walks to the museum after eating a lunch she doesn't taste, and then stands in front of the door for nearly five minutes, trying to stop shaking. Ezekiel Pitt isn't interested in her. The worst he'll do is tell Byron, and she isn't afraid of Byron. Byron's power over her is only a matter of her skin and the old stupid rules about possessing it. Nothing here can hurt her, so why can't she move?

Because she's afraid. She's afraid of Ezekiel Pitt; she's afraid of the museum where he dens. Her fear is brutal, terrible, so vast she can't even run from it. She stands, wooden and helpless, on the sidewalk until a voice says, "Are you all right?" and breaks her stasis.

It's the woman from the beach, the pale, mousy woman who was watching the sunrise and crying, and this time the selkie is close enough that even a stupid human nose can catch her scent. "Oh!" the selkie says involuntarily. "You're . . . " The woman the artist is cheating on with me. The woman I smell on him, although he claims you're hundreds of miles away.

"Magda Fenton," the woman says. "And you're Dale's new model. Russet, isn't it?"

The selkie nods.

And then a thought seems to strike the woman; she tilts her head to one side, like a bird, and says, "How did you know who I was? Dale showed me his sketches, but he hasn't drawn me in years."

"I smelled you." And then her heart stutters in her chest, because of all the things she shouldn't have said . . .

"You *smelled* me?"

"On him. I'm so sorry."

"He's sleeping with you." She doesn't sound surprised, or even angry. Only tired. "That explains a great deal."

"I really am sorry," the selkie says; she feels sick. Because she can't claim she didn't know the artist was cheating on his wife. She can't even claim she didn't know it mattered. Not when that's why she was sleeping with the artist herself. Because it's the only thing she can do that hurts Byron at all.

"Dale's decisions aren't your fault," the woman says, almost kindly. "But . . . you *smelled* me? How? I don't wear perfume, and I haven't . . . "

The selkie knows she should lie. But she doesn't. She's hurt this woman already, and the woman has not tried to hurt her in return. She has behaved like a sister, not a hunter.

The selkie turns her hands palms up, spreading the fingers. And she says, "I'm a selkie." It's the first time she's ever spoken the words.

The woman becomes very still for a moment, staring into the selkie's eyes as if she could find truth in them. Then, slowly, she bends her head to look at the selkie's hands, the webs between her fingers, the rough skin of her palms. And then she looks up again, her pale eyes like rock, and says, "Where is your skin?"

The selkie blinks hard against the salt burn of tears. "In there," she says, nodding toward the museum. "Byron hid it in there."

201. Figurehead. Wood. 35" x 20". American, ca. 1850-1860. Figure of a woman, her hands crossed at her breast. Ship unknown.

I BELIEVED HER.

Dale would have laughed at my gullibility, but I was astonished at how little I cared. I saw the truth, not in her webbed fingers, but in her eyes, which were dark and sad and much older than her face. She was a selkie, a seal-woman, and her soul was trapped in the museum just as the figureheads were.

We walked through the museum together, the only visitors, while she told me about Byron and her skin and in return I told her about the figureheads. Neither one of us mentioned Dale. We didn't go into the figureheads' room, but stopped in front of a diorama, dusty and crude, of an Inuit ice-fishing.

"They're imprisoned," I finished. "Does that seem like nonsense to you?"

"They're man-built things," she said. "I don't see how the ocean can possibly be their home."

"Because they're inanimate?"

"Because men built them," she said with an impatient shrug.

"Not all men are like Byron."

"But you're all . . . " She waved her hand in an angry, inarticulate gesture and said again, "They're man-built things."

"And the works of human beings have no souls?"

"Man-made souls," the selkie said. "Souls that belong with men."

"Souls that would profane your home," I said, understanding.

"You got that right," she muttered, a pitch-perfect imitation of the sullen girl she appeared to be.

There was nothing I could say. I stood silently, helplessly, wondering if it would be worth the effort to try to convince her to come look at the figureheads, or if it would simply be wasted breath. And what, I asked myself, did I think she could do anyway? She was a creature out of a fairytale, but that fairytale had nothing to do with me and my self-proclaimed duty. She had her own problems.

She'd gone from standing hipshot in front of the diorama to leaning on—no, pressing against the glass.

"Russet?" I said.

"My skin," she said, her voice no more than breath and pain. "It's in there."

"In there?" I stared at the mannequin dressed in stiff, moth-eaten sealskins. My double-take was hard enough to hurt.

"How can I get in there?" the selkie said, and I looked away from her yearning hands flattened against the glass.

"There's a door in the back wall, but—" And then I remembered Ezekiel Pitt emerging from a door marked Employees Only. "Come on!"

I wasn't sure she would follow me, but she did. We were halfway down the aisle between the figureheads when she balked, stopping as if she'd been brought up short by an invisible wall. "Are these . . . " I heard her breath catch. "Are these what you were talking about?"

"These are the figureheads, yes."

"I knew I hated Ezekiel Pitt," she said, then shook herself and looked at me, eyes sharp. "Okay, do you have any bright ideas?"

"You mean you—"

"I was wrong, okay?" she said, glaring at me. "I thought you were just, you know, telling stories. It's what you people are good at."

I wasn't sure for a moment who "you people" were. "Don't selkies tell stories?"

'It's not the same. But I *get* it, okay? I'm with the program. Nobody made their souls, and they don't belong here. And you want to help them. I get that, too. And—" She broke off, glowering, daring me to laugh at her. "I didn't think you people cared—didn't think you *could* care, and I was wrong, and I'm sorry. Okay? Now what are we gonna do about it?"

I had an ally, however unwilling and irritated, and I felt some measure of dread lift away from me. "We should start with your skin."

She looked startled, so I elaborated, "We know what to do there." And then, when her expression didn't change, "I care about that, too."

"Oh." She shook herself and said, brusque efficiency to cover embarrassment: "Yeah, okay. Through here, you think?"

"Unless you'd rather just break the glass," I said, teasing gently, and she responded with a smile as brief and brilliant as a flash of lightning.

"Let's not even get started on what I'd rather do. For now, I'm gonna go with hoping this door isn't locked."

It wasn't. We slunk through it like characters in every bad spy movie I'd ever stayed up watching, long past midnight, instead of trying to sleep in the same bed with Dale. Or with his absence. The hallway was deserted, and the selkie didn't waste any time working her way back along to the diorama's access door.

It wasn't locked, either.

"You realize I can only do this because you're with me," she said. "I mean, I'm scared out of my mind here."

"I wouldn't have thought you'd care about breaking the law."

"I don't. I care about that creepy motherfucker Ezekiel Pitt." She slid into the diorama as smoothly as if the air were water, and was back in ten seconds, shutting the door behind her left-handed; her right hand was clenched white-knuckled in a limp, ratty-looking sealskin.

I knew it was her skin as well as she did; it took my breath away to look at her. Her colors were vivid, her lines clean. She was bright instead of dull, focused instead of blurred. Everything in this town was faded, but not the selkie, not anymore.

"Are you frightened of Ezekiel Pitt now?" I said, curious.

She laughed. It was a strange sound, not merely because she sounded like a seal barking, but because it was so obviously a learned response. "Right now, I'm not afraid of anything," she said. "Let's see what we can do for your figureheads."

Ezekiel Pitt was waiting on the other side of the Employees Only door.

"Byron called me when he couldn't reach you," he said, looking past me to the selkie. I wasn't even sure he'd registered my presence. "In a tizzy as usual. I told him I'd see what I could do about pulling his chestnuts out of the fire." He expected her to be afraid of him. It was in his voice, his posture, the way he looked at her. He knew it was her fear of him that had kept her imprisoned, and he didn't imagine that could change.

"I wouldn't worry about Byron's nuts if I were you," the selkie said and shoved me gently forward into the figureheads' hall. "You have other problems."

"Do I? Seems like you're the one with the problem, miss. All I have to do is call the cops."

"No," the selkie said. She reached out, caught his wrist. And held. He brought his arm up to wrench away, and he couldn't. "You're a greedy man, Ezekiel Pitt. You're holding what doesn't belong to you. And you need to let go."

"You're confusing me with Byron," Ezekiel Pitt said, still trying to wrench free, and still failing. "And I admit Byron should know better than to think he can hold a—"

"No." He stopped talking, his mouth hanging slightly open, and she said, her voice flat and calm, "Let them go."

He didn't try to pretend he didn't know what she was talking about. "What do you want me to do? Throw them all in the sea? They're valuable, you know, and the museum—"

"The wood isn't what matters. The wood is only what holds them here. Let them go."

Her grip tightened on his wrist. He was whining now, like a neglected dog: "I can't. I don't know how. I don't know what—"

"Yes, you do." She walked over to the green ecstatic-eyed maiden, bringing Ezekiel Pitt with her. She was a wild creature, and the truth of her nature shone through her like sunlight through glass. He was nothing next to her.

She put his hand on the figurehead's forehead. He was whimpering, and the noise was both pathetic and repulsive. The selkie was inexorable. She said, "Let them go home, Ezekiel Pitt."

His face twisted—a snarl of fury, a grimace of pain—and he cried out, "Goddamn you, you bitches!" as if he could make even freedom into a curse.

The figureheads were free.

In the silence, the selkie let Ezekiel Pitt go.

He backed away from her, from the figureheads which now were nothing but wood, man-made things without even man-made souls. He was cradling his hand against his chest; his mouth was working, though no sound came out until he was five feet from the selkie, out of her reach, and then he hissed, "I'm calling the police, you . . . you bitch!" He turned and bolted, shouldering past me as if I, too, were inanimate wood.

The selkie looked at me, bright-eyed, gleeful, and said, "Let's get the hell out of here."

181. Figurehead. Wood. 36" x 18". American, ca. 1850. Figure of a woman holding a sword. Ship unknown.

THE WOMAN, who is so much more than the artist's wife, comes with the selkie to the beach. The selkie is glad.

They stand together just above the rush and retreat of the

tide, and the silence between them is awkward, painful, a human silence.

The selkie can feel her sisters swimming out in the cold sea; she can feel her wooden sisters, too, singing without sound in the darkness of the deeps. Silence with her sisters won't feel like this, won't be wrong.

She says, "You could come with me. If you wanted?" She wants. She wants this woman to be her sister.

The woman blinks, her pale lashes making it look more like a flinch. "I'm a good swimmer, but—"

"The wood isn't what matters," the selkie says.

"You mean . . . "

"Your wooden sisters will welcome you. I'll bring your seal sisters to meet you."

"Am I so trapped?" the woman murmurs. She looks at her hands. "Is this a wooden prison?"

"I didn't mean it like that."

"Dale would agree with you," the woman says, catching the selkie with her pale eyes. "I'm no more than a figurehead to him."

"Dale's an idiot," the selkie snaps, and the woman laughs. "I didn't mean you were trapped. Dale doesn't have your skin. I just meant, if you *wanted* to . . . "

The woman smiles, a smile as warm as a sister's love. "Thank you. But the ocean isn't my home. It might become my prison."

The selkie nods. She does understand. "You won't go back to Dale, will you?"

"Not a chance," her sister says and laughs, the ecstatic laughter of a child.

"If you ever see Byron, you can tell him from me to fuck off. I'm going home." She strips her clothes off as the sea washes around her feet. Carrying her skin, she wades out up to her waist; then,

SOMEWHERE BENEATH THOSE WAVES WAS HER HOME

with one last kick of her human legs, she jack-knifes into the water and clads herself in her true skin. She surfaces fifty yards out, already hearing her sisters' joy, and glances back.

Her sister is standing on the shore, waving good-bye.

—⊙⊙⊙—

Darkness, as a Bride

The inventor built the town a virgin.

He had objected, but the mayor, the town aldermen behind him, prevailed. They needed a virgin to make a bargain with the sea monster who hunted the waters off their coast, and they were not willing to sacrifice their daughters. And the inventor, a cripple, both guest and prisoner, knew what would happen to him if he refused. The town doctor was a cold man, all black and white with a cruel red mouth, and he would not balk if the mayor told him to take the inventor's eyes.

The inventor was not a brave man. He made a virgin as he was told.

She was a monstrous thing, charnel and clockwork, though comely enough to look upon. Only at very close range could one observe the unyielding chill of her flesh, the mechanical regularity of her breath, the blind stone of her eyes. The darkness within her, where others had light. The inventor gave her a name, but no one ever asked him what it was.

He taught her to walk, to speak, to eat and excrete. He taught her to listen, taught her to dance.

He taught her she was a monster by the way he did not answer certain questions, by the way he did not ask certain others. By the way, when she touched him, he always withdrew and always apologized for it, fumblingly, uncomfortably.

He could not teach her to love, but he did not need to.

The mayor and the aldermen were pleased, by her silence as much as her prettiness, by her obedience as much as her virginity.

They agreed, not bothering to lower their voices, not caring if she could hear them, that she was a fair and reasonable sacrifice, and at dawn on the first day of spring they took her to the cold coast, the town doctor pushing the inventor in a great wheeled wicker chair, and chained her to an ancient boulder. The town doctor pinched his fingers in the aged and rusty manacles and swore savagely.

She could not bleed, but the mayor had brought a vial of his own daughter's blood, which he made a fussy little ceremony of pouring into the sea. Then the aldermen retreated to a safe distance, taking the inventor with them, and they waited, the aldermen passing around a flask, the inventor huddled into his chair, the virgin standing straight, unyielding, against the boulder, her blind eyes staring at the sun.

When the sun was a handspan above the horizon, the sea monster arrived, a massive creature, whiskered like a catfish, maned and mantled. Its eyes were great lamps in its ponderous skull, its teeth like scimitars. It drew itself partway out of the sea, its webbed front feet splayed against the rocky beach, and looked under its magnificent tufted eyebrows from the huddled group of men to the virgin standing straight and unyielding against the rock.

The monster leaned forward and snuffled with great dignity at the cold pale skin of her arm. She did not flinch; her breath did not catch, and her eyes continued to stare stonily ahead, unblinking.

"Harrumph," the monster said at last, pulling its head back. "Yes. An ingenious cheat."

"Am I?" said the virgin. Her voice revealed her nature, as harsh and unmodulated as the cry of a crow.

But the monster did not seem to mind. "Oh, yes, my poor monstrous patchwork child. Yes, indeed."

"I *am* a virgin."

"I'm certain that you are," the monster said kindly. "But you aren't a sacrifice."

"They chained me to this rock."

"And felt not one shred of reluctance, not one ort of regret. You are no sacrifice, for it costs them nothing to give you to me."

"So you will not bargain with them."

"No. I will not."

The virgin said nothing for a time; the monster, amiable, curious, waited.

She said, abruptly as all her utterances were abrupt, "Could *I* make a bargain with you?"

"You could, for you are a virgin. But—forgive me, my dear— have you anything to sacrifice?"

"I love," she said, in her harsh inhuman voice. "It is all I have. I would give you that."

"Ah," said the monster and leaned forward again, this time snuffling at her hair and face, at her blind unblinking eyes. "So you do. And if I took this love, what would you want in return?"

"I want to be free," she said, and although there was no emotion in her voice or on her face, the monster smelled her fierceness all the same. "I want to be free of this town and those men and the purpose I was made for. I want to be free of the one who made me."

"The one you love."

"He will never love me back. And if he who made me cannot love me, I should not love."

"That, I think, is not true. But your love for him is a worthy sacrifice. Is this what you want, my dear?"

"Yes," she said. "Yes. I want to be free."

"Very well," the monster said, and it dug its claws into the rocky beach, lowered its head, and arched the tremendous length of its tail out of the water, and then, as swift as the blade of a guillotine, brought it down.

The virgin and her rock and the cliff and the men standing on it were drenched, but what mattered was the earthquake that answered a long moment later, a sullen grumbling grinding voracious snarl that split the cliff asunder beneath the inventor's great wheeled wicker chair and ran thence, creating a jagged, parlous canyon, to the town and to the town hall and to the cramped back room where the inventor had lived and had taught the virgin to live as well.

In the aftermath, the virgin stood, still pale and unyielding, her wrists still manacled but chained to nothing. And walking up the beach toward her was a young-old man, dressed gorgeously in silks the colors of the sea and sun, with a wild white mane of hair, tremendous tufted eyebrows, and mustaches like those of a catfish. His eyes were great inhuman lamps, though the virgin, of course, could not see them.

She felt his approach, and tilted her head, a little, to listen to the sound of his bare clawed feet against the rocks and sand. "Are they all dead then?"

"Most of them."

She considered that. "Should I be sorry?"

"Would you have chosen differently?"

"No."

"Then no. You are what they made you."

"I feel cold," said the virgin. "Broken. My love is gone."

"Yes," said the monster.

"But you are still here."

"Yes," the monster said again, smiling a wide white scimitared smile. "The virginity is as important as the sacrifice, you understand."

The virgin made no response for a moment—she was not human, to nod, or draw back, or make a noise with no meaning to it. Then she said, "Yes," and began to undo the buttons of her dress.

The monster broke the manacles off her wrists before they made love on the remains of the rock those manacles had chained her to.

For monsters can love.

Did you doubt it?

KATABASIS: SERAPHIC TRAINS

snow falls in her open eyes

HER NAME is Clair. She wears black, no jewelry, and has long straight hair, dyed a dark reddish-purple, the color of the foundries' breath against the night sky. If she feels any emotions, her eyes never reflect them. She does not talk about herself, and she has never cried.

Her apartment is enormous and bare, and your footsteps echo hollowly off the parquet floor, giving the impression of even greater vastness, greater emptiness, as if you walked through a palace made of ice, cyclopean and uninhabited. The walls and the few pieces of furniture are stark, sterile white, like untouched snow. Clair moves like a shadow through the whiteness of her rooms.

your hatred, like a sleeping beast

IT WAS a great city once, and powerful. It has power still, dark, corrosive power like smog. The foundries and factories are mostly shut down now. Those that still operate stain the sky with billows of black and gray; in some quarters of the city their roaring can be heard all night long, and they throw bruised and blurry rainbows against the clouds. A river flows through the city's heart, sullen and sluggish, but brown and hungry and strong. And the city itself is a snarl, a brawl, a festered wound. It seethes and roils and bides its time.

the stings of winter wasps

BEYOND THE WINDOW, snow fell like frozen drops of poison.

Clair looked at him, her eyes clear and pitiless. "It's very nice, Sean," she said.

135

"Nice?" he said. "That's it? Just 'nice'?"

"Oh, darling, I'm sorry." Her laugh, the sound of icicles shattering. "It's lovely, Sean, of course it is. I'm very impressed."

"It isn't finished," he said desperately. "I mean, I know there's weak spots, and I . . . "

Her eyes were a strange color, milky gray with touches of blue and green: dirty, dead-of-winter ice. Her gaze always upset him, dazed him; in the depths of his heart he knew that it had enchanted him. Now, cold and hard and full of light, her gaze silenced him, and when she was sure he would not speak, she said, "I'm not saying you're not talented, Sean, because clearly you are. But I think you've maybe overreached yourself just a trifle. It's such an *ambitious* project. I know you're very serious about it, but I think—"

"You think it's no good."

"I didn't say that."

"But it's what you meant, isn't it? *Isn't it?*"

And she looked at him, not alarmed by his nearness, his anger. His gaze dropped first. "I think it's awfully . . . traditional."

"You mean clichéd."

"Do I?"

"Well, don't you?"

"You're still young, Sean. It's all right to model yourself on the poets you admire."

"But I'm not!"

"Oh, please. Darling, I don't want to be cruel, but there's no sense in letting you delude yourself. You're dripping T. S. Eliot from every page."

"Thank you, Clair," he said with stiff irony.

"You're *young*," she said. "Give yourself time."

"Are you saying my writing's immature? Come on, Clair, say what you mean!"

"I thought certain passages were just a little . . . naïve," she said, and the cold clear eyes watched his reaction without changing.

"I'd better go," he said, aware of the blood mounting to his face, aware of the hot prickle of starting tears

She let him leave; only as he was opening the door of her apartment did she say, softly, almost laughing, "You'll be back."

silver ribbons for my love

THE RIVER RUNS through the heart of the city, and braiding around and over and under the river, the city's rail system is a welter of tarnished silver ribbons. The tracks sear through the city with a fine disregard for its geography, soaring above and plunging below the streets as the whim takes them, sometimes following the lines laid by the major boulevards, sometimes running alone through empty lots, sometimes cutting a swath through residential districts so that top floor tenants could, if they were so inclined, reach out from their back windows and have their arms ripped off by the force of the passing trains.

It is said in those districts that not all the trains which run on the city's tracks are listed in Metropolitan Transit's compendious schedule. The residents will tell you that after midnight, on some nights, there will be other trains, trains whose cry is different, the bellow of some great beast fighting for its life. And if you watch those trains go past, behind those bright flickering windows you will see passengers unlike any passengers you have seen when riding the trains yourself: men with wings, women with horns, beast-headed children, fauns and dryads and green-skinned people more beautiful than words can describe. In 1893, a schoolteacher swore that she saw a unicorn; in 1934, a murderer turned himself into the police, weeping, saying that he saw his victims staring at him from a train as it howled past the station platform on which he stood.

These are the seraphic trains. The stories say they run to Heaven, Hell, and Faërie. They are omens, but no one can agree on what they portend. And although you will never meet anyone who has seen or experienced it, there are persistent rumors, unkillable rumors, that sometimes, maybe once a century, maybe twice, a seraphic train will stop in its baying progress and open its doors for a mortal. Those who know the story of Thomas the Rhymer—and even some who don't—insist that all these people, blest or damned as they may be, must be poets.

starless night

FOR DAYS after Sean's suicide, Bram Bennett walked around without being aware of what she wore, what she ate, what she did. Her whole head burned with words to which no one would listen. She looked at the people she knew on campus and was dully astonished at how little she liked them. The idea of talking to her parents was merely ludicrous, and she had gladly lost contact with the few friends she had had in high school. There was no one she could tell, no one who would understand her grief. She felt like a woman standing in the aftermath of Hiroshima, surrounded by debris and corpses, the only living thing for five miles in any direction and herself dying, dying of the radiation she could neither see nor feel.

the twilight water

THE SUBWAY STATION is a long, barrel-vaulted hall, an echo chamber for sounds which seem to have no origin. No passengers board trains here. The iron benches sit desolate, their only company the illegible sheets of newsprint which fly and flap and skitter and scuttle from one end of the platform to the other.

Those who disembark at the Court of the Clockwork Kings do not linger.

velvet death

THE INTERIOR of the train car (Bram thought) was a very good imitation of a Metropolitan Transit train done by someone who'd never actually been inside one. All the colors and shapes were right, but the textures were wrong. The walls were papered with something silvery that felt like velvet; the seats were upholstered in blue satin. The floor was carpeted in black brocade, the ceiling was pressed tin, and Bram wasn't sure, but she thought the poles and safety fittings were solid silver. It made her feel small and grubby and excessively herself. Her black clothes were too obvious, and surely everyone in the car could tell she dyed her hair, that her light hazel eyes would never belong with hair that black. The rings in her ears and nose felt like something she'd done merely because everyone else did. She was morbidly certain that the black rose tattoo on her back, safely covered by her T-shirt and leather jacket, was nonetheless radiantly visible to everyone who looked at her. She sat on one of the blue satin benches, worrying that she was getting it dirty, and clutched her guitar in its case across her lap.

The other occupants of the car mostly ignored her. There was a horde of children with cat-heads—kittens, she supposed, since none of them could be more than four years old—playing some elaborate game up and down the aisle; she counted two Siamese, three brown tabbies, two tortoiseshells, and one white Persian. They were dressed like Victorian children in velvet suits with broad lace collars. Their round eyes, green and amber and gold, looked at her with perfect trust and perfect indifference; to them, she was merely one more obstacle to be incorporated in their game.

At the far end of the car from where Bram sat, there was a woman, naked except for an opal choker around her neck, green-skinned, her eyes the luminous white of clouds—so beautiful that her beauty was like pain. She was clearly watching the child-kittens, with sharp attentiveness rather than the amused tolerance of a stranger, and Bram wondered if this woman, whom any culture in the mortal world would have worshipped as a goddess, was employed as a child-minder by a group of cat-headed parents.

Just down from the green-skinned woman were a group of creatures who looked as if they were made out of tree-roots; twisted, hunched, and knotted, they huddled together and talked in high, scratchy voices, like twigs against a windowpane. Bram couldn't understand what they were saying, and from the vindictive cunning in their tiny red eyes, she was quite sure she didn't want to. Across the aisle from them was a giant, black as moonless midnight, with a bull's head and hooves, his horns brushing the roof of the car, his long, rat-like tail sweeping out into the aisle and restlessly curling and uncurling itself around the nearby poles. The child-kittens treated the tail like a hurdle, jumping over it with exaggerated, giggling caution. The minotaur ignored them completely; he was immersed in a small, crumbling book bound in cracking green leather.

At the other end of the car sat two tall, grave, chalk-white gentlemen, dressed in chalk-white business suits and each with his hands folded over a chalk-white briefcase in his lap. Bram would have taken them for angels, remembering the stories Sean had told her about the seraphic trains, except for the crusted blood at the corners of their mouths. Their eyes were of no color that she could discern; they looked and spoke only to each other, studiously ignoring everything else in the car, including, on the bench nearest them, a group of giggling young women, golden-haired and warm-eyed, dressed in old rose and gold and burgundy velvet, their ears as delicately pointed as cathedral spires. Every time Bram looked at these young women, one of them was looking at her, and she had the horrible feeling that she was the cause of their giggles.

And directly across from Bram, there was a dead girl. The girl's hair was lank and brittle, her eyes sunken, her nails dark and splintered against her pallid, blue-tinged skin. And Bram could see the ragged, black-edged hole in her temple, not quite concealed by her hair.

The fifth or sixth time Bram snuck a glance at the dead girl, she met her eyes. Red-faced, ashamed, Bram twitched a smile at her. The dead girl looked down at once, and Bram fixed her gaze resolutely on the silver pole opposite and slightly to the right of her.

And then the dead girl raised her head, and Bram's gaze was instantly drawn back to her. They stared at each other, and Bram could not help feeling kinship with this girl, the only other mortal in the car, even if she was dead.

"Your music's really neat," said the dead girl.

"Thanks," Bram said, blushing again. "Thank you. Really."

"It's a stupid thing to say."

"No, it's not. It's nice of you."

"No, really. You don't need me telling you you're good. I mean, the train stopped for you, didn't it?"

"That's not what caused it," Bram protested. That couldn't be true; she, Bram, could not have succeeded where Sean had failed.

The dead girl glanced up at her and away, and Bram felt the force of her disbelief even through the filmy congealed deadness of her eyes. "Oh, come *on*," the dead girl said. "You gotta know how good you are. What else were you doing out there playing at the trains anyway?"

"I'm looking for someone."

"*Looking* for someone? Either you're on crack or you're pulling my leg."

"No, I mean it. Someone . . . someone like you."

The dead girl's eyes were like stones behind the filthy curtain of her hair. "Someone dead?"

Bram took a deep breath and let it out. "Yes."

"That's fucked up."

"Can you help me? Can you tell me how to find him?"

"I can tell you you don't want to."

"I *have* to. Please."

The girl leaned forward and put her dead, grimy hand on Bram's knee. "Please, chickie, believe me. You don't want to. You want to go with those girls who are checking you out and live forever in Faërie or some shit like that. Or don't get off the train. Just go right the fuck back where you came from and get a record deal. You don't want to go to the Court of the Clockwork Kings."

"Is that where I'll find him?"

"Are you even listening to me?"

"I am, I promise, and I really appreciate your concern. But this is what I have to do."

"And I thought *I* was fucked in the head. But whatever it is you've got is way worse than a bullet. Okay. Yes. That's the stop you want. The Court of the Clockwork Kings. But, I mean, really, what good do you think it's going to do?"

"I'm going to bring him back," Bram said, articulating for the first time the plan which had sprung full-formed into her head as soon as she had seen the open doors of the seraphic train, and the dead girl, after a disbelieving moment, rocked back on the bench and went into a terrible dry spasm of laughter that sounded like someone choking to death on a bone. The two tortoiseshell child-kittens stopped a moment, staring at her with grave wonder, but the green-skinned woman called to them, and they ran to her.

"Man, you are just fucked up," the dead girl said, and after that she would not speak to Bram again.

KATABASIS: SERAPHIC TRAINS

our story crumbles in my hands

WHEN YOU GO to the office of the city's oldest paper, the *Telegraph-Clarion*, and ask to see their archives, you will be admitted to a room crammed to bursting with the huge black ledgers in which the city's entire journalistic history is preserved. In those grim and brittle ledgers, you will find births and deaths and marriages, records of parades and speeches—a relentless marching army of facts that will not surrender up the answers you can sense, like rats in the wainscoting, behind the bland, prosperous wallpaper of the articles' words.

But even the *Telegraph-Clarion* has not always been able to flatten the oddity out of the city's dark flourishing. In the 1870s a factory girl living in Prosper Park was reputed to tell the future. Not major events such as wars or assassinations or stock-market crashes, but predicting the number of kittens in a litter, or how many tries it would take a boy to hit a target with a stone. In 1877 she threw herself under one of the Metropolitan Transit trains and died. The brief popularity of apocalypse preachers at the end of '77 can hardly be coincidental, a fear that her tiny, trivial talent had shown her something too dreadful to be borne. But no such calamity ever occurred.

Similar cases abound: a classics professor who chased rainbows until his disappearance in 1964; Caroline Hayward, who was discovered weeping in Asherton Park in October of 1905, her hands stained with blood that was not hers. No victim was ever found, and Caroline Hayward could speak, stammering, sobbing, only of falling leaves.

And there is the story of Phoebe Gruenstahl.

Phoebe Gruenstahl was institutionalized in 1909; she was

seven years old. Her parents told everyone that she had died, and in time, freed from their strange, mute, savage child, they came to believe it. She was an inmate of St. Catherine's for twenty-nine years, and then one sweltering August night in 1938, she escaped. No one, then or later, ever discovered how.

The city was in a panic for seven days. It became generally accepted that she had gotten into the sewers, and there were expeditions with dogs and rifles to bring her out again, but no luck. In fact, there were no confirmed sightings of Phoebe Gruenstahl until February 1939, when her body was dragged out of the river less than half a mile from the then newly completed Enoch J. Hopkins Bridge, the first bridge to allow the Metropolitan Transit trains to cross the river above the ground.

Cause of death could not be determined.

Everyone who examined the corpse remarked on its astonishingly beautiful smile. In life, Phoebe Gruenstahl had never smiled, never once.

your face, dark behind the glass

SEAN LACROIX was born and raised in Prosper Park, one of the city's oldest and grimmest neighborhoods. When Sean was seven, his parents moved the family from their increasingly cramped apartment to a house backing onto the Metropolitan Transit tracks. Sean had a tiny bedroom to himself, at the rear of the house; if he stuck a broom handle out his window, he could bump the tracks with it. The noise and shaking of the trains bothered him at first, but quickly became a mere fact of existence.

One night in July, Sean sat by his open window, watching the trains go past and trying not to listen to his father yelling at his mother in the room below. The trains roared by, and Sean pretended they were fabulous monsters, but he knew they were just trains.

At 1:39 a.m. he heard an approaching train, although the next train wasn't due until 1:50. Curious, he leaned forward even as the train let out a chuffing yowl like the hunting cry of some great beast.

It roared past in no more than five heartbeats, so fast that Sean had no idea of it overall, but individual images, like fragments from a kaleidoscope, lodged in his heart and would stay with him until the moment of his death.

A dead woman, wrapped in a blood-stained shroud, tenderly stroking the hair of a sleeping child.

Two tall, beautiful people—whether men or women he could neither then nor later decide—dancing together, their wings trailing behind them like iridescent gossamer.

A saber-toothed tiger yanking at its chains with human hands.

Two queens, crowned and jeweled and with the heads of foxes, playing chess.

In the last car, a man with the head of a white stag. The man wore black velvet, and on every branch of his wide-spreading antlers a tiny white candle burned serenely, anchored in its own wax. The man's dark, lambent eyes met Sean's, and Sean knew, then and ever after, that that stag-headed man understood him and loved him as no one in his life ever would.

And then the train was gone.

wings, torn from cloudy moths

LYING TOGETHER in the darkness.

They had just had sex, awkwardly and uncomfortably, on Sean's narrow dorm-room bed. It had not exactly been Bram's first time, but it couldn't count as more than her second. She hadn't said anything about that to Sean, but she was afraid he'd been able to tell anyway.

"Sean?" she said into the darkness.

"What?" Sean said. He sounded sleepy, maybe a little irritated.

"Oh, nothing. I just . . . was I okay?"

"Sure. You were fine. We aren't being graded, you know."

"I didn't mean that. It was just . . . " She lost her nerve and said, "The bed's pretty narrow."

"Hey, we didn't fall off. Ten points out of ten."

"Okay," Bram said, although she was only partly reassured.

But Sean was awake now; Bram felt him shifting position, sitting up against the headboard with the pillow behind his back. She stayed as she was, lying on her side, pressed against the wall, her head inadequately supported by what she would later find to be a pair of Sean's roommate's sweatpants.

Sean said, "What do you want your music to do, Bram?"

"What?"

"Your music. What do you want to do with it?"

"I don't know. I guess I'm not sure what you mean."

"Don't you have any aspirations?" Sean said, a stinging flick of contempt in his voice.

"Of course I do. I just . . . they're hard to articulate, you know?"

"No, they're not. Not if they're real."

"Well, what's your aspiration then?" Bram said, defensive and yet hoping that perhaps Sean was working around to asking her to read his poems.

"The city," Sean said. "I want to capture the truth of the city."

And when she asked him what he meant, Sean told her about the seraphic trains and the river and the city's tenebrous history. But he did not show her his poems.

Katabasis: Seraphic Trains

her blood

Things Lost in the City and Never Recovered:

- 3 canvases by the American surrealist painter, Frank Attwater: *The Sum of All Objects in the Room*, *The Dirigible Eaten by Stars*, *The Andiron*
- the diary of the novelist Susan Kempe (burned by the author before her suicide in 1988)
- St. Roque's Hospital (destroyed in the fire of 1922)
- a key to the secret room in the house at 549 Grosvenor Avenue
- 7 life-size wooden marionettes, representing Henry VIII and his 6 wives: Catherine of Aragon, Anne Boleyn (with detachable head), Jane Seymour, Anne of Cleves, Catherine Howard (with detachable head), Catherine Parr
- a packet of Agathe Ombrée rose seeds
- a stained kidskin left glove missing the index finger, said to have belonged to the Confederate spy Rose O'Neal Greenhow
- the Maupin Boulevard subway station

the moon's pyre

BRAM CLIMBED the stairs from the subway station and emerged in the middle of a brick-paved plaza. There were benches around the edges of the plaza, and tall, ornate streetlamps; the plaza was almost disappointingly normal, except for the fact that it was underground. The air was cold, but stuffy, and the sweetish scent of dust was everywhere.

She looked up, but the streetlamps did not cast enough light for her to see if the ceiling of this place was natural or man-made. She squeezed the handle of her guitar case, for reassurance, and started to walk toward the edge of the plaza opposite the head of the stairs. She wished, a tired, aching thought, that she had any idea of where she was going.

Bram walked through the Court of the Clockwork Kings. The houses loured on either side, crammed cheek-by-jowl, tall and narrow-fronted and stern. There were no lights behind any of the windows, but she could not shake the faint, frightened impression that the houses were not deserted, that the rooms behind those staring windows were not empty, and that those who waited in those airless, dusty rooms (and waited for what?) were watching her as she went past. She walked a little faster, but that made the echoes of her footsteps mime the increasingly rapid and panicked rhythm of her heart, and she had to slow down again.

After a time—she did not know how long, and she was afraid to look at her watch—she saw a different kind of light up ahead. It bloomed like a rose against the darkness, not the right color for a fire, although it was naggingly familiar. She got a little closer and realized it was pink neon, as lurid and tasteless as anything one might see on Jefferson Avenue. Bram stopped, bewildered, suddenly afraid in an entirely new way.

And it was at that moment that she became aware of a hand on her arm.

She jerked away and turned, in one motion, and found herself staring at something that looked like a man but wasn't one. It was tall and deathly white—not the same white as the chalk-white gentlemen in the train, this was a dead white, like the undersides of rotting fish—and wrapped in trailing black that might have been a cloak or a shroud or a pair of nebulous wings. Its eyes were blood-red slivers of glass.

"What are you?" Bram said, her voice shrill and shaking. "What do you want?"

"We are the noctares," said the creature, and Bram looked around wildly, but there was nothing like it in sight; its words, though, were blurry, echoing, as if it spoke with more than one voice. "We serve the Clockwork Kings. What do you seek, you who breathe, in the Court of the Clockwork Kings?"

"I . . . I'm looking for someone."

Its head tilted, slowly and jerkily, like a rusty piece of machinery, to the left. It said, "You do not belong here, you who breathe. Go back. Go home. Walk beneath the sun and stars and taste the air of the world. Do not walk in this city of darkness."

"I can't. I'm sorry, but I just can't. I have to find him."

It stared at her, its red glass eyes unfathomable, and said, "If you will not go, we must take you before the Clockwork Kings. We who do not breathe and never have, we beg you: go now. Do not look back. Let go of that which does not breathe."

"Wh . . . what will they do to me?"

Its head tilted, with the same slow jerkiness—clockwork, Bram thought and then wished she hadn't—to the right. It said, "The Clockwork Kings do no harm."

"Then I will see them. I am not afraid." A lie, a lie, but she could not go back, not without Sean.

It bowed its head. "You have made your choice. Come with us." And its hand, as white and cold as death by freezing, took Bram's arm just above the elbow. This time, Bram could not pull away.

those cold mirrors

CLAIR WAS the only person Sean had ever loved. When she kissed him, when she smiled at him, he felt almost breathless with awe. He told her things about himself he had never and would never tell a living soul. The first time he had seen her, the first time he had looked into her eyes, he had thought he saw his Stag of Candles reflected there. He had been trying to find that reflection again ever since, but all he ever saw was himself.

———

bone needles

SEAN SAT in the dusty dimness of St. Christopher's small parish library. He was working on a poem about St. Christopher's, his own parish church, for *The Stag of Candles*; he had spent the afternoon looking through the contents of a box labeled simply FROM CONVENT. Most of it was incomprehensible to him, but down at the bottom, he found an accordion file of documents relating to the case of a nun who was committed to St. Catherine's in 1942. She claimed she heard angels singing in the roofs of the transepts—this, the last in what was apparently a long history of visions and voices, some of them distinctly secular, all of them highly suspect. Moreover, in a letter written to her sister but apparently never sent, she gloried in the fact that only she could hear the angels, her tone that of a spoiled child gloating over a birthday present. When she would not recant—when she became blasphemous and violent before the Bishop—she was committed to St. Catherine's. She died of pneumonia nine years later, insisting to the end that angels had sung to her from the roof of St. Christopher's.

Sean jotted down some notes; as he was starting to tidy the contents of the box, the ancient and almost senile Sister Mary Bartholomew tottered over to the table, peered at Sean's pile of documents, and nodded to herself.

"Did you know her, Sister?" Sean asked, not hopefully.

"Her and her angels." Sister Mary Bartholomew snorted. "We all heard them—but only Sister Mary Jude was fool enough to say so."

And she tottered away again, leaving Sean staring after her. He was suddenly very cold.

long-held breath

IT WAS PAST ELEVEN on the fifth night after Sean's death. Bram crossed the campus without seeing the stark, strange beauty of the bare oak trees against the sky. She made for the nearest Metropolitan Transit stop, bought a ticket she had no intention of using, and climbed the narrow, scaffold-like staircase to the platform.

She was following Sean as best she could. Her grief was too raw and black to admit of any other course of action. But she intended her suicide also to be a memorial, a testament to the tremendous jagged void Sean left in the world. Sean had told her about the seraphic trains, had told her some of the stories about them, and she had heard the longing in his voice. She could not end things until she, too, had watched a seraphic train sweep by and leave her behind, scorning her offering.

She lifted her guitar out of its case, tuned it, and began to play. She paid no attention to the passengers waiting for the next train, no attention to the cold air or the bad lighting; nothing existed except the music and the trains that roared and howled and gibbered their way past. Each of them was an ordinary train, and Bram kept playing.

She started with folk songs, some Bob Dylan, Beatles songs that she'd been playing since her first guitar lesson at the age of eight. She segued into her own stuff when fingers and voice were warm, when she could feel the strength of the music all the way down her spine. It would be cheating not to play her best, and she knew it would make no difference. No seraphic train would stop for her. Midnight came and went, and she was still playing. She stopped only to get drinks of water. She felt that her heart was opening wider and wider, that it was pushing open the stone carapace of grief and her music was soaring out like dragons.

There was no self-consciousness left when she started playing "Why Do You Linger?", a song she had half-despaired of ever finishing. But tonight she understood it; tonight it was as clear and brutal and precise as a glass dissecting-knife. Tonight she understood what the song was trying to say, that the truth was still beautiful, even if it came out of something painful and ugly and heart-breaking.

The song ended; she looked up, arming sweat off her forehead, and saw the train standing at the platform, doors open; there were faces at every window, looking at her, and not a single one of them was mortal.

A seraphic train had stopped for Bram Bennett.

my love waits for me in green

THE FAIRLAWN MEMORIAL GARDEN is always deserted. Funerals are held here, the grounds are immaculately kept, but, no matter when you visit, you will never see another living soul.

The Thiboudeau Hill Cemetery is noted for the yearly funeral procession of the city's fifth mayor, Henry Hamilton Carr. Cemetery workers from all over the city gather at sundown on March eleventh to watch the spectral procession, though no one now knows who the mourners are.

The city's most famous (or infamous) resident, the poet and critic Francis Burnham, is buried in St. Mary's Cemetery. Stories were whispered throughout the city of his debauched ways: his orgies, his absinthe and opium, the fortunes he squandered and the young men he ruined. He went mad at last—and the reasons given for his madness are as many and varied as the people who tell the story—and hanged himself in the cupola of his house on Grosvenor Avenue, where his last sight would have been of the city below him. His house now belongs to the city's most influential judge, who does not welcome sightseers.

The Three Oaks Cemetery, though sadly neglected, has some of the country's finest examples of nineteenth-century funerary sculpture. The weeping angel on the tomb of Hester Lyall repays the effort it takes to climb the overgrown path, and the sad, somber dignity of the family group which marks the Addison graves is undiminished by the ivy which twines around their lower bodies. Some long-ago vandal made off with Mrs. Addison's head, and every St. Valentine's Day a posy of belladonna is left by persons unknown on the stump of her neck.

The city has one crematorium, which operates only at the dark of the moon, and what is done with the ashes it is better not to ask.

singing home the rooks and ravens

SEAN STOOD at his dorm-room window, staring out at the quadrangle. Behind him on his desk, a poem lay abandoned in the middle of a line. He was thinking about Clair.

More and more frequently these days, as he tried to work on *The Stag of Candles*, he found himself thinking about Clair. Her delicate face, her Medusan eyes, came between him and the page, leaching the strength out of his words. He was aware that he was writing less, and what he wrote came harder, and, when it did come, it was feeble, thin, twisting restlessly away from what he wanted it to be.

It's Clair, he thought, and although his eyes were looking at the fountain in the quadrangle, mute and desiccated with the winter, and his hands were clenched white-knuckled on the window sill, in his mind he saw only her, felt the silkiness of her hair beneath his fingers. Somehow, in some way he could not describe or explain, he was losing his poetry to her.

He had felt this, uneasily, not quite consciously, for months; although he could not stay away from her for long, he had been trying to find ways to distract himself from Clair. He had even, in the extremity of his desperation, starting going to open-mike nights at Café Xerxes. Everyone was tremendously impressed with his poems, and although he loathed himself for it, he could not help being flattered, gratified. One of them, hero-worship all over her face, had even made a shy, clumsy, stammering pass at him the week before. He had turned her down, but not unkindly. Bram Bennett was actually a pretty good songwriter, and she was a fierce little Goth; she made a good shield against the talentless and overwrought.

But no matter how he felt about them, their reaction was so different from Clair's, the difference between water and salt. Clair let him read his poems to her, the poems that awed the children at Café Xerxes, but her cold indifference was never shaken. And that hurt—it was the slow torture of the rack—but he also knew those poems weren't his best work. *The Stag of Candles* was stronger, stranger, unafraid. But he had shown that to no one.

And he couldn't stop thinking about Clair. I have to break her spell, he thought. I have to win free, face her as an equal.

There was an open-mike at Café Xerxes that night. Sean decided he would go and read, and if Bram Bennett was there, maybe he'd buy her a drink. And maybe, when *The Stag of Candles* was ready, he would give it to Clair to read.

dead leaves

THE MOST NOTORIOUS CASE of suicide off the Liliard Bridge is that of Mr. Horatio Prynne. On the night of Friday, November second, 1894, dressed in complete and impeccable evening wear, Horatio Prynne started across the Liliard Bridge from the west, stopped at the highest point of the bridge's arc, set down his cane, removed his hat and overcoat, and without visible distress or hesitation, stepped up to the parapet and leaped off. A cabman witnessed the event and summoned the police; when the body was at last recovered, at two a.m. on Saturday, November third, it was discovered that the deceased was wearing a money belt laden with silver dollars. There was no doubt that his death had been intentional.

As the Prynnes mourned, the police set about retracing Mr. Prynne's movements on the last day of his life. He had gone driving with his sister in the morning, and had seemed quite normal. He had lunched with friends, who likewise testified to his calmness and good-humor. He had then gone to visit his fiancée, Miss Lucasta Fremont, and had spent much of the afternoon walking with her in the gardens of the Fremont house on Grosvenor Avenue. Miss Fremont, though prostrated with grief, explained that she and Mr. Prynne had talked of their upcoming wedding and that she had told him details of her family history in which he had expressed an interest. Nothing had occurred to upset or alarm him, and he had left very much in his usual good spirits.

The Fremont butler remarked that Mr. Prynne had appeared to be in a great hurry.

At a quarter to five, he walked into the First Municipal Bank on Sheldon Avenue. The bank-teller testified that Mr. Prynne was "visibly agitated" and "very white about the eyes." He had withdrawn four hundred dollars from his account and had insisted that the money be given him in silver dollars. The teller counted out the money, and Mr. Prynne took it away.

That evening he attended the opera with his fiancée, his sister, and his cousin, Mr. Tobias Kingsley. Although Miss Fremont claimed to have noticed no difference in his attitude toward her, Miss Prynne and Mr. Kingsley agreed that he had seemed less attentive to Miss Fremont than usual, and both of them remembered wondering if the couple had quarreled. Mr. Kingsley further testified that on one occasion when Miss Fremont's hand brushed Mr. Prynne's shoulder, Mr. Prynne quite visibly flinched. Miss Prynne had not witnessed this awkward moment, and Miss Fremont explained that Mr. Prynne had apologized in the intermission, telling her that he, not expecting the accidental touch, had believed it to be a spider.

After the opera, the three agreed that Mr. Prynne had mentioned a headache and a desire for fresh air. He told them to return home and that he would take a cab when he was ready. No further witnesses to Mr. Prynne's actions could be found until he appeared at the west end of the Liliard Bridge at a quarter to midnight.

Horatio Prynne left no note, and the final verdict was suicide while temporarily unbalanced in his mind. The *Telegraph-Clarion* described his death as a great loss, both for the Prynnes and for the city, and a custom was established of leaving flowers at the spot from which he had leapt. This custom eroded with time and had ceased entirely by the end of World War II.

In 1896, Mr. Tobias Kingsley married Miss Lucasta Fremont. The wedding was small and private, but the guests remarked that both Mr. Kingsley and his new wife seemed radiantly happy. They honeymooned quietly in the Kingsleys' summer home on Lake Michigan. It was when they returned that Tobias Kingsley's slow decline began. He became quieter and more withdrawn even as his wife, blooming and vivacious, gained a reputation as a sparkling society hostess. Finally in 1905, he was committed to a private rest-home, where he quickly lapsed into catatonia, dying in 1910 at the age of forty-two. The last words he was known to have spoken were to his lifelong friend Mr. Barnaby Munroe, who visited him in the rest-home in the autumn of 1905.

Mr. Kingsley had not spoken to anyone for a week, and for some time he did not speak to Mr. Munroe, either. But finally, as the shadows were drawing down and Mr. Munroe was preparing to leave, Mr. Kingsley looked up at him and said, "Finally I understand poor Horry."

Only this and nothing more.

lying under the gallows-tree

THE NOCTARES BROUGHT BRAM to a building she recognized; she had to cram her fist against her mouth to keep back a spasm of hysterical giggles. Of all the things she had expected to see in the underworld, the absurd Victorian gazebo from Lafayette Park had surely been last on the list. But there it sat, a debutante in an abattoir, looking self-conscious against a dark byzantine tangle of girders and pipes whose function Bram could not imagine.

Then she saw the figures waiting beneath the gazebo's arches, and her laughter withered and turned to dust in her mouth.

There were twelve of them, tall men robed in dark blood-red. As she came closer, she could see that they each wore the same mask, a stark, stylized face in unpainted white porcelain. The eyeholes of the masks were empty, but behind them she could see gears and cogwheels meshing and turning. She swallowed hard and stared at the steps of the gazebo to keep from being mesmerized by the endless spinning clockwork. The noctares let go of her arm, and when she looked around, it had vanished.

One of the twelve Clockwork Kings stepped forward and said, "I speak for all." Its voice was the voice of a clockwork mechanism, full of rust and oil, dust and dead spiders and fragments of macerated time. The other eleven bowed their heads and stepped back into the shadows of the gazebo, but she could still see slivers of light glinting off the moving clockwork in their eyes.

There was silence; unlike mortals, the Clockwork Kings did not shift or grumble or even breathe. Only the clockwork, ever moving, revolved and revolved, but it made no sound.

Bram licked her dry lips and said, "I'm looking for someone. Sean Lacroix."

"And what will you do when you have found him?" said the Clockwork King.

"I want . . . " She had to stop, wrench her gaze away again from the whirling gears. "I want to take him back with me. To the world."

"He is dead."

"There's ways around that, aren't there?" Bram said and flinched at her own boldness.

"A few. But why should we do this for you? Why is your love greater, your pain deeper, than that of any of the thousands of people grieving in the city above?"

"The train stopped for me," Bram said, knowing it was not enough.

"It stopped for your music, not your errand." One of the other Clockwork Kings made some tiny motion, a bare rustle of fabric, and the first said, "And yet you have answered our question. Play for us."

"Play for you?"

"Play for us. And if your music pleases us, we will let you talk to your friend, and you may take him back if it is what he wishes."

Hands shaking, barely daring to breathe, Bram took out her guitar, tuned it, and began to play. She played a song of her own, "Soaring Jilly," that she'd played often and always to generous applause. But the rapture that had possessed her on the Grandison Station platform was gone; she was aware that her playing was no more than adequate and her voice was thin and strained and tending to sharp, and the Clockwork Kings were watching her with their arms crossed. She began to imagine she could hear a clock ticking, and then to be sure that she really did, although she could not tell where the sound came from; she had only a limited amount of time to catch the Clockwork Kings' attention before they would dismiss her and her request, and she would have to go back to the world, to life, alone.

A strange thing happened then, and unlike the other events of that terrible night of wonders, it happened in Bram's head. The situation flipped upside down, and she realized that that ticking clock, imaginary or otherwise, was running every time she stepped up in front of an audience. There was always that narrow window of opportunity to make them care, make them listen, and, despite everything, this was no different. She straightened up, took a better breath, and vamped her way down from "Soaring Jilly" into the song of hers that Sean had always liked best, "Cast Shadows." And now she'd got to the place inside herself where she needed to be; the music opened up and let her in. She felt the difference, and she could tell that the Clockwork Kings felt it, too; they were listening now, not judging, and she knew she had won.

When she had finished, the Clockwork Kings bowed their heads gravely in thanks, and their speaker said, "Are you sure? Our kingdom holds other pleasures."

"I want Sean," Bram said.

Again the Clockwork Kings nodded, and they all said, with the single great voice of a tenor bell, "As you wish."

the starling's path

REGARDLESS OF WHAT you may be told, there is no phantom in the city opera house.

corrosive kisses

IT WAS A NIGHTCLUB in a city where night never ended. The dance floor was packed with writhing, twisting, gyrating bodies which did not sweat and did not breathe. They were young men and women, beautiful in death, powerful because they did not live. They made way for Bram, separating as she came near, turning to stare at her with lightless, filmy eyes, like the dead girl in the train car. Bram asked for Sean, and they shook their heads and slipped away to other parts of the dance floor. She became aware of their scent, faint and sweet and reeking.

Finally, the twentieth or thirtieth or hundredth time she said, "I'm looking for Sean," the boy she had approached, a tall snake-sinuous blond with a livid rope-burn around his neck, nodded and pointed. There were alcoves along the walls, and in one of them, she now saw, there was a group of people dancing together, creating their own world of rhythm and sound.

"Thank you," she said, but the blond boy was already gone. Bram crossed to the alcove through the dancers, aware of their dead, empty gazes on her back. As she approached, the people dancing in the alcove felt her presence and turned. There were six of them, beautiful and dead: three girls, two boys, and the sixth was Sean, like a king in their midst. There was a tattoo across his chest that had never been there in life, the stylized mark of train tracks, and Bram felt suddenly cold and queasy.

"Sean?" she said, in a tiny voice.

"Bram?" Sean's eyes widened, but they weren't his eyes—not the rainwater gray eyes, full of light, that she had loved. The rest of Sean had become brighter, straighter, more beautiful, but his eyes had truly died These were dull gray stones, dry as drought-parched earth.

"It's me," Bram said. "I . . . I came to find you."

"You aren't dead." Sean and his cadre of dancers drew away from Bram a little, as if her vitality might be contagious.

"No. I . . . " But she had to say it; Sean would figure out the truth anyway. "A seraphic train stopped for me."

"Did it?" Sean said, with a bark of laughter as dead as he was. "And you came *here*? *Why*?"

"For you, Sean." Unnerved, scared, she rushed into speech. "The Clockwork Kings say you can come back. I played for them, and they agreed to it. You can come back with me."

The silence lasted until she realized that the throbbing, thrashing music was no longer playing. She turned around; the dancers were all standing still now, watching her with their dull, dead eyes.

She turned back to Sean. There was no joy on Sean's face, no relief, no gratitude. He was staring at her as if he had never seen her before.

"Sean?"

"What? Am I supposed to say thank you? Am I supposed to fall at your feet weeping with gratitude, a good little Eurydice? Has it occurred to you, Bram, that I might not *want* to go back?"

"You don't? But—"

"No. It's over, Bram. Clair doesn't love me—I realized that at last. And I'm not a poet. I'll never be one. There's nothing left up there for me except defeat and pain, and I don't want those."

She did not know who Clair was. "But, Sean . . . "

"What?" Sean said. He was smiling a little. Two of his cadre came up beside him, a girl on the left and a boy on the right. Snake-like, they twined their arms around his waist, and he put his arms across their shoulders.

Bram felt the anticlimax coming and could not help it. There was nothing else left for her to say. "I love you."

"Do you?" Sean said, without interest. "And why do you imagine that matters?"

It was a terrible echo of the Clockwork Kings' question. She said, "It's love. It has to matter. Sean, look, I know I'm not like you. I know I'm not really worth your while. I'm a poser, a wannabe, wearing black like it was peacock feathers. My name isn't even Bram. It's Michelle, all right? I don't know why the train stopped for me. It shouldn't have. It should have stopped for you. But I love you, and I came here to bring you back, and don't you even *care*?"

From all the dead dancers in the nightclub, there was a long, mocking round of applause. Bram stood still beneath it, her cheeks burning, stubbornly refusing to drop her gaze from Sean's face. And Sean looked back at her, with those murky gray eyes that were not his, and said, "Honestly, Bram—Michelle, if you like—no, I don't. Your love meant nothing to me when I was alive. It means even less to me now. Go back to the world, Bram. There's nothing for you here." He turned to the girl on his left and they kissed, open-mouthed, imitating passion they could no longer feel.

Bram flinched back, and Sean's cadre moved in between them, Sean's armor against life and risk; from somewhere, the music started again. Bram was left with no options, nothing to do except turn around and leave. She stumbled through the throng of young men and women, who would never age, never be ugly, never grow, never be able to open their hearts to anyone or anything. And even as they writhed and strutted, the dead dancers watched her all the way to the door.

why do you linger?

SEAN CLIMBED OUT the window of his old bedroom and scrambled onto the roof of the house; it was five to midnight, but the dark didn't bother him. Once on the roof, he opened his backpack and took out a flashlight and the battered manuscript of *The Stag of Candles*. Clair's scent was still on it, or perhaps that was just his memory of what she smelled like.

He stood, holding *The Stag of Candles* to his chest, and waited for the 11:59 train.

It howled past in a stink of oil and stale air. Midnight. Sean turned on the flashlight, folded the top page of the manuscript back against its binder clip, and again waited, like a captain's wife on her widow's walk, watching the sea for her husband's sails. When he heard the next train coming, the 12:20, he began to read in a hard, clear, angry voice.

Sean read a poem from *The Stag of Candles* for each train that passed. He kept his voice level and firm, although after about 1:45, he crouched down on the roof between trains and sobbed in choking whispers, clutching the manuscript to him like a hurt child.

At 3:12, a seraphic train screamed by. It did not stop, and the people inside did not even turn their heads. Sean scrubbed his eyes with one grimy hand and waited for the next train.

He read poems about the foundries, poems about the art museum and the coldly echoing rotunda of the public library. He read the poem about St. Christopher's, and another poem about his own confirmation and the angels that did not sing to him. He read poems about the interstate, about the city's storm drains, which were supposed to prevent floods but never quite did. He read a long poem in Spenserian stanzas about St. Catherine's. He had written a corona of eight poems, one for each of the city's eight public parks, and he read the corona to the trains, which were no more impressed than Clair had been. He read his sequence of sonnets about the river. Now, nearly 6 o'clock, he was no longer stopping between trains, just reading and reading from this bloated leviathan of a manuscript, which he had been working on in one form or another since he was fifteen.

At 6:39, a second seraphic train hurtled past; the roar of its passage sounded like mocking laughter. Tears were running down Sean's face, but he kept reading, embarked now on the long narrative poem about Sophia Walters, the early twentieth-century mystic who predicted the terrible fire of 1922 and died in it.

At 7:29, Sean read the last poem in *The Stag of Candles*, a villanelle dedicated to Clair. He stood on the roof, dry-eyed now, although his eyes and throat and nose were raw. It was over; there was nothing. He had been tested, and he had failed. The seraphic trains would not stop for him. His poetry was a bouquet of dead, rotting roses, a sickness, a canker, a stupid, self-indulgent delusion. There was no worth in him.

At 7:31, the sun rose.

At 7:32, the first daylight train passed the house at 2981 Lynn Street. Still clutching *The Stag of Candles* in a white-knuckled grip, Sean threw himself off the roof and onto the tracks just before the wheels of the train.

The pages of the manuscript flew free briefly and then were swallowed by the city, which would not mourn. *The Stag of Candles* became another sacrifice.

Lost in the city and never recovered.

the company of stone-eyed watchers

There are nine sundials in Lytton Park, each purchased and installed by the philanthropist W. W. Maddox, who died in 1920. By the terms of his will, there were to have been four more sundials installed, for a total of thirteen, but as the Maddox estate was immediately and inextricably mired in litigation between his second wife and his son, each contesting the inheritance of the other, this ambitious scheme was never brought to fruition. Both the son and the second wife accused their opponent of encouraging Maddox in his passion for sundials, which the son described as "morbid" and the second wife stigmatized as "unnatural," and as the Municipal Park Board confessed that in its heart of hearts it did not desire any more sundials, that clause of the will became part of the complicated evidence adduced by both sides to prove Maddox was not of sound mind, and was eventually, thankfully, dropped.

If you acquire a map of Lytton Park and plot the positions of the sundials, you will see that the form an incomplete circle. The third sundial is set awkwardly into the side of a hill, and the sixth is buried in deep shade among a stand of cypress trees. You may begin to wonder whether Maddox's beneficence had some darker, ulterior motive, but if either the second wife or the son knew anything about that, they never said a word.

Not one of the nine sundials shows the correct time.

roses she gave me, and columbines

BRAM BENNETT RETURNED to the mortal world on a seraphic train that was empty except for her and a man crouched in the corner, sobbing and sobbing. Looking at the two livid, bloodless wounds running from shoulder to waist on either side of his spine, she could understand why. It was all she could do not to join him.

The train stopped again at Grandison Station in the cool, serene darkness before dawn. Bram got out. No one had to tell her that the seraphic trains would never stop for her again. She knew it in the marrow of her bones and the beating caverns of her heart.

She stood on the platform, her guitar at her side, and wondered what to do. She supposed wearily that she could throw herself under the next train to come along, as she had originally planned, but that seemed stupid and futile; even this terrible spiny knot of pain, compounded of grief and humiliation and anger, was better than the mechanical frenzy of the pink neon nightclub.

She made her way along the platform to the stairs. She remembered that she had finished "Why Do You Linger?" in the night, and it was still in her head, raw, vital, imperfect—but complete. She could go write it down; maybe later, when the mute, stupid weight of grief had lessened, she could play it. But not at Café Xerxes. She would not go back there; it was as barren and futile as the nightclub, and she realized that that was why Sean had gone there: because it might be dead, but it was safe.

Somewhere dangerous, she thought, going down the stairs. Somewhere alive. Somewhere *new*.

The oak trees saluted her with their stark but living branches, black against the luminous sky. Suddenly, laughing, Bram raised her arms and saluted them in return.

reaching for your reflection

CLAIR STANDS in front of her picture window, gazing out across the night-bejeweled city. It is impossible to tell if she has posed herself deliberately, aware of the picture she creates, or if the angle of her raised arm, the geometry of her fingers against the curtain she holds back, the tilt of her head, the position of her feet, are merely accidental. And you would not dream of asking her.

In a moment Clair will turn away, turn back to you where you watch her from the long, low, white couch, but for now she stands, gazing out at the city which is more truly her beloved—her lover, master, servant, self—than any mortal who has ever touched her.

FIDDLEBACK FERNS

"Are these fiddleback ferns, Mommy?" Cindy asked.

"Fiddle*head*, honey," Marjorie said absently. "Fiddlebacks are nasty spiders." It was only later that she would realize that Cindy, for once in her vacuous Barbie-obsessed life, had been exactly right.

Fiddleback ferns indeed.

Marjorie dismissed them as weeds at first—the plants she cared about bloomed prettily and smelled nice—rooted them out, planted pansies instead. But a week later, the pansies were dead, and those nasty purple-green shoots were visible again.

"Darn it," said Marjorie, who never swore, and dug them out again.But the more of them she uprooted, the more there seemed to be. Their smell was like something burning rather than something growing, and it was strong. Ron complained of headaches and did even less yardwork than usual. Marjorie consulted her gardening books, consulted Mrs. Higgins next door, even got Daniel to show her how to Google. But she couldn't find anything that looked like the things growing in her yard. Daniel, who watched too much TV, said, "Maybe they're alien spores or something," and Marjorie said, "Do your homework."

Cindy and Daniel were sick more often that spring than Marjorie could ever remember them being. Allergies, the doctors said. Asthma, they said, when Cindy started having trouble breathing. "Will you buy me another Barbie 'cause I'm sick?" was all Cindy cared about.

And then Cindy was in the hospital with a tube in her throat, and Ron was out getting drunk with "the boys," because that was how Ron coped in a crisis. Daniel was supposed to be doing his homework, but he was watching TV. Marjorie stood in her spotless kitchen and thought about the strange plants that had taken over her flowerbeds.

Fiddleback ferns.

Alien spores.

"*Fuck*," said Marjorie, who never swore.

"Mom?" Daniel said, turning away from the TV.

But Marjorie wasn't there.

She stood on her front lawn in the twilight, staring at them. "Why?" she said. "Why here? Why *us*? The most important problem in Cindy's life was that her Barbies were too big to ride her My Little Ponies! If you're going to beam down from outer space and kill some poor little kid, shouldn't it be Einstein or Gandhi or somebody?"

The ugly purple-green fronds ignored her and unfurled another millimeter.

"Ignore *this*, Audrey," Marjorie muttered.

"Marjorie honey?" said Mrs. Higgins next door. "Is that *gasoline*?"

Marjorie ignored her, and Mrs. Higgins went inside to call 911. But Marjorie lit the match before the police got there.

Daniel stood on the sidewalk, watching his mother capering like a witch before their burning house, watching the greenish oily smoke rising up from the flowerbeds, and when the policeman asked him why his mother had done it, he said, "An exorcism, like in that movie."

"Too much TV," the policeman said, and went to radio for a fire truck.

And Marjorie went to ask Mrs. Higgins next door if she could borrow some salt.

Three Letters from the Queen of Elfland

WHEN PHILIP OSBOURNE found the letters, he did not do so by accident.

Since the birth of their son, he had become worried about Violet. In the evenings, when they sat together, he would look up and find her staring at nothing, her hands frozen above her embroidery. When he asked her what she was thinking about, she would smile and say "Nothing." Her smile was the same lovely smile that had first drawn him to her, but he knew she was lying. At their dinner parties, where formerly the conversation had sparkled and glimmered like a crystal chandelier, there were now silences, limping faltering pauses. He would look around and see Violet watching the reflections of the lights in the windows, with an expression on her face that frightened him because he did not know it.

He had come to believe, in the fullness and flowering of his love for her, that he knew Violet's every mood, every thought; but now he seemed to be losing her, and this sense that she was drifting away, borne on a current he could not feel, made him angry because it made him afraid.

THE FIRST LETTER:

Dearest Violetta,

I have obeyed your prohibition. It has been a year and a day. I have not spoken to you, I have not come near you, I have not touched your dreams. It is my hope that you have changed your mind. My garden is not the same without you. My roses still bloom, for I will not let them fade, but the weeping willows have choked out the cherry trees, and all the chrysanthemums and snapdragons have become love-lies-bleeding and anemones and hydrangeas of the deepest indigo blue. You are missed, my only violet. Return to me.

On that afternoon in late May, Violet Strachan had been in her favorite place beneath the oak tree, a cushion stolen from her mother's boudoir protecting her back from the tree roots. She was writing poetry, an activity her mother disapproved of. Happily, as Mrs. Strachan abhorred anything closer to the state of nature than a well-tended conservatory, she did not come into the garden. Her daughters, Violet and Marian, spent much of their time in the little grove of trees along the stream.

Violet was never sure what made her look up—a noise, a movement, perhaps just the faint scent of honeysuckle. Something tugged at her attention, causing her to raise her head, and she saw the woman standing barefoot in the stream. She knew immediately, viscerally, that the woman was not mortal. Her eyes were the deep, translucent blue-green of tourmaline; her hair, held back from her face with cunningly worked branches of golden leaves, was a silken, curling torrent that fell to her hips. Its color was elusive—all the colors of night, Violet thought, and then did not know where the thought had come from. Neither then nor later could Violet ever describe the inhuman perfection of her face.

Violet's notebook fell from her hand unheeded. She knew she was staring; she could not help herself. The woman regarded her a moment with a bemused expression and then waded delicately across the stream, saying, "Our gardens abut. Is that not pleasant?"

"Beg pardon?"

The woman came up onto the bank, her sheer silver-gray dress instantly dry, its hem lifting a little with the currents of the air. She flashed Violet a breathtaking smile and said, "We are neighbors. What is your name?"

Violet had known the neighbors on all sides of the family estate from infancy, and this woman could not be imagined to belong to any of them. Yet she found herself saying, "Violet. Violet Strachan."

"Violet," the woman said, seeming almost to taste the syllables. "A lovely name, and a lovely flower." The tourmaline eyes were both grave and wicked, and Violet felt herself blushing.

"What . . . " she faltered, then recklessly went on, "What am I to call you?"

The woman laughed, and the sound made Violet feel that she had never heard laughter before, only pale imitations by people who had read about laughter in books. "I have many names," the woman said. "Mab, Titania . . . You may pick one if you like, or you may make one up."

Her words were only confirmation of what Violet's instincts had already told her, but they were nonetheless a drenching shock. While Violet was still staring, the Queen of Elfland came closer and said, "May I sit with you?"

"Yes, of course," Violet said, hastily bundling her skirts out of the way. "Please do."

"I have not walked among your world for decades," the Queen said, seating herself gracefully and without fuss. "I cannot reconcile myself to the clothes."

"Oh," Violet said, pushing vaguely at the masses of cloth. "But you're here now."

The Queen laughed. "I told you: we are neighbors." Her long

white hand reached out and touched Violet's, stilling it instantly. "Have you chosen what to call me, Violet?"

"I cannot," Violet said, staring at their hands where they met against her dark blue skirt. "I know of no name that suits you."

"You turn a pretty compliment," the Queen said. She sounded pleased, and Violet felt even more greatly bewildered, for she had not meant to flatter, merely to tell the truth. "I would tell you my true name, but you could not hear it if I did. 'Mab' is by far the simplest of the names mortals have given me, and I find it has a certain dignity to it. Why do you not call me Mab?"

"No," Violet said, struggling against the weight of embarrassment—and a queer, giddy feeling, as if her blood had turned to glowing champagne. "Nyx is closer." For surely the Queen's beauty was the beauty of Night.

The Queen was silent. Looking up, Violet saw the beautiful eyes staring at her, the perfect brows raised. She saw that the Queen's eyes were slit-pupiled, like a cat's. "You speak more truly than you know, lovely flower. Very well. I shall be pleased to answer to 'Nyx' from your mouth." And she smiled.

For a moment, Violet's heart stopped with the impact of that smile, and then it began trip-hammering. She could barely breathe, and the world did not seem wide enough to contain the Queen's eyes.

The Queen lifted her hand from Violet's skirt to touch the piled chignon of her hair. "You have beautiful hair, Violetta. But all those pins with their cruel jaws! Why do you not let it free?"

"I couldn't," Violet said, purely by reflex—she was so dazed that she only knew what she was saying when she heard her own voice. "Mother would have a fit."

"Your mother need not know," the Queen said, her fingers as light as moths on Violet's hair. "I assure you, I am skilled enough to replace these ugly dragons when the time comes." And then, leaning closer so that the smell of honeysuckle surrounded Violet, she whispered, "I dare you."

Later, Violet would wonder how long the Queen had watched her—weeks? months? years?—before she had made her presence known. Certainly it could be no accident that she had found so exactly the chink in Violet's armor, the phrase she and Marian had used since childhood to make each other braver, stronger, less like the daughters their mother wanted. By the time Violet caught up with what her own hands were doing, they were already teasing out the second pin. And then it seemed there was no going back. In moments, the pins were out, resting in a natural hollow in one of the oak tree's roots, and the Queen was gently finger-combing Violet's hair.

"Beautiful hair," she said, sitting back. "It is the color of sunset, my flower. I can feel dusk gathering in your tresses."

Violet had not had her hair down in the daytime since she was a child. The feeling was strange, unsettling, but the champagne in her blood seemed now to have twice as many bubbles, and, as she felt the breeze tugging against the warm weight of her hair, she was hard-pressed to keep from laughing out loud.

"Now," said the Queen, "I feel I can look at you properly. Tell me about yourself."

It was an invitation, but from the Queen of Elfland, even an invitation fell on the ear like a command. Violet found herself pouring out her life's history to the Queen: her father's quiet, scholarly preoccupation; her mother's ferrous dissatisfaction; her sister Marian; her friend Edith; the callow boys who came calling; Violet's own true desire to write poetry and have a salon and never to marry, except perhaps for love. And the Queen listened, her knees drawn up to her chin, her eyes fixed raptly on Violet's face, only asking a question from time to time. Violet could not remember ever being listened to with such care, such fierceness.

Only when Violet had done speaking, made shy again by those brilliant, inhuman eyes, did the Queen move. She sat up straight and gently pulled free a strand of Violet's hair that had caught in the oak tree's bark. Still holding the strand between her fingers, she said, "And you have no lover, Violetta? I find that sad."

"The young men I know are all boring."

"And one's lover should never be boring," the Queen agreed. She was winding Violet's hair around her fingers, being careful not to pull. "What about your friend Edith?"

"Edith? But Edith's . . . " *A girl,* she had been going to say, but the Queen knew that already. Involuntarily, Violet looked at the Queen; the Queen was watching her with pupils dilated, a cat ready to pounce. "We couldn't," Violet said in a thin whisper.

"It is not hard," the Queen said, releasing Violet's hair. She caressed Violet's cheek. "And you are made to be loved, Violetta." There was a pause. Violet could feel a terrible, immodest heat somewhere in the center of her being, and she knew her face was flushed. The Queen raised perfect eyebrows. "Do *I* bore you?"

"No," Violet said breathlessly. "You do not bore me." The Queen smiled and leaned in close to kiss her.

Philip waited for a day when he knew Violet would be out of the house. She made very few afternoon visits since Jonathan's birth, but he knew she would not refuse her childhood friend Edith Fairfield, who had been so ill since the birth of her own child. At two o'clock he told his clerk a random lie to explain his early departure and went home.

He was not accustomed to being home during the day; he was disturbed by how quiet it was. The housemaid stared at him with wide, frightened eyes like a deer's as he crossed the front hall. The carpet on the stairs seemed to devour his footsteps. He had climbed those stairs a thousand times, but he had never noticed their breadth and height, the warmth of the glowing oak paneling, the silken run of the bannister beneath his hand.

He stopped on the landing. There was a bowl of roses in the window, great creamy-golden multifoliate orbs, seeming to take the sunlight into themselves and throw it out threefold. Their scent had all the sweetness of childhood's half-remembered summers, and he stood for a long time gazing at them before he turned down the hall toward Violet's bedroom.

Her bedroom was not as he remembered it. Standing in the doorway, he tried to identify what had changed and could not. The room, like Violet herself, seemed distant. It was the middle of the day—he thought of the torch-like roses—yet Violet's room seemed full of twilight and the cool sadness of dusk.

For a moment, like a man standing on the brink of a dark, powerful river, he thought that he would turn and leave, that he would not brave the torrent rushing in silence through Violet's room. For a moment he recognized, in a dim wordless way, that the name of the river bank he stood upon was *peace*.

But it was not right that Violet should have secrets from him, who loved her. He took a deep, unthinking breath and stepped into Violet's room to begin his search.

LATER, VIOLET WOULD RECOGNIZE that the Queen had in fact enchanted her, that first afternoon by the stream. But by then she had come to understand the Queen of Elfland as well as any mortal could, and she was not angry. The Queen had done as she had seen fit, and the enchantment had not made Violet behave in ways contrary to who she was. It had merely separated her temporarily from inhibition, caution, guilt . . . so that the feel of the Queen's mouth on her naked breasts, the feel of the Queen's cool fingers between her legs, had brought her nothing but passion.

Only at twilight, as she was hastening up to the house, praying that her buttons were fastened straight and that there were no leaves caught in her hair, did it occur to her to wonder what had possessed her, to imagine what her mother would say if she were told even a tenth of what the Queen had taught Violet that afternoon. Her face was flushed with shame by the time she sat down at the dinner table. Luckily, her mother assumed her heightened color was due to sun, and therefore Violet received only a familiar diatribe about the quality of a lady's skin. She bent her head beneath her mother's anger without even feeling it, her mind full of the throaty purr of the Queen's laughter.

That should have been the end of it—the encounter should have been a momentary aberration, from which Violet returned, chastened and meek, to her senses—but the heat the Queen had woken in her would not be damped down again. She found herself imagining what it would be like to kiss Edith, or Marian's beautiful friend Dorothea, or even Ann the housemaid. At night she fantasized about the heroines of her favorite books, and sometimes her hands would creep down her body to touch the secret places the Queen had shown her. Two weeks after their first meeting, Violet went back to the spinney. The Queen of Elfland was waiting there, her hands full of roses.

PHILIP FINALLY FOUND the letters hidden in the back of a photograph of Violet and her sister Marian, who was now in India with her husband. He had never liked the portrait, had always wished Violet would get rid of it, but it was the only picture she had of Marian. He did not like the dark directness with which the sisters looked out of the frame. It seemed to him unpleasant—and most unlike Violet. That girl's face, remote and delicate and somber, had nothing to do with the woman he had married.

He picked it up, turned it over, pried loose the back with a savage wrench.

The letters fluttered out like great helpless moths and drifted to the floor. He dropped the portrait heedlessly and picked them up, his hands shaking.

There were three of them; he could tell by the ink, which darkened from the terrible crimson color of blood, through a rich garnet, to a red so dark it was almost black. The handwriting was square and flowing, elegant yet as neat as print. The paper was translucently thin, as if it had been spun out of the great richness of the ink.

He looked first, viciously, for a signature. There was none on any of them, only an embossed signet, the imprint of a linden leaf. It meant nothing to him.

He put the letters in order, darkest and oldest to brightest and newest, and began to read.

The second letter:

Violet, my song,

I dream of your breasts, their small sweetness. I dream of your thighs, of the nape of your neck, of your fragile hands. I dream of the treasure between your thighs, of its silken softness beneath my fingers, and its warmth. I dream of your kisses, my Violet, of the taste of your mouth, the roughness of your tongue. My truest flame, my mortal queen, I dream of the feel of your lips on my skin, the feel of your fingers in my hair. I dream of your laugh, of your smile, of your velvet-rich voice.

You asked me once if I would not forget you. I could see in your eyes that you believed I would, that you thought yourself no more than an amusement, a toy with which I would soon become bored. I could not tell you then that it was not true, but I tell you now. I have not forgotten you. I will not forget you. You are more to me than you can imagine. Return to me.

After he had read them all, Philip crumpled the letters in his shaking hands and hurled them away as if they were poison. His brain seemed full of fire. When he bent, automatically, to pick up the portrait, he found another object wedged in its back, an elaborately woven knot of hair, as firm and soft as silk; its color seemed to shift with the light, from ink to ash to fog. It had to be the token the final letter spoke of.

He was standing with it in his hand, staring at it in a dry fury, when he heard the rustle of Violet's dress in the hall. As she came in, her face already surprised, his name on her lips, he shouted at her, "*Who is he?*"

She looked from him, to the crumpled letters, to the portrait, to the token in his hand. The expression left her face, as if she were a lake freezing over. She said, "No one."

"Who wrote you these letters, Violet?" he said, striving to keep his voice low and even. "You said you hadn't had suitors before me."

"I hadn't," she said. "I did not lie to you, Philip."

"Then what are these?" He pointed to the letters.

She looked at him, her eyes as dark and direct as the eyes of the photographed Violet lying on the floor. "Mine."

He was so jolted he took a step backwards. It suddenly seemed to him that he was facing a stranger, that this woman standing here, her red-gold hair gleaming in the sunlight from the windows, was not his wife, Violet Strachan Osbourne, but some almost perfect replica, like a Madame Tussand's waxwork come to life. "But, Violet," he said, hating how feeble he sounded even as he said it, "I am your husband."

"Yes," she said. "I know."

"Then why won't you tell me the truth?"

"It would not help." She looked away from him, not in embarrass-ment or shame, but merely as if she were tired of thinking about him. "If you will leave me now, in an hour I will come downstairs, and it will be as if none of this ever happened. We can forget it."

He did not want to talk to this Violet, so cold and patient and indifferent. He wanted to take her offer. But . . . "I cannot forget. Who is he, Violet?"

She came into the room, picked up the letters and carefully smoothed them out. She came past him, picked up the photograph, returned the letters to its back. She turned to him then and held out her hand, her eyes level and unfathomable. He surrendered the token. She put it with the letters, then replaced the back of the frame and returned the photograph to its accustomed place. Only then did she say, "I wish you would reconsider."

"I cannot," he said, with greater certainty now. "I will forgive you, but I must know."

She looked into the distance for a moment, as if she were thinking of something else. "I do not think I have asked for your forgiveness, Philip."

"Violet—!"

She looked back at him, her eyes like stone. "If you insist on knowing, I will tell you. But I do not do so because I think you have a right to hear it, or because I want you to 'forgive' me. I do so because I know that I will have no peace otherwise."

"Violet . . . "

"You married me two months after we met. I was glad of it, even gladder when I became pregnant so quickly. I thought she would lose interest then."

"*She?*"

The look Violet gave him was almost pitying. "My lover, Philip. The Queen of Elfland."

In fear and fury, he erupted at her: "Good God, Violet, do you expect me to believe this nonsense?"

"No," she said, and the flash of her dark eyes went through him like a scythe. "I don't care what you believe. You may hear nothing, or you may hear the truth. I will not lie to you."

"I thought you loved me," he said in a failing whisper.

"I wanted to. And I like you very much. But she was right. I cannot forget her, though God knows I have tried."

It came to him then clearly, terribly, that she was not lying. Those letters with their strange paper and stranger ink, the knot of hair with its shifting colors, the fabulous roses—all those things forced him to face the idea that Violet held secrets from him, that there was something in her he had never even guessed at.

"She found me," Violet said, and he knew dimly that she was no longer speaking to him, "when I was eighteen. There was a spinney at the bottom of our garden with a stream running through it. Marian and I went there to read novels and write poetry and do other things Mother disapproved of. Sometimes we would talk of what we meant to do when we were grown. We would never marry, we told each other solemnly. I wanted to be a poet. Marian wanted to be an explorer and find the source of the Amazon. But that day I was alone."

It was another thing he had never known about her. He had never known that she wrote poetry at all, much less that she had dreamed of poetry instead of marriage. It was another fragment of her that he had not held, when he thought he had held everything that she was.

She had drifted across to the mirror, the massive heirloom cheval glass in its mahogany frame. She was running her fingers over the carved leaves and flowers; her reflection in the glass seemed like a reflection in dark water.

"I can't remember what I was doing. I just remember looking up and seeing her. She was standing in the stream. I knew what she was."

The eyes of her reflection caught his eyes. He watched Violet remember where she was and to whom she spoke; her face closed again, like a door slamming shut.

"She seduced me," Violet said, turning to face him. "We became lovers. At night I would sneak out of the house and cross the stream to her court. One week, when my parents took Marian to visit her godmother, I told the servants I was staying with Edith, and I spent the entire time with . . . with *her*. She begged me not to go back, but I could not stay. Do you understand, Philip? *I could not stay.*"

She seemed to see in his face that he did not understand, and the vitality drained out of her again. "The night before I married you, I asked her to let me go, to give me a year and a day to try to be your wife. She did as I asked."

"But then she began writing letters," he said, because he had to prove, to Violet, to himself, that he was truly here.

"Yes. I have not answered them. I have been faithful to you."

He held up his hands, palms out in a warding gesture, as if the bitterness in her voice were something he could push away. But he could not keep the reproach from his tongue: "You kept the letters."

"Yes," Violet said, her tone too flat to be deciphered, "I kept the letters."

THE THIRD LETTER:

Violet, my only heart,

I know that your silence must mean you will not return, that you have chosen your other life. I could compel you to return, just as I could have compelled you to stay. I hope you understand that my choice not to do so is itself a gift, the only way you have offered me to show you that I love you. I do not know what there is in your life to treasure: your husband, as blind and senseless as a stone? your fat, stodgy infant who will surely grow up to resemble his father? the mother whose love you cannot win, the father who has never noticed you? your sick and clinging friend? the infrequent letters from a sister who thinks of nothing but her husband?

You know the wonders and joys I can offer you. You know that in my realm you will be honored as you are not in your own. Violet, it is pain to me to know how you are treated, how little those around you see you—much less recognize your beauties—even as they use you and destroy you. I know that you will not heed me; I feel in your silence that your mind is made up. You are better than the mortal world deserves.

I will give you three gifts then, since you will not let me give you more. Your freedom, even though you turn it into slavery; this token—I wish that perhaps you will wear it next your heart; my roses, that your house, too, may become a garden. And I give you, still, my hope that you will return.

THE SILENCE in the bedroom was as heavy as iron, heavy as lead. Philip could not find the strength to lift it. In the end, it was Violet who straightened her shoulders and said, with an odd, crooked smile, "Well, Philip?"

"You don't love me," he said.

The smile fell from her face. "No. I am sorry."

"What about Jonathan? Your *son*?"

The Queen's careless description, "your fat, stodgy infant," hung unspoken between them. Finally, Violet said, "I will do my duty by him."

"My God, Violet, I'm not talking about duty! I'm asking if you *love* him!"

"You are asking too much." The color was gone from her face; for the first time, he was forced to admit that the solemn photograph captured something that was really part of Violet. Before he could compose himself against that realization, another hit him: that he did not know her, that the sparkling, marvelous conversations, on which he had founded his love, had given him nothing of her true thoughts, nothing of her heart. He had worshipped her as her suitor; he had worshipped her as her husband. But until now, he had come no closer to her; truly, as he had thought earlier, she was a stranger to him.

In the pain of that revelation, he said, "You used me. You're *using* me and Jonathan." Then, with a gasp, "You're using my love!"

"I have given everything I have to give in return!" Violet cried. "Is this all there is, Philip? Have I no choice but to give everything to her, or to you? Either way, what is there left for me?"

"Violet—"

"No," she said, so harshly that he was silenced. "I see that I am like Ulysses, caught between Scylla and Charybdis. To neither side is there safe haven."

He looked away from the bitter anguish in her face. He still loved her. He did not think he would ever forgive her for what she had done, but her despair struck him like barbed arrows. "I am sorry," he said at last. "I did not realize I was asking so much."

"You have asked no more than any man asks of his wife." She sank down slowly onto the chair by the window, resting her forehead on her hand.

"I did not wish to . . . to crush you," he said, fighting now simply to make her hear him. "I did not know you were so unhappy."

"I am not unhappy," she said without raising her head. "I chose between love and duty, and I am living with my choice. I had not . . . I had not expected to be offered that choice again. That makes it harder."

"Will you go back to . . . *her*?"

"No. I cannot. Her love will destroy me, for I am only mortal, a moth, and she is like the sun. My poetry was immolated in her ardor, left in her garden with my heart, and I cannot sacrifice more to her." He thought for a moment she would go on, but she said only, again, "I cannot."

"Will you . . . will you stay with me?"

She raised her head then to stare at him; her face was set, like that of someone who looks on devastation and will not weep. "Have I a choice?"

"No, I mean . . . I meant, only, will you *stay*? With *me*?"

"You know that I do not love you."

"Yes, but . . . " He could not think how to express what he wanted to say, that he needed and loved her whether she loved him or not, and was forced to fall back, lamely, on, "You are my wife. And the mother of my son."

"Yes," she said, her voice inflectionless. "I am."

He said, in little more than a whisper: "Don't shut me out, Violet, please."

"Very well," she said. Her smile was a faded reflection of its former luminous beauty. "What is left is yours." She turned away, but not before he had seen the brilliance of tears in her eyes.

He wanted to comfort her, but he no longer knew how. He stood, awkward in the fading afternoon light, and watched her weep.

On the landing, the roses of the Queen of Elfland, as clamorous as trumpets, continued to shout their glory to the uncomprehending house.

─────⊗⊗⊗─────

Night Train: Heading West

In the lounge car, the insomniacs:
a woman playing Solitaire,
the conductor
telling three Minnesota ladies
about his past lives,
a teenage boy, protected
by headphones, staring into the vast
darkness beyond the windows.

The cards
growl through her hands;
she lays them down,
making patterns, looking
for some small meaning.

The Black Death, the conductor
tells the ladies.
It was the third time I had
died in Rome.

The pattern comes to
nothing. She sweeps
the cards together,
shuffles brusquely,
lays them down again.

Egypt, says the
conductor. I
was a priest of Anubis.
I spent my
days among the dead.

A snarl,
a failure.
With impatient hands, she
gathers the cards, lays them down.

The teenage boy rocks
gently to the music only
he can hear. The night
pours past, another river,
like the Mississippi
they have already crossed.
But the night is a river
we are all still crossing.

I was a woman
once, the conductor says.
A Cherokee woman. I died
on the Trail of Tears. I remember
how tired I was, and
how everything tasted of destruction.

She picks up the
cards and deals again.

THE SÉANCE AT CHISHOLM END

"I BEG YOUR PARDON, my dear," said the ugly little man in the amazing waistcoat, "but could you do me the inestimable honor of lending me a hand?"

Harriet Winterbourn paused in the doorway. "You're the medium, aren't you? Mr. Venefidezzi?"

"*Doctor* Venefidezzi. At your service." He really *was* a most remarkably ugly little man, pug-nosed, with a wide, flexible mouth, and wide-spaced eyes of a nearly colorless blue. His fine, flyaway hair, too long for current fashion, was reddish-blond going gray. His diction was perfect Oxonian; despite his exotic name, Harriet suspected uncharitably that English was his native language. He was dressed with unexceptionable propriety in dark gray broadcloth, except for the black silk waistcoat embroidered in a barbaric welter of crimson and gold dragons. "It really won't take but a moment."

"What do you need?" Harriet said by reflex. For five years, she had been the paid companion of old Mrs. Latham—and unpaid seamstress, secretary, and general factotum for the younger Mrs. Latham and her daughters, Virginia and Claudia—and sometimes thought that helpfulness was the only personal characteristic remaining to her (if one could even call it that), all the others having been pressed to death between old Mrs. Latham's venomous and ceaseless misanthropy and young Mrs. Latham's iron dominion over the household of Chisholm End.

"It's the epergne," said Dr. Venefidezzi. "I don't like it."

Looking at the epergne, Harriet could not blame him. The room the younger Mrs. Latham had chosen for the night's séance was the second-best drawing room, known in the parlance of the house as the Blue Room. It was supposedly haunted; no one seemed to know by whom or what, though the servants muttered that old Mrs. Latham had brought something with her when she married into the family. The Blue Room was unpopular, both with the family and with the servants; consequently it served as a sort of oubliette for furnishings unsuitable to the rigorously careful taste of the rest of the house. The epergne, Harriet remembered dimly, had been a present from old Mrs. Latham's cousin Emmeline, who lived in Bath. It was the size of a Russian samovar and looked like the unfortunate offspring of a pineapple and the palace of Versailles.

"I was wondering," Dr. Venefidezzi said, after a moment's pause as if to let the vileness of the epergne speak for itself, "if there might be some place to which it could be relocated. The bottom of a nice, deep mine shaft would be my first choice, but I imagine that notion would not be well-received."

"No, but there's a closet under the servant's stair where it won't come to any harm. Does it disturb the vibrations?" Five years at Chisholm End had also given Harriet a good working knowledge of the parlance of mediums and mystics, both the dubiously genuine and the out-and-out fakes, and she asked mostly from malice.

Dr. Venefidezzi gave her a look of comic appallment which made her want to laugh, despite the tension throbbing in her head. "Well, of *course* it does, dear girl. Not to mention it would scare a gorgon into spasms. Where's this closet of yours?"

"This way," said Harriet. He picked up the epergne and followed her to the left down the hall, through the baize doors, to a low, white-painted door. "Here," Harriet said. "Just remember to tell Mrs. Latham or Mrs. Brennigan what—"

"HARRIET!" The voice echoed only dimly down the stairs, but Harriet jumped as if she'd been shot.

"I have to go," she said and scurried away, abandoning the medium and the epergne in the middle of the hall.

WHEN HARRIET came panting back up the stairs with the embroidery frame Mrs. Latham had sent her to retrieve, she closed her heart against the old woman's abuse and offered no explanation of her "dawdling." Mrs. Latham was a devotee of Spiritualism, in the same way another woman might have been a devotee of the theater; the information that Dr. Venefidezzi had asked Harriet's help might well have appeased her. But Harriet found herself reluctant to talk of that brief encounter, the way the little man had treated her, as if she was a reasonable member of the human species, just as he was himself. She feared that anything she said might betray her liking of Dr. Venefidezzi. Mrs. Latham, who approved the plodding, dreary courtship of the fat curate, Mr. Benfelton, would instantly accuse Harriet of being "sweet" on Dr. Venefidezzi, smug in the knowledge that this tactic would prevent Harriet from showing the slightest interest in the medium ever again. Harriet was twenty-nine and plain, and she loathed being teased and pinched at as if she were a girl of Claudia Latham's age.

Moreover, Mrs. Latham would make sure that the calumny reached the ears of Mr. Benfelton, and he would come to talk to Harriet in maddeningly vague terms about marriage and respectability and his ambitions—and doubtless contrive to stay long enough that he had to be invited to tea. This evening's one mercy, Harriet reflected as she dressed for dinner, was that he would not be here. Mr. Benfelton was a high-minded man, and he did not approve of mediums.

The Séance at Chisholm End

That dinner turned out to be one of the least uncomfortable meals Harriet had sat through at Chisholm End; ugly and gaudy he might be, but Dr. Venefidezzi talked brilliantly. He told stories of Italia and Graecia and Macedonia, stories about werewolves and vampires and ghouls, and had the entire Latham household hanging breathlessly on his words. He even, at Claudia's pleading, took off his coat and rolled back his sleeve to show them the scars on his arm, where a werewolf had bitten him. Harriet kept to herself the idea that any large dog could have done the same.

By the time the company rose from the table to make their way to the Blue Room, Virginia and Claudia were wide-eyed and peering nervously into the shadows. The younger Mrs. Latham was pretending indifference, but the way her head snapped around at the creak of a floorboard betrayed her. Old Mrs. Latham wouldn't have been fazed by finding a vampire in her bed, and Mr. Latham had no imagination and scorned his wife's habit of séances in any event. He took himself off to his study; Harriet, bringing up the rear of Dr. Venefidezzi's little procession, wished she could have done the same.

Her place, however, was dancing attendance on old Mrs. Latham. She carried the candelabrum into the Blue Room and closed the door behind her at Dr. Venefidezzi's request. The medium took some time arranging the Latham ladies around the table; Harriet examined the room, noting approvingly that Dr. Venefidezzi was what she thought of as a "sensible" medium. There were no cabinets for him to be locked into, no array of ropes, none of the paraphernalia that would indicate the tiresome manifestations of ghostly hands and ectoplasmic cheesecloth. His props consisted simply of candles placed on the sideboard, and a bowl with a plain robin's-egg-blue glaze, filled with water, which was sitting in the middle of the table where the epergne had been.

Old Mrs. Latham was asking about the bowl, in a tone indicating she was ready to be offended at the banishment of her cousin Emmeline's valuable gift.

"It is necessary," Dr. Venefidezzi said, handing Claudia to a chair. "My control, you see, was drowned as a child."

Virginia and Claudia shrieked and twittered with pleasurable alarm, but old Mrs. Latham was satisfied. Without old Mrs. Latham's satisfaction, nothing happened at Chisholm End; Harriet could not quite tell, from the medium's face, whether he had deduced that for himself or not.

He seated Harriet last, in the chair next to his own. She observed that he had contrived to place old Mrs. Latham as far from himself as possible, with her daughter-in-law beside her, so that the circle, starting from Dr. Venefidezzi and proceeding widdershins, went: the medium, Harriet, young Mrs. Latham, old Mrs. Latham, Virginia, Claudia.

Dr. Venefidezzi asked them to take hands, as mediums always did. Harriet's right hand was pinched and prodded by young Mrs. Latham's rings; her left hand found the medium's hand, broad and stubby-fingered, warm and dry, unlike the hot, moist hands of Mr. Benfelton.

Dr. Venefidezzi said, "I will ask you not to break the circle, no matter what I may say or what strange sounds you may hear. Nothing in this room can harm you unless you let it."

That was rather less comforting than the normal line of patter. Harriet felt a faint stirring of unease, a sense that perhaps Dr. Venefidezzi was not what she thought him. But she glanced sideways at his astonishing waistcoat, his ugly, good-natured face, and told herself not to be a goose.

"My control's name is Francis. He is a child, and I will ask you not to frighten him. Ask him your questions, ladies."

Dr. Venefidezzi lowered his head. They sat in stiff, uncomfortable silence for several minutes before the medium threw his head back and cried out, a shout with no words in it. Harriet and Claudia both flinched involuntarily and probably would have broken the circle, except that Dr. Venefidezzi's hands had tightened on theirs, and he was stronger than he looked.

His eyes came back into focus, but he was someone else. He looked around the circle, wide-eyed and pleased, and said, "Tell me your names!" The voice was a child's treble—a young child, no more than eight—and the accent sharper, harsher than Dr. Venefidezzi's perfect Oxford English. A city child, Harriet thought, even a Cockney. The women around the table, nervously impressed by this demonstration of Dr. Venefidezzi's powers, said their names, and the child repeated, "Harriet, Cecilia, Esther, Virginia, Claudia— pretty ladies! What do the pretty ladies want to know?"

"I want to speak to someone, please," Virginia said. "James Milverton is his name." James Milverton had died of influenza four years ago, two months before he and Virginia would have been married. It was the only good thing Harriet knew of Cecilia Latham, that her passion for Spiritualism was at least partly caused by her desire to bring Virginia some comfort.

"Miss Virginia wants Mr. James," Francis said. "Mr. James is here."

That was fast, Harriet thought, her unease growing. The medium's face changed again; it seemed to narrow and lengthen. A trick of the shadows, Harriet told herself desperately. That was, after all, why mediums liked to work by candlelight. But then the medium spoke.

"Ginnie?" he said. His voice had dropped nearly an octave from Dr. Venefidezzi's normal register, and his vowels had shifted again.

"James!" Virginia gasped.

"Ginnie, I want you to stop this séance nonsense."

"Oh, James!"

"You're wasting your life," the spirit said sternly.

"But, James, I promised. I promised I'd always love you."

The smile was James Milverton to the life. If Harriet had not been sure herself, the quick indrawn breaths of young Mrs. Latham and Claudia would have told her. "That doesn't mean you have to be married to my grave."

Virginia's eyes were wide, brilliant in the candlelight with her tears. She whispered something, too softly for anyone else to hear it, and managed a small, tremulous smile.

"Good girl," said James Milverton. Then the medium's face shifted; the child returned. "Mr. James is gone," he announced. "Another lady, ask a question! Mrs. Esther? Miss Claudia? Miss Harriet?"

Harriet nearly jumped out of her skin when Francis turned toward her. Before she could come up with any kind of an answer, he said, "There is a spirit who wishes to speak to Miss Harriet. It is an unhappy spirit, Miss Harriet."

"Oh, go on, Harriet," Claudia said, giggling.

"Very well," Harriet said.

The medium's face changed; she recognized it immediately, painfully: the frowning eyebrows, the drooping mouth. "Papa?"

"Harry, are you all right? I am so sorry."

"I'm fine, Papa. Really." She locked her jaw and throat and treacherous heart against the things she wished to say.

One eyebrow quirked. "Are you warm, my daughter? Are you warm?"

And Harriet could not help smiling back. "Quite warm, King Frost."

"You're a good girl, Harry. I shouldn't have left you like that. I am sorry."

"It's all right, Papa. I . . . " She could not say she forgave him, but perhaps that was not what either of them needed. "I love you."

And her father smiled through the medium's face and was gone.

"Another question?" said the child.

The Latham women said nothing, Virginia and Claudia and their mother eyeing Harriet as if she were some unexpected and exotic species of snake. The elder Mrs. Latham, as complacent as a snake herself, a well-fed python, was quite visibly storing away Harriet's revealed weakness for later use. Harriet's weary hatred of her rooted itself another inch deeper.

But Francis was waiting. After a moment, Harriet managed to say, her voice only slightly unsteady, "Thank you, Francis, but I think maybe we've had enough for the night."

"You're sure, Miss Harriet?" He leaned a little closer and whispered, "He likes you." Then he straightened, looking around the circle again. "Are you sure, pretty ladies? No more—"

He stiffened suddenly, his hand clamping down on Harriet's; from the gasp, she thought the same thing had happened to Claudia. "There is another spirit."

If Harriet had not been so disconcerted, first by her father's return and then by that whispered confidence, she might have been able to stop the séance simply by freeing her hand from young Mrs. Latham's. She wondered, later, if it would have done any good, or if it had already been too late.

The younger Mrs. Latham said, by rote, "To whom does the spirit wish to speak?"

"Mrs. Esther." Francis's voice was shaking and shrill.

"I am here," said old Mrs. Latham. Her expression was sneering, and Harriet knew she still thought this was just an act.

"Mrs. Esther, be careful," the child moaned, and then he was gone.

"So you married that moron Latham, did you?" said a new voice, a young woman's voice, merry and light. "Oh, how the mighty are fallen. I'd have thought, once you got me out of the way, you'd at least have landed that poor chinless viscount. What was his name?"

"Who are you?" demanded old Mrs. Latham.

"Oh come now, Esther," the young woman said with a trill of laughter. "You know who I am."

"Dr. Venefidezzi," old Mrs. Latham said, "I insist that you stop this nonsense at once."

"He can't, Esther. I'm afraid I've frightened his control. I can't imagine why." She smiled with Dr. Venefidezzi's face; while her voice was light and charming, the effect of the smile was grisly, like the rictus of a skull.

Mrs. Latham pulled her hands free with an angry snort, her granddaughter on one side and her daughter-in-law on the other uttering identical gasps of protest.

"Don't be silly, Esther. It seems as if I've been waiting forever for this chance to talk to you. You don't think I'd let some silly medium's silly mumbo-jumbo get in my way, do you?" She let go of Harriet's and Claudia's hands and held her own up, laughing again.

"What do you want?" old Mrs. Latham said.

"Revenge, darling, revenge. Shall I tell your granddaughters what you did? Shall I tell them about their Great-Aunt Enid?"

"I don't know what you're talking about, and I think this joke is in exceptionally bad taste."

"You always *were* pig-headed. She murdered me, my dears. Poisoned me. What was it, Esther? I'm afraid I never had the faintest idea. Arsenic? Strychnine? Deadly nightshade?"

"I don't know what you're talking about," Mrs. Latham repeated obdurately.

"Dr. Venefidezzi," said the younger Mrs. Latham, "I really think this has gone far enough."

"And I'm sure Dr. Venefidezzi agrees with you," Enid said. "But the matter is no longer in his hands. I have been waiting to have this conversation with my sister for forty-five years."

"I have nothing to say to you," old Mrs. Latham said, getting up. "Cecilia, if you pay this man, you're a bigger fool than I take you for. Come, Harriet." She left the room as magnificently as a man o' war under full sail.

"I hope her pig-headedness isn't hereditary, or you're going to have an awful time marrying those girls off," Enid said to the younger Mrs. Latham. "Don't worry. My business is with Esther, not any of you." And she was gone. Dr. Venefidezzi fell forward across the table, his head narrowly missing the blue bowl. And, perfectly predictably, Virginia Latham went off in strong hysterics.

The séance was over.

The medium had fainted, Harriet was told by Wilson when she brought the tisane that Mrs. Latham claimed kept off her "spasms."

"Out cold," the housemaid said, her air of concern marred by the ghoulish delight in her voice. "They thought he was faking—Mrs. Cecilia said that was all his séance was, parlor tricks and such—but he wasn't. Mr. Latham told Jasper to go fetch the doctor."

Mr. Latham, Harriet reflected, taking the tisane to old Mrs. Latham, had the virtues of his defects. Cold-blooded, phlegmatic, and unimaginative, but he did not lose his head in a crisis, nor ever doubted the right course of action. She tried not to imagine how they might have "proved" that Dr. Venefidezzi wasn't faking, and felt sick and cold.

It had taken over an hour to pacify Mrs. Latham. The old lady was not, so far as Harriet could tell, in the least frightened; she was enraged, accusing the medium of prying and meddling and mockery. Harriet was not quite sure what it was that Dr. Venefidezzi was supposedly mocking, but she knew better than to ask. She said nothing but, "Yes, Mrs. Latham," and "No, Mrs. Latham," cramping her fear and grief and worry—her self—into a box as small and dark as a coffin.

You have nowhere else to go, she said grimly to herself, just as you have had nowhere else to go any time these past five years. Nothing has changed.

But something had. When Harriet was finally able to escape from Mrs. Latham, she went up to her small, drab room, propped the chair beneath the doorknob, and sat down on the bed, intending to calm her mind by reading her Testament—the only book she could own in Chisholm End without questions and disapproval and Mr. Benfelton's opinions on education for women. She was quite accustomed to opening the limp leather-bound book and beginning to read perfectly at random, a species of *Sortes Biblicae* which had never offered her any insights into either the future or the ethereal plane. But this time, the book fell open and Harriet stared at the page without reading it, her mind full of crimson and gold dragons, of an ugly little man smiling at her, of a dead child's voice whispering, *He likes you.* And, a nagging thread of disquiet, those terribly specific facts offered by something that claimed to be Esther Latham's long dead sister. Harriet knew all about Mrs. Latham's viscount; he had been carried off by a pleurisy of the lungs before he ever actually breathed a word of devotion or commitment (or even, from what Harriet could tell, inclination), but it was accepted family history that Claudia and Virginia had almost been descended from a viscountess. Mrs. Latham hadn't mentioned the lack of chin.

Harriet thought, coldly, If Dr. Venefidezzi wasn't faking, then he was telling the truth.

Decisively, she smacked the Testament down on the bedside table, bounced off the bed in an unladylike fashion, swung the chair aside, and went back downstairs. She pretended to herself that she was on an errand for Mrs. Latham—a story which no one in the Latham household would dare to disbelieve—and walked briskly into the library as if she had every right to be there.

It was deserted; from the noise, she guessed the center of the crisis had moved belowstairs, with an outpost in Virginia Latham's bedroom, where she was doubtless weeping on her sister's shoulder while her mother watched helplessly, faced with the only problem her iron decisiveness could not solve.

They won't throw him out, Harriet thought, not sure why she was offering herself reassurance. Mr. Latham sent for the doctor.

She knew where the family Bible was, and knew that it had been the Grimshaw family Bible before it had come to the Lathams. Harriet knelt, opening the glass-fronted bookcase, and pulled the Bible out. It seemed to weigh as much as a small child. She opened the Bible to its flyleaf, where the long decorous progression of Grimshaw ancestors was inscribed, with Mr. Latham, his wife, and his daughters added in old Mrs. Latham's crabbed, ungenerous script.

Harriet looked at the lines above and found there what she had known she would find: Enid Charlotte Grimshaw, born the same day as her sister Esther, dead at the age of twenty . . . forty-five years ago.

"What was it, Esther?" Harriet quoted softly. "Arsenic? Strychnine? Deadly nightshade?"

She shuddered and slammed the book shut, as if it contained some evil thing which might escape, even though she knew that whatever evil there might be in Chisholm End was already abroad.

THE HOUSE HAD CHANGED. It was nearly ten o'clock; there was no reason to be disquieted by darkness. But the shadows seemed too thick, too heavy. After returning the Bible to its rightful place, Harriet paused uneasily in the doorway of the library, and a whispering noise, like the sound of her skirts and petticoats, seemed to run on and on into the corners and there to die in sly susurration. She closed her mind against the conclusions that waited, circling like carrion crows, but instead of retreating upstairs, she went in search of the medium.

She found him alone in the housekeeper's sitting room, white-faced and wild-eyed. He whirled as she opened the door, and all at once he was clutching her hands, staring up into her face. "Miss Winterbourn, you have to help me. I have to get out of here."

He was fully clothed, and the doors were not locked. "What . . ."

"The bowl. I have to get the bowl back, and *they won't tell me where it is.*"

He seemed half-mad between fear and fury. Carefully, Harriet disengaged her hands and stepped back. "Dr. Venefidezzi—"

"That isn't my name! Surely you know that isn't my name!"

"What *is* your name?"

"Far. Far Faithwell."

"Mr. Faithwell, then, what is in this house?"

"It's *her*," he said, for a moment sounding and looking like Francis. "That iron-plated bitch's—I beg your pardon. The elder Mrs. Latham's sister."

"Enid Grimshaw."

"If that's her name, yes."

"Yes. Mrs. Latham's twin sister."

"*Twin*?" She'd thought he was pale before, but now his face was paper-white, and his hand shook as he crossed himself.

"Yes. Does it matter?"

"It . . . oh, never mind. I can't explain. But it isn't . . . it is not good news."

"Can't you do anything?"

"Miss Winterbourn, I am a medium. Only a medium. Not a clairvoyant, not an exorcist. Please, I have to get out of here, but I have to have the bowl."

Grimly, Harriet throttled the reflexive response of, How can I help? "Why?"

"Why?" he echoed blankly.

"Why do you have to get out of here, and why do you need the bowl?"

"Francis. Francis is screaming in my head."

Harriet went cold. "Francis? Your control?"

"My twin brother. Drowned in the Thames at the age of eight. Our father was a boatman."

"Oh," Harriet said, but it was as if a dam had broken inside him, and the words were pouring out, the Cockney in his voice growing stronger by the syllable.

"My mother had the second sight. Born with a caul. She knew I was like her. She knew what happened when twins . . . when one was . . . She took me to an old woman, older than Eve, I used to think, and she taught me how to . . . how to . . . but I have to have the bowl, or I can't do anything!" His voice was almost a howl by the last word. He stopped, ran one hand over his face, then said more quietly and with his vowels smoothed out again, "I can't comfort Francis. And if that girl should happen *not* to be satisfied by her sister's death . . . I'm the medium, Miss Winterbourn. The circle was broken, and I'm vulnerable to her."

She understood, although she wished she did not. "Can she really . . . ?"

"Yes. Whatever you're thinking, she can. Vengeful spirits,

unlike most others, grow stronger as the years pass, and that girl . . . " He shuddered visibly. "If you ask me, it was only a matter of which one of them made her move first."

"I have to warn Mrs. Latham."

He grabbed her hands again before she could move. "You can't!"

"I have to."

"You hate her. I know you hate her. You couldn't *not* hate her."

"That doesn't matter," Harriet said, disentangling herself again. "I have to warn her."

"She won't listen to you."

"That doesn't matter, either. But once I've done that, I'll get you your bowl. I think I know where they'd put it."

He was silent a moment, eyes shut, forehead furrowed with pain. "I'll come with you."

"I beg your pardon?"

"She might . . . I might be able to convince her. I don't know what she can do, even if she does believe us. But you're right. We have to try."

"Thank you," Harriet said and smiled at him. The smile felt strange for a moment before she realized that it was the first time in years that she had smiled at someone and truly meant it. "This way."

He followed her uncomplainingly, although he became perceptibly more frightened as they approached Mrs. Latham's bedroom. At the top of the stairs, he whispered, "She's waiting for midnight," so softly that Harriet wasn't even sure he knew he'd spoken aloud.

She tapped on Mrs. Latham's door and was rewarded by, "What do you want? Cecilia, I've told you before you cosset—"

Harriet opened the door. "It's I, Mrs. Latham."

The old lady, sitting stiffly upright in bed, gave her a glare compounded of incredulity and wrath. "What on earth do *you* want? If you want to have hysterics like the rest of the fool women in this house, I suggest you go downstairs."

"No," Harriet said and stepped aside so Mr. Faithwell could enter the room behind her.

"*You!*" Mrs. Latham said, with magnificently withering contempt. "How you can have the nerve to show your face—"

"Mrs. Latham," Harriet said, "he isn't a charlatan."

"Don't be a nitwit, Harriet. I knew you weren't bright, heaven knows, but I never took you for a prating fool like my granddaughters."

"Then listen to me. He—Dr. Venefidezzi isn't a charlatan." Carefully, she proceeded, "I don't know if what that spirit said is true—"

But not carefully enough. "How dare you even suggest such a thing! You ungrateful vixen!"

"I'm trying to *warn* you! And if we are to speak of ingratitude—"

"Miss Winterbourn," Far Faithwell said. Harriet choked on her own words. Mrs. Latham said nothing, silent as a spider waiting for a fly to come too close; her malevolence was like water in the air. Despite that, despite the fact that he was coming apart even as Harriet watched, Far stepped forward and said, "Mrs. Latham, we cannot force you to believe us. But I swear before God that what I tell you is true. That spirit is real. Her anger is real. And her vengeance will be real before dawn tomorrow. I am sorry, but—"

"Get out," said Mrs. Latham. "Both of you. Get *out!*"

"Mrs. Latham, please," Harriet said desperately, "I'm sorry for what I—"

"Are you deaf, Harriet? I said, get out, and take your damned mountebank with you. What was the plan? Terrify us all into locking ourselves into our bedrooms and then make off with the silver? If you don't get out this instant, I will have you *put* out. And don't think I can't."

She could. Harriet knew all too well that Mrs. Latham's word was law in Chisholm End. She said stiffly and coldly, "Am I to understand that you are dismissing me from my position?"

"I'm certainly not going to keep you around."

"And you will not listen to our warning?"

"*OUT!*" shrieked Mrs. Latham, yanking furiously at the bell-pull. Harriet turned and bolted, Far at her heels.

She found herself saying ridiculously as they clattered down the stairs, "They'll never give me a character now. Never in a million years. Never never never." The front hall was deserted; the servants were doubtless, as Mrs. Latham had said, indulging themselves in hysterics in the servants' hall.

"Wait!" Harriet said, catching Far's sleeve. "Your bowl."

"You know where it is?"

"I think so. This way."

And sure enough, in the breakfront in the formal dining room, there was Far Faithwell's simple blue bowl, incongruous among the Sèvres vases and Dresden figurines.

Far tried the door. "It's locked."

"But I know where the key is," Harriet said, still with maniacal giggles welling up under her breastbone. "The housekeeper's supposed to keep it on her ring, but she never does. It's too fiddly, and she says she's afraid she'll lose it. Here."

It was hidden carefully in another present from Cousin Emmeline in Bath: a hideous crenellated silver salt-cellar which leered at the room from the top of the breakfront. Harriet unlocked the door, stood aside to let Far lift out the bowl himself—and she noted with what care he did so, using both hands, as if it were the Grail—then locked the door again and put the key back in the salt-cellar. There was no need to get Mrs. Brennigan in trouble.

Far was standing in the middle of the room, his head bent over the bowl.

"Mr. Faithwell? Are you . . . "

"Better," he said, and gave her a smile that was like a dim reflection of Francis.

They returned to the front hall; there were still no signs of life. Wilson, Harriet reckoned, would have gone pelting up the backstairs as soon as the servants noticed the bell ringing, but by then there was a sporting chance Mrs. Latham would have rendered herself incoherent. But still, she and Far didn't have long, and she was grateful for the evening's alarums, which had so thoroughly disrupted the household that the butler hadn't yet locked up for the night. Harriet and Far wrestled the door open and half-fell out into the cool night air.

Far cradled his bowl carefully in his right arm and offered Harriet his left.

She accepted it, her giggles deserting her. "Is Francis . . . are you all right?"

"Yes, thank you."

They started together up the long drive. Far said, with an effort at lightness, "This is the first time I've ever actually been thrown out of a house before."

"It is not an edifying experience."

"No, but one must strive to keep from stagnating." He glanced over his shoulder and said in a completely different tone, "Are those your *footmen*?"

Harriet looked back. Peter and Jasper were just emerging through the front door, a matched set of giants. "She's probably told them you stole the silver. Can they see us?"

Her question was answered by a shout from Jasper. Together, they ran, Far clutching his bowl to his chest, Harriet bundling up her skirts in both hands. The footmen were unwilling to follow them far in the dark, doubtless imagining a whole team of burglars, and Harriet and Far emerged on the main road breathless but in good order.

The moon was near full; by its light Far looked at Harriet quizzically. "What will you do now?"

"I don't know." The enormity of it crashed in on her all at once. "She *fired* me. No character, no warning. My things . . . Oh dear God—"

"Don't get hysterical now, I implore you."

"I beg your pardon?" Harriet said as icily as she could, and then couldn't help returning Far's grin.

"Look. Your situation is my fault—" He held up a hand, forestalling Harriet's protest. "Please. I'll buy you a train ticket to wherever you want. If you'll accompany me to the train station, of course."

"You have money?"

"I do. No one was crass enough to empty my pockets while I was unconscious."

"Perhaps there's something to be said for breeding, after all," Harriet said, and they laughed together, shakily. "The train station's this way. Though I'm afraid it's a good five miles."

"I have nothing better to do, and I cannot imagine a more charming companion."

They walked in silence for half a mile. Far was still shivering; Harriet herself felt on the verge of tears. She said, "Did you mean it?"

"Mean what?"

"When you said her vengeance would be real before dawn."

"Yes. Harriet, you aren't still—" He broke off, his eyes widening. "Miss Winterbourn, I beg your pardon."

"I've just been thrown out of a house with you. I think we can, without loss of decorum, establish ourselves on a first-name basis."

He smiled back at her. "Harriet, then. You aren't still—"

"Of course I am. I always will. But I know that you're right. She would not listen, and I don't suppose, even if she would have let me, that staying in her room all night would have helped."

"No," Far said. "Believe me. I know of *nothing* you can do. She broke the circle, you see."

The simplicity with which he said it chilled Harriet to the bone. "I understand. And I won't be sorry that she's dead. But . . . "

There was another long silence. Harriet's feet began to hurt.

"If anyone I've ever met deserves what that woman has coming to her," Far said, "she's it."

"Yes," Harriet said desolately. Far away and dim, from the house they were leaving behind them, she could almost hear Enid laughing.

They reached the train station in the coldest, bleakest hour of the night. There were no passengers waiting; the booking clerk was asleep in his coffin-sized office. Far said, "Let's not wake him yet," and drew her over to sit on one of the benches.

He looked at her sidelong, an odd half-grimace of a look, and said, "Where will you go?"

"Beg pardon?"

"The train ticket. Where will you go?"

"I . . . I don't know. I haven't any family. I don't—"

"I . . . " He cleared his throat nervously. "I have a suggestion."

"A suggestion?" She could not help her eyebrows lifting, and he blushed fiery red.

But he stuck to his guns. "You could come with me."

"Come with you where?"

"Well, I have an engagement in York on Tuesday."

"You're serious."

"I am."

"But what . . . "

"I have no designs on your virtue. I promise. But I have wanted to hire an assistant for some time."

"An assistant?"

"Yes."

"If this is because I've been dismissed—"

"No! Well, I mean, yes, but not like that. Do you know how few people there are who genuinely believe me?"

"Oh, but surely . . . "

"They half-believe. Some three-quarters. But people who genuinely believe that I hear the voice of my dead twin brother in my head? Who genuinely believe that the dead speak to them through me? Not one in a thousand. So. Will you?"

He was watching her anxiously, an ugly, tired little man, ashen-faced and shivering a little.

She said, "Francis said you liked me."

He almost flinched, but he met her eyes. He said, "Yes. Yes, I do."

She was throwing away her respectability—but, then, she had already thrown it away, left it behind with her limp leather-bound Testament in Chisholm End. And, she thought, her heart suddenly seeming to expand in her chest, she had left behind Mr. Benfelton, as well.

"Yes," said Harriet Winterbourn, and she and Far Faithwell smiled at each other, like children waking from nightmares to wish upon a star.

<hr />

No Man's Land

He wakes up tasting dirt.

A voice, hissing, "Jesus, Cluny, are you okay?" and hands grabbing his shoulders, dragging him away from ... away from ...

Away from what?

And who the fuck is Cluny?

He jerks free of the hands, wipes sweat and blood off his face with the sleeve of his uniform jacket—except no way is that his uniform and that can't be his arm, and he presses hands that don't belong to him against a face that isn't his either and comes closer to screaming than he has since he was eleven and stepped in a yellow-jackets' nest. Back on Earth.

"Cluny! *Cluny!*"

He looks up, because he knows a sergeant's voice when he hears one, and a hand grabs his jaw, tilts his head. It's a woman's hand, and the yellow-brown eyes staring at him are a woman's eyes. *Oh Jesus who is this bitch?* He doesn't know her, and she's wearing the wrong uniform, just like he is.

She lets him go and says, "Jesus, girl, your head must be solid rock. That poor bastard of a Yoggo gets his skull smashed to smithereens and you aren't even bruised."

He stares at her. *That poor bastard of a Yoggo ...* He jerks around, hard enough and fast enough to hurt his neck, and looks back, into the tunnel she just dragged him out of, and sees the rockfall and a bright splash of blood and then there's the body and oh fuck oh Christ there's the *right* uniform and he knows those boots with the duct-tape holding together the left heel and he knows that outflung arm with the darn on the elbow of the jacket and the scar across the back of the hand and oh sweet Jesus that's *him*, he's lying out there dead, dead and fucked to Kingdom Come.

Except that he's *here* and the woman with the yellow eyes is shaking him and saying, "Come on, Cluny, we got to move."

And he follows her back to where the rest of the squad is crouching, because she's a sergeant, and he can't think around the voice in his head screaming, *Koth, I'm a Koth, fuck me Jesus, how can I be a KOTH?* Because he hates them and fears them, and he doesn't know what the fuck happened that he's stuck in the body of a Koth-bitch private, but he just keeps putting one foot in front of the other because he's a grunt and that's what you do.

He keeps with the squad, keeps his head down. Being a grunt is being a grunt, and he's even kind of comforted by that, when he can forget for two minutes together that he's on the wrong fucking side. He squints sideways at names, matches them to faces and the sergeant's harsh voice. The sergeant's name is Livingstone. She's a big dark woman, grip like a trash compactor—he can feel where she left bruises dragging him out of the rockfall. The other grunts don't give him any shit, and that's good. Makes it easier to keep himself together. He watches and listens. Really, he keeps expecting to fall down dead.

But he's still alive four hours later, when they make it back to the Koth camp, and Livingstone says, "Cluny, come on. The rest of you, dismissed." He follows her, because she's his sergeant, and at least in this fucking mess, he knows who his sergeant is—*and you fucking pussy, does that actually make you feel BETTER?*

Yeah, actually. It does. And then it occurs to him that "pussy" is maybe not something he wants to be calling himself anymore, and he doesn't feel better at all.

Livingstone leads him straight to the med-tent and shoves in shouting, "Doc! Doc!"

"Sergeant Livingstone, I presume." A tall, skinny, snarky man, older than any of the camp-docs he's seen in a year or more. Koth must take better care of them. "What can I do for you, sergeant?"

"Take a look at Cluny here," Livingstone says. "Piece of tunnel came down on top of her.

Oh shit. "I'm fine," he says, and dear Jesus is that his *voice*? The last word trails up into a squeak like a dog-whistle, and he starts coughing.

"Yes," says the doc, "I can see how fine you are. Come on, Cluny, you know the drill."

He doesn't, but he gambles on it not being different from what he's used to, and it seems like it must not be. He takes off his boots and his uniform jacket, and Christ he hadn't imagined they *made* uniforms this small, and steps over where the doc is waiting and smirking at him like a dried-up vulture. He's not trembling, he tells himself, and it's not like he has anything to be afraid of now. The doc shines a light in his eyes the way they always do, and listens to his heart, and prods at his stomach and kidneys and all the vulnerable bits between the ribs and the hips. Which he hates, and it's even worse in this body because he can't let go of knowing how close the doc's long cold fingers are to his tits. Well, not *his* tits, but this body's tits. Which aren't very big, but still. He doesn't want the doc touching them. Doesn't want the doc touching *him*, and he can feel his hands balling into fists, feel that cold sweat starting on the back of his neck and in his armpits, and it's just fucking great that it feels the same in this skinny little body as it does in his.

He tells himself not to flip out, not to be a sissy, but he knows it's not doing any good, and then a movement, just a little one, drags his attention back to the tent-flap, and he realizes Livingstone's still standing there, arms folded and one hip canted. She doesn't trust the doc, either, and she isn't going to leave. And he thinks he shouldn't be as relieved by that as he is—*you fucking sissyboy*—but he can't do anything about it.

And finally the doc straightens up and steps away and says, bored, "Nothing wrong here." He gets his jacket and boots back on, and feels better for it.

"Good," Livingstone says. She jerks her head at him and he follows her back out into the camp. He tries to identify things as they pass: the showers, the quartermaster's tent, and oh Christ somewhere in this mess is *her* tent, Cluny's tent, and what the hell is he going to do about *that*?

Burn one bridge at a time. Which is something his own sergeant says, and God he hopes Sarge is okay, and the other grunts, and it was just him that went down in that rockfall. And the Koth didn't get them.

And then he remembers he *is* a Koth.

Livingstone comes to the mess-tent, and he follows her in. Sees her unit—his unit?—at one of the long tables, and they wave and make space. He follows Livingstone through the line and over to the table. They sit down, and Livingstone says, "We should donate Cluny to science. Hardest fucking head in the universe."

"You okay, Miriam?" One of the other grunts, guy named Chang. Bald-headed, slant-eyed, big motherfucking tattoos. And Cluny's first name is Miriam. Good to know.

"I'm good," he says, and keeps his attention on his tray, listening to them talk about Yoggos and trying to make himself process that they're talking about guys like Sarge and Riley and Markowitz. And him, before. They sound about like Sarge and them talking about the Koth, like they're tired of the war and wish the enemy would just sit down and surrender already.

And then dinner's over and he's still wondering what the fuck he should do with himself, when Chang comes up to him and says, "Come on and hit the showers with me."

"You saying I stink?" he says, and the grin feels a little funny on this face. He wonders what he looks like.

"I'm saying you're covered in dirt," Chang says.

"Jesus, you're picky," he says, and Chang laughs and jerks his head at him in a come-along kind of way, and he goes along because, well, he *is* covered in dirt, and it itches.

Koth camp doesn't have much more in the way of showers than what he's used to, but he's glad for at least a little privacy for his first face-to-face with his new body. He goes in the cubicle—corrugated iron, bare bulb, nasty draft, just like home—shuts the door, strips off boots, socks, jacket. Bare feet on the wet unevenness of the floor, grit against his toes. Hesitates a moment over the t-shirt, then yanks it off over his head. No bra. He feels the dog-tags shift against his chest, feels something pulling, binding, as his shoulders move, and surely even with tits it shouldn't feel that weird, and he looks down.

And just about pukes. He knows the difference between scars you get in a fight and scars you get because someone holds you down and makes them, and these are the second kind, Xs of knotted gray-white tissue, crossing over what used to be her nipples and are now just lumps.

He stares, the same way he'd stare if it was a woman in his unit and she'd taken off her shirt in front of him. He doesn't want to, but he reaches up with one hand, and god his fingers are shaking, and he touches the lump where her left nipple used to be. He can feel his own fingers, sort of, or at least he can feel that *something's* there, but even though he knows his fingers are like ice, they don't feel cold or hot or anything against the scarring. He moves his fingers to a bit of unscarred flesh, puckered and strained by the ugly mess around it, and swallows a yelp because his fingers *are* like ice, and that piece of skin isn't shy about saying so.

He knows, in a distant sort of way, that he's got to keep moving, that Chang'll be waiting for him and how long can you take in the fucking shower anyway? He watches his hands—*her* hands—unfasten her pants, shove them down over her hips, and fuck she's skinny, he can practically count every fucking rib and her hips are like caltrops, and then there's just her undies, and it's weird to think that this morning a woman named Miriam Cluny pulled those things up and now it's him hooking his thumbs in them and pushing them down. Weird and scary and sad, and if he could give Miriam Cluny her body back, he would.

And then, staring down at scarred chest and long skinny legs, he realizes that if her tits look like that . . . Fuck. He's got to check out his own cunt.

He's no virgin, so he at least knows what it ought to look like. He bends his head, cants his hips forward. From the pale tangle of pubic hair, he's probably a blonde now. And he's not . . . he doesn't have . . .

He swallows hard.

It's a woman's body. And he knew that as soon as he looked at that arm that wasn't his, back in the tunnel with his own dead body. So it's not like he's *surprised* that his balls and cock aren't between these long, pale, skinny legs, but it's still . . . it's just . . .

He bites the side of his hand to keep from moaning loud enough for Chang to hear through the partition. With his other hand, he reaches to touch the folds of skin between his legs and feels like he ought to apologize, although he's not sure who to.

"Sorry, Miriam," he whispers, and then his cold fingers part the lips of his pussy, and he bites down hard on his knuckles, hard enough to taste blood.

Clit's still there, at least, but Jesus God what did they fuck her with? A chainsaw? He reaches and feels more scars around her asshole. She must've been damn near fucked to death, and he's never going to ask who did it, because he knows. Wasn't his unit—and he gives a dizzy little giggle when he realizes he doesn't have to worry about whether he raped himself. Sarge doesn't like that kind of thing, and the grunts do what Sarge tells them. But it might've been friends of his.

It might have been Charlie, big red-faced balding Charlie, strong as an elephant and the nicest guy in the battalion. Might've been Ahira or Ratcliffe or Young. Or all of them. Probably all of them, and he could imagine it if he let himself think about it, imagine that shoving pack of bodies in the dark, holding her down, probably with a knife to her throat because everybody knows those Koth bitches are hellcats, calling her *slut* and *whore* and *cunt. Come on, you cunt, we know you want it.* They're the enemy. You call the women cunts and the men fags, because it's war and it's what you do.

He wonders why they didn't kill her when they were done, and then he does puke, bile burning his mouth and nose, and he spits into the drain, over and over, because he knows why. They didn't kill her because they thought she was already dead.

He turns on the water and shoves himself under it, knowing it's going to be ice cold and feeling like he deserves it. He scrubs himself roughly, trying not to think about it, trying not to think about hands on his body, holding him spread-eagled, fists slamming into his stomach. Trying not to remember the jeering voices, the things they called him. Trying not to remember the doctor's uninterested voice tallying up his broken bones. He'd been lucky—they hadn't cut on him. He hadn't had scars like Cluny's.

But now he does. Now they're his scars.

Ain't no difference, he thinks, coming out from under the shower, grabbing the standard-issue strip of toweling, harsh as sandpaper. *Me and her. Us and them. Ain't no difference except somehow we ended up picking sides. Like kids playing softball.*

And he wishes that was all there was to war: kids playing a game, and at the end of the day you pick yourself up, brush the dust off, and go home.

He wishes he could go home.

He wishes Cluny could go home, too.

But they can't, so he gets dressed and goes to war instead.

NATIONAL GEOGRAPHIC ON ASSIGNMENT:
MERMAIDS OF THE OLD WEST

THE MERMAID PRESSED her hands flat against the wall of the tank, baring her teeth at the crowd. There was a surprised murmur, and several people near the front stepped back hastily. She was from Lake Mead, hauled writhing and screaming out of its clear blue depths by a DNR-crewed boat, and you could see that she had been a catfish, before.

Now she was an aquarium attraction in San Francisco.

I wanted to tell her it wasn't so bad; if she'd been netted by private interests, she might have ended up like her sisters I'd photographed in Las Vegas, decked out as Mermaids of the Old West. Annie Oakley and Calamity Jane. They'd been taught to do tricks, like the orcas at Seaworld. It was enough to make me want to hand out prints of the photograph I'd taken in the North Atlantic, a mermaid stretched out dead on the deck of a trawler. She'd been a shark, before. They hadn't wanted to kill her, the trawler-crew told me, but she'd bitten one of them before they realized she was trapped in their net, and they'd had to break her jaw to get her to let go.

It had killed her. Mermaids are more fragile than you'd think.

The Lake Mead mermaid beat her fists against the glass, a curiously human gesture. I sighed and trained the camera on her clenched hands, on the cold fury in her small, shining eyes, on the shadows of the crowd against the glass.

And took the picture.

A NIGHT IN ELECTRIC SQUIDLAND

SOME DAYS, Mick Sharpton was almost normal.

Those were the good days, the days when he did his job and went dancing after work, days when he enjoyed eating and slept well and sang in the shower. Days when flirting with a good-looking man was fun, even if it didn't lead to sex, and he didn't lose his temper with anyone unless they deserved it. Those were the days when he liked himself and liked his life, and some months there were more of them than others.

The bad days were when the world wouldn't stay out of his head, when everyone he looked at wore a swirling crown of color, and everything he touched carried the charge of someone else's life. Those days were all about maintaining his increasingly precarious control, snarling and snapping to keep anyone from getting too close. Trying not to drown. Sometimes he succeeded; sometimes he didn't.

Today was a good day. He could almost pretend he wasn't clairvoyant. His head was clear, and he felt light, balanced. He had not remembered his dreams when he woke up, and that was always a positive sign.

Mick and his partner were wading through a backlog of paperwork that afternoon. The sheer monumental bureaucracy was the downside of working for a government agency like the Bureau of Paranormal Investigations; left to his own devices, Mick would have let it slide, as he had always done with schoolwork, but Jamie had a stern, Puritan attitude toward unfinished reports, and it was useless to argue with him.

It was always useless to argue with Jamie Keller.

But the perpetually renewed struggle to find the right words—where "right" was a peculiar combination of "accurate" and "decorous" as applied to descriptions of interrupted Black Masses and the remains left on the subway lines by ghoul packs—was both tedious and frustrating, and Mick was positively grateful when the phone rang, summoning them to Jesperson's office. Jesperson would have something for them to *do*.

"It'll just be more paperwork later," Jamie warned.

"Oh, bite me, Keller."

"Not my thing," Jamie said placidly.

When they came into his office, Jesperson was leaning over a ley line map, spread out on the big table and weighted down with a fist-sized chunk of the Tunguska meteorite, two volumes of the *Directory of American Magic-Users*, and a lumpish pottery bowl with a deep green glaze, made for him by his daughter Ada and used for keeping paperclips and sticks of red chalk in. Ada lived with her mother in Seattle; Jesperson saw her for one week each year, at the Winter Solstice, and nothing was more sacred in the office than Jesperson's annual week of vacation, even if most of his employees politely pretended they had no idea why.

Jesperson looked up and said, "*There* you are," as if they should have known to be somewhere else, and waved at them impatiently to sit down.

They sat; Jesperson stalked over to stand between them and glowered at them both impartially. "What do you know about Electric Squidland?"

"It's a nightclub," Mick offered. "Goth scene. Lots of slumming yuppies."

"And?" Jesperson said, looking from one to the other of them.

Mick had told him all he knew—Electric Squidland had always

been too trendy for his taste—and it was Jamie who finally said, reluctantly, "They get into some heavy shit on the lower levels."

"You've been to Electric Squidland?" Mick said.

"Used to work there," Jamie said and became unaccountably interested in the backs of his own hands.

"You *worked* at—"

"Sharpton."

"Yes, sir. Sorry, sir."

Jamie said, not looking up, "This is about Shawna Lafayette, ain't it?"

"It might be."

"Who's Shawna Lafayette?"

"A young woman from Murfreesboro. Three years ago— just after the Carolyn Witt scandal, if you remember it—she disappeared off the face of the Earth."

"Just like that?"

"She went into Electric Squidland," Jamie said in a low voice, "and she never came out."

"Vanished without a trace," Jesperson said, "and now it's happened again. Maybe."

"Maybe?" Jamie said. "You mean somebody *sorta* disappeared?"

"Actually, yes," Jesperson said and allowed himself a small, crooked smile at their expressions. "What we have are the remains of half a person."

"Um, which half, sir? Top? Bottom?"

"The right half, I believe, Mr. Sharpton."

Mick and Jamie looked at each other. "Well, that's a new one," Mick managed after a moment.

"Quite," Jesperson said dryly. "We got a tip this morning. Anonymous, of course. Here."

He pressed the play button on the tape recorder that sat, as

220

always, on the corner of his desk, and a woman's voice, drawling with a hard nasal edge, spoke into the quiet room: "There's something y'all need to see. Right now it's out in the Sunny Creek Dump in a big black garbage bag, but I don't know how long it'll be there, so you better hurry. And if you wanna know more about it, go to Electric Squidland and ask 'em what happened to Brett Vincent." A solid clunk of metal and plastic as she hung up the phone, and Jesperson pushed the stop button.

And then both he and Mick were staring as Jamie lurched to his feet and said in a strangled voice, "I'll be right back." He almost fell against the door on his way out. Mick glanced at Jesperson for permission and followed him.

Jamie hadn't gone far; he was leaning against the wall next to the water fountain. Dark-skinned as he was, he couldn't go pale, but he was definitely gray around the edges. "Jamie?" Mick said, half-expecting his friend to slide to the floor in a dead faint.

"Sorry," Jamie said. His eyes were closed, and Mick thought he was doing one of the breathing exercises he'd learned from practicing yoga.

"About what, exactly? Are you okay?"

"I'll be fine. Just wasn't expecting . . . "

"Well, I wasn't expecting any of it, so I'm not sure how that gets you out here in the corridor looking like you're about to have a heart attack. You're not, are you?"

That got Jamie's eyes open. "Mick!"

"You look bad enough. And if you are, I want enough warning that I can call down for a gurney or something."

"Christ. No. I am *not* going to have a heart attack. I just wasn't ready for . . . "

"Oh," Mick said, feeling like an idiot. "You knew the guy, didn't you? Brett whatsisface?"

"Vincent. Yeah, I knew him." Jamie smiled, but there was neither mirth nor pleasure in it. "All too well."

After a moment, Mick said, "I didn't know you were bisexual."

"What I am is monogamous," Jamie said—mildly enough, but it was a clear warning to back off.

"We're going to have Jesperson out here in a minute," Mick said obediently.

"Yeah," Jamie said. "You go on. Lemme get a drink of water. And, yes, you can tell him about me and Brett."

"Okay," Mick said, touched Jamie's shoulder lightly, awkwardly, wanting to give comfort but knowing he was no good at it, and went back into Jesperson's office.

"Jamie, um, had a relationship with the deceased," he said to Jesperson's raised eyebrows.

"Did he?" Jesperson said, and added just as Jamie came through the door, "Then perhaps he can identify the body."

AN HOUR AGO, this had been a good day. Now, it was beginning to feel more like a nightmare.

Mick and Jamie were in the BPI morgue. Cold, echoing, the lights harsh on gray tile and metal, the psychic residue of death like dirt on every spotless surface. Mick hated it.

He hated it more today, watching Jamie's grim impersonation of a hard-as-nails, ice-cold BPI agent. He wasn't fooling his partner, and Mick doubted he was fooling himself, which meant he was hanging onto the act because it was either that or go off in a corner and have a meltdown.

Mick spared some hate for Jesperson while he was at it.

He understood the logic, and Jesperson wouldn't have been competent to run the BPI's southeast hub if he didn't grab every advantage he could get and wring it bone-dry. But knowing that didn't make it any more bearable to watch the way Jamie's hands, carefully clasped behind his back, tightened and released against each other again and again, like the beating of some murderously overworked heart.

The morgue staffer seemed to catch the mood, for she was silent as she led them to the autopsy table, and remained silent as she pulled the sheet back.

Mick had to turn away. Even the mental images conjured up by the phrase 'half a body' had not prepared him for the reality: the raw, ragged edges of bone and skin; the way what remained of the internal organs spilled untidily out of the body onto the table; the way that one staring dead eye was somehow even worse than two.

Jamie regarded the body for a long time, perfectly silent, then said in a level, almost uninterested voice, "Yes. That's Brett Vincent. I recognize him, and he's got the tattoo."

"Tattoo?" Mick said; his voice, unlike Jamie's, was a wavering croak.

"We went and got 'em together," Jamie said, touching Mick's shoulder to get him to turn around. He did, carefully not looking at the table, and saw that Jamie had rolled his right sleeve up, was indicating the bend of his elbow, where the Wild Hunt who rode in somber, frenetic glory the length of his arm broke like sea waves to either side of a design clearly the work of a different artist. For a moment, Mick couldn't make sense of the lines, and then it resolved into a circle made of two snakes, each biting the other's tail. Without knowing he was going to, Mick reached out and touched the tattoo gently, as if it might still be sore all these years later. His finger was shockingly white against Jamie's dark skin, and they both pretended they couldn't see how unsteady it was.

Jamie said, "Anyway, that body's got Brett's tattoo right where Brett had it. It's him."

"I'll write up the report," the morgue staffer said. "Thank you." Jamie was unhurriedly rebuttoning his cuff. "And I guess we go see what Jesperson wants us to do now."

Jesperson wanted them to go to Electric Squidland.

"Never thought I'd see the day when the Old Man would send us clubbing," Jamie said when he picked Mick up that evening.

"Never thought I'd see the day when the Old Man would send us on a date," Mick countered, and was delighted when Jamie laughed.

They left the Skylark three blocks from the nightclub and walked the rest of the way, enjoying the mild night air. At 10:07 p.m. (Mick noted the exact time from force of habit) they walked into the Kaleidoscope, the first level of Electric Squidland, mirrors and colored lights everywhere, and were greeted with a loud cry of, "Jamie! Lover!"

Mick stared disbelievingly at Jamie, who winced visibly before turning to greet an extremely pretty young man who was making the most of his Hispanic heritage with a pair of pale blue satin toreador pants. Mick, observing the pretty young man with the eye of an expert, saw that he was not as young as he was trying to appear, and he would be prettier if he admitted it.

"Ex-lover, Carlos," Jamie corrected, but he let Carlos kiss him.

"Oh, nonsense, darling. Once I let a man into my heart, he *never* leaves. But who is your Marilyn Manson here? This your new flame, sweetie?"

Mick opened his mouth to say something withering about blue satin toreador pants, but Jamie's abashed, apologetic expression stopped him. He swallowed his venom, said, "Mick Sharpton," and endured Carlos' cold fish handshake. He and Carlos understood each other very well.

"Mick's never been to Electric Squidland," Jamie said, adroitly avoiding the issue of whether Mick was or was not a 'flame.' "So I said I'd show him around. Suzanne working tonight?"

"Is it Wednesday and is the Pope Catholic?" Someone across the room was trying vigorously to attract Carlos' attention. He said, "We'll catch up later, sweetie. When you're not so busy."

When you've ditched your gothboy, Mick translated and was not sorry to see the last of Carlos. "I'll assume Carlos has hidden qualities," he said in Jamie's ear.

"Me-*ow*," Jamie said, and Mick felt himself blush. "C'mon. We won't find what we're looking for up here."

"What *are* we looking for, exactly?"

"Gal who has the Wednesday night show in the Inferno."

"Oooo-kay."

Jamie grinned. "The two lower levels are Members Only. And I don't think Jesperson's going to let us put membership on our expense accounts. But Suzanne can get us badges, if she has a mind to."

"And will she?"

"Will she what?"

"Have a mind to?"

"Oh, I think so," Jamie said, and there was a private joke in there somewhere. Mick could feel it, and it made him a little uneasy. But only a little. He trusted Jamie, in a way he'd never been able to trust a partner before. He'd wondered sometimes, the first two years he was with the BPI, why he kept torturing himself, spending his days—and sometimes his nights—with a series of agents who disliked him, distrusted him—some of them had openly hated him, and Mick had hated them back, fiercely and with no quarter given.

He had expected Jamie to be more of the same, Jamie with his bulk and his heavy hands and his deceptive eyes. And he still didn't understand what was different about Jamie, massive, gentle Jamie with his night-dark skin and his tattoos like clouds— didn't understand why Jamie had decided to like him and made that decision stick. Mick was painfully aware that he didn't deserve Jamie's liking—ever a proponent of 'hit back first,' he had been unconscionably nasty to Jamie in the early days of their partnership, until Jamie had proved, immutably, that he would not be nasty back. So whatever it was Jamie was waiting to spring on him, he knew it wouldn't be too bad.

He followed Jamie obediently from the Kaleidoscope down the open corkscrew staircase that was the centerpiece of Electric Squidland's second level, the Submarine. The Submarine was classier, the level for those who fancied themselves Beautiful People. No disco balls here, and the music was dark, very techno, very European. Mick bet the bar on this level went through a lot of synthetic absinthe.

Jamie used their descent of the staircase to reconnoiter, and at the bottom, he grabbed Mick's elbow and said, "This way."

"Your gal's here?"

"Yup."

"Is she drinking synthetic absinthe?"

"What?"

"Never mind." By then, he could see the woman Jamie was aiming for, a petite woman with long plum-red hair, dressed in trailing, clinging black. The liquid in her glass was lurid green, and Mick moaned quietly to himself.

She looked up at their approach. Her eyes widened, and then she said, with apparently genuine delight, "Jamie! A very long time, and no see at all!" And then she gave Mick a once-over, seeming to take especial note of Jamie's hand on his elbow. "Are you attached to this delectable creature?"

"At the hip," Jamie muttered, only loud enough for Mick to hear, then said, "Sorta. I'm showing him around tonight."

"Well, you can just leave him to me." Suzanne extended a hand, the nails as long and black as Mick's own, and said, "Hi. I'm Suzanne."

"Mick." He did not let Suzanne's hand linger in his, although he knew he probably should have.

"Sit down, please," Suzanne said. "How have you been?"

"Oh, fine," Jamie said. "Listen, Suzanne, I really want Mick to see your act tonight."

It was hard to tell in the Submarine's dim lighting, but Mick thought Suzanne blushed. "Jamie, how sweet of you."

Jamie kicked Mick's ankle; resigned, Mick picked up his cue: "Jamie's told me the most amazing things."

She *was* blushing. "He's probably exaggerating. But . . . " She looked at them, an expression in her eyes that Mick couldn't read. But whatever she saw pleased her; she smiled and said, "I'd hate to let you down. Let me see what I can do."

She left with a generous sway of her hips, and Mick leaned over to hiss in Jamie's ear, "She *can't* think I'm straight."

"I'm sure she doesn't." He shifted guiltily. "Suzanne, um. She has a thing for . . . "

"She's a fag hag," Mick said, several things falling into place; Jamie winced, but did not dispute the term. So that was Jamie's private joke. Mick grinned. "You son of a bitch. And you want me to—"

"Jesperson wants information. Of the two of us, I'm the one who knows where to look, which means you get to play distraction."

"But do I have to distract *her*?"

"You *can* distract her. And if you're distracting her, I can tell the bouncer at the Inferno's side door I'm running an errand for her, and he's likely to believe me."

"Your plan sucks," Mick said.

"It's the only one we've got. And anyway, she's coming back, so it'll have to do."

"Your leadership technique *also* sucks," Mick said and forced himself to smile at Suzanne. Suzanne had brought them two pin-on black badges, each saying *Inferno* in fiery letters. "I've got to run and get ready," she said. "Sit where I can see you, and I'll talk to you after, okay?" It was clear to both Mick and Jamie which one of them she was talking to, and Mick only barely managed not to sigh audibly.

"Be glad she brought two badges," Jamie said, then hesitated. "Suzanne's really not that bad. She's like a lot of the kids here— thinks it's exciting and sexy to work in a nightclub with a reputation. *She* doesn't know what goes on in the Neon Cthulhu."

"And you do? What did you do, when you worked here?"

"Chief bouncer for the Inferno. Adler called me Cerberus and thought he was being funny."

"You must've been good at it. Why'd you quit?"

Jamie smiled widely, mirthlessly, the same smile he'd had when he'd confessed to knowing Brett Vincent. "Because they were gonna give me a promotion."

"Most people," Mick said, cautious now because he didn't know this mood on Jamie, didn't know which way Jamie would jump, "don't find that offensive."

"They wanted to put me on the door of the Neon Cthulhu, the lowest level. And I wasn't stupid enough to be interested. Inferno's bad enough, and it's really just play-acting." He held up one broad palm, anticipating Mick's objection. "Nothing illegal in the Neon Cthulhu. Leastways not out in the open. It's all consensual, and they got a license for public occultism. But it is *nasty* shit. I was only down there once." And he shuddered, as if even the memory made him ill.

"Jamie?" Mick said uncertainly. "You okay?"

228

Jamie shook his head, a weary gesture like a bull goaded by flies. "Don't like it here," he said. "Lot of real crappy memories."

"I'm sorry," Mick said helplessly, and was relieved when Jamie smiled at him, even if the smile was thin and forced.

"Not your fault, blue eyes. C'mon. Let's go to Hell."

SUZANNE, IT TURNED OUT, was a class eight magician; her act was very good, very smooth. She had a rather pretty young man as her assistant, and looking at him, looking at Suzanne, Mick saw his own twenty-year-old self and understood what Jamie had been trying to say about Suzanne. So eager to be wicked, but with no clear idea of how to go about it, so ready to admire anyone who seemed to have the secret information she lacked. He was able to relax a little, though, more confident that she would not turn out to be the sort that would try to get him into bed.

After her curtain calls, Suzanne came and sat at Mick and Jamie's table, instantly making them the cynosure of all eyes; she preened herself, and Mick felt his patience with her slip another notch. Jamie, with his customary talent for evading the spotlight, went to get drinks, then muttered something about the restroom and disappeared.

Leaving Mick alone with Suzanne and several dozen interested spectators, including her seething pretty boy. Mick knocked back a generous swallow of his screwdriver, and offered the first conversational gambit, asking a simple question about how she accomplished one of the effects in her act.

An hour later, he was wishing Suzanne's pretty boy would just go ahead and slip strychnine in his glass, because it would be less excruciating than this. The boy was hovering, green with jealousy; Suzanne, well aware, was flirting with Mick in a way he could have put paid to with a few pithy words, except that he was supposed to keep Suzanne distracted until Jamie got back, and where the hell was Jamie anyway?

Shouldn't have let him go running off to play James Bond on his own, Mick thought, while acknowledging ruefully that there was nothing else he could have done. He smiled at Suzanne—a little too hard, but she wouldn't notice in the dim light—and choked on his screwdriver when she asked, a trifle too nonchalantly, "Have you been Jamie's partner long?"

The coughing fit was merciful; by the time he recovered, and Suzanne was saying, "I'm so sorry, I didn't mean to embarrass you," he'd realized what she meant. She thought he and Jamie were lovers; her curiosity was prurient, not professional.

"You just surprised me," he said. "I didn't realize you . . . " and as he hesitated, trying to decide what he ought to say, whether he ought to play along, or whether he ought to tell her about Jamie's girlfriend, the image crashed into his mind, brutal as an SUV through plate glass—blood, black in lurid green light, and the harsh scent of cedar incense.

"Shit!" he said, setting his glass down hard enough to slop orange juice and vodka onto the table. "Jamie's in trouble."

Suzanne looked as if she couldn't decide whether to be offended or alarmed. "What, are you psychic or something?"

"Yeah, actually. Three-latent-eight."

She and her pretty boy stared at him with identical wide-eyed expressions.

"And I mean it," Mick said. "Jamie is in serious trouble. Will you help me find him?"

"But where would he . . . ?" She twisted around, and only then seemed to realize that Jamie was not lurking anywhere nearby.

"*Fuck*," Mick said between his teeth. But Jamie needed him, and he knew he'd never find his partner without help. He gambled on the truth. "We work for the BPI. We're investigating the death of Brett Vincent, who was found out in Sunny Creek this morning."

"BPI? Jamie Keller went to work for the *BPI*?"

Mick wondered tangentially what Jamie had been like when he had worked here, and if that was why he'd been so unhappy to come back. "Yeah."

"And Brett?" Her eyes had gone even wider, and under her makeup, she'd gone pale. "Brett disappeared a week ago. Adler said he'd taken vacation, but Brett hadn't said anything about it, and that's not like him."

"Jamie identified the body. It really was him."

Suzanne thought a moment, her teeth worrying her lower lip, then turned to her pretty boy and snapped, "Give him your Cthulhu badge."

"But, Suzanne—"

"Do it!"

Pouting, frightened, the boy unpinned the badge—black like the Inferno badge, but with *Cthulhu* written on it in lurid green black-letter.

"Trade," Suzanne said. "Nobody wears both."

Mick did so quickly, lucky to avoid stabbing himself to the bone with the pin.

"Good. Come on."

"You don't have a badge," Mick said, getting up to follow her.

"I've worked here for years. They won't stop me."

Neither the bouncer at the top of the stairs, nor the bouncer at the bottom seemed at all inclined to argue with Suzanne. This was the job Jamie wouldn't take, Mick remembered and showed his Cthulhu badge. The bouncer waved him on with no further interest, and Mick felt a pang at how completely Jamie would have been wasted on this job.

He got out, he reminded himself fiercely. And you'll get him out again. Get him out and not come back.

Then he got his first good look at the Neon Cthulhu. Mick was no stranger to S&M, and although he was not himself a magic user—and had no desire to be—he had been trained to recognize the more esoteric byways of the various disciplines. But the Neon Cthulhu still rocked him back on his heels—almost literally—and it took him a moment to realize Suzanne looked as shocked as he felt. He remembered Jamie saying she didn't know about the Neon Cthulhu, and it appeared that had been the truth.

"Stop looking like you're about to puke," he said, low and fierce. "C'mon, Suzanne. Pull yourself together."

"God," she said. "I mean, I knew it was a heavy scene down here, but—"

"It doesn't matter," he said, resisting the urge to shake her. "Help me find Jamie, and then you can get the hell out of Dodge."

"Okay." She took a deep breath and said it again, more firmly, "Okay. But where . . . "

Mick looked around, a quick, comprehensive glance. "That door," he said, with a jerk of his head toward the only other door that had a man on guard. "Can you distract the bouncer for me?"

"Can I . . . "

"For Jamie," Mick amended hastily, and that seemed to steady her. She nodded. "Good. Then pretend like this is all part of your stage act, and let's go."

That got her spine straight and her face, finally, settled, and they stepped away from the door together.

Having gone through all the stages from raw newbie to elite inner circle at more than one goth club, Mick knew perfectly well that the second most obvious sign of a tyro—after the wide-eyed gape—was the overdone look of blasé nonchalance. The trick was to look appreciative but not shocked, and he could manage that if he pretended strenuously to himself that the occult signs and mutterings and bits of ritual were just exceptionally impressive window-dressing for the S&M scenes being enacted in cages and on altars at various points around the room. He also reminded himself that Jamie had said Electric Squidland had a license for public occultism, and thus nothing going on here was illegal.

They stopped by a cage in which an ecstatic young man was being flogged by an Asian woman whose long braids snapped around her like another set of whips, and Mick pretended interest while Suzanne sashayed over, all hips and sex appeal, and engaged the bouncer's attention. Mick ghosted forward, aided by a sudden rapturous scream from the man in the cage that turned everybody's head for a split-second. Then Mick was at the door, wrenching the knob with clammy fingers, and then he was through, the door closed behind him, feeling his way down a much darker staircase, the bite of the cedar incense almost enough to make him cough. And he knew Jamie was close.

He could hear voices; as he reached the bottom of the stairs, his eyes adjusting to the darkness, he realized that the stairs were masked from the room beyond by a curtain. Green-tinged light seeped around its edges, and he drew close enough to make the voices come clear.

" . . . he must know something, or he wouldn't be here!"

"Could've been just listening to the rumors again. You always were a gossip, weren't you, Jamie boy?" A heavy thudding sound and a grunt: somebody had just kicked Jamie in the ribs. Mick's hands clenched.

"He's a threat, Adler," the first voice insisted.

"And I'm going to deal with him."

A beat of loaded silence, and the first voice said, appalled, "You're not going to give him to Brett's—!"

"I really don't think it will care." Adler sounded amused. "*He* certainly won't. At least not for long."

"We're not ready," the first voice said. "After last night . . . "

"Oh, Jamie will keep. No one's likely to come riding to *his* rescue."

Wrong, asshole, Mick thought with considerable satisfaction, listening as Adler and the other man, now discussing logistics and supplies for what sounded like a very complicated ritual, moved away from the stairs, growing distant and more muffled, until finally, with the click of a closing door, they became inaudible entirely.

Mick pushed the curtain aside only enough to slip through. The room beyond would have seemed ordinary enough—a waiting room with benches and chairs along the wall—if it had not been for the terrible greenness of the light, and Jamie Keller lying like a foundered ship in the middle of the floor, wrists bound, ankles bound, mouth stopped with a ball gag that could have been borrowed from any of the scenes going on in the Neon Cthulhu's main room.

There was blood on Jamie's face—it looked like it was from his nose, and Mick was cursing Adler viciously under his breath as he dropped to his knees beside Jamie and fumbled at the buckle of the gag, trying not to pull Jamie's already disordered braids, trying not to hurt him more than he'd already been hurt.

He eased the ball out of Jamie's mouth, and Jamie took a deep, shuddering breath, and then another; Mick hadn't been the only one with visions of asphyxiation. Then Jamie let his head roll back on the carpet as Mick started working on his wrists, and croaked, "How'd you find me?"

"Had a flash," that being Jamie's term for the times when Mick's latent eight blindsided him.

"No shit?" Jamie sounded amazed and delighted, as if Mick had given him a birthday present he'd always wanted but never dared to ask for.

"Yeah," Mick said, and the leather thong around Jamie's wrists came loose. "But enough about me. What happened to you?"

"Being a Grade-A Prime fool, I walked slap into Mr. Henry Adler on my way back to the stairs."

"On your way back?" Mick said, untying Jamie's ankles. "Did you find out—"

"Yeah," Jamie said, his voice tight with the pain of returning circulation. "Only let's get out of here before we have Story Hour, if you don't mind."

"You could hardly have suggested anything I would mind less," Mick said and braced himself to help Jamie up. Jamie was perfectly steady on his feet, and Mick hoped that meant he had not been hurt too badly, despite the blood. He was glad to let Jamie take the lead as they proceeded cautiously into a positive rabbit-warren of storerooms and access tunnels.

"You are in a maze of twisty little passages, all alike," Mick quoted uneasily. "Where the hell are we going?"

"Back door. Heck of a lot easier than trying to get out the way we came."

"And where's it gonna get us? Atlanta?"

Jamie laughed, and Mick was ridiculously glad to hear it. "Alley in back of the Kroeger's on Lichfield."

"That's three blocks away!"

"Halfway to Atlanta," Jamie said dryly.

"Adler can't own everything between here and there."

"Steam tunnels. Hell, Mick, you know how this city is. *Every-thing's* connected underground."

"Fucking ghouls." Much of the undercity of Babylon had

been constructed in the late nineteenth century by a series of Reconstruction mayors who had preferred the local necromancers' money—and at a choice between the necromancers and the carpetbaggers, Mick wasn't entirely sure he blamed them—to the safety of their citizens. It was the ghouls, though, who kept those tunnels clear, as patient and industrious as moles.

"Works in our favor this time," Jamie said, and a voice said in answer, "It might."

Mick and Jamie both whipped around, and then Mick shied back, right into Jamie's unyielding bulk. He might have screamed; later, he could not remember and could not bring himself to ask.

The thing that had crept into the corridor behind them had once been human. It might still be able to pass, to anyone except a clairvoyant, although the way Jamie's arms tightened around Mick for a breath-stealing moment before letting him go suggested otherwise. Mick could see the broken wings it dragged behind itself, black as tar and shadows, and the way its eyes glowed fitfully sodium orange in the dim light. But the way its voice blurred and doubled, as if it were neither one person nor two, but perhaps one and a half—that, he thought, registered on the material plane, where Jamie could hear it just as well as he could.

And then there was the way it crawled, like a spider or a crab, and the fact that its legs ended in stumps where the ankle bones should have been; even if it could have passed for human, it could never have passed for normal.

Jamie said, his voice unnaturally steady, "You used to be Shawna Lafayette, didn't you?"

"'Used to be'?" Mick said, hearing the shrillness of his own voice. "Then what the fuck is she now?"

"I am ifrit," the thing said, its eyes flaring brilliantly, its voice warping and splintering, and it raised itself up like a cobra preparing to strike. Then it sank back again, the light in its eyes dulled. "And I think that, yes, this shell was once called Shawna. Much is lost."

There were several thousand questions demanding to be asked, and Mick couldn't find the words for any of them. Jamie cut straight to the heart of the matter: "What do you want?"

"I am hungry," the ifrit said in a plaintive, unconvincing whine. "I am hungry, and I am tired, and I am starting to lose my grip on this shell. You carry pain with you. You could release it to me." It licked its lips, not like a human being, but with the darting, flickering motion of a snake.

"No, thank you," Jamie said. "I did figure out what they're doing with the Neon Cthulhu, you know. You got all the pain—and all the sex—you ever gonna need."

It hissed, again like a snake. "It would be better this way. Brighter."

Mick suddenly figured out what they were talking about and lurched back into Jamie again.

"He is eager," the ifrit said, its voice warbling with its own eagerness.

"*He* is scared out of his mind, thank you very much," Mick snapped. "Jamie, what—"

"Shut up, Mick," Jamie said, and very gently put him aside. "I have a better idea," he said to the ifrit, advancing slowly. "Why don't I help you let go of that body, before things get *really* ugly, and then you can go your way, and we can go ours?"

"Jamie—!"

"Shut *up*, Mick."

"You will not kill this shell," the ifrit said. "You know its name." It sounded certain, but it had backed itself against the wall, and it was watching Jamie with wide unblinking eyes, very orange now.

"And if you understood thing one about human beings, you'd know that's why I'm willing to kill you. That body's in misery, and it used to be someone I knew." He stopped, just out of arm's reach, and stared down at the ifrit. "It'll be quick, and then this whole clusterfuck will be over."

"I do not want . . . " But the ifrit's voice trailed off, as if it could no longer be certain what it did want, or didn't want; Mick remembered for no reason that mongooses were supposed to mesmerize their prey by dancing for them.

"Hold still, Shawna," Jamie said, his voice terribly kind, and then he moved.

Greased lightning had nothing on Jamie Keller, and Mick was still shocked at the idea that anyone so big could move so fast when he realized that small dry noise he had heard, like a twig breaking, had been Shawna Lafayette's neck. The body was just a body now, slumped and broken. The ifrit was gone.

"Is it dead, too?" Mick said hoarsely.

"Fucked if I know," Jamie said, and it was clear he didn't care, either. "Shawna's better off, though. I'm sure of that."

THEY REACHED THE SKYLARK half an hour later, without another word being exchanged; Jamie folded down into the driver's seat with a sigh of relief and reached for the handset.

Mick caught his wrist. "Tell me first—are you okay?"

"Yeah. Adler got me down with a hex, not a cosh. Hadn't gone face-first, I wouldn't even have the bloody nose." He sounded disgusted at his own clumsiness.

Mick hadn't really meant physically. "Jamie . . . "

"I'm fine, Mick. Let's report in and get this over with, okay?"

Mick couldn't argue with that, although he had a vague feeling he should. He listened as Jamie called in; neither of them was surprised when Jesperson's voice interrupted to pepper Jamie with questions. Jesperson really *didn't* sleep, and he almost never went home. The first was the result of being a class nine necromancer—a necromancer dux, they called it in Britain—even if officially non-practicing; Mick often wondered if the second was as well.

"Did you find out what killed Brett Vincent?"

"Yes, sir. And Shawna Lafayette, too. Well, part of Shawna Lafayette, anyway."

"I'm not going to like this, am I?"

"No, sir. Because Adler's hosting ifrits."

Jesperson's vocabulary became briefly unprintable. "Are you sure? Adler's only . . . "

"Class four, yessir. *That*'s what happened to Shawna Lafayette. And Brett Vincent."

"That . . . oh. Oh, bloody hell."

"Yessir. Adler and his boys, they're talking 'bout it like a ritual, and I know for a fact Henry Adler ain't got the math. He can't figure a tip without a calculator."

"I like this even less than I thought I would. How long do you think this has been going on?"

"Dunno, sir. But I know what happened to Brett Vincent's body was on account of them getting the phase wrong, and the stupid bastards didn't even know the word."

Becoming aware of Mick's goggle-eyed stare, he covered the mike with his palm and hissed, "*What*?"

Mick just shook his head, and Jesperson said, "'Brett Vincent's *body*.' You don't think—"

"I think Brett Vincent's been dead for a long time. Same way I would've been if Echo hadn't come and got me out."

"Yes, what *was* November Echo's part in this evening's escapade?"

"Echo was invaluable, sir," Jamie said, and elbowed Mick hard in the ribs to make him stop laughing.

"Good," Jesperson said. A pause, probably while he wrote something on one of the legal pads that littered his office like shed snakeskins. "How many ifrits do you think there are in Electric Squidland?"

"There can't be that many," Mick said, and now it was Jamie's turn to look goggle-eyed at him.

"How do you figure that, November Echo?"

"Yeah," Jamie said. "How *do* you figure that?"

"Well, you said it yourself—and how did you get to learn so much about necromancy, anyway?"

"*I* don't spend my off-hours fornicating like a bunny rabbit. Go on—what did I say?"

"That they didn't know what they were doing. I mean, I don't either, but if they had to repeat the spell every so often—?"

"Yeah. 'Bout once every five years. Ifrit starts losing its grip, and that ain't pretty. Well, you saw."

"Yeah. And they've fucked up twice *that we know about* in the last three years—they can't be maintaining an army of ifrits, or we'd be up to our asses in Missing Persons."

"They must've lost the person who knew what they were doing."

"Carolyn Witt," Jesperson said, startling them both badly. "She was part owner of Electric Squidland. Sold her share to Adler just before her arrest. And she was class seven. I think a word with Ms. Witt might clear up a great many questions."

"Yessir," Jamie said and yawned.

"Go home, November Foxtrot and Echo," Jesperson said, and for a moment the rasp in his voice sounded less like irritation and more like concern. "You can finish the paperwork when you've got some sleep."

THE BPI RAIDED Electric Squidland that same night, discovering things in the rooms beneath the Neon Cthulhu that would keep the state Office of Necromantic Regulation and Assessment busy for years. Suzanne Parker was not among those arrested; she had taken Mick's advice and gotten the hell out of Dodge.

At 11:34 the next morning, Mick set two cups of coffee on the desk he and Jamie shared, and sat down opposite his partner. Although his head was clear this morning, and the world was coloring within the lines, Mick had a gloomy feeling today was not going to be a good day at all. They were facing a mountainous stack of paperwork, including the closing of a file on an seventeen-year-old boy named Daniel McKendrick who had disappeared from a Nashville suburb in 1983. His fingerprints matched those of Brett Vincent.

Jamie pushed back from the desk, stretching until his spine popped.

"Lila going to forgive you?" Mick asked.

"Maybe," Jamie said dolefully. "She hates my schedule."

"That's because you don't have one."

"Bite me." Jamie took a generous swallow of coffee and said, "Do you think we're right to say that body is Daniel McKendrick?"

"It *is* Daniel McKendrick."

"Not like that. I mean, his family's gonna be notified, and they been thinking he's dead all this time, and now they get half a fucking body to bury? Aside from which, Daniel McKendrick *has* been dead all this time—or at least most of it. That body was . . . somebody else, if it was a person at all."

"You mean, you think when you were sleeping with him . . . "

"Oh, I'm sure of it. Because he didn't give a shit when Shawna Lafayette disappeared, and now I know why."

"Do you want to talk about it?" Mick asked, red-faced at his own stupid clumsiness.

"No, but I'm gonna have to put it in the report anyway." Jamie sighed, took another slug of coffee. "It's the reason I quit Electric Squidland. Well, one of the reasons. Shawna was a waitress in the Kaleidoscope. She caught Adler's eye, because she was pretty and not very bright, and I was worried about it—because she was pretty and not very bright. And then she disappeared, and nobody cared, and I asked Brett if he didn't think there was something strange about it, and he essentially told me to mind my own business. And, you know, I'd seen him talking to Shawna before she disappeared. Talking to her *a lot*."

"Persuading her."

"Seducing her," Jamie corrected. "And I don't know how many other people he seduced like that, or why he didn't try it on with me."

"Jamie, you're not helping yourself—"

"You know, that's the worst part. He let me go."

"Sorry?"

"*He let me go*. Oh, he tried to make me stay on, but when I wouldn't, he was okay with it. He never used magic on me, or tried to get me to play Adler's little games. Hell, he never even asked me to go down to the Neon Cthulhu with him, and he must have known I would have. I think about the shit he could have pulled on me and the fact he didn't pull it, and the fact that he fucking let me go, and . . . Well, fuck it, Mick, I don't know. Was I just not worth it? Or do you think ifrits can love?"

"I don't know," Mick said, wanting desperately to give a better answer but simply not having one. "I really don't." And hesitantly, almost cringing, he reached out and put his hand over Jamie's, feeling the warmth and the strength and the roughness of Jamie's knuckles. And Jamie turned his hand over, folded his fingers around Mick's hand.

They sat that way for a moment, saying nothing. Jamie squeezed tighter, then let go and said briskly, "This ain't getting the paperwork done." But his eyes were clearer, as if some of the pain knotting him up had been released, and Mick returned to his share of their report feeling better himself.

Today might turn out to be a good day after all.

—◦◦◦—

IMPOSTERS

THEY WERE PULLING OUT of the parking lot of St. Dymphna's Psychiatric Hospital when the radio crackled into life. Mick answered. Dispatch said, "There's been another one."

"Shit," Jamie said. They'd developed a rule that the partner not holding the handset did the swearing for both of them. Mick said to Dispatch, "Give us an address, and we're on our way."

There was a hesitation, infinitesimal, but years long in Dispatch-time, which they understood when the dispatcher said, "Langland Street subway station. He jumped."

"Christ," Mick said, racking the handset.

"That makes what, three jumpers?"

"Three jumpers, a bullet to the brain, and Mrs. Coulson back there in St. Dymphna's. I think the police are right. This one's paranormal."

"Evidence or hunch?"

"Hunch mostly. But. People don't just 'go crazy' out of a clear blue sky, you know. And here's four people—five now, I guess—no history of mental illness, going zero to psychosis in sixty seconds flat. Something is very definitely wrong with this picture. And it feels paranormal to me."

Mick's 3(8) esper rating wasn't quite high enough for his intuition to be admissible legal evidence, but Jamie had never known him to be wrong. "Then we'd better start trying to figure out what these people had in common."

"Nothing," Mick said, pale blue eyes staring an angry hole in the dashboard. "Absolutely fuck all. Aside from the fact that they all went crazy, of course."

"Well, and crazy in the same way," Jamie said, determined not to let this blow up into a fight, not even to make Mick feel better.

"Yeah." Mick sighed, offered Jamie a sidelong, apologetic smile. "What did she say? 'I stole her life.'"

"Yeah," Jamie echoed softly and shivered, trying not to imagine what it would be like to wake up one morning believing himself to be an impostor. He didn't blame any of them for committing suicide, nor Mrs. Coulson for trying.

"Must be hell on earth," Mick said, and they drove the rest of the way to Langland Street in troubled silence.

PAUL SINCLAIR WAS BROUGHT UP off the subway tracks one piece at a time. Jamie kept a weather eye on the progress of that operation and its delicate balance between speed and thoroughness; the last thing anyone wanted was for ghouls to be drawn out of the tunnels by the smell of blood. But although dealing with the ghouls if they appeared would be his and Mick's responsibility, they'd only be in the way of the morgue workers if they went over there now. They were listening to witnesses instead.

Eye-witness testimony was notoriously volatile, but allowing for the inevitable variations in what individual witnesses perceived, Jamie was getting a fairly clear picture of the last two minutes of Paul Sinclair's life.

The witnesses agreed that he'd been nervous and jerky in his movements when he came down the stairs from the street. A homeless woman who panhandled in the station on a regular basis remembered noticing him the day before, and he hadn't looked well then, either. Jamie would have dismissed that as embellishment, a natural desire to stay in the limelight a little longer, but Mick said she was telling the truth.

Paul Sinclair—bank manager, aged thirty-two, single—had

advanced to the edge of the platform, where he'd set down his briefcase and waited, attracting attention by his fidgeting and the way he moved sharply apart from the other people on the platform. "Like we were dirty and he didn't want to touch us," said a teenage boy who probably should have been in school, but that wasn't Jamie's problem and he wasn't asking. When the 10:43 D train made itself heard approaching the station, its ghoul-ward howling, Paul Sinclair said, very audibly, something like, "Don't try to save me. I'm not me." And he jumped straight into the path of the D train, which tore him to pieces.

When the police opened his briefcase, it contained nothing but a suicide note along all too familiar lines. Paul Sinclair, in handwriting Jamie had no doubt would be proved conclusively to be that of Paul Sinclair, asserted that he was an impostor. *I have stolen his life,* he wrote, echoing Marian Coulson and the other victims. *I don't deserve his life.* The note was not signed—poor bastard, Jamie thought, what name could he use?—but scrawled at the bottom, a painful afterthought: *Please take care of Mr. Sinclair's dogs. Their names are Leo and Bridget.*

"Just like the others," Mick said. He sounded—and looked—ill. "Even the same phrasing."

"Definitely paranormal."

"You say that like you think it helps."

"It *is* the first thing Jesperson told us to do."

"Well, hooray for us." But there was no anger in him now; he just sounded defeated.

"It's better than nothing."

"Tell that to Paul Sinclair," Mick said, and Jamie was glad to be called away to talk to the morgue crew.

After a hurried and unenthusiastic lunch, they spent the afternoon going through the case files again, correlating and cross-checking, trying to narrow down the possibilities. Mick remained subdued, which increased their efficiency, but Jamie found himself perversely wishing for Mick's usual argumentative and scattershot approach to this kind of work. It did not reappear, and Thursday was more of the same, as they conducted interviews with witnesses and survivors and Marian Coulson's bewildered husband, and if Mick strung three words together into a sentence, it was as much as he did all day.

At 3:32 Friday morning, Jamie's cellphone rang, waking him from a confused dream in which the BPI was being moved into his old elementary school. He had the phone open and to his ear before he was even sure where he was, and his "Foxtrot-niner" was as clear and crisp as if he were in his office rather than up on one elbow groping for the lamp on the nightstand.

Lila mumbled something, but Jamie's attention was focused on the silence from his cellphone. "Hello?"

More silence, but the distinct sound of someone breathing, too rapidly and hard.

"Who is this? Look, if you don't say something, I'm going to have to assume you have hostile intent, and we don't none of us want that paperwork. So come on. What do you want?"

Thin thread of a voice: "Jamie?"

"Mick? What the fuck?"

"Jamie, how do you know you're you?"

Jamie felt every separate blood vessel in his body go cold. "Where are you, blue eyes?"

"I, um, I don't know. On a bridge."

Jamie rolled out of bed, yanking sweatpants on over his boxers, shrugging into a flannel shirt one arm at a time, so he didn't have to put the phone down. "Which bridge, blue eyes? Come on. How'm I supposed to come get you if I don't know where you are?"

"You're going to come get me?"

Mick sounded dazed, the way he did when his esper hit him hard.

"Course I am." Shoes. Shoes. Goddammit, they had to be here somewhere. "Can't leave you freezing your ass off all night."

"But I'm not . . . "

"*Yes, you are*," Jamie said, as forcefully as he thought he could without spooking Mick. "You're just confused, blue eyes, that's all."

"Are you sure? Are you sure I'm me?"

It was all too easy to imagine Mick standing on one of Babylon's bridges, hunched around his cellphone, his long dyed-black hair straggling across his face. Jamie tried to keep that imaginary Mick firmly on the pavement, but it was even easier to imagine him standing on the railing, one arm wrapped around a stanchion, teetering out over the black water.

"I am absolutely certain you're you," Jamie said, cramming his feet into his sneakers. "You trust me, don't you?"

"Yes," Mick said promptly.

"Good, blue eyes, that's good. Now can you tell me where you are?"

"I, um . . . "

"Jamie," Lila hissed, "what on *earth* is going on?"

"Mick's in trouble," he said over his shoulder, heading down the short hallway to the living room to find his keys. The Saturn was Lila's, and he didn't normally drive it, relying on buses and subway trains to get him to and from work, but there were no buses this time of night, and he couldn't leave Mick out there in the state he was in.

"I should have guessed. God knows you wouldn't race off like this for your mother." Mick and Lila had not taken to each other the one time they'd met.

248

"Can you find a street sign?" he said to Mick.

A long pause, during which Jamie did not panic because he could still hear Mick breathing. He and Lila stood staring at each other, neither one of them quite willing to have the argument they were on the brink of.

"Rossiter!" Mick said triumphantly. "I'm on the Rossiter Street Bridge."

One of the jumpers had gone off the Rossiter Street Bridge; Jamie wondered if Mick had remembered that, or if this was just unhappy coincidence. "Good, blue eyes. Now, don't hang up, okay? It'll take me ten minutes to get to you, but I'll stay on the phone the whole time. You can talk to me. Okay?"

"Okay," Mick said. He sounded lost again. "But why would you ..."

"Why would I what, blue eyes?" Jamie asked, buttoning a couple of random buttons on his shirt. Lila tsked, rolled her eyes, and came over to do the buttons up properly.

"I stole his life. Why would you help me?"

There was the confirmation Jamie hadn't needed. "Because you need me," he said. "Besides, remember you trust me? And I don't think you stole anybody's life."

Lila finished buttoning his shirt, stepped back with a firm pat to his chest. "You can make it up to me later," she said in a sultry whisper and turned to make her way back to bed.

"Blue eyes?" Jamie said. "You still with me?" He left the apartment, took the stairs two at a time.

"I, um . . . yeah. You'd tell me, wouldn't you? If you really thought I wasn't me?"

"Course I would," Jamie said. "But that's not what I think. I think you *are* you." Out into the crisp night air, around to the back of the building and the parking lot.

"Oh," Mick said, a barely voiced exhalation.

Jamie unlocked the Saturn, wedged himself in. "Talk to me," he said to Mick. "When did you start feeling funny?"

"I've always been fake," Mick said, his voice thin and desolate and eerie. "Glass eyes."

It was something Jamie had thought more than once himself, pale as Mick's eyes were against his unnaturally black hair. "You didn't think you were fake yesterday."

"Of course I did. I've always been fake. It just didn't . . . it didn't bother me before."

Jamie whipped the car around in the tightest three-point turn that parking lot had ever seen, and put his foot down. This time of night, traffic was sparse, and he drove hard and fast, all the while encouraging Mick to keep talking, asking questions, trying both to keep him from jumping—for there was never the slightest doubt in Jamie's mind that that was why Mick was on the Rossiter Street Bridge—and to get more information, some hint as to the parameters of the thing they were dealing with. He wondered if it was Mick's esper that had made it hit so hard, so quickly. Wondered if in another three or four days, it would be *him* on the bridge.

He left the car half on the sidewalk on the north bank of the river and walked, carefully not allowing himself to run, out to the midpoint where Mick was standing, leaning against the railing like a drunk.

At least he wasn't *on* the railing, and Jamie took what felt like the first breath he'd had in years.

He hung up the phone only when he saw Mick glance at him, and in another three strides, he was standing beside his partner. The Rossiter Street Bridge wasn't very high, but it was high enough.

"Hey, blue eyes."

Mick was looking carefully at his hands where they rested on the bridge railing. He whispered something.

"Sorry, what?"

"You can tell now, can't you? That I'm an impostor?"

"Oh, *Christ*, Mick," Jamie groaned, although it wasn't Mick's fault, and he knew it. Except, said a mean and entirely reasonable voice in the back of his head, that he won't go for the esper training like Jesperson's been on at him . . .

A sudden, blessed inspiration. "Come on. We're going to go see Jesperson."

"Jesperson?"

"You remember, the nice man we work for? Class nine necromancer. No impostor could ever get by him."

And to his relief, Mick said, "Okay," and let himself be shepherded to the car.

AT 8:30 THAT MORNING, Jamie was leaning against the wall of the BPI clinic, watching Mick sleep the sleep of the heavily drugged. Jesperson had wasted no time in calling out the night-shift decon team, and then had torn strips out of Jamie's hide for not thinking to do the same. Jamie was too relieved to mind, too relieved, now, to do anything but stand and watch Mick sleep and occasionally remember to take a mouthful of lukewarm coffee.

"Well," said Jesperson, scaring the living daylights out of him, "at least we know considerably more than we did." And he added, almost under his breath, "Damn and blast the boy," making the ritual sign to nullify his words with his free hand.

Jamie eyed the stack of reports in his other hand with foreboding. "What do we know, sir?"

"It's definitely a curse, and it was definitely laid *on* Sharpton, rather than being transmitted by a curse-vector. But there's no structure to it."

"Meaning?"

"This isn't the work of a magic-user," Jesperson said grimly. "It's not even really a curse, in the technical sense. More like an extremely powerful ill-wishing."

"Thought those went out with the bustle."

"That's just the problem. Ill-wishing is much less common these days, thanks mostly to improvements in public education, but by its nature it will always happen—if only among the ill-educated and the very young."

"You don't think a *child* did this?"

"I was speaking in general terms. And, no, this curse is not the product of a child's psyche."

"So it must be someone without much education?"

"Or someone whose mind is not well-controlled at the moment. There is a reason necromancers fear senile dementia above all other illnesses, you know."

Jamie frowned, trying to figure out where Jesperson was headed. "Mrs. Coulson? But—"

"She and Sharpton are the only two who have survived. And Sharpton only survived because something—training or motherwit or God knows what—impelled him to call you before he—"

"Did anything stupid," Jamie finished hastily; his memories of the Rossiter Street Bridge were still too vivid for comfort. "So you want me to go see Mrs. Coulson again?"

"At the very least, that ill-wishing needs to be raised. I'm giving you Juliet-seven until Sharpton's back on his feet. She can take care of that part."

"Yessir," Jamie said without enthusiasm. Juliet-seven was Marie-Gabrielle Parker, one of this year's crop of rookies.

"She's a class two necromancer," Jesperson said, amused. "And *someone* has to blood the tyros, Keller."

"Yessir. But Mick's gonna be okay?"

"Oh, yes. The ill-wishing is lifted. Dr. Sedgwick just wants to let him sleep off the residue. He should be gadflying about again by tomorrow."

"Thank you, sir." Jamie pushed off from the wall. He might as well go find Parker and get this over with.

"Oh, and Keller—"

"Yessir?"

"Be careful. I don't know if our ill-wisher is Mrs. Coulson or not, but whoever it is, he or she is . . . " He hesitated a moment, as if he could not find the right word. "Ill-wishing is made of anger. Someone out there is very angry indeed."

"Yessir," Jamie said. "I'll keep it in mind."

BUT JESPERSON'S SUSPICIONS were wrong.

Primed with the knowledge gained from Mick's case, Parker lifted the ill-wishing, if not easily, then at least without making a huge production number out of it. And she and St. Dymphna's staff magic-user—a lowly class three magician, but good at his job—agreed: Marian Coulson was a victim here, not a perpetrator. Parker said pithily, "She doesn't have the strength of will to ill-wish a mosquito." And looking at the soft-eyed, frightened woman blinking around at her strange surroundings, Jamie could only agree. She hadn't succeeded in committing suicide because she didn't have the guts.

He questioned her gently; she was afraid of him, but eager to help, willingly telling him everything she could remember about the events of the previous week. Jamie took notes, although he had no real hope that Mrs. Coulson would remember anything useful, working on autopilot until the words *Langland Street* brought him back with a thump.

"How did you get to Langland Street, ma'am?"

"Oh, I took the subway." Remembered irritation creased her forehead and made her voice peevish. "I really wish the city would do something about cleaning up the subway stations. There was a dirty old woman there, asking everyone for money—"

"Thank you, ma'am, you've been a great help," Jamie said, scrambling to his feet, and led the bewildered Parker nearly at a run back to the car.

He was lucky enough to get Avery when Dispatch patched him through to Records, and Avery didn't fuss or ask questions, but found out what Jamie needed to know. What he already knew.

All of the victims had been on Langland Street in the week before their deaths.

"Son of a *bitch*," Jamie said. "All right, Parker, hang on." And he floored it, wondering how many people, like Paul Sinclair, he was going to be too late to save.

SHE *WAS* a dirty old woman, as Mrs. Coulson had said, and Jamie was ashamed to realize he didn't remember her name. Avery in Records had that, too: Veronica Braggman. Old and dirty and shapeless beneath layers and layers of ragged clothes, her eyes small and bright and half-mad. She was tucked into a corner of the Langland Street Station, her crudely lettered cardboard sign in front of her like a shield: CANT WORK / GOV TOOK MY PENSHON / PLEASE HELP.

She saw him coming—he would have had to be a class nine necromancer like Jesperson to have any hope of concealing himself—and heaved herself to her feet. "You stay away from me, nigger!" she cried. "I was respectable once—I don't have to talk to you!"

That answered one question: why her ill-wishing had landed on Mick instead of him. He hadn't been worth her anger.

"Miz Braggman?" he said politely, carefully. "We just need to ask you a few more questions."

"I ain't talking to you!" she said, still with her high voice pitched to carry.

"Ma'am, there's four people dead. You don't have a choice."

Her head lowered, and she looked at him sidelong, like an ill-tempered, cunning animal. "Ain't my doing. I didn't push 'em."

"Yes, you did, and you know it," Jamie said. The stench of her body was nothing compared to the stench of her mind, and he didn't need esper to feel it. "You hexed 'em."

Hex was an old word, his Great-Granny May's word, and he saw from the way she blinked that it was Veronica Braggman's word, too. "I can't hex nobody, nigger. Just a poor old lady, that's all I am."

He cut her off before she could get well-launched into that rehearsed whine. "Why'd you do it?"

"Didn't do nothing," she said sullenly. Then suddenly, she was shouting again, "Get him away from me! Get this nigger away from me! Ain't there no decent God-fearing folks anymore?" Jamie realized they'd attracted an audience, and one of them was a woman in the uniform of the BMPD, who was already pushing her way through the crowd toward him.

He turned carefully, not letting Veronica Braggman out of his sight, and said, "I'm with the BPI. If you'll give me a moment, I can show you my ID."

"He's a liar!" shouted Veronica Braggman. "A filthy liar!"

Jamie slowly reached into his hip pocket, slowly brought out his ID folder, slowly opened it for the policewoman's inspection. He saw her face change, and Veronica Braggman saw it, too, for she changed her tactics. "They're all against me, all the gummint! Just want to keep a poor old lady down so the niggers and the white-trash can walk all over me. They took it all away from me, so I ain't got nothing. And now they gonna take that, too!"

The policewoman said, "Do you need any help, Mr. Keller?"

He saw the incandescent fury light Veronica Braggman's face and instinctively backed away from her. But nothing seemed to happen; she slumped back against the wall, muttering, "It ain't no use, none of it. Can't never get back my rights. Can't never get what they stole from me."

Marie-Gabrielle Parker's voice said, from the midst of the crowd, a little unsteady but admirably clear, "Keller, we've got the evidence we need. And we need to get you back to headquarters before that ill-wishing has time to sink in. I don't think I can handle it myself."

He turned back to Veronica Braggman. "You just hexed me?"

Her head came up; there was nothing sane in her eyes at all. "*You stole my life,*" she said, and it was the snarl of an animal goaded past endurance, the wail of a lost child, the cry of a woman who had nothing left, *nothing*, and who sat on the cold tiles of the Langland Street subway station every day, watching people go past, people with jobs and families and homes to go to, people with lives . . . people who saw her, if they saw her at all, merely as a nuisance, as dirt to be cleaned up.

She lunged at him; he had played football from the time he was an eight-year-old bigger than most ten-year-olds, and he could read her body language. She expected him to fall back, to leave her space to twist through the crowd, to throw herself off the edge of the platform like Paul Sinclair. And part of him wanted to let her do it. Even if she didn't break her neck in the fall, and she didn't land on the third rail, and a train didn't kill her, the ghouls would take care of her before she'd gone half a mile in the darkness of the subway tunnels. Like a garbage disposal.

Jamie put his hands out and caught her—and narrowly avoided being bitten to the bone for his pains. And then Parker was there, and they were getting handcuffs on her; she went limp, weeping great maudlin crocodile tears, and Jamie knew no matter how long he spent in the shower, he'd never really get the stink of her off him: madness and hate and despair and the terrible bewilderment of not knowing how she had ended up like this. He did not want empathy with her, but he could not help understanding. Blame the government at first, but the government is faceless, far away. It's the people who walk by you every day and don't make eye-contact, who call you names and talk about needing to "clean up" the subway stations; they're right there, and it must be their fault. They're the ones with lives they don't deserve; they're the ones who have stolen your life. They're the impostors, because under their clothes and makeup, their cellphones and iPods and the hard shell of security, they're *just like you.*

Jamie shuddered, and Parker said, with surprising authority, "Come on, Keller, move your ass."

She was all right, Parker was.

HE ENDED THE DAY where he'd begun it, in the BPI clinic. Mick was awake now, a little owlish still with the sedative and somewhere between mortified and furious at what Veronica Braggman had done to him.

The decon team had lifted the ill-wishing off Jamie, although it had taken them three tries before they were sure they had all of it, and somewhere else in the BPI's sprawling bulk, that lady was doubtless being fingerprinted and tested and, Jamie hoped, fed.

"Ironic that she's probably going to end up better off," Mick said.

"'Less she goes to the electric chair."

Mick shook his head. "She'll be found insane, and they'll put her in Leabrook."

"You sound awful sure."

"I was . . . well, I wasn't in her head, exactly, but something like it. The reverse of it, maybe. She's insane."

"And four people are dead."

Mick raised his eyebrows. "You sound like you think your halo's a little tarnished on this one."

"Fuck off, Mick." He couldn't leave—they wanted to keep him under observation overnight, and Lila'd had a fit about that, too—but he got up to pace. Up and back, the room not really long enough to accommodate his stride, but it was better than sitting still with Mick sneering at him.

"Jamie?"

He swung round to give Mick a glare, and maybe a piece of his mind, but Mick was looking at him wide-eyed, solemn and a little taken aback, and Jamie's anger drained out of him.

"I'm sorry," Mick said. "You wanna tell me what I did?"

"You were just being your usual charming self. I'm sorry. Shouldn't've flown off the handle like that."

"I don't mind. Except you usually don't. It's more my speed, isn't it?"

Jamie thought of some of the tantrums Mick had pitched and grinned reluctantly. "I just . . . she's not a nice old lady, you know."

"Parker gave me the highlights," Mick said, rather dryly. "But I don't see why that's got your tail in a knot. You caught her, you know. Justice will be served."

"Yeah, but she was right."

"I'm sorry?"

"All those people walking past her every day. Probably most

of them ain't nice, either. Who says they have any right to good clothes and a warm place to sleep? Who says they deserve it more than her?"

"Nobody," Mick said. He was eyeing Jamie cautiously now. "You still feeling like yourself, Keller?"

"It ain't that," Jamie said and started pacing again. "It's just, how come she ended up the villain here?"

"Because she started killing people."

"You said it yourself. She's crazy. And she's crazy because somehow she got fucked over and spat out in little pieces. Blame The Victim isn't a nice game, Sharpton."

"Nor is Pin The Blame On The Donkey." Mick slid off the bed, gawky and angular in the clinic's ugly. He approached Jamie slowly, put one bony hand on Jamie's biceps. "Jamie, it isn't your fault."

"I know that. Nobody's fault, really. Or everybody's. Just another clusterfuck of modern life."

"We do the best we can, instead of the worst," Mick said. "That's all we can do."

"I know," Jamie said, not turning to face Mick, because he knew the particular kind of courage it took for Mick to offer comfort and just how fragile that courage was. "I just hate it that that's not enough sometimes, you know?"

"Yeah," Mick said, his hand warm and heavy and vital on Jamie's arm. "I know."

STRAW

MOSTLY, NOW, they leave us alone.

We aren't news any longer; we have been wrung dry of "human interest"; even the tabloids have given up hoping for a miracle to put us back on the front page. Generally, someone shows up around the anniversary, but they are not allowed to see us, and I do not know what they write. Harry asked once if I wanted him to tell me, and I said I did not.

We are the debris left after you save the world: broken bricks and dirty straw. I spent three years waiting to be tidied away, cast into the fire like chaff, but last night I had a dream.

FOR THREE and a half months after the flash, I was in a coma.

And for every day of those three and a half months, Harry talked to me.

He did not sit beside the bed and hold my hand—neither he nor I could have borne that, even if they would have let him—but we had been left, like two abandoned walkie-talkies, tuned to the same frequency. The effect has faded with time, though never entirely disappeared; we must converse aloud like ordinary mortals, but I do not have to ask to know how he is feeling.

The only memory I have for nearly six months after the flash that is neither pain nor grief is that interior sound of Harry's voice: scratchy, careless, tender.

It was how I knew, as soon as I woke, that Harry was no more responsible for what he had done than I was.

Once, almost a year ago now, Harry said in the middle of the night, knowing I was awake, "They let me have a mirror today. I'm like the Elephant Man, only not as cute."

"Then I won't be sorry I can't see you," I said.

A beat of silence. Then we both started laughing, and it was some time before we could stop.

THE DAY the troubles began—although I would not know they had begun until the next morning—I had a screaming argument with my piano teacher and stormed out into the quad to sulk. I would not have put it that way, of course; I fancied myself an artist, and fancied that my selfishness and temper tantrums were "temperament" when they were nothing but pure childish egotism.

I remember lying on my back in the grass, staring at the pure warm blue of the sky and thinking about the comet that had everyone so excited. We didn't know then that it wasn't exactly a comet.

We didn't know what it was going to do.

HARRY AND I have different names for the nursing home in which we live. Some days we call it the Bastille or the Château d'If, other days Bedlam or Arkham Asylum. On very bad days, Harry calls it the Gulag, but I don't think, even then, that he means it. Once, bitterly, I called it the Trianon, and then had to explain to Harry what I meant.

It is a comfortable prison, ours. "One of the best private care facilities in the country," the lawyer my mother hired said proudly. The fees are paid by the federal government, which wants to keep Harry where they can see him, and does not want (with careful prompting from Mother's lawyer) to appear ungrateful toward me. Our room is spacious, more than big enough for the two of us, with windows everywhere; I can still feel the sunlight, even if I cannot see it. There are gardens in which we do not walk, a swimming pool in which we do not swim. For my twenty-first birthday Mother sent a grand piano, and the staff very obligingly cleared a room for it. I told them to let the other inhabitants use it—and it was only Harry's warning nudge in my mind that kept the word from coming out "inmates." I would not even let Harry take me to inspect it. I have not touched a piano since that last screaming argument with Madame Vautelle.

The nurses are cheerful, kind, and efficient. We know them all by name; they talk to us, sometimes, like human beings.

I asked Harry once, on a very bad day, why he had talked to me when I was in my three and a half month coma. "Wouldn't it have been better to let me die?"

"Maybe," said Harry, "but how was I supposed to know that?"

"But why did you care?" The selfish, spoiled child I had been, demanding attention, answers, never letting go of what she wanted.

But before I could open my mouth to say, *I'm sorry. Never mind*, Harry answered me.

"Everyone I loved was dead, kid. Everyone. And I probably killed them, although I don't remember it. Don't remember much, in case you were wondering." Bitter sarcasm, and I could not quite control the flinch of my hands. "I remember the smell of blood and ozone. I remember the screaming. God help me, I remember what it felt like to crush a man's skull between my bare hands."

He stopped, and I didn't dare say anything. After a moment, he said, "Sorry. You didn't deserve that. But the investigators found *pieces* of my wife's body. *Pieces*. I didn't ask them which ones, and they were nice enough not to tell me. They wouldn't let me out of the hospital to go to my daughters' funeral. You know, I still have dreams that I'm buried with them—and then I wake up and realize that the coffin I'm trapped in is my body."

He came closer. Not close enough to touch, for we do not do that unless we have to, but close enough that I could feel his body, hear his labored breath. "I talked to you because you were the only one left."

I can't cry any more. The flash burned that out of me, too. But I said, "I know, Harry. I'm sorry." And just for a second, his scarred, lumpy fingers brushed across my hair.

I UNDERSTAND that the scientists and the philosophers, the mystics and the UFO-chasers, the psychiatrists and the madmen, still argue about what they were: demons, aliens, mass hallucinations, spaceborne viruses, gods. A hundred thousand theories, none more implausible than any of the others.

I gave my theory in my testimony, when I was finally well enough to speak. The Commission liked my theory well enough to bury it in political doublespeak and jargon and call it their own. I am a little bitter about that, but not as bitter as I am about the fact that I told them the truth, and they listened because the truth happened to be convenient.

Templates. That's what we were infected with, Harry and me and the woman in India and the two men in South Africa and all the others whose names I never learned. We were reformatted, like computer disks. Set to run a series of programs and then, like something out of an old spy show, to self-destruct.

It might have been carelessness, or the deterioration of very old technology, or some other mistake, that kept Harry and me from dying like the others. It might have been my fault for refusing to complete the program. When he sank to his knees in front of me, weeping, and cried in a voice that was nothing but ashes and pain, "Kill me!" and I did not. Could not. Perhaps that was what the flash could not consume: Harry's guilt and my compassion.

Or maybe it was simply the punchline of a very cruel joke.

IN THE EARLY DAYS, when they were still trying to find a new template to fit us into, the reporters tried to make a romance between Harry and me. The idea made us both feel slightly ill, and not merely because we could neither of us bear to be touched. "It would be like screwing my sister, if I had one," Harry said later, after everyone had gone, "and pardon me for saying it, princess, but you just aren't my type."

"You aren't my type, either, Harry," I said, and I felt his affection like the smile his scarred face could not make and my scarred eyes could not see.

I SAVED THE WORLD.

Nineteen years old and I saved the world.

Very heroic, except for the fact that it wasn't me. The hero wasn't me, any more than the villain was Harry McLaughlin, forty-year-old forest ranger and father of two. We were just the matrices that held the pattern, the straw and clay from which the myth was built. And now that we are only straw and clay again, the world does not know what to do with us.

My mother sent lawyers and a piano, but she has never come to visit. The reporters came to try to make a story and went away defeated. *You can't use the same straw twice,* I wanted to tell them, but they would not have understood what I meant.

There's not supposed to be anything left after the end of the world, even if the end of the world doesn't quite happen.

But I am beginning to think maybe it wasn't a mistake, or a

joke. In my coma I had Harry's voice, and did not die. Last night, I had a dream.

IN MY DREAMS, I can still see, and in this dream I am walking among the ruins of a house, skirting crumbled piles of mellow red-pink bricks. It's very peaceful, and the sky is the same blue I remember from the last day of my old life. I hear someone singing, a wordless crooning little tune, and I follow the sound until I come to a man sitting beside one of the piles of bricks.

Every brick he touches turns into straw, and as I watch, he takes the straw and twists and plaits it into marvelous multi-pointed stars. He's utterly unhurried, utterly content; as he finishes each star, he balances it on his palm and gives it a little flip up, and when I look at the sky, I see his stars shining.

What are you doing? I ask.

He looks up at me. It's Harry, unscarred and unhurt, his eyes shining as brightly as the stars he has made. And he says, *You can use the same straw, kid. You just can't expect it to come out as bricks.*

TODAY I SAID, "Harry, take me to the piano."

ABSENT FROM FELICITY

FORTINBRAS IS NOT HAMLET.

I wish with all my heart that he were, wish even that I could close my eyes and pretend. But he is a swarthy, swaggering Pole, broad-shouldered, with a warrior's heavy muscle. His hands are hard with calluses; Hamlet's were soft, narrow, the hands of a scholar. Hamlet liked to discuss philosophy in bed, the light rambling voice like a counterpoint to the explorations of those soft, clever hands. Fortinbras does not waste his breath.

FORTINBRAS COMES TO ME after the funeral, where I stand beside Hamlet's grave. My throat is raw from tears, from words, from the cold, bitter wind of Elsinore.

He says, "You were more than friends."

It is not a question; I do not answer it.

His hands are on my shoulders; his breath tickles my ear. He is standing too close, too close, but I cannot move. I have followed Hamlet for so long, so blindly. Now that he is gone, I do not remember how to walk on my own.

Fortinbras says, "You must be very lonely."

A trite, obvious line, suitable for chambermaids and serving girls. I bow my head, choking back bitter laughter. We are alone in the graveyard, alone with the dead, and I know Fortinbras does not fear the dead. Unlike Hamlet, he is not an imaginative man.

The hands settle into a hard grip. He says, "I am lonely, too. It is difficult to find someone to trust, here in Denmark." I shiver at the disjunct between the voice, with its gentle platitudes, and the hands, the punishing weight, the blunt fingers digging for nerve and bone. I do not know which to believe.

"We do not have to be lonely," Fortinbras says, and under the pressure of his hands I sink to my knees. "I am told that Prince Hamlet was a lonely man. You must have helped with that, Horatio." A shove, quick, brutal, and I only save myself from sprawling across Hamlet's grave by catching at the headstone, a graceless block of granite he would have hated.

Fortinbras says, "Show me."

THE DANES do not quite know what to make of Fortinbras: the child of their old king's enemy, but a strong man, a man for whom decisions are easy, policy is clear. After the short and serpentine rule of Hamlet's uncle Claudius, Fortinbras comes as a relief to the court of Denmark. The soldiers and common people are only grateful that perhaps this winter they will not have to die.

I WEAR BLACK NOW, as Hamlet did. The court ignores me, as they ignored Hamlet. In Elsinore, if you do not want to see something, then you do not see it. It explained so much about Hamlet to me, when I came to Elsinore: the frenetic brilliance of his wit, his hunger for attention, the way he would touch me, a light pat on shoulder or cheek, just to get me to turn and look at him. He was not the child his father had wanted, and I could imagine him becoming steadily more outrageous as he grew up, constantly devising new schemes to get his father and his father's court to acknowledge his existence.

I am not Hamlet. I do not care if the court notices me or not. I wear black for grief; I wear black for him.

I BRING FLOWERS to Ophelia's grave.

I hated her.

Hated her doe eyes and her little soft grasping hands. Hated her for being able to flirt, demurely, with Hamlet when I could do nothing but stand to one side and watch. The loyal friend.

And I hated her because she loved him. I hated her for her pain, her grief. I hated her for going mad. And I hated her most of all for dying. I stood, the loyal friend, and watched Hamlet leap into her grave. Later, I held him while he cried, neither of us knowing that he had less than a day to live. I kissed his tear-damp cheeks and told him I loved him and knew he did not hear me.

If she had risen from her grave in front of us, I would have killed her myself.

I bring her flowers because she loved him, because she died for him. Because he would not let me do the same.

I SHOULD LEAVE. I know I should leave. Fortinbras has a country to rule, an uncle to placate. He would not stop me, though he would not help me, either. But if I leave Elsinore . . . I cannot go back to Wittenberg, where every hallway, every street corner, will have some memory of Hamlet as he was. I could not protect that bright Hamlet from his father's dark hand. I cannot face Wittenberg without him. And I have no family, no kin, no place where I can truthfully say I belong. I hoped when I came to Elsinore that it might prove to be such a place, that because it was Hamlet's home, it might become my home as well. But Hamlet died in Elsinore, died *of* Elsinore. It will never be my home.

But I cannot leave. I cannot leave the pain, the cold, the darkness and the damp and the constant stench of death. I cannot leave Fortinbras, for at least he notices that I am alive.

I WANT to be haunted. I go up to the battlements at midnight, slipping out of the new king's bed. The sentries eye me warily and skirt wide. The wind scours the tears from my face, but I taste them at back of my throat, bitter as graveyard dirt.

I stand there until dawn, waiting, but he does not come.

THE WORLD WITHOUT SLEEP

I. *In the Night City*

IN THE JANUARY that I turned thirty-five, sleep became a foreign and hostile country. I had never been more than what one might call a refugee in the country of sleep; one of my earliest memories is of my nurse telling me that if I did not go to sleep, the goblins would get me, and of waiting all that night for the goblins to appear. They did not, of course, but even so I am not sure that she was wrong.

I have always been an insomniac, but in that January 'insomniac' itself began to feel like the wrong word. When I slept at all, in sporadic cat naps lasting between fifteen minutes and an hour, my dreams would be vividly senseless, and I would be plagued with images from them for hours afterwards. The other archivists and curators remarked uneasily on my bloodshot eyes and bruise-dark eye sockets; I said truthfully that I often had trouble sleeping, and they left me alone.

I could not sleep between midnight and dawn. It was not even worth the effort, and I grew to loathe my bedroom, then to loathe the study, the living room . . . Finally, desperate for peace of mind even if I could not rest, on the last Friday in January, I put on my coat and went walking. If I was robbed or assaulted or murdered, I felt vaguely that it would be no more than I deserved.

But this quarter of the city was antique and genteel; not only were there no miscreants abroad, there was no one at all, no one but me. The only sound was the echoing of my footsteps; the only lights were the street lamps. No one else was awake; they slept the sleep of the just and innocent. Like Satan in the Garden of Eden, I looked at their darkened windows and was consumed with envy.

I paid no attention to the routes I took, nor to how far I went. Some part of my mind, better regulated than the rest, seemed always to contrive that I should return to my own front door around dawn, so that I could shower, shave, sleep soddenly for three quarters of an hour, and eat breakfast before going to work. One afternoon in early February, I found myself doodling the hubristic Gothic outline of the Nicodemus Kent Building on my desk blotter and realized hollowly that I must have walked halfway across the city the night before. And yet I had no memories of leaving my own neighborhood, no recollections of the poorer neighborhoods, the financial district, the massive Mycenaean bulk of the Public Water Utility, which I must have passed to reach the Kent Building. Could I in fact be sleeping even as I walked?

The idea was so unsettling that I very nearly locked myself into my apartment that night. But I could not stand the oppressive familiarity of the patterns made by the shadows on the floors, the relentless ability of my ears to catalogue every strange sound the building made in the deep watches of the night. I decided instead to choose a goal and to pay attention as I walked, to prove to myself that I was not slipping into some unnatural fugue state in my perambulations. I further decided that I would walk to the Public Water Utility; it was an achievable goal, and even in the darkness, it was readily recognizable as itself.

I felt better for having formulated a plan, even a plan as ultimately meaningless as that one. I set out into the nighttime streets, feeling a certain cautious optimism that I could at least contend with this piece of the wider and apparently insoluble problem that beset me.

I became lost.

In itself, I do not suppose this is either alarming or surprising. My sense of direction is not particularly acute, and in their dark desolation, the streets of the city all looked remarkably similar. Against this stood the fact that I had known where I was going and that it was a walk I had taken before in daylight. I confess to a certain morbid affection for the Public Water Utility, surely the most graceless piece of civic architecture in America. And, paying attention or otherwise, I had become accustomed to the city's nocturnal streets; they no longer seemed unfathomable to me.

And yet I was lost. The buildings did not look familiar; the street signs, when I found them, were for streets named Boulevard de la Lune, Nyx Place, Umbra Road—streets which I had never seen before in my life, and I was born in this city.

"I must be asleep," I said to myself, muttering under my breath simply for the comfort of hearing my own voice. I did not believe it, but there seemed no other explanation, no other method by which I could have walked out my apartment door into a city of such absolute unfamiliarity. If I was dreaming, I reasoned— tenuously and uncomfortably—then I must have been dreaming all those previous nights, and the best strategy for finding my way out of the dream was to do what I had done before. I had an uneasy sense that there was a fallacy somewhere in that piece of logic, but I turned down Umbra Road because standing by myself under the street sign was becoming increasingly nerve-wracking, and I knew I was in danger of beginning to imagine that things were watching me from the shadows.

I decided to keep walking as if I could come to the Public Water Utility, hoping that I might wake up when I arrived there, or that my failure to do so would somehow shake me out of this frightening maze. I knew I would not find it, and so I do not know the right words to express my complete bewilderment when I did.

There it was, looming out of the darkness like a prehistoric temple idol, its entryway looking as always like the lowered head of a bull before the monstrous bulk of the main building. It was incontrovertibly the Public Water Utility.

And yet I was standing on the sidewalk of—I walked to the corner to check the street sign—Artemis Street, and I knew as well as I knew my own name that the Public Works Utility brooded over the south side of Fairlie Road between Jackson and Godolphin. Artemis Street at this point claimed that it crossed Nocturne Street.

I sat down, quite without meaning to, at the base of the signpost. It is one thing to suspect yourself of going mad; it is another thing entirely to discover that your suspicions are correct.

I wondered drearily what would happen if I sat here until dawn. Would I wake up in my own bed? Would I wake up at the corner of Fairlie and Jackson? Would I not wake up at all, but find myself admiring the sunrise from Artemis and Nocturne? Each option seemed more repellant than the last.

It was at that nadir in my thoughts that I noticed the light. In all the vast darkness of this city, there was one light burning. I surged to my feet and started toward the light.

I walked a block and a half down Nocturne Street and found myself opposite a church. The light came from a lamp hung over its doorway. The church was brick and homely, and as I climbed the steps, I saw it was dedicated to St. Christopher, patron saint of ferrymen, protector against floods, fires, earthquakes . . . and bad dreams. When I tried the door, it was unlocked. I pulled it open and went in.

The interior of the church was a great, gloomy vault. I realized after a moment's bewilderment that it was not fitted for electricity; the only light came from candles, in sconces on the walls, crowning great candelabra on the altar, offered as votives in the two chapels that flanked the nave. I could see stalagmites of wax beginning on the floor beneath the sconces that flanked the front door.

I was still standing, unable either to sum up the courage to penetrate farther into the tremendous darkness of the church or to maintain the resolve to turn and walk out again, when a voice called, "Is someone there?"

It came from near the altar; seeing movement, I realized that what I had taken for a deeper patch of shadow was a man, now in the act of getting to his feet from the first row of backless pews. At first I could not make sense of his shape, but then he moved into the light and I saw that he was winged, marble-white feathers rustling softly from his shoulders to his heels.

"You need not fear," he said, starting down the aisle. "Our doors are left unlocked for a reason."

As he came closer, I saw that he was a young man—probably four or five years younger than I—and that his resemblance to a marble angel in a cemetery did not end with his wings. He had the high forehead with the bar across the supraorbital ridge, the straight, patrician nose, the proportionally weaker mouth and chin, which nonetheless held an expression of great gentleness and sweetness. His skin was alabaster pale; his hair, curly and overlong, was tow-colored. As he passed through a puddle of candlelight, I saw the final, capping, dreadful resemblance: his wide-set eyes were blank, perfectly white, like the eyes of a classical statue whose colors have been washed away by centuries of rain.

"Are you an angel?" I blurted.

His laugh was enchanting, self-deprecating and rueful. "A demi-angel, only. But you cannot be one of my parishioners."

"No, I beg your pardon. I did not mean . . . that is, I am . . . " I hesitated, and decided on the stark truth. "I am lost."

"Lost," he said thoughtfully, as if the word had some deeper meaning of which I was unaware. "Will you come sit down and tell me? The nights are long and lonely here, and I," and his lips curved in a gentle smile, "I am unquenchably curious about travellers in our city."

"I . . . I'm not . . . that is, I don't think I am a, er, a traveller. I'm just lost."

"All the more reason to speak to me," he said. "Perhaps I can help you become found again. I am Clement, the dominie of St. Christopher's."

"My name is Kyle Murchison Booth," I said.

Clement found a pew with a light sweep of his right hand. He sat, his wings wrapping round him like a cloak, leaving space for me; I sat beside him. He smelled of vanilla and nutmeg. His hands, folded restfully in his lap, were as beautiful as his face, long-fingered and smooth. I clasped my own hands, with their knobby joints and chapped knuckles and ink-stained fingertips, between my knees, and told Clement as best I could about my insomnia and my walks and the strange city I now found myself in. He listened without any trace of restlessness or impatience, although his feathery brows drew together slightly as my tale unfolded.

"Do you know, er, the other city?" I said. "Have you heard of Fairlie Road?"

"No," he said.

"I feared as much."

"But it is possible that I can help you all the same. If you will help me in return."

"I will do anything I can," I said, knowing it was rash, but also knowing that I did not have a choice in any meaningful sense of the word.

Clement smiled at me radiantly. "It is not as difficult as your voice suggests you fear. But it is most desperately important. You see, the goblins have stolen St. Christopher's Glass."

"St. Christopher's . . . I'm sorry. I, er . . . "

"It is our relic."

"Relic." I supposed it was foolish of me to be surprised. Clearly the boundary between this nightmare city and the waking world was all too permeable; if random persons such as myself could cross, why not the remains of saints?

"It's a glass ball, about the size of my thumb joint. Warm to the touch. It contains one of St. Christopher's tears, and the sunlight reflected in it."

"It . . . I'm sorry. I don't think I understand you."

"This is the night city," Clement said, his beautiful face sad. "We have no sun. It is why the vampires are so strong."

"Vampires? You, er, do mean the blood-drinking sort, not some other of which I am unaware?"

"They leave the city at moonrise to hunt. I am told it is terrible to witness."

"I'm sure," I said faintly.

"The city is theirs, you see. The shadows are their thralls, and we cannot travel without protection."

After a moment, I realized that his 'we' was the demi-angels. "Are you all blind, then?"

A tactless question, but he did not seem to notice. "Yes. We stay in our churches, where the vampires cannot come, and do what we can to help the shadows." His wings drooped as his shoulders slumped. "Sadly, it isn't much."

"Why can't one of these, er, shadows go after your relic?"

"The vampires would notice their absence," he said, seeming shocked that I had to ask. "They are very strict overseers."

"Ah. And you—the demi-angels—cannot go because of your blindness, and it's obviously useless to ask the vampires."

"Oh, they mustn't know it's gone," Clement said earnestly. "It's the only thing that keeps them in check at all."

He had boxed me in very neatly with the solution he wanted, although I did not think, looking at that beautiful, gentle face, that he was aware of his own manipulation. "Very well," I said, although I could not quite repress a sigh. "I hope that you can at least tell me where I must go."

"Shift ends very shortly, and the shadows are allowed an hour before they have to sign the registers of their dormitories. One of them will show you the way. But, please, I would hear more of your city, if you would tell me."

It would have been difficult to resist his shy entreaty, and I reflected that I would probably get more useful information from the shadows. So, shy myself, I told Clement about the museum, and the neighborhoods I walked in on the weekends; the library, the zoo, the Alethea Wing Parrington Botanical Gardens. I described the Nicodemus Kent Building and the Public Water Utility, and the city's other architectural marvels, both the beautiful and the grotesque, and some that were both. I told him about the Resurrection Hill Cemetery, where my ancestors were buried, and a little about the old, gracious neighborhood in which I had spent my childhood. I described the city to him as I knew it, and both of us became wide-eyed as children with the wonder of it. I managed to forget so thoroughly where I was and what was being asked of me that I jumped and flinched when the church door opened, and a voice called, "Dominie Clement?" It was a soft voice, a little asthmatic, indeterminate as to sex.

"In the nave, my child. Come here, there's someone I want you to meet."

The patter of bare feet, and I turned to watch the shadow come into the church proper. It was child-sized, very pale, limbs long in proportion to the torso, giving it an unpleasantly spidery appearance. It wore its pale, cobwebby hair scraped into a topknot, which looked incongruously savage juxtaposed with the sober, tidy laborer's clothes. The face was unremarkable next to Clement's beauty, the eyes large and dark and much inclined to blink.

They blinked at me, puzzled and reproachful, and the shadow said, "'Oo—Who is this?"

"Is that you, D-7-16? This is Mr. Booth, who has very kindly agreed to retrieve St. Christopher's Glass for us."

The look of alarm had to be due to the goggle-eyed blinking, I decided, for D-7-16—if that was indeed the creature's name—said, "That's very nice of you, sir," and sounded sincere and even eager.

"Mr. Booth is a stranger to our city," Clement said, "so I need you to show him the way to the Goblin Door."

"It'll have to be now, sir."

"Yes, I know. D-7-16 will take good care of you, Mr. Booth."

I looked at the blinking eyes, the sly thin-lipped mouth, and was not so sure. But there did not seem to be any way I could say so; therefore, I got up—this time the blinking was definitely in alarm, as D-7-16 backed hastily away from my gangling height—and said, "Thank you. I'll do my best."

"Oh, I'm sure you will succeed," Clement said, almost gaily. "The goblins are nasty little brutes, but they're not really *dangerous.*"

How would you know? inquired an unpleasant voice in my head, but I bit my tongue and did not say it.

"This way, sir, please," said D-7-16, making urging motions without actually approaching me. "There's not much time."

I wished I had a better option, but I did not. I followed D-7-16.

THE NIGHT CITY, as Clement called it, was not less *unheimlich* for having a companion. D-7-16 padded unspeaking on long pale feet, only nodding in a self-important manner at the other shadows we met or passed. They were all indistinguishable to my eyes, with their pale topknots and subfusc clothes and fish-like blinking eyes. And no less so when the street lamps were lit, as they were by other shadows, just as pale and goggling—though I could not tell if the lamps were meant to signify day or night.

I felt terribly tall and awkward and out of place—which differed from my waking life, I supposed, only in that no one here would expect me to feel otherwise. The thought was queerly emboldening. I said to D-7-16, "Do all shadows have, er, names like yours?"

The blink this time was clearly contemptuous. "That isn't my *name.*"

"Oh. I beg your pardon. Then, er . . . "

"It's my designation. Factory D, seventh level, technician sixteen."

"Oh. And your real name?"

"The vampires have that," D-7-16 said, sounding scandalized that I would feel it necessary to ask.

"The vampires have your *name?*"

"Shhh!" D-7-16 said, rather frantically. "Never know who's listening." But oddly—for I knew it did not like me any better than I liked it—it must have wanted to answer my question, for it said, "It's why we work for them. Earning our names back."

"But how did they get your names in the first place?" I was wondering if I had been mistaken in what type of vampires these were. Onomastic vampires?

"Protection," D-7-16 said. "We give 'em our names when we're born, and they protect us from the dragons. And we can earn our names back working in the factories—as adults, of course."

I firmly put aside the temptation to ask about shadow child-labor laws. "And, er, what happens when you do?"

"The dominies have a system. We give them part of our wages every month, and whenever anybody buys their name back, the dominies take money out of the kitty and buy 'em passage on a ship to Heft Averengh."

I was about to ask if that happened very often when D-7-16 stopped short. "If I go any farther, I shan't get back in time to sign the book. Just keep following Clair, though—"and it jabbed a long skinny finger at a sign proclaiming this to be CLAIR STREET—"and you can't miss it." And it bolted like a rabbit, not so much as pausing to wish me good luck.

But when I turned to continue in the indicated direction, I saw why D-7-16 had been in such a hurry and cursed it as not only a rude and sullen rabbit, but a cowardly one as well.

It must have smelled the vampire coming.

I cannot describe the vampires of the night city in any way that will truly convey the experience of meeting one. To begin with, the miasma that surrounds them if one gets too close—a stench of blood both fresh and very old, compounded by a cloying reek of roses that I guess to be the scent of the vampires themselves—is like nothing I have ever encountered, before or since.

They are somewhat like the demi-angels in shape, being tall and well proportioned and winged. And they are pale-skinned, pale-haired: albino.

But their wings are the naked leathery span of the bat, and their faces, too, have nothing that is human or beautiful about them.

Round faces, almost chinless, with a nose that is nothing more than nostrils, and a lipless inverted V slash of a mouth, the sharp teeth plainly visible with every word spoken. They eyes are round and bright, very red and very old.

I yelped at finding myself face to face with such a creature, the yelp only not a scream because the stench of roses and blood choked me; the vampire winced, its hands going up as if to protect its ears, and said in a lovely, perfectly modulated mezzo-soprano, with only the slightest trace of a lisp, "I beg your pardon. I did not mean to startle you."

Somewhat incoherently, I begged pardon in return, chiding myself inwardly for being surprised that such an ugly creature should be female. But I could not help it: I *was* surprised, as if her sex ought to make her exempt, as if something that hideous could only be male.

She said, "You are a stranger here, are you not?"

"Yes."

Her head tilted, and her mouth moved in an expression that I thought was intended as a smile. "And let me guess. Dominie Clement has talked you into going after that tiresome relic for him."

The expression on my face made her laugh, and if her voice was beautiful, yet her laugh was the shrieking, tittering noise her bat-like physiognomy suggested. The passing shadows, all of whom were carefully on the other side of the street, covered their ears and walked faster.

"But please," said the vampire, collecting herself. "I forget my manners." She extended her hand, very long and very white, and the fingers plainly tipped with claws, not nails. "This is the correct observance? And we tell each other our names."

"Only if I won't have to pay to get mine back," I said.

"Your name is entirely safe," she promised, and for some mad reason I believed her.

It required a considerable effort of will to take her hand. But her skin was warm, her palm furry against mine, and she was very careful of her claws, so that I felt only the slightest tickling scratch against my wrist. "Kyle Murchison Booth," I said.

"Mirach," she said in return, and I hoped I hid my relief adequately when she released my hand. "That is a most charming ritual."

"I, er, that is, I'm glad you find it so."

"And it means we are not enemies," she said triumphantly, "so you need not fear any longer that I will bite you." For one heart-stopping second, she bared her teeth at me, as sharp as if they'd been filed, and I knew she could have torn my throat out in a single snapping mouthful of blood and skin and gristle. And then she relaxed and stepped slightly away from me, and after a moment I was able to relax, too. Infinitesimally.

"Come," said Mirach. "Walk with me."

I was not certain whether it was invitation or command, but it seemed wiser to obey, regardless. I followed the vampire through a wrought-iron gate, out of which she must have emerged to intercept me, down a long, wide spiral of stairs circling a great empty space like a ballroom in which no one had ever danced, and then through another gate and onto a brick-paved promenade beside a river which, after one glance, I tried not to look at too closely. There were others strolling along the river-walk, but they were vampires, and they did not approach us.

Presently, Mirach said, "The dominies still think we don't know, don't they?"

"Er, yes . . . how *do* you know?"

"This is our city. Very little happens in it that we are not aware of. And the dominies are transparently bad liars."

I thought of Clement's beautiful, expressive face, and nodded my understanding.

"They also trust the shadows to keep their secrets, and shadows do not keep secrets, Kyle Murchison Booth. They whisper to each other all day long in the factories, whisper whisper whisper like mice in the wainscotting, and what they whisper to each other, sooner or later, one of them will whisper to us. An increase in status, a bonus for the week . . . they fear us, and they will tell you they hate us, but they whisper their secrets to us all the same."

"You don't seem, er, terribly perturbed about the loss of the relic."

"Why should we be? And, yes, Kyle Murchison Booth, I do speak for my siblings in this. It is distasteful to us, this relic, and goblins love bright things. They mean no harm and will do no harm."

"Then you've, er, come to stop me?"

"I came to *meet* you. The dominies are not the only ones who are insatiably curious about travellers from far lands. And, no, I shall not prevent you from going through the Goblin Door."

I struggled with it, but in the end said humbly, "I don't understand."

"Let us sit," said Mirach, indicating a wooden bench beside the promenade. I was not entirely comfortable with the proximity to her this plan entailed, but she had promised not to bite me, and therefore I felt I had no valid grounds for complaint. I sat.

She sank down gracefully beside me—like the pews in the church, the bench was backless—and after some moments of breathing carefully through my mouth, I began to acclimate to her appalling scent. I do not know if she could tell I was on the verge of asphyxiation, or if she merely needed time to order her thoughts, but it was not until I was breathing more normally that she began to speak.

"I said that the dominies are bad liars, and they are. But they are very skilled at something which is not lying, but which obscures the truth just as surely.

"What a dominie does not wish to see is not seen."

"But—"

"I am not speaking literally, although we have sometimes wondered, we vampires, if their physical blindness is a punishment for this other, willful blindness. We are predators, Kyle Murchison Booth. We see clearly whether we wish to or not. But the dominies were blind when we met them. We do not know if our story is true—or merely a story."

"What is it that, er, the dominies do not wish to see?"

"This city," said Mirach and gestured with her long, white, horrible hands. "They imagine that it is we who rule, the shadows who toil for our pleasure, and they themselves, the dominies, our helpless, passive captives, who do what they can to help the shadows and resist our evil. Yes?"

It was a not inaccurate summation of what Clement had told me; I nodded.

"The truth is that without the dominies, the shadows would have revolted against us long ago."

I gaped at her; like an animal's her face was expressionless except when she remembered to contort it, and her round red eyes gazed back at me somberly.

"It is the dominies who teach the shadows to be patient, the dominies who assure them their service will be rewarded. The dominies taught the shadows how to dream, and it is that above all that keeps them obedient."

"You are cynical," I managed.

She shrugged magnificently, a gesture that involved her wings as well as her shoulders. "We are vampires. What else could we be?"

"But you don't tell the dominies." For I did not doubt that the vampires could make the demi-angels see this truth, if they chose to.

"We love the dominies. Though we are cynics. Though they call us monsters. We would not make them unhappy for all the worlds we know. And thus," and she thought to smile, although the expression was no less disturbing the second time, and I wished she had not, "if Clement wants to send you clandestinely to retrieve his unpleasant little toy, we shall not stop you."

"Um," I said. "Thank you."

"It seemed unkind to let you continue fearing us and our potential intervention," she said, answering a question I had not succeeded in articulating. "We decided we could trust you not to hurt the dominies."

"Thank you," I said, with greater assurance. However they had decided I was not a practitioner of pointless cruelty, I was ridiculously glad to have the vampires think well of me.

"Very well then," said Mirach, rising in a single fluid motion. "I will escort you to the Goblin Door. I would accompany you further, but if I did, you would never see so much as a single goblin fingertip. They remember the days when we used to hunt them."

I opened my mouth to ask what the vampires hunted now, then thought better of it. I was afraid that if I asked, she would tell me.

Other vampires watched as we walked, their eyes reflecting the lamplight in flat red disks, and Mirach murmured their names to me: Sadalsuud and Taraapoz, Suhail and Nashira and Menkalinam.

"Why did you meet me, and not one of them?"

"We have demesnes—parishes—just as the dominies do, although they would be appalled to learn that we have borrowed their word. Clement is a dominie of my parish; thus my interest was judged greatest. My brother Alhaior was most displeased. He has actually been to your world once—or to what he thinks was your world—and he had a great many questions he wished to ask."

"Er," I said. But the mention of 'your world' had reminded me, and I asked: "Do you think the dominies can truly send me back? To, er, my world, that is?"

"If they cannot, we can take you," Mirach said, clearly regarding the matter as one of no importance, and I stopped in my tracks as if she had shut a door in my face. "*You* can take me? Then why—?"

"Please, Kyle Murchison Booth," Mirach said, her face screwed up in a wince, "moderate the loudness of your voice."

I apologized, but stuck to my point: "If you can return me to my world, why am I going on this . . . this treasure hunt?"

"Because Clement wants his relic back, and I cannot retrieve it for him myself."

There was something terribly stark in the way she said it, an acknowledgment of the hopelessness of the vampires' love for the demi-angels, and at the same time a resolute dignity that rejected pity. I apologized again, and she waved it away, the graceful gesture of her left arm echoed by an equally graceful gesture of her left wing.

"We are exploiting you," she said, and I knew beyond the slightest shadow of a doubt, that if I asked her what she preyed on, and if she reveled in its death, she would answer me with truth. "You have reason to be upset."

We had reached the end of the promenade, ascending back to street level by means of a corkscrew stair, iron and rusting. Mirach let me out through a turnstile and said, "There, across the street, is the Goblin Door."

I would not have known it without her guidance, and I wondered again just how eager D-7-16 truly was to have St. Christopher's Glass returned. It was the sort of door any small commercial establishment might have, wood-framed glass with brass fittings, and a neat brass plaque saying PUSH. I noticed as we approached that the lower portion of the glass was smudged and smeared, as if with the fingerprints of small children—also that, indubitably, Mirach cast a reflection. Her mirrored image was, if anything, more hideous than her physical self, for it looked like a waxwork, some Gothic marionette given animation without life.

I turned my head with a jerk, almost a wince, and Mirach said softly, "You cannot travel through mirrors if you can meet your own eyes in them."

"Is that how you move between worlds?"

"One way," she said, with a hard carelessness that told me further questions would be futile. "But your way lies through the door, Kyle Murchison Booth, not the mirror. Someone will be waiting to guide you to St. Christopher's when you return."

For a weak, childish moment, I wanted to beg her to be here herself, but I throttled the impulse grimly and said merely, "Thank you."

I did succumb to the urge to extend my hand again; her head tilted, and she said with great interest, "It is appropriate at parting also?"

"Yes."

"I am charmed," she said, and clearly was. We shook hands; it was easier by far to touch her than to look at her, though I had never imagined finding myself in a situation where I could say that truthfully. But her touch was like the touch of an animal, not like the touch of another person.

Then she turned, drifting across the street with her easy, unhurried stride, and I took the deepest breath my nervousness would allow and pushed open the Goblin Door.

II. Through the Goblin Door

I had had a nanny until I was five years old. I remembered her scent more clearly than anything else: a warm sweetness of rose water and cornstarch. She had seemed a giantess to the child I had been, though doubtless I would tower over her now. She had been wide-hipped, soft-bosomed, her hands small and chapped. Her name was Martha Mulcahy.

And I remembered her stories about goblins. They were her method of discipline; as an adult I could see their crude manipulation, the meretricious effects she achieved by playing on a child's gullibility. But that knowledge, that adult awareness, did very little to dull my childhood fear. The goblins ate naughty children's eyeballs, Martha Mulcahy had told me. They were attracted by the sound of children crying, and would pinch them black and blue. And, of course, they stole children who would not go to sleep. What they did with the children then, Martha Mulcahy had never said, but my imagination had had no difficulty in filling in the gaps.

And all those stories, her cautionary tales and my own fevered imaginings, were crowding back now. Neither Mirach nor Clement had seemed to consider the goblins a threat, but of them, one was blind, reclusive, and naïve, and the other was a vampire and doubtless had a skewed perspective on the whole notion of 'threat.' Though I was sure they had both been truthful according to their lights, I did not feel their opinions could be trusted.

The Goblin Door had opened onto a marble foyer, a trough worn down the center of the floor between the door and the head of the stairs with their flanking Corinthian columns. I was finally free of the reek of vampire; the foyer, and the stairs as I started down them, smelt of cool stone and dust, slightly of water and more strongly of the earthy musk that had to be the scent of goblins.

The stairs were broad and shallow, with the same trough worn down the middle. I descended carefully, holding onto the banister, and realized with a sinking sensation of doom that I should have asked Mirach for some sort of light.

At the bottom of the stairs, I stopped, unable to pry my fingers off the reassuring marble weight of the banister, and there I stood, as if turned to stone, while around me the darkness settled and deepened. I knew I had to move, even if it was only to go back up the stairs and beg someone for a flashlight or a lantern or a torch, but I had reached the end of my capacity for action; I stood and clung and quailed hopelessly at embarking on any course I could think of.

After a time, I saw a light. It had turned a corner, I thought, to come into view, and as it grew nearer, accompanied by a strange snuffling, shuffling, tapping noise, and great lambent green-gold eyes, I saw that it was a little tin lantern with what looked like the sort of cheap candle used on children's birthday cakes. It was at the height of my thigh, the eyes being slightly higher.

All at once, the lantern stopped, and the shuffling and tapping stopped, and the eyes became very wide and still with alarm, and a growly little voice whispered penetratingly, "There's a *bloke* on the stairs!"

A babble of whispers and little outcries, and another voice said, "'S it a domino?"

A third, palpably frightened: "'S it a vamp?"

"Nah," said the first voice. "Dun' got no wings, does 'e? Can't be a thing what got wings if you don't got wings. Stands to reason."

"Awright then," said the third voice. "Should we go closer, d'you think?"

This question occasioned a great deal more muttering and shuffling, and the snuffling of their breathing became more pronounced. At last, as it seemed they were not going to reach a decision on their own, and as with the best and most timorous will in the world, I could not construe them as a danger, I said, "I beg your pardon, but are you goblins?"

"Oooh!" they all said and went back a step en masse.

After a moment, one of them whispered, "'E ast if we was goblins."

"Whaddo we tell 'em?"

I was becoming accustomed to their Greek chorus method of conversation; I said, "I shan't hurt you. I promise."

"Easy to say," one said, and for a moment the green-gold eyes were full of menace. Then another said, "Nah, 'e's a nice bloke. Look at 'im!"

They all did, shuffling closer; I retreated half a step involuntarily, forgetting that I was still standing on the stairs, and nearly fell, saving myself only by sitting down hard.

My small interlocutors earned my instant and eternal goodwill: they did not laugh.

They had come close enough now that I could see them in the light of their little tin lantern. They were stocky-bodied, short-limbed. They were as goggle-eyed as the shadows; their faces were broad, wide-mouthed, pug-nosed. Their ears were pointed, wide-spread; their hair, black and coarse, they wore in long braided scalp locks like Red Indians. Their hands were small in proportion to their bodies and oddly delicate. I looked at their feet and understood the tapping sound I had heard; they were cloven-hooved, like sheep, and I realized—as, daring, they approached closer still—that the strange shape of their heads was not due to the poor light. They had horns lying along the curve of their skulls, like the mountain sheep displayed in the Parrington's Hall of Natural History.

They were all clothed quite tidily, if shabbily, shirts and trousers cut down for their small size, and vivid red suspenders that, by the way they tended to stand with their thumbs tucked behind them, were clearly their pride and joy.

"'E *looks* all right," one said.

"An 'e ain't a vamp," said another, "so if he *ain't* all right, we can handle 'im."

I guessed there were twenty or so of them, clustered around me now like homely children around a performing dog, so I was inclined to agree with that assessment.

"Okay, then," said the one holding the lantern, whom I surmised to be their leader. "We're goblins. What of it?"

"I've come to, er, ask you to return St. Christopher's Glass."

Frowns of what looked like genuine incomprehension. "Wot's that, guv?"

"The, er, relic of St. Christopher's. A little glass ball with—"

"The shiny!" one of the goblins said, in tones of the greatest enlightenment, and was echoed in a jumbled mutter by the others.

"But we don' have the shiny," said their leader.

"I was told you'd, er, taken it."

"Thass not right, guv!" the leader said indignantly, and the chorus picked up the theme: "'S not true! . . . 'S a lie, innit? . . . We din' do that!"

"Oh," I said, feeling foolish and distinctly at a loss. "Do . . . er, do you know who did?"

Wide-eyed, solemn, they shook their heads. "Shouldn't go round stealing the shiny," somebody muttered from the back. "Ain't right," somebody else agreed.

"We wouldn't steal the shiny," the first goblin said, clearly still miffed. "Not ours. Don' want the dominoes mad at us."

"*Or* the vamps," another goblin said, and they all nodded fervently; I noted with interest that the goblins understood the true balance of power in the city above them.

"Musta been a shadder," said a goblin standing on the other

side of the banister, and made me startle, for I had not realized any of them had crept that close.

"Musta been . . . sorta thing they'd do, innit? . . . Sneaky, they are . . . " Their Greek chorus was in consensus, and I wondered if they were right. I had no doubt that they were telling the truth to the best of their knowledge and ability. They struck me as creatures who would have to practice in order to tell a lie.

But assuming that the goblins were telling the truth left me in a difficult position. I knew, without any need to test the hypothesis, that Clement would not believe the goblins so readily, and the resulting impasse would not get me any closer to finding St. Christopher's Glass and being able to return home.

There was a tug at my sleeve. The goblin holding the lantern, green-gold eyes grave, said, "The shiny's gone?"

"Er, yes. Someone stole it from the church."

"Dominoes must be unhappy."

"Dominie Clement is very, er, distressed."

They shuffled from foot to foot, little hooves tapping and scraping at the stone. "So, said the first goblin, "if we found the shiny, it'd make the dominoes happy?"

And the Chorus chimed in: "Would it make 'em like us? . . . Would they like us like they like the shadders?"

I felt a pang of empathy; I knew all too well how it felt to want love and have no idea how to earn it. I said carefully, not wanting to mislead them, "I'm sure Dominie Clement would be very grateful. And perhaps he would, er, reconsider his opinions."

They nodded, and I hoped they understood how little I was promising. "We'll find the shiny," their leader said. "An' bring it to the church." And they pattered away.

" . . . Thank you!" I called after them, rather disconcerted by the speed at which they moved once they had made up their minds about something, and turned to labor back up the stairs through the great breathing darkness beneath the night city.

As MIRACH HAD PROMISED, there was a vampire waiting for me when I reemerged from the Goblin Door. In fact, there were two, glaring at each other like rival tomcats. I wondered if the vampires' division of the city into parishes was simply an imitation of the demi-angels as Mirach had implied, or if perhaps vampires were as territorial as the cats these two resembled.

They both started forward when I came through the door, and I had to curb my instinct to retreat. I found myself with my back pressed against the door's cold glass, so I was not entirely successful.

Both vampires checked their stride, looking uncertainly from me to each other. "Greetings, traveller," said the one to my right in a stentorian bass. "I am—"

"Oh, no, you don't," the other cut in, tenor, strident, almost shrewish although the vampire was clearly male. "Mirach sent *me*, and I'm not going to—"

"Don't be ridiculous," said the first and (I thought) elder vampire. "Mirach and I are kindlings—" at least, I thought that was the word he used— "and she would never—"

"But she did!" the second cried in vindictive triumph. "She told *me* to come meet him, so you can just *go away!*"

They were facing each other now, almost audibly snarling. "Er," I said, and broke off when they both turned to stare at me accusingly, red eyes round and shining. "Er. Who are you?"

The elder began, "I am Alhaior—"

"And I am Dafira," the other cut in defiantly. "Mirach sent me—"

"A mistake," said Alhaior. "I would be delighted to escort you to St. Christopher's. Do you have the relic?"

There was a certain unworthy satisfaction in saying, "No," and watching the two vampires do double-takes like cinema comedians. "The, er, goblins do not have it."

Alhaior merely stared at me, but Dafira, quick-minded, said, "Then who does?"

"I, er, I don't know."

"Well, *we* don't have it."

"No. I, er . . . " I decided even as I spoke not to mention the goblins' self-appointed quest. "I thought perhaps . . . that is, Dominie Clement may know—"

"How do you know the goblins do not have it?" Alhaior demanded. I had already noticed how the depth and sonority of his voice made his every utterance majestic and authoritative. In this instance, he sounded very much like a cross-examining lawyer.

"I . . . er . . . they, that is, they told me so." I sounded feeble-minded to my own ears, but both vampires seemed to consider that quite adequate testimony and to take it most seriously.

Alhaior's tongue traced his upper lip nervously, a gesture which unnerved me so badly I could not look at either of them. "But if the goblins did *not* take the relic . . . "

"I imagine," Dafira said, "that that is why this gentleman wishes to speak to Dominie Clement again."

I nodded, not looking up.

"Then I shall take you," Dafira said. "Alhaior, why don't you tell Mirach and the Wisdom of this new development?"

Still staring at the scuffed toes of my shoes, I felt the clash of wills between them. The balance of power had shifted; Dafira was sure of himself, and Alhaior gave way. I felt him leave more than I heard him, and the reek of vampire diminished noticeably.

There was a silence between Dafira and me; then the vampire

said, almost shyly, "Mirach said you might be willing to share your name with me. I swear I will nor hold nor use it."

I forced my head up. To my eyes, Dafira looked no different from Mirach, any more than either of them was distinguishable from Alhaior. Their individuality was all in their voices, Mirach's elegance against Alhaior's gravitas against this abrasive earnestness.

"My name is Kyle Murchison Booth."

Dafira did not attempt to smile, but he bowed to me over his folded hands in a Japanese fashion. "I am honored. Shall we proceed to St. Christopher's now?"

I acquiesced and followed him on a route very different from the one Mirach had taken. Dafira went up, leading me via fire-escapes and jury-rigged bridges from roof to roof across the night city. After negotiating the third rope and plank bridge with the steadying help of Dafira's hand—like an iron armature under the shirred velvet of his pelt and I almost did not notice his scent any longer—I asked, "Do you, er, fly?"

His wings flexed and spread as if woken by the question. "We do," he said slowly, choosing his words with care, "but rarely within the city. For the dominies cannot—not without our guidance, which they will not accept—and we are . . . fearsome in flight." He furled his wings sharply, almost as if he were trying to hurt himself, and I remembered abruptly, as if from a conversation held years previously, Clement saying how terrible he had been told it was to see the vampires leaving the city to hunt. And since all the demi-angels were blind, and it was clear Clement did not talk to the goblins, he could only have been told by a shadow. The shadows told the demi-angels, and the demi-angels, cruel in their innocence, told the vampires. And the vampires did not fly within the city.

Pursuant to the train of thought thus started, I said, "Have matters always been so, er, fraught between you and the . . . the dominies?"

"There's St. Christopher's," Dafira said, pointing at a nearby spire, and I thought he was avoiding my question. But after a moment, he said, "No. Our relationship has never been easy, for we cannot change our nature, any more than they can, and thus we hunt and they disapprove, and it will always be so, but it used to be that they would come to the doors of their churches to speak with us if we knocked. It used to be that they would walk with us in the city, even if they would not fly."

"When did the change occur?"

"I don't know." He supported me carefully down a final fire escape, almost as steep as a ladder, and we emerged from an alley between two brownstones to stand on the sidewalk directly across from St. Christopher's. "Clocks, whether elaborate or simple, do not keep time in this city, and time itself . . . " He made a gesture, his hand closing into a fist and then spilling open again, as if unable to hold that which he sought to keep. "It cannot be measured. The only variation we have is the arrival of visitors like yourself, and even at that, I cannot tell you whether the last one appeared two days ago, or two hundred years."

"Have the shadows and the goblins been here as long as you have?"

"The goblins, yes. The shadows came later . . . I think."

I asked the question I had not gotten to pose to D-7-16: "Do any of them every actually leave?"

"Oh, yes," Dafira said, almost cheerfully. "They take passage on the trading ships to Heft Averengh, once they earn their names back."

"But, er, I beg your pardon, but if you have no method of keeping time, how do you know when they have done so?"

His eyes widened; I saw his pupils expand and contract like those of a cat about to pounce, and noted to myself the stupidity of disconcerting a predator. He turned his head away sharply, refusing the instinct that told him a threat must be fought and killed and eaten. He said, his voice uncertain, a little muffled, in telling contrast to the lethal certainty of eyes and teeth and clenching hands, "I don't know. I *thought* they left. The dominies have such elaborate plans . . . "

"Mirach told me the dominies taught the shadows how to dream. It, er, follows that they have learned to deal with . . . that is, a dream does not lose its strength for never being realized."

"Oh," Dafira said, his fingers now pressed against the triangular slash of his mouth. "You think . . . time doesn't pass here, does it? We just go round and round and nothing ever happens because nothing ever *can*."

"But something *has* happened," I said. "Someone has stolen St. Christopher's Glass."

DAFIRA COULD NOT ENTER the church. I stood beside him in the portico, and we took it in turns to knock, until Clement finally opened the door, saying with bewilderment and a touch of irritation, "The church is always open." And then his nose wrinkled as he caught Dafira's scent.

"Except to those who cannot come in," I said and was startled at my own waspishness.

"Mr. Booth! I did not expect you so soon. But why . . . ?"

"Matters have become, er, complicated."

"Complicated? Do you have the relic?"

"No, because the goblins aren't the ones who stole it."

"The goblins aren't . . . Of course the goblins stole it!"

"You sound awfully certain for one who did not witness the theft," Dafira said. He had regained his composure, and his eyes were bright with interested malice.

"I expected a remark like that from a vampire," Clement said witheringly, and I had to intervene before they descended into an unbecoming exchange of personalities.

"The goblins did not steal the relic," I said as firmly as I could, "and I have discovered a number of other questions that need answering."

Clement tilted his head, his beautiful face perplexed but willing. "What do you want to know?"

"Come out and, er, sit down, dominie. I feel that this may take some time, and you are likely to have other visitors before we are finished."

Clement hesitated, apprehension and uncertainty visible in every line of his body, in the awkward half extension of one wing.

"There is nor trick nor treachery," Dafira said abruptly, harshly.

"Very well," Clement said.

The portico was flanked with backless benches. Clement settled awkwardly on one; Dafira, back stiff, wings twitching as if they wanted to mantle and he would not let them, perched on the edge of the bench opposite.

I sat down next to Clement, for I did not want him to feel that Dafira and I were allied against him. And my gesture did seem to lessen his unease, for he said, "I do not understand, but I do not believe you would lie to me. Do you believe you can retrieve the relic?"

"I, er, hope so," I said, thinking of the goblins. "As I said, there are questions I must ask."

"Ask them," Clement said.

Invited so directly to speak, I stammered and fell silent. Dafira, having waited politely for a few moments, said, "You were asking me if any of the shadows have ever succeeded in buying back their names."

"Well, of course they have!" Clement said indignantly.

"Have they?" Dafira asked, leaning forward. "Have any of your parishioners done it?"

"Well . . . no. But I'm sure—"

"Do you know, personally, of any shadow who has taken passage for Heft Averengh?"

Clement opened his mouth to respond, but Dafira said, "*Personally,*" with great emphasis, and the demi-angel subsided again.

"I don't either," the vampire said after a moment.

"But what are you saying? That you're exploiting your workers? We've been saying that all along!"

"I have another question," I said hastily, and then had to think of one. "Er. That is, what do your factories produce?"

"I beg your pardon?" vampire and demi-angel said together.

"The factories where the shadows work. What do they produce?"

"I have no idea," Clement said, as one who was above such crass concerns. I looked enquiringly at Dafira, who blinked, clearly surprised that anyone would need to ask, and said, "They manufacture night."

"They . . . I beg your pardon." I felt as if I had been hit in the head with the cognitive equivalent of a brick. "They manufacture *night*?"

"Of course," Dafira said, still as a missionary explaining good hygiene and Sunday church-going to an unwashed savage. "We are nocturnal, and a very little sunlight will prove fatal to us. The sun blinds us, and burns us, and the daylight dragons who hunt us find us laughably easy prey. So we hired the shadows to make night in our factories."

"Do they know that's what they're doing?" Clement said.

"It isn't a secret," Dafira said, tilting his head worriedly.

"You mean that they knew," Clement said in a low, terribly even voice. "All the time that they were pleading for our sympathy at how harshly their masters treated them, they knew. They *knew* that the work they did ensured that those masters would retain their power." The demi-angel came to his feet, his wings beating so wildly that I was obliged to crouch down on the floor to avoid being knocked senseless, and his voice rose into a shriek: "They *lied* to us! Selfish conniving *beasts!*"

I discovered Dafira was on the floor next to me. "I've never seen a dominie lose their temper," he said, sounding rather awed.

"Can you, er, do anything?"

"I shouldn't think so. But I can't imagine this will last long. He'll exhaust himself, if nothing else."

Indeed, the frenzy of wings was already slowing, and I could hear Clement's breath laboring in his chest beneath his howling rage. And then, abruptly, it was over; the demi-angel sagged back onto the bench. Dafira and I stood up cautiously, but Clement merely buried his face in his hands and wept, his wings wrapped protectively around his shoulders. Dafira took my elbow and tugged me down the steps.

"Mirach said she trusted me not to be cruel," I said.

"You were not cruel. You asked a question Clement should have asked for himself long ago."

"It looks like cruelty from here," I said, gesturing at the bitterly weeping demi-angel.

Dafira tilted his head. "You are asking questions which we have not thought to ask ourselves, vampires as much as dominies. It is not surprising that you are causing disturbances, but neither is it your fault."

"Is it not?"

Dafira tilted his head the other way, round red eyes unreadable. "We have found, in the past, that no traveller comes to this city without a reason. In general, those reasons have been their own, burdens they carried with them whether they knew it or not. But perhaps you have come here, not on your account, but on ours."

"You, er, ascribe to me an ability I am quite sure I lack."

The round eyes blinked consideringly. "And yet you have already made me consider a question I would never otherwise have thought to ask. Does our manufac—"

But what Dafira's question was, I did not then learn.

I felt the vampires before I heard or saw them. They were silent as owls; when I looked up, searching for the source of the crawling oppression I felt, they were there, great pale shapes against the endless night. As I watched, they dropped lightly to the sidewalk around us one by one, a series of bat-winged Samothraces. I assumed that one of them was Mirach, but there were at least three female vampires among them, and I had no hope of telling them apart. And then their massed miasma hit me, and as I choked on it, the panic-white awareness of them as predators sent me to my knees, a foolish rabbit surrounded by foxes.

There was a perturbed muttering and shifting among them, and I quite clearly heard Mirach say, "Why is Clement weeping?"

"I told him the truth," Dafira said dryly.

"About what?"

"About what our factories produce. The gentleman wished to know."

"I thought his business was recovering the dominie's relic." Her voice was cold, laden with threat. I could not catch my breath, could not stop making dreadful undignified noises like a cat afflicted with a hairball. Could not defend myself, explain myself.

Dafira said, "It is not so simple. For if the goblins did not steal the relic, the shadows must have. And there are other matters."

I realized that the softness brushing my hair and neck was the membrane of Dafira's wing. He had put himself bodily between Mirach and me. I had not and would not have expected such a gesture, would never have expected a vampire to be my champion.

"*Other* matters?" Mirach said, as if she felt the matters already on the table were more than sufficient.

Dafira asked her, as he had asked Clement, "Do you personally know of any shadow who had succeeded in buying back their name?" And, raising his voice slightly, "Any of you?"

There was the faintest uneasy shuffling, and I managed finally to control my breathing. I did not, however, dare to raise my head, but remained as I was, sheltered behind Dafira's wing like a child behind his mother's skirts.

The silence stretched, twisted. No vampire spoke, though it was clear that each of them *wished* to; like Clement and Dafira before them, they could not. No one knew of a shadow who had sailed to Heft Averengh; no one knew of a shadow who had earned back its name.

"And that would be the answer," Dafira said softly, "if we asked every vampire, dominie, and shadow in the city. It has never happened. *Never.*"

"But what does that signify?" one of the other vampires said. "We haven't *prevented* them from doing so."

"We quite intended them to do so, in sooth." A third vampire, older, not as stentorian as Alhaior, but with a mellow, resonant voice, "and thus the fact that they have not is disturbing, if nothing more."

"As is," said a female vampire who was not Mirach, "the fact that no one has noticed."

"Including the shadows themselves," said another vampire, and then they were all talking together, theorizing and exclaiming and arguing.

I got very carefully to my feet, and Dafira murmured, "Are you well?"

Are you warm, my daughter? Are you warm? "Quite well, thank you. I, er . . . I apologize for . . . "

"Most sentient creatures react that way to a blood of vampires. Only sapient creatures are foolish enough to try to apologize for it." His tone was teasing rather than offended, and I managed a weak smile in appreciation of the distinction he was making. Then another vampire caught his attention; he turned away, and, not wishing to remain where I was, I mounted again to the portico and reclaimed my seat beside Clement.

"It is I," I said quietly.

"What's happening?" Clement whispered.

"The vampires are, er, arguing." I thought of what it must be like for him, surrounded by the reek of charnal roses and the babel of voices and unable to see for himself what they were actually doing. "Do you, er, want to go back inside?"

"They won't hurt me," he said confidently, perfect faith transmuting to perfect arrogance. Although I knew it was wrong to feel sympathy for the vampires, I could not help it. The dominies had trapped them as neatly as any predator, and they had not even the reprieve of death to hope for. I wondered if any of the vampires—clear-sighted as they were—had yet realized that. I said nothing in answer to Clement, merely sat and waited for the vampires to come to some resolution.

I was still waiting when there was a clatter of tiny hooves and a triumphant bellow of "We got the shiny!" and a throng of goblins boiled out of the neighboring building's cellar, a shadow struggling in their midst.

The vampires reacted like a flock of pigeons beset by an unexpected cat; they scattered and sought higher ground. Two of them ended up in St. Christopher's portico, and it was at that moment I realized I had lost track of Dafira in the confusion and had no hope of finding him again unless he chose to approach me.

The goblins, oblivious to the effect they were having, surged to a halt in the middle of the street; above their babble, I could hear the shadow protesting stridently but ineffectively, until one of the goblins cuffed it across the back of the skull. It said, "Ow!" and fell silent, sulkily rubbing its head.

With the streetlights lit, it was easy to identify the goblins' leader; trousers that had seemed merely dark by the light of the little tin lantern were revealed to be bright purple, and it was that goblin who stood forward from the rest and shouted, "Where's the bloke wiffout wings?"

Immediately, all the vampires were staring at me, politely appalled by the company I chose to keep. I felt myself blushing, but there was nowhere to hide, nothing to do but stand up and say, "I . . . er, I'm over here."

They thronged around me like small children or dogs, both of which make me terribly nervous. But the goblins were purposeful; their purple-trousered leader said, "Cough it up, shadder," and the others jostled threateningly, not quite butting but clearly ready to. And the shadow, a spindly creature even more exophthalmic than D-7-16 and with a look in its pop-eyes that boded trouble, dug unwillingly in its pockets and held out on its fishbelly palm a lump of glass, roughly spherical, with a mote of brightness dancing in it, a mote I might have thought a mirage of my own eyes if it had not been for the vampires, who had gathered close, shying violently, arms and wings both coming up to shield their vulnerable eyes. There were even one or two yelps of protest, high-pitched as the cries of bats, and I distinctly saw the look of malicious satisfaction that flitted across the shadow's face and was gone.

I closed my own hand over the glass as quickly as I could, flinching away from the clammy touch of the shadow's fingers. The vampires began cautiously to straighten; the glass was warm against my skin, smooth and uneven. I turned; Clement was standing, wings half spread, expression hopeful, frightened.

I said carefully, "The, er, goblins have found St. Christopher's Glass for you, Dominie Clement. A shadow had it."

And as Clement stretched out his hand and I gave him the relic, being careful not to expose the vampires to it again, the purple-trousered goblin said, "Tell 'im 'oo you are," and the chorus chimed in: "Yeah . . . Give 'im your number . . . Speak up, shadder, don't be shy." I turned back and saw the goblins blocking the shadow's attempts to sidle away. It looked more than a little panicked, and its pale pop-eyes blinked up at me beseechingly.

I found myself unmoved, and merely raised one eyebrow in my best imitation of my terrifying prep school Latin master.

The shadow quailed quite gratifyingly and blurted, "E-9-35."

The vampires hissed, open-mouthed feral displeasure, and I clenched my hands until my fingernails bit into my palms to keep from succumbing to panic again. A female vampire came forward. I thought it might be Mirach, but her voice when she spoke was high and sweet, and cold with fury. "You are of my demesne," she said, and the shadow looked quite ill with terror. "How did the relic come into your possession?"

It shook its head wildly, its mouth compressed so tightly it all but vanished. The vampire's face did not change, but I read incredulity as well as rage in the movement of her shoulders and wings. She took a single step forward; the shadow shrank back, cowering against my legs and whimpering. I jerked away in disgust, and the vampire's hand shot out, closing in the shadow's collar, dragging it forward. It let out a shriek and began babbling, a torrent of words at first indecipherable, but gradually resolving into sense.

I did not fully follow the complexities and ramifications of the shadow's explanation—although it was clear from their grim nods that the vampires did—but I got the general gist. It seemed there had been dissension among the shadows. Although they had not recognized the root of the problem any more than the vampires had, they had been becoming increasingly discontent, and had been unable to agree on how to proceed. I gathered, although E-9-35's rhetoric became obfuscatory at this point, that most of the shadows favored the rational, reasoned approach of appointing a spokesman and petitioning for an audience with the Wisdom of the vampires, which seemed to be their ruling council. But this course of action—again for reasons I did not fully understand—was very slow, and some shadows, mostly low ranking technicians like E-9-35 itself, had become impatient. They had thought negotiations might proceed more swiftly and more in their favor if they had some leverage. And thus they had stolen St. Christopher's Glass.

It had been D-7-16's plan, E-9-35 insisted, and I was no longer surprised that D-7-16 had so cheerfully led me off on a wild goose chase. D-7-16's plan, executed by a whole cadre of shadows, and the relic given into E-9-35's safekeeping while they tried to figure out a way to use it. But since they could not come up with a plan that would not reveal their own guilt, it had been seeming increasingly likely that the relic would never be used at all.

The shadow's voice faltered and trailed off; the vampires were closing in around it, eyes bright and opaque and implacable, and I thought, shivering, that revenge was a concept natural to predators. The female vampire hauled the shadow closer, her forearms cording and her mouth opening. But I was distracted at that moment by a tug on my sleeve.

I looked down; the purple-trousered goblin looked up at me and whispered hoarsely, "D'you think the domino will like us now?"

I said to the goblin, trying to sound kind instead of merely squeamish, "Let's find out."

Clement had withdrawn into the corner of the portico, his hands closed tightly around St. Christopher's Glass, his wings spread like a screen.

"Dominie," I said, "the goblins, er, wish to know if you will like them now."

Clement's white-blind eyes were falsely bright with tears. He said, sounding genuinely surprised, "Do the goblins *wish* me to like them?"

The heat and mass of small bodies was all around me, the weight of their yearning almost as palpable.

"Yes," I said for them. "They do."

Clement slipped St. Christopher's Glass into his sleeve and said, "I have been wrong about so many things. Perhaps I have been wrong about them as well." He sank gracefully to his knees, wings fanning wide for balance and surrounding us all with the scent of nutmeg. "Come," he said, and his smile was breath-taking. "Let me meet these goblins who wish my friendship."

They pressed past me, though I noticed they were careful not to crowd Clement. Their leader said, "Ta *very* much, guv," and then I was on the outside of the newborn community of goblins and demi-angel. I had to remind myself sharply that I wanted to return to my home, not to be adopted by the goblins of the night city.

The vampires had moved away with their victim, and matters in that quarter were ominously silent. I sat down on the steps of St. Christopher's to wait, and wished wearily that there were any point in waiting for dawn.

THE LAMPLIGHTERS HAD COME around to extinguish the street-lights, averting their eyes with obsessive care from the clustered blood of vampires, before anyone, goblin, demi-angel, vampire, or shadow, remembered my existence. But finally a single vampire approached the church; when he spoke, I knew him for Dafira, and I tried not to notice the darkness staining his mouth and chin and spotting the collars of his shirt.

"We have decided. We shall destroy the night factories and give the shadows back their names."

"All at once?"

"If we try to take our time over it, it will not happen at all," Dafira said grimly. "We may be short-sighted selfish fools, but we have at least learned that much from experience."

"Ah. . . . Er, yes."

"Will you come with us? We must explain to the dominies and the shadows, and we thought perhaps you would like to watch the destruction of the factories. It should be quite spectacular."

It was kindly meant, and I could not deny that I was curious. "But then you will take me home?"

"Yes," Dafira said without hesitation or hedging.

"I will trust you," I said, and shook hands with my second vampire.

AFTER THE DRAGON

for Elise Matthesen

AFTER THE DRAGON, she lay in the white on white hospital room and wanted to die.

The counselor came and talked about stages of grief and group therapy, her speech so rehearsed Megan could hear the grooves in the vinyl; Megan turned the ruined side of her face toward her and said, "Do you have a group for this?"

She felt the moment when the counselor dropped the ball, didn't have a pre-processed answer, when just for a second she was a real person, and then she picked it up again and gave Megan an answer she didn't even hear.

The doctors talked about reconstructive surgery and skin grafts, and Megan agreed with them because it was easier than listening. It didn't matter; they could not restore the hand that had seared and twisted and melted in the dragon's heat. They could not restore the breast rent and ruined by the dragon's claws. They couldn't stop the fevers that racked her, one opportunistic infection after another like the aftershocks of an earthquake. Her risk of thirteen different kinds of cancer had skyrocketed, and osteoporosis had already started in the affected arm and shoulder.

They could not erase the dragon from her body, and she hated them for it.

IN DEATH, a dragon reverts to the minerals from which it rises into life. Rhyolite, iron, bright inclusions of quartz, and—stabbing through—the dragon's terrible obsidian bones, every edge sharper than cruelty.

No dragon can be moved from where it dies; the last profligate expense of heat welds it to the geology of its death. The dragon that died on that strip of beach in Oregon turned the sand to glass for fifty yards. Strange glass, black and purple and green, twisted in shapes no glassblower could imagine. The government brought their Geiger counters, but there, they were lucky. This dragon had not risen from Trinity or the Nevada Proving Ground or Pikinni Atoll. Its poisonous heat did not survive it.

AFTER THE DRAGON, her mother would not look at her.

She came, and she yanked the curtains back, dazzling Megan's aching eyes. She turned her smile like a *call-me-Nancy* searchlight on nurses and orderlies and doctors and interns; no one could escape, least of all Megan. She gossiped ruthlessly about women Megan knew, women who were healthy and successful and happy, women who were not lying in a white on white on white hospital room, women who had never seen a dragon. She brought flowers, daffodils and gaudy tulips and vast red roses, and the hospital room took them in and made them look fake and shrill, like her voice.

Nancy came in and out like a cyclone, and she never looked at Megan. Megan lay and tried to remember the last time Nancy *had* looked at her, had seen her, had known her, and the next time Nancy came, Megan got her answer. "I found this picture of you, sweetie, and I thought you might like it."

Megan squinted and managed to focus on the picture; she hadn't lost the burned eye, but it had almost no vision. From the portrait frame, her eighteen-year-old self smiled at her as dazzlingly as sunlight, unharmed and unaware that harm could come to her. She still called her mother "Mom," not knowing yet the protection of irony, of distance, of pretending not to care. There was no dragon in her flat glass-protected world.

And of course that was the daughter Nancy wanted to see when she was not-quite-looking at Megan: eighteen and blonde and going to prom with the boy she'd dated for three years. Going to college. Surfing just for something to do on the weekends, a way to hang out with her boyfriend and his friends. Even then, it hadn't been true—even then the boys called her "Surfer Girl" more as a warning than a joke—but Megan had believed she could make it be true just as much as Nancy had. And she'd worked so fucking hard at it. Even when she quit school, got a job as an instructor, as her hair went sunbleached on top and brown underneath, she hid her failure from her mother as much as she could. For fifteen years, she'd hidden it, from her mother, from herself, and now she knew just how well she'd succeeded.

Nancy said, "I'll just leave this here where you can look at it." She was gone before Megan got her eyes open again. Her eighteen-year-old self smiled at her from the bedside table. Megan snarled back.

THE BEACH IN OREGON had no name. There was no need; it was just another piece of coastline, a narrow strip of sand hedged about by rocks. Sandpipers and sea lions knew it but did not name it, and if the whales gave it a name, they told no one but their children.

It still has no official name, but it has a designation: DI-2009-002-177. The 177th dragon incursion known to the Department of Defense to have occurred on American soil, the second such in the year 2009. There was a polite skirmish between the federal government and the state of Oregon, which the state of Oregon won; DI-2009-002-177 remains public land.

Inevitably, locals and tour books and websites begin to call it Dragon's Beach.

For a long time after the dragon, she hated in the same way that she breathed. She hated the doctors and the nurses. She hated everyone who visited her. She hated herself. Above all else, she hated the dragon, the smell of it that would not leave her nostrils, the bright lidless regard of its eyes. She hated it for not killing her, for leaving her trapped in this ruined mockery of a body. She hated it for dying and leaving her to face the world alone.

Her physical therapist was a rangy blonde woman who looked like her name should be Astrid or Olga. Actually, it was Jenny, and she was a third generation Los Angelina who spoke Spanish on the phone with her husband. She insisted that Megan move her arm in ways it no longer moved, insisted that she walk the length of the hall outside her room, and when she finished and collapsed, sweating and dizzy and nauseated, Jenny said, "Good. Tomorrow we'll do it twice."

Before the dragon, Megan could have kept up with Jenny easily—she could have run Jenny into the fucking ground. Now that was as far gone from her as picking up a water glass with the hand she no longer had.

No one knows the total of the dragon's devastation. Human beings can be counted: five dead. Domestic animals can be counted: one dead, a Labrador retriever who died in the same instant as her owner, neither of them with even a chance to understand the death that stooped for them on silicate wings. Trees large enough to be landmarks can be remembered, although there is nothing left of them, only ashes. But even the best photographs, the most careful computer-generated reconstructions, can only guess at the squirrels which might have lived in the trees the dragon burned, the insects which were in its path, the earthworms which died beneath the heat and weight of its feet. There are craters left where the dragon stood, and the earth in them is scorched and lifeless.

AFTER THE DRAGON, after the surgery, after all the therapy, she still wasn't whole.

They let her go home to a musty, dark apartment she almost didn't recognize as hers. It was like walking through the home of someone who had died.

Me, she thought. *I died.* She went into the bathroom, stared, frowning and only half seeing at the brightly colored poppies on the shower curtain. A dead woman had chosen that curtain, and now she could not remember what being that woman had felt like. The woman in the mirror would never have chosen that shower curtain. The shiny skin along her jaw creased strangely when she tried to smile, and the eye looked as false as glass. Her hair was growing out again, though it was still not long enough to cover the warped cartilage of her ear.

"At least you won't frighten small children anymore," she said, her voice strange and hoarse and deep. The dragon had dropped her voice from soprano almost to tenor, and she could not accustom herself to it. Could not abide with it.

"This isn't me!" she cried, harsh as a crow. "I died—I died! This isn't me!"

The mirror shattered, great pieces falling into the sink and onto the floor. Her hand was bleeding. She looked at it for several moments, watching the blood welling red and reproachful in the cup of her palm, before she remembered what to do next.

SIGHTSEERS COME to Dragon's Beach, but they don't stay long. The rough glass of the beach is too dangerous to walk on, the earth crumbles horribly beneath your feet, and besides, there isn't anything to *see*. Just a weird rock formation and some holes in the ground. If you're stubborn, you can chip away a piece of the glass as a souvenir, but word gets around that it always, *always* draws blood, and anyway it's dull and ugly when you bring it back home.

Then there's an internet scare that the glass is carcinogenic, and after that the sightseers don't even get out of their cars.

AFTER THE DRAGON, she tried things she'd never tried before.

It began with the mirror, which had broken into three large shards and seven smaller ones, along with all the bits too small to count. And she knew that she should simply throw them away, counted and uncounted, that the mirror was broken and that was that, but she couldn't. She saved them instead and remembered her father teaching her to do jigsaw puzzles. After he had died, when Megan was nine, Nancy had thrown out puzzles by the armload.

Megan kept the shards of the mirror, despite the eerily accurate echo of her mother's voice in her head: "Sweetie, you don't know the first thing about working with glass, and you know you've always been so *clumsy* . . . " She kept the pieces of mirror and began, not idly, to look at DIY and crafts websites.

JENNY HAD EXPLAINED in careful and appalling detail the possible effects of failing to keep up with the prescribed exercise regimen, and Megan would not give more of herself to the dragon now that the fucker was dead. She went to the gym three times a week—the *gym*, god help her, which she'd always considered as a feeble second best to surfing or running or rock climbing, any of the things she couldn't do now, might not be able to do ever with her newly friable bones—dragging her wreck of a body like a reluctant dog on a leash. At first it was a nightmare, one more new nightmare to add to the stack, but she said grimly to herself, *If you survived the dragon, you can survive anything,* and kept going. And no one was cruel. They tried not to stare where she could see them, and after a couple of weeks, the body builders began, very respectfully, to give her tips. She was both startled and grateful, and after another week she began to remember how to say, "Hello" and "Have a nice night."

And then she met Louise.

Louise was Nancy's age, but where Nancy was soft and feminine and restless, Louise was wiry and fiercely androgynous and had the strength of her own inner stillness. Louise was a cancer survivor; one breast was gone, and there were pain lines on her face that never entirely smoothed out. But what first attracted and held Megan's attention were her tattoos. They started on her forearm and swirled up to her shoulder and then down both sides of her body beneath the tanktops she wore. The colors were vibrant, triumphant, and when Megan finally found the courage to ask to see the rest, she learned that the colors and the beauty and the pageantry of Louise's tattoos were all emanating from a lion tattooed over her heart. The tattooist had used the topography of Louise's chest, the scars and concavity, as guidelines, and the result was grotesque but also beautiful.

"Why a lion?" Megan asked, and then was afraid it was a rude question. Before the dragon, she'd never had this sort of conversation, about real pain and disaster and how you lived with being broken.

But Louise just grinned, a little ruefully, and said, "Strength in the Tarot. And Aslan from the Narnia books. And I'm a Leo."

"It's beautiful."

Louise looked down at herself. "Yeah," she said; she sounded almost surprised. "Yeah, it is."

THE WORLD RETURNS slowly to the glass beach.

There is a graduate student writing her dissertation on the ecological effects of dragon incursions; she has a grant, and she walks out to the beach every day and takes notes and samples and pictures. She measures the craters; sends the ashes to be analyzed and compared with the ashes from the most recent California wildfire, with the ashes from Mount St. Helens, with the ashes from other American dragon incursions, all the way back to the dragon of 1869, the first dragon for which such samples had been kept. She walks out with white-knuckled care to the obsidian bones and only once lays her hand open on their merciless edges.

She is lonely, but she doesn't mind. Her work is important.

On the day she sees the first cautious returning kildeer, she comes back after dark with a bottle of tequila. She pours a libation—not to the dragon, for the dragon is destruction and death and needs no homage—but to the Earth who heals herself if given half a chance, and then proceeds to get royally hammered.

AFTER THE DRAGON, she put things back together as best she could.

From her mother, Megan had learned to judge herself by marking points off from perfection. But now, looking at herself in the fractured, crazy-quilt mirror she'd made, perfection didn't make any sense. She wasn't sure what did.

"What do you like about yourself?" Louise said one day at the gym.

"What do I *like* about myself?" Megan said blankly.

"Yeah," Louise said, not pausing in the steady rhythm of the rowing machine.

"Louise, have you *seen* me?"

"Megan," Louise said back, just as snippy, "did I say anything about your *looks*?"

Megan didn't have an answer to that, and she went to swim laps with the question still bouncing around inside her head. Later, when she joined Louise in the jacuzzi, she said, "My mother always said it was a good thing I was pretty because what else did I have to offer a husband?"

"So your mother is who? June Cleaver in hell?"

Megan felt guilty about laughing, but god, there was no way she could stop herself. And Louise just grinned.

"I'll tell you what I like about myself," Louise said. "I like my tattoo. I like that I'm strong. I like that I'm entering a marathon next year, and I don't think I'm gonna place, but I know I'm gonna finish. I like that my sister's kids hug me hard, and I hug 'em back. I like that I don't give a shit anymore how my hair looks."

She raised her eyebrows at Megan. For a moment, Megan didn't think she had anything to say, and then she blurted, "I like my legs."

"They're cut," Louise agreed. "You gonna take that tai chi class?"

"Maybe," Megan said, and they finished their soak and walked back to the locker room lazily arguing the pros and cons.

Megan showered, put her street clothes on. T-shirts now, always T-shirts, because as awkward as it could be pulling them on, it was better than the humiliation of fumbling with buttons. And it wasn't like she had anything left she could win by being chic and femme and a copy of Nancy. She looked in the locker-room mirror and saw somebody who was so far from perfect the word didn't make sense. Somebody who was going to have to live with it.

Somebody who *could* live with it.

She waited, awkwardly, until Louise was dressed, and then said in a rush, before she could change her mind, "Louise, will you introduce me to your tattooist?" And when Louise looked at her, clearly startled, she said, "I want . . . I like the fact that my body is still alive. And I want it to know that."

"Of course," Louise said, and in her smile Megan saw beauty that no mother, no dragon could touch. "Of course."

Story Notes

Many of my short stories, including the title piece of this collection, come from necklaces or earrings made and named by my friend Elise Matthesen <elisem.livejournal.com/>. Elise's work is gorgeous, inspiring, thought-provoking . . . there's a reason this collection is dedicated to her.

Draco Campestris

"*Draco Campestris*" took me a long time to write because it only unveiled itself slowly and in non-contiguous pieces. The tipping point, though, was when I realized it was about a taxonomist. (It is also, like my stories featuring Kyle Murchison Booth, about my slightly uneasy love for museums.) But the intertwined stories of the taxonomist, the lady, the tithe-children, and the Museum itself were never either complete or linear strands in my head; they were always fragmentary and jumbled, as they are in the story itself.

"*Draco campestris*" is also the first story in a series that Elizabeth Bear and I seem to be . . . I don't know whether the right word is "writing" or "playing," because it's the closest to jazz improvisation that I think writing can come. I wrote "*Draco campestris*"; Bear wrote "Orm the Beautiful" <clarkesworldmagazine.com/ bear_01_07>; I wrote "After the Dragon (which is the last story in this collection, and, yes, that's a deliberate framing choice); Bear wrote "Snow Dragons" <subterraneanpress.com/index.php/ magazine/summer-2009/fiction-snow-dragons-by-elizabeth-bear>; and there are further stories, unpublished, unfinished, unwritten. But each story plays off the others, and each story comes from something Elise Matthesen has made. It's fun and it's challenging; I love each story, mine and Bear's, separately, and I love the sequence they make when you put them together.

QUEEN OF SWORDS

"Queen of Swords" is an early story, and I think it's pretty clear I'd been reading Angela Carter. I love stories that work with fairy tales, either retellings or subvertings or using the language of fairy tales to tell a different kind of story, and this is my attempt at that form.

LETTER FROM A TEDDY BEAR ON VETERANS' DAY

This was the first short story I ever successfully finished. It comes from an Elise Matthesen necklace, so it also marks the beginning of my friendship with her. It is also the story of mine that is most explicitly about the part of America in which I grew up: all the place names are real.

I have a theory that the category of "things you can do with words" lies on a spectrum from poetry to novels, and that short stories wobble back and forth across the tipping point. Some of them are like very short novels; others are like unpacked poems. This is one of the ones that is like an unpacked poem, and it may be the story of mine of which I am most proud.

It was a *bitch* to write.

UNDER THE BEANSIDHE'S PILLOW

This one's even farther toward the poetry end of the spectrum, and it comes from a pair of Elise's earrings with wooden skulls and tiny silver acorns.

Story Notes

I like to believe that we are all capable of transcending human nature, and I see no reason why I should not extend that belief to those whose natures are not human.

The Watcher in the Corners

This story, on the other hand, is more like a small novel.

Lilah Collier started out as a very minor character in a piece of juvenilia, and this story was originally a spin-off: what happened to her when she escaped her father's house and her psychopath of an older sister. But the juvenilia never managed to fledge into an adult story, and the spin-off put down good strong roots and bloomed.

(And if that's not a mixed metaphor, I don't know what is.)

I'd love to know what happened to Lilah after she left Mississippi, but she's never come back to tell me.

The Half-Sister

What happens after the story's over? is probably the question my stories most persistently return to and wrestle with. I'm always more interested in what happens after you save the world or slay the dragon and about who has to pick up the pieces when you're done. I'm interested in costs and consequences. And I'm interested in the people who aren't heroes, the people who stay home and keep the lamps clean.

Ashes, Ashes

Four stories of mine come from a single one of Elise's necklaces. The necklace is called *Why Do You Linger?* and so is one of the stories (in press, as of this writing, with *Subterranean Magazine*).

Another story is "Wait for Me," which can be found in *The Bone Key,* my collection of interrelated stories featuring the character of Kyle Murchison Booth. The third story is "Katabasis: Seraphic Trains," which I'll talk about a little later on. And the fourth story is "Ashes, Ashes," which I think it's fair to call my Daphne du Maurier homage.

The woods behind the narrator's house are the woods behind my childhood home; I can remember consciously visualizing the dry creek bed when I was writing this story. The history of those woods, however, is purely imaginary.

SIDHE TIGERS

This is another story that is very close to being a poem. It comes from a necklace of the same name, of very pale green beads.

A LIGHT IN TROY

I was thinking about the fall of Troy (you know, like you do). More specifically, I was thinking about Euripides' *The Trojan Women,* which is about what it's like to be a woman on the losing side of a war. And I was thinking about Andromache and the various stories told about what happened to her after the fall of Troy.

And then I was thinking about feral children.

Why these two trains of thought should have collided to produce this story, I don't know. But, as best I can reconstruct it, that's what happened.

AMANTE DORÉE

A little alternate history here . . . a little genderfuck there . . . And somehow it came out a spy story.

SOMEWHERE BENEATH THOSE WAVES WAS HER HOME

The Field Museum in Chicago has a collection of figureheads which are beautiful and slightly sad. Elise made a necklace called Somewhere Beneath Those Waves Was Her Home. The selkie was originally in a different story, but it turned out she needed to be in this one. If you're getting the idea that short stories generally happen by virtue of two or three random things colliding in my head, you're not wrong.

DARKNESS, AS A BRIDE

There was a challenge involved in the genesis of this story. I know it had something to do with rocks, because the challenge also produced Elizabeth Bear's excellent "Love Among the Talus" <*Strange Horizons*: strangehorizons.com/2006/20061211/talus-f. shtml>. I was obviously thinking about the rock that Andromeda was chained to and about what happens if Perseus never shows up. I was also obviously thinking about the ballet *Coppélia*—and about the Hoffmann stories it's based on—and what that story looks like from the doll's point of view.

Also, I love the sea monster in this story with all my heart.

KATABASIS: SERAPHIC TRAINS

Every writer gets one Orpheus story. This is mine.

It's also a Tam Lin story, and an urban fantasy—in the literal sense that it is a fantasy about a city. The moment that sparked the story was riding the El from the outskirts of Chicago into the city itself, and seeing how close it comes to the houses along its path. It was also a chance to nest several tiny stories inside the larger one.

The section headers are lines from the song "Why Do You Linger?" Like the sections themselves, they are not in linear order, but you can put them together to find the outline of the song, which is itself one of those tiny nested stories.

FIDDLEBACK FERNS

I don't write much science fiction, and I don't write satire at all, but this story turned out to be both. I love some of the turns of phrase in it, and I like the fact that it gets in, gets the job done, and gets the hell out of Dodge.

THREE LETTERS FROM THE QUEEN OF ELFLAND

Another Elise necklace: this one turned into my first published and most successful story. It is my most reprinted story, and it won the Gaylactic Spectrum Award for Short Fiction in 2003.

NIGHT TRAIN: HEADING WEST

Believe me, no one is more surprised than I am that I wrote this poem. But the twined images—reincarnation and Solitaire—didn't have a story around them, which pretty much means you're stuck with a poem, and I did the best I could.

The conversation on the train really happened, but it was about UFOs, not past lives.

THE SÉANCE AT CHISHOLM END

I write a lot of old-fashioned horror, because I love it. This story is old-fashioned horror, with the séance and its off-stage aftermath; it's also, very quietly, alternate history.

And from a different angle, it's as close as I'm ever likely to get to writing like Georgette Heyer. Which is to say, not very close at all.

No Man's Land

I get many of my stories from my dreams, which tend to be very vivid and also very narrative. This is one of those stories, although it took a lot of reworking and polishing to get it into the shape of a story. It originally started out in a sort of stock fantasy setting, with swords and kings and suchlike, and had to be rewritten from the ground up because all the fantasy trappings kept getting in the way of what the story was *about*. So it ended up as one of my very rare science fiction stories. Really, I'd call it science fiction magical realism, which surely puts it in a subgenre of its own.

National Geographic on Assignment: Mermaids of the Old West

Mermaids of the Old West is one of Elise's necklaces. I'd been reading a lot of *National Geographic magazine*s (where by "reading," I mostly mean "looking at the pictures"). You wouldn't think the two would go together, and yet, they do.

A Night in Electric Squidland
&
Impostors

. . . I don't even know how to begin to explain Mick and Jamie.

There are three stories about them: these two, and a third, "Blue Lace Agate," which is, as of this writing, in press with *Fantasy Magazine*. I also have a bunch of other ideas about Mick and Jamie that are just waiting for me to get around to them.

Mick and Jamie live in a Lovecraftian alternate universe, in Babylon, Tennessee (which seems to be more or less what would happen if you slapped Memphis down where Chattanooga is and added ghouls for good measure). They work for the BPI, the Bureau of Paranormal Investigations, and you should imagine their boss, Otho Jesperson, as being played by David McCallum circa 1985.

They're my excuse to write little buddy-cop movies for myself.

STRAW

I woke up one morning from a particularly weird and vivid dream, and by lunchtime I had turned the dream into this story. I think that's the fastest I've ever written anything.

ABSENT FROM FELICITY

The centerpiece of my doctoral dissertation is the chapter on *Hamlet*. And after I finished that chapter, I found that I still had something to say about *Hamlet*. And Hamlet. And poor Horatio. And about what happens after the story's over.

THE WORLD WITHOUT SLEEP

I love H.P. Lovecraft even when he drives me crazy. And of all his stories, I think my favorite may be *The Dream-Quest of Unknown Kadath*, partly because it's so wildly inventive and partly because it takes the monsters from *another* of my favorite Lovecraft stories, "Pickman's Model," and looks at them from a different angle. When I was writing "The World Without Sleep," I told everyone it was my Marxist Dream-Quest of Unknown Kadath with Vampires story, and that's still pretty much what I have to say about it.

The narrator of "The World Without Sleep," is Kyle Murchison Booth, the narrator-protagonist of the stories in my collection, *The Bone Key*. *The Bone Key* is much more traditional Lovecraft/M.R. James horror than "The World Without Sleep," but if you like Booth, that's where to go to spend more time with him.

AFTER THE DRAGON

After the Dragon, She Learned to Love Her Body is a sculptural necklace that Elise showed me the first time she showed me her workroom, most of ten years ago now. *Healing Is Not About Pretty* is a necklace made of deformed hearts that I bought from Elise in 2008 or 2009. The two came together to spark this story—which is also a story about what happens after you save the world. Or slay the dragon.

And with that, we've come full circle: from dragon to dragon. Thank you for reading.

—∞—

ACKNOWLEDGEMENTS

"*Draco campestris.*" *Strange Horizons* (August 2006). Reprinted in *Best American Fantasy*, eds. Jeff and Ann VanderMeer and Matthew Cheney, Prime Books, 2007.

"Queen of Swords." *AlienSkin Magazine* (November 2003).

"Letter from a Teddy Bear on Veterans' Day." *Ideomancer* 5.3 (September 2006).

"Under the Beansidhe's Pillow." *Lone Star Stories* 22 (August 2007).

"The Watcher in the Corners." [originally published on author's blog].

"The Half-Sister." *Lady Churchill's Rosebud Wristlet* 15 (January 2005).

"Ashes, Ashes." [first publication]

"Sidhe Tigers." *Lady Churchill's Rosebud Wristlet* 13 (November 2003). Reprinted in *Glass Bead Games*, ed. Elise Matthesen. Minneapolis: Inner Magpie Press, 2008.

"A Light in Troy." *Clarkesworld Magazine* 1 (October 2006). Reprinted in *Best New Romantic Fantasy*, ed. Paula Guran. Rockville, MD: Juno

Books, 2007. Reprinted in *Realms: The First Year of Clarkesworld Magazine*, ed. Nick Mamatas and Sean Wallace. Wyrm Publishing, 2007. Reprinted in *Podcastle* (March 9, 2010).

"Amante Dorée." *Paradox* 10 (Winter 2006): 4-11. Reprinted in *Trochu divné kusy* 3, ed. Martin Šust, Laser-books, 2007.

"Somewhere Beneath Those Waves Was Her Home." *Fantasy Magazine*. Prime Books, 2007.

"Darkness, as a Bride." *Cemetery Dance* 58 (2008).

"Katabasis: Seraphic Trains." *Tales of the Unanticipated* 27 (2006).

"Fiddleback Ferns." *Flytrap* 9 (June 2008).

"Three Letters from the Queen of Elfland." *Lady Churchill's Rosebud Wristlet* 11 (November 2002). Reprinted in *Trochu divné kusy* 2, ed. Martin Šust. N.p.: Laser-books, 2006. Reprinted in *So Fey: Queer Faery Fiction*, ed. Steve Birman. Binghampton, NY: Haworth Positronic Press, 2007. Reprinted in *The Best of Lady Churchill's Rosebud Wristlet*, eds. Gavin J. Grant and Kelly Link. New York: Del Rey, 2007. Reprinted in *Glass Bead Games*, ed. Elise Matthesen. Minneapolis: Inner Magpie Press, 2008. Gaylactic Spectrum Award for Best Short Fiction, 2003.

"Night Train: Heading West." *The Magazine of Speculative Poetry* 7:2 (Spring 2005). Reprinted in *The Year's Best Fantasy and Horror XIX*, eds. Ellen Datlow, Kelly Link, and Gavin J. Grant. New York: St. Martin's Griffin, 2006.

ACKNOWLEDGEMENTS

"The Séance at Chisholm End." *Alchemy* 3 (May 2006).

"No Man's Land." *Fictitious Force* 5 (2008).

"National Geographic On Assignment: Mermaids of the Old West." *Fictitious Force* 2 (Spring 2006).

"A Night in Electric Squidland." *Lone Star Stories* 15 (June 2006). Reprinted in *The Lone Star Stories Reader*, ed. Eric T. Marin, LSS Press, 2008.

"Impostors." [first publication]

"Straw." *Strange Horizons* (June 2004).

"Absent from Felicity." [first published on author's blog].

"The World Without Sleep." *Postscripts* 14 (Spring 2008).

"After the Dragon." *Fantasy Magazine* (January 2010).

ABOUT THE AUTHOR

Sarah Monette grew up in Oak Ridge, Tennessee, one of the three secret cities of the Manhattan Project, and now lives in a 105-year-old house in the Upper Midwest with a great many books, two cats, and one husband. Her Ph.D. diploma (English Literature, 2004) hangs in the kitchen. Her first four novels were published by Ace Books. Her short stories have appeared in *Strange Horizons*, *Weird Tales*, and *Lady Churchill's Rosebud Wristlet*, among other venues, and have been reprinted in several Year's Best anthologies. *The Bone Key*, a collection of interrelated short stories featuring her character Kyle Murchison Booth was published by Prime Books in 2007. A cult favorite, it was re-issued earlier this year in a new edition. Sarah has written two novels (*A Companion to Wolves*, Tor Books, 2007; *The Tempering of Men*, Tor Books, 2011) and three short stories with Elizabeth Bear, and hopes to write more. Her next novel, *The Goblin Emperor*, will come out from Tor under the name Katherine Addison. Visit her online at www.sarahmonette.com.

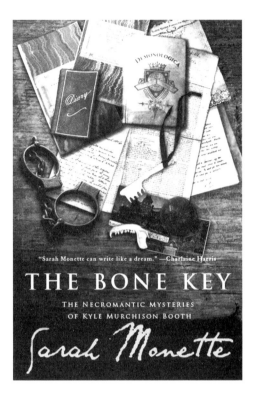